Pum Pum Rock

There's No Place Like Homo

Written by

Leslie Anne Frye-Thomas

Copyright @ 2020 by Leslie Anne Frye-Thomas
Published in the United States by Reel Stories Creative, Inc.
All rights reserved.

Library of Congress Cataloging-in-Publication Data is available upon request.
ISBN
978-1-7363149-1-3
Cover design by Alex (Ander) Mahler of alexanderyves.com

Acknowledgments

When they made you they broke the mold
And O' what a sight to behold
Out came sparkles, glitter, and gold
Fairy dust
Like a piñata that had just gone bust
You could not be contained
Nor reigned in
You an unbridled unicorn
And me — too afraid to give in
Cuz mama always said it was a sin
No matter if you were a stem, bull dagger, dyke or femme
But you didn't care
You were proud to be queer
Came face to face with corrective rape
You've been disowned, unfriended
Hell, you've been locked up for just existing
From Buggery Laws in the Caribbean
To Sodomy Laws in the states
Let the record show
To identify as queer in this time and space
Is to gamble with your
Life. Love. Liberty.
Then sprinkle in race
Shit
The system wasn't built to sustain our dreams
How do I know?
Cuz, fam, we're on the same team
Hinges kicked clear off the closet door
I've had all that I can stand
We not taking no more
So when you pledge your allegiance to the rainbow flag
Rest assured
They may call you fag
But you'll never be stag

United we stand
In perfect precision
A beautiful, rainbow coalition of ambition
Consider this my rendition
A token of gratitude
An acknowledgement of debt
To chosen family
Bound by persecution, perseverance, and pride
A love letter to my wife for loving me every step of this bumpy ass ride
To mom for showing up more and more each day
To friends and family who pushed every step of the way
To my creative team for helping manifest this dream
To the ancestors for being the engine, providing the steam
And to the Lord above
The epitome of love
You planted the creative seed
Proving day in and day out
You're all any of us truly need

CONTENTS

Learn more @PumPumRockBook
LeslieAnneFrye.com

Part One

Unhinged

Chapter 1

Dear God

Adorned in her private school uniform, twelve-year-old Natalia Higgins stared out the luxury sedan's window as her mother, Cassia Higgins weaved in and out of Montego Bay traffic. "Just because they say I like girls, doesn't make it so," the preteen spoke with a sweet Caribbean twang that interrupted the car ride's deafening silence.

"Have you seen yourself?" Cassia scoffed. Her accent was just as thick. "Most days you look more like my son than a daughter," she sucked her teeth.

"It's not like that," Nate whined as she turned to face her mother. She then removed an ice pack from her mouth, revealing a fat, bloodied bottom lip. "I hate that school and everyone there," she sulked, remembering the conversation that they'd just concluded with Nate's school principal: "I've told Natalia this a thousand times," Nate's principal continued, "her bandmates would stop teasing her if she simply changed how she dressed and acted a little more, well, normal." By normal, the principal had, of course, meant girlie. Nate shook her head in disgust as her mother's nagging jarred her from the principal's office and back to the passenger seat.

"So obstinate!" Cassia rolled her eyes. "I just hope our new addition don't give as much grief," she said, rubbing her belly. You couldn't tell it by looking at her, but the woman was three months pregnant. "Sometimes, I feel like some duppy done curse me." It took no less than three miscarriages, but Cassia finally got pregnant with Nate. After years of high priced fertility treatments and trying the old fashioned way, Cassia was again with child. "You will be my saving grace," she said, rubbing her belly. Nate stared at her mother's burgeoning baby bump as Cassia accelerated and made a hard right turn.

"Your father and I hand everything to you on a silver platter. You choose to repay us by being a laughing stock. Don't you care what people think?" Nate glanced at the speedometer as Cassia clocked in at twenty miles over the legal limit. "There are places we can send you," Cassia's tone softened. "Places that will fix you."

"I not broken!" Nate protested emphatically.

"You know it's a sickness, Natalia. A sickness and a sin!" Cassia swerved around an SUV into what would have been oncoming traffic, had the road ahead not been clear.

"You don't understand—you never will," Nate grumbled under her breath.

"You can be cured. We can correct this," Cassia protested.

"Why can't I live with Auntie Earlene?" Nate pouted as Cassia grew quietly humiliated that her daughter preferred the company of her sister-in-law.

"You must be mad," Cassia said, cutting her eyes at Nate. She then veered around a slow truck, only this time, she ran directly into an oncoming passenger van. Moments later, the mangled sedan lay head over heels in a nearby ditch, spewing flames and exhaust into the baby blue sky.

"Mom!" Nate screamed for Cassia, who had already unbuckled her seat belt and slid out of the car.

The last thing Nate remembered was begging Cassia for help. Although battered and bruised Cassia made absolutely no effort to save her firstborn from the smoldering, wrong side up vehicle. When Nate awoke in the hospital bed, her thighs were bandaged due to the second-degree burns she'd endured and Auntie Earlene was by her side to deliver the heart-wrenching news.

"She lost the baby, Natty." Auntie Earlene gently rested her heavy body atop Nate's as they grieved the life of a child they never knew. "He's with the angels now."

#

Haunted by the memory of her childhood, 28-year-old Natalia Higgins tossed and turned in bed as she relived the tragic accident that had claimed her unborn brother's life. In the sixteen years since his death, Nate had grown distant from her family and had started a brand new life in California. Her two-bedroom apartment was small, but because she was a minimalist, it was all she needed. The view of Echo Park Lake, accompanied by Los Angeles' distinct skyline, provided just the right amount of street chic. The walls were covered with a bevy of Buddhas and West African masks, and the air wafted with the faintest combination of Nag Champa and weed.

Her government name was Natalia Higgins, but depending on the circumstance, she also went by Nate, Natty or her podcast moniker, Natty One. The Montego Bay native had moved from Jamaica fourteen years ago and hadn't been back since. In typical fashion, the podcaster and aspiring music producer had fallen asleep under an ice, gold and green throw in her apartment's converted recording studio. Its contents: a mixing board, keyboard, two computers, a futon and wall-to-wall framed posters of reggae and electronic dance music legends.

Nate's face was partially shielded by a set of wireless headphones and bleach-blond dreads. Yet, the outline of her body was still quite visible: a pair of long brown limbs tucked awkwardly into a fetal position, and a rear-end round enough for a baller, yet sensible enough to be seen on a Senator's arm. Suddenly her smartphone rang, and Nate stopped snoring. She was groggy and had a crick in her neck courtesy of the well-worn futon, but she still managed to answer the phone by its third ring.

"Hello?" Nate cleared her throat and opened her eyes partially, sliding the headphones off her ears and on to her neck.

"Natty. Hi, this is." The woman took a beat to collect herself. "This is Ms. Ruth. Your Auntie asked me to call you."

"Ms. Ruth?" Why was Auntie Earlene's closest friend calling Nate and so early in the morning at that? Nate sat up straight and threw her legs over the edge of the futon. She then listened intently as the woman who knew Nate well enough to call her by her pet name, "Natty," continued.

"She's not doing so well." Ruth paused for a beat. "She's sick, Natty. Doctors say..."

"I'll take it from here, Ruth." Barrington Higgins, Jamaica's Minister of Youth and Culture, stopped Ruth mid-sentence and came on to the phone.

"Daddy?" It had been a good three months since Nate had talked to her father and even longer since she'd spoken to her mother. Officially freaked out, Nate turned the speaker function on and began to pace. Her silhouette breezed past the living room's picture window overlooking Echo Park Lake as the sun slowly made its debut across Los Angeles' expansive horizon.

"Hey, baby girl," Barrington's deep, island-tinged voice permeated Nate's apartment, causing her pause. "Auntie Earlene's not doing well. Natty, you need to come home straight away."

"What's wrong with her?" Nate emerged from the shadows and slipped into the growing patch of sun on the hardwood floor.

"They're running some tests." Barrington lowered his voice to a hush and Nate listened as his dress shoes clicked across the tiled hospital floor. "She's been at the hospital for weeks now," Barrington choked up as his voice began to tremble, "It's pancreatic cancer. The test will tell us how advanced."

"Cancer?" Natty stammered in disbelief as her heartbeat intensified, and tiny beads of sweat began to grace her temples. "Why am I just now hearing about this?"

"Auntie didn't want to worry you. She's stubborn as an old ox. You know that," Barrington joked, trying to lighten what had become an exceptionally solemn mood.

"Listen, little brother, I'm sick, not deaf," Auntie Earlene's voice resonated through Nate's speakerphone. "I asked you to call the girl for me. The phone now, please, Barry."

Exasperated, Barrington sighed and conceded to his only sibling. "Please, Earlene. Relax." He said, handing Auntie Earlene the phone. "It's bad enough you stopped treatment."

Earlene sucked her teeth defiantly, and Nate listened from her apartment as her aunt sounded off in her customary fashion. "First of all, I am relaxed, so don't vex me!" Nate couldn't help but laugh aloud at the irony of Auntie Earlene screaming about how relaxed she was. "And second, ain't nothing so serious that the Lord Almighty and some bush tea can't remedy." Earlene hadn't skipped a beat. She sounded just as sassy as she'd always been. Nate felt suddenly soothed as her heart rate began to normalize. Maybe Auntie Earlene did have a fighting chance.

"My talented niece, Natty One," Auntie Earlene spoke into the cell phone. "You know I play that last CD you sent me 'til it couldn't play no more." Earlene's laugh turned quickly into a cough.

"I'm glad you liked it, Auntie, but daddy says you been in the hospital for weeks. You should've told me. And what's this about you stopping treatment?" Nate put the call on speaker and then used her tablet to search for flights home.

"Now, hold on, Natty. Catch your breath," Auntie Earlene insisted. "Let me hear it."

"I'm safe. I'm breathing. I got this." Nate ran through the mantra that her Auntie Earlene had taught her years ago.

"Very good, Natty." Auntie Earlene paused as Nate ran through the mantra one last time and then she continued, "Treatment made me feel worse than I already did. I just need a small break. Then I'll be back at it."

"I can be there tonight or tomorrow morning." Nate clicked around the page, checking departure times and fares, just as a calendar alert popped onto the screen: Brown Bag Cutie—Show Open Pitch—Simon and Chad Herbst—Four PM, Tuesday.

"Meh say hold on." Earlene's gentle yet firm tone got Nate's attention. "There's no need to rush back. Get here by Friday, that's when doctors will have the results."

"You sure, Auntie?"

"Natalia," Auntie Earlene sighed. Calling Nate by her government name meant she wasn't playing. Nate knew better than to make Auntie Earlene repeat herself.

"Yes, Auntie." Nate clicked the flight search close.

"Until then, all I ask is that you pray for your Auntie. You'll do that for me, right?"

"Of course, Auntie."

"Good. Now, your daddy wants to talk, but y'all make it quick. I won't have you running up my minutes."

"Yes, Auntie," Nate laughed as Auntie Earlene passed the phone back to Barrington.

"Email me your flight info, and I'll send a car," Barrington said, hopping back on the call.

"I'll catch a cab," Nate quickly declined the offer.

"Nonsense," Barrington maintained his position.

"Fine, daddy. Thanks."

"Mommy and I can't wait to see you."

"I'll email you." Nate hit the end call button before Barrington could finish his goodbyes.

"Love you, Natty," Barrington spoke into the phone, although Nate had already hung up.

Suddenly lightheaded, Nate's cell phone slipped from her grip as her stomach did summersaults. Her hand covering her mouth, Nate reached the half bath just in time to hurl. After heaving for a few minutes, she flushed last night's leftovers away and tried best to compose herself. Nate grasped the porcelain throne firmly and then slowly rose to her feet. Next, she grabbed her fanny pack from the hook behind her. She then pulled out a CO_2 reducing inhaler and took several deep breaths. Nate had come to rely on the inhaler ever since discovering it on a late-night infomercial. She'd struggled with panic attacks after surviving a violent assault in Jamaica and had depended on the device's anxiety-reducing effects along with Auntie Earlene's mantra ever since: "I'm safe. I'm breathing. I got this."

Auntie Earlene having cancer, was horrible, but the thought of seeing her parents face to face after all these years had brought Nate to her knees. Nate was scared and gripped instantly by panic. Thankfully, with the help of her inhaler and a reassuring phrase, she was able to force those emotions down. Hell, she had to! Albeit self-diagnosed and largely untreated, the fact of the matter was Nate had endured years of posttraumatic stress and a bulk of it stemmed from her parents abandoning her when she needed them most.

Rocked by the tragic death of Nate's unborn little brother, the family exuded a brave exterior, but on the inside, they were crumbling. Even two years after the tragedy, Barrington and Cassia insisted that they did not have the emotional bandwidth to support a lifestyle Nate could always, as they put it, "choose to correct." Unable to deal with her budding love for women and its potential to affect their standing in the community, at the tender age of fourteen, Nate's politically entrenched family shipped her to California to live with relatives. Her relationship with her parents all but flat-lined, Auntie Earlene had been the only one who remained consistently close. She had been there for Nate since birth, and although she refused to fly, Auntie Earlene had for years kept tabs on Nate.

Nate used a hair tie situated amongst the beaded bracelets on her wrist to gather her dreads into a loose topknot. Next, she let the faucet run for a beat, then doused warm water on to her face and the back of her neck. As the water ran, it was as if Auntie Earlene was standing right beside her. "All I ask is that you pray for your Auntie. You'll do that for me, right?"

Auntie Earlene's instructions were as clear as the water that cascaded down Nate's wrists onto the bath mat on which she stood. "Of course, Auntie." Nate turned the faucet off and then slowly raised her head. She allowed her face to drift up to the mirror and then locked eyes with her own reflection. Nate smiled at how much she did, in fact, resemble a younger version of her sassy Auntie Earlene, although she had no idea how deep their kinship indeed ran. Nate soaked in this image of self for a beat and then shut her chestnut-colored eyes as tight as possible. She took a deep breath and then started to pray. "Dear God."

Chapter 2

Brown Bag Cutie

Beside a Jacuzzi atop a downtown Los Angeles rooftop, Nate scanned the expansive skyline. Since she'd hung up the phone with her family earlier that morning, her mind had been clouded with thoughts of Auntie Earlene's diagnosis. A welcomed distraction, Nate gripped her boom microphone firmly and silently thanked God for work. It was past morning rush hour, but the downtown streets below were still bustling as the skeleton film crew assembled for their first shot of the day on the most asinine dating show to ever hit reality TV. While she pursued her musical ambitions, Nate had found work as a boom operator and sound engineer at Herbst Studios on that very same dating show. The show was called "Brown Bag Cutie" and its premise was simple—one picker chooses between several masked daters.

This was Round One of the competition, and by its end, the pool of five potential mates would be reduced to one female picker and four male daters. Two of the men sported authentic Lucha Libre wrestling masks, while a couple rocked customized brown bags and the final contender, also known as the wild card, remained bare faced. The goal was to see whether winning personalities or striking physicality carries the most weight when looking for a potential date.

"Okay, fellas, congrats and welcome to Brown Bag Cutie," the female picker squealed.

"Cheers!" The group clinked their glasses together and toasted mimosas as Nate angled the boom microphone in their direction. "Now this may be a little premature, but I want to see whose got the best victory dance," she demanded.

"Nothing premature about me!" Dater #1 exclaimed. Nate rolled her eyes at the proclamation as the unmasked dater hopped from the Jacuzzi and commenced a rhythm-less two-step.

The director hung back, offering camera cues as the date unfolded on a series of monitors. "Camera Two, go tight on this idiot. Camera One, you stay wide," she whispered into the camera operators' earpieces.

"I'd actually rather take a victory lap," Dater #2 responded. He then plunged below the water's surface and headed straight for the picker's thighs.

"Camera One, slow zoom on Mr. Two Left Feet and Camera Two, same move on the picker," commanded the director. Nate held the boom as steady as possible. In her earphones, the indisputable moaning of the female picker grew intense. Was Dater #2 really doling out underwater head?

"Man, just cut! Cut already!" The bare face dater yelled and then stormed off as Dater #2 emerged and waved goodbye.

"Later, dude," The second dater laughed.

"I suggest you gargle, dude!" The bare-faced dater screamed while pulling up faded jeans over his swimming trunks. "Y'all don't pay me enough," he said, bolting toward the exit. Nate was in shock as the busty blonde pushed Dater #2's head back underwater. The director was thrilled. "Follow him to confessional," the director ordered as the producer leaped to her feet and trailed behind the frustrated contestant. "Camera One, go wide. Camera Two, keep rolling on the picker."

After several hours of day drinking and crude commentary disguised as getting to know each other, it was Round Three and the picker had narrowed her choices down to two daters. Dater #2, his identity still obscured by the traditional Mexican wrestling mask, had remained charming throughout the day and seemed to genuinely connect with the picker. Although his face was hidden, you could tell he worked out. Plus, the way that the setting sun saluted his bronze skin had Nate betting he was a shoo-in. His competition—an alpha male rocking a bedazzled brown bag and an over-the-top television persona. While the wannabe reality star had a solid physique, he'd managed to irk the hell out of everyone on set. His first faux pas, shorting out a wireless microphone because he felt the need to cannonball into the infinity pool. Idiot.

Chapter 3

Affirmative Action

"So who did she pick?" asked twenty-seven-year-old Karina Zakaryan, leaning in—more buzzed than curious. She and Nate had been friends since high school, and even back then, Karina liked to get what she called, lifted.

"Mr. Brownbag," Nate replied, lowkey annoyed at the increasing difficulty inherent in their conversation.

"The frat boy? No!" Karina screamed, slamming her hand down hard on the glass table for emphasis. She was loud and doing way too much for a Monday night.

"Girl, yes." Nate scanned the down-home Armenian restaurant, locking eyes with curious customers and waitstaff. "And please keep your voice down," she continued. "You just got off work. How are you this lit?" Nate squeezed fresh lime into her Vodka tonic and took a sip.

Out of nowhere, Karina's nose began to run, making it apparent to Nate that Karina's sudden case of the sniffles was actually a California cold. She then watched as Karina scanned the popular Eurasian restaurant. Other diners did their best but were unsuccessful in averting their gazes. Karina laughed hysterically, enjoying the attention. Although she had gained a noticeable twenty pounds in the last few months, Nate knew better than to mention it. Thick or thin, the woman was striking. Karina was a full-figured, first-generation Armenian-American with fair skin, dark hair and a smile that rivaled the night sky's brightest constellation. She was also intoxicated.

"Don't get your burka in a bunch," Karina joked. She then poked at the ice in her cup, while gesturing for a waiter.

"Yes, ma'am." The waiter approached.

"One more Vodka on the rocks for me," Karina instructed.

"And you, Miss?" The waiter asked, smiling in Nate's direction.

"I'll have another," Nate accepted, her eyes trained on Karina. For as long as she could remember, her long-time friend had been a functioning addict. Presently, her drug of choice was cocaine, but back in high school, her addictive personality revolved around boys, booze and homemade sizzurp. In fact, it was no secret that for a few months during sophomore year Karina sold the mixture of Codeine, grape soda and jolly ranchers to students. Luckily for Karina, her parents were big-time donors, so she never got into any real trouble. Even when the cops busted her for selling on school grounds, her family's lawyers were able to make the entire situation go away.

"Loosen up," Karina laughed, tearing off a piece of lavash and tossing the traditional flatbread in Nate's direction.

"I've been working through a lot today, plus this meeting with Simon has me so anxious. If he likes my track and uses it for the Brown Bag Cutie show open, I will legit lose my shit."

"How could he not like your music? I've been talking you up nonstop since we ran into each other at Runyon last week," Karina squealed, strategically omitting critical details about her strained relationship with Simon. "He's a gatekeeper—if you get this right, you'll be scoring movies, TV, touring. And it'll all be thanks to me!" Karina bragged.

"Oh, so you after your ten percent?" Nate was only partially joking. She and Karina had been friends since high school and one thing she knew for sure about her dear old friend was that Karina rarely did something for nothing.

"I just want to see you win," Karina maintained.

"Simon and his brother Chad are just so connected," Nate said, sipping her cocktail. "Especially, Simon. I still can't believe he left Masquerade Records to take over for his pops."

"You're meeting with the newly named joint heads of Herbst Studios," Karina continued. "It would be weird if you weren't at least a little nervous, but no worries. You got this. And by the way, Simon Herbst is a teddy bear." A grizzly bear was more like it! Karina again stretched the truth; however, it would take Nate several days to discover it for herself.

"I've spent the day listening to my parents complain about how I'm not as dedicated to real estate as my brother while you've spent the day surrounded by hot boys and D-cups," Karina teased.

"You're ridiculous," Nate smirked. Karina had a point. Nate's job was pretty cool on paper, but in truth, being a black woman working production on a reality TV show was far from transcendent.

"You should be grateful. People would kill to be in your position. And speaking of positions, see if that were me, Lucha Libre or not, I would have been all up on the brown-skinned brotha with the chiseled chest. Yum-my!"

Some things never change. Growing up, Karina had a real fetish for black boys and black culture. In truth, the only thing that came easier than hooking up with black guys was high school track. The summer before her sophomore year, she'd discovered that cocaine not only made her feel great but was also an appetite suppressant. After shedding some weight, the formerly chubby teen found that her long limbs and athletic build made her a natural at the sport. So for two years of high school, she ran and got high. She liked getting high for obvious reasons—being inebriated felt phenomenal, plus escaping reality was a definite incentive.

Eventually, Karina came to enjoy track. Competition was thrilling, but in all honesty, the brothas were her primary motivation. To Karina, their swag was even more intoxicating than the Codeine laced concoction she slang in the cafeteria. As politically correct as her parents pretended to be, they did not want their daughter dating outside of her race or religion. They never outright said it, but Karina knew that her infatuation with black boys got under their fair skin, which to her made dating guys named Jahvon and Tre all the more enticing.

"What did he look like under the mask anyway?" Karina wrapped her crimson painted lips around the straw and began to suck.

"I guess you'll just have to tune in and see," Nate replied, eying Karina curiously. Inebriated or not, she was more than fine. The woman oozed sex appeal without even trying. And sure, they were besties, but Nate was first and foremost a lesbian with very real needs. Sitting across from Karina, she couldn't help but think back to the one time these needs almost got the best of her. It all happened late one night, a year ago. After partying with some friends in Karina's downtown loft, Nate volunteered to help clean up. Eventually, she and Karina ventured to the rooftop Jacuzzi, where they indulged in one too many shots of premium Vodka.

Laughter led to lust, and the next thing Nate knew, Karina was straddling her in the warm water and kissing her deeply. The kiss was a mystical, drunken blur of which Nate stopped as soon as she considered the repercussions of hooking up with her best friend. No matter how one-sided their friendship sometimes was, it meant more to Nate than any fling ever could. Besides, Karina was straight, and from experience, Nate knew that getting involved with straight girls, even if they asked for it was a headache waiting to happen.

"So let's talk Simon," Nate said, leaning in. "Tell me everything." She shifted her focus from her off-limits friend to the matter at hand.

"Like I said, he's a teddy bear," Karina shrugged.

"Go on." Nate signaled the waiter as Karina continued.

"We met at an all-white party, Memorial Day weekend." Karina used the straw to draw figure eights in the short, fat glass as she told the story of how she'd met Simon several months ago. "My parents were hosting a party for some of their VIP clients on the Queen Mary and Simon was there. His dad had just purchased his third home in Malibu through our agency before he passed."

"Tragic," Nate said, shaking her head somberly.

"I know, right? We almost didn't get the commission because his fourth wife hated the house, but my dad was like, no backsies, boo," Karina snickered.

"I was referring to the tragic car crash that took his life, but hey, a deals a deal," Nate's sarcasm was palatable.

"Basically," Karina replied and smiled at the waiter as he approached, cocktails in hand.

"One Vodka tonic and one on the rocks. Can I get you ladies anything to eat?"

"I never eat past seven," Karina replied while using her smartphone as a mirror to primp.

"That's a lie," Nate laughed aloud. "Another order of lavash and hummus, please."

"So anyway, the Queen Mary was cracking. Simon was hanging with his brother and a couple other guys," Karina continued.

"We started talking about that plastic surgery reality show you guys produce, what's it called?" Satisfied with her appearance, Karina asked, placing her phone back on the table.

"Replace My Face," Nate retorted, mortified at the roster of absurdity that she'd helped to produce. However, she had faith that her big break was just around the corner.

"Replace My Face," Karina chuckled. "That's the one! Anyway, Simon told me how three female producers had just up and quit. So I mentioned Troy."

"T-Roy? You hooked him up with your dealer?" Nate queried.

"So what! Troy is the truth and you know it," Karina declared. "I mean, sure he deals, but he's freelanced for years. So I worked my magic and hooked a brotha up—401K, PTO, the whole deal." Karina took a long swig, proud of herself. "That's what I call affirmative action."

"I wouldn't go that far, but it's cool you were able to get him in," Nate paused for a beat before continuing. "He's lost out on permanent positions to other freelancers with half his experience on multiple occasions." Nate sighed, annoyed as she could relate to the feeling of being passed by and overlooked.

"Now, boo, you know better than anyone, skills don't matter. At least not much." Karina reached over and placed her hand atop Nate's. "It's all about who you know. That is why you asked me to link you with Simon, right?" Karina didn't stop long enough for an answer. "Simon knows Troy, and as of tomorrow, he'll know you too. Affirmative action," Karina chirped.

"Okay, Kar. I'm going to need you to make a full stop. Affirmative action corrects years of systemic racism and sexism. What you did was hook Troy up. Big difference," Nate said, throwing what was left of her cocktail back like a shot.

"Is it really that different?" Karina softened. "A hook up is a hook up. Besides, I'm color blind. Always have been, always will be."

Color blind? Was she serious? Nate's skin crawled at the audacity and utter place of privilege that Karina was coming from. Between her Aunt's diagnosis and upcoming meeting, Nate just didn't have the bandwidth to explain to Karina why being color blind was a fallacy and in fact, a smack in the face to people of color. Although her family was Eurasian Muslim, which came with a whole host of unfair stereotypes, Karina didn't necessarily look the part. She could just as easily pass for Italian as she could Armenian. Unlike Nate, Karina had never been profiled or unjustly pulled over by the police. This was indeed a teachable moment, based on embracing diversity as opposed to disregarding our differences. Alas, Nate lacked both the energy and desire to mount her soapbox.

"For the sake of my sanity, let's table this discussion and get back to Simon." Nate sat up straight in her chair, eyeing one of her oldest and most out of touch friends.

"Affirmative," Karina replied sarcastically, which for her was a way of life.

"Kar," Nate rolled her eyes.

"I'm kidding," Karina smirked, tossing long, brunette extensions over her shoulder. Much like a cheap lace front wig, she was tough to pin down. On the one hand, Karina could be the most progressive person in the room, but in an instant, she'd change course, hurling micro-aggressions as indiscriminately as slugs from an AR-15. "So you and Simon only hung out that one time, on the ship?" Nate redirected their conversation.

"Actually I saw him a few days later. We checked out a house in the hills," Karina said, recalling the viewing: "Here's to the first of three beautiful homes we'll see today." Still curvy, but noticeably leaner, Karina raised her champagne flute and toasted Bellinis with Simon. "Follow me," she instructed.

"Anywhere," Simon smirked and followed Karina deeper into the palatial, two million dollar Hollywood Hills mansion. Rocking a tightly quaffed bun, black pencil skirt and money green blouse, Karina's look was polished, poised and professional.

"Tell me more about the wood." Simon rested his glass atop the fireplace. "You were saying it's durable and decay resistant," He asked, unbuttoning his blazer.

"Because of its rugged strength, Ipe wood is the number one choice for commercial and residential decking," Karina affirmed. "And the coloring, well, look for yourself." Karina squatted down and ran her fingers over the tight wood grain. "It's beautiful and the foundation for this incredible home."

"Breathtaking," Simon replied, standing over Karina. As she attempted to stand, he placed his hand on top of Karina's shoulder. "That's enough shop talk for one day, don't you think?" He asked, smiling perversely.

Karina was used to men coming on to her, so she typically knew how to play it, but this time was different. This was Karina's first property over one million dollars and although she was really counting on the commission, degrading herself had never been part of the plan.

"I'm flattered, but Simon, we can't." Karina tried not to handle the executive's fragile ego with care. "Let me show you the rest of the house." She stood up, smoothed her skirt and walked further into the vast home.

Unable to resist and unaccustomed to being turned down, Simon took the opportunity to grab a fistful of Karina's perky rear. And with that, she lost it along with any hope of cashing in on the biggest commission she had ever come close to making.

"Simon, stop!"

"Come on," Simon cackled, completely turned on by the perceived game of cat and mouse. "What happened to the party girl I met a couple of days ago?" Sure, Karina and Simon had done a couple of lines on the infamous party boat, but this was Los Angeles and indulging with strangers was not something Karina considered abnormal.

"It's not happening!" Karina stood her ground as Simon again invaded her personal space. His musky cologne was equally, if not more offensive than he was.

"Just let me show it to you," he moaned, grabbed his crotch and motioned for his zipper.

"What did you say?" Her face quickly grew flush, and although her tone was calm, Karina felt her blood boil. Although Karina was months removed from the encounter as she sat across from Nate in the Armenian restaurant donned in Halloween decorations, she became gripped with that same fear that she felt as Simon relentlessly propositioned her. Vacillating between fright and fury, the sound of Nate's voice diverted Karina's attention back to the moment at hand.

"Well, what did you say?" Nate rolled her eyes, convinced that Karina had zoned out and was simply too high to pay attention when in reality, she was undergoing genuine post-traumatic stress caused by Simon's assault.

"What?" Although Karina had watched Nate's lips move, she hadn't heard a word.

"I said, what did you say to Simon about me?" Nate questioned Karina, staring into her noticeably rounder face. She had no idea that the woman sitting across from her had spent the last six months emotional eating and binging cocaine in hopes of healing from the assault.

"I told him you were a talented musician with a stellar work ethic and that he'd be a fool not to put you on," Karina replied before scanning the room and pulling out her snuff bullet. Next, she inhaled two quick bumps sending a scorching plume of white-hot fire through her nasal cavity. Fast and discrete, the girl was a pro when it came to mood stabilization. "He's looking forward to meeting you. If you play it right, I'm sure he'll introduce you to the heavy hitters at Masquerade Records."

"You're the best!" Nate shrieked in excitement at the thought of getting one step closer to her goal of becoming a successful music producer.

"I know you're tired of holding that boom mic all day," Karina said, forcing a smile and trying her best to stifle memories of the horror she'd endured with Simon.

"Got the arms looking right, though." Nate flexed her right bicep, causing it to stiffen and jump on command under her button-down.

"I see you," Karina laughed and then inhaled a couple more bumps of the illegal substance. "So what you plan on wearing tomorrow? You should throw on a dress."

Nate laughed so hard it was now her turn to gain unwanted attention from neighboring tables. "Yea, not gonna happen," she sneered.

"Just asking. Because if you want, I could lend you something," Karina smirked.

"Yea, that's a hard no." Nate's smile exposed a pair of perfectly straight teeth, compliments of her well-to-do parents and the braces they insisted on. "Halloween's your favorite holiday, not mine," she joked. "I have no need for a costume, but thanks for the laugh. I needed that." The waiter approached their table and placed two more cocktails in front of them, along with the traditional bread and hummus. Karina waited for him to be out of earshot before speaking.

"So, what else is up?" Karina asked, genuinely concerned. "You're hella tense and I know it's not just meeting Simon that's got you on edge."

"What gave it away?" Nate asked, sipping her cocktail, which after the fourth one, tasted more like limeade than premium Vodka.

"Well, for one, you're going toe-to-toe with me, not that I'm counting." Karina raised her glass and Nate conceded, knowing full well that she was drinking more than usual.

"I got a call from my Auntie Earlene this morning. She's not doing well."

"Auntie Earlene with the bomb guava tarts?"

Nate sipped and nodded affirmatively. "It's cancer. She's been in the hospital for a couple of weeks now. They're running tests to see how far along it is."

Karina joined Nate on her side of the booth and Nate instantly let her head fall into Karina's comforting arms. "I'm so sorry, sis."

"Thanks, Kar." Stoic, Nate fought back tears. "I'm flying back at the end of the week."

"Good," Karina replied, while she tenderly stroked Nate's back. "How she holding up?"

"Still cussing folks out, so she's good, I guess," Nate grinned. "Typical island woman, trying to treat her stomachache with herbs and bush."

"Bush?" Karina asked, unfamiliar with the term.

"Auntie basically boils whatever herbs and roots she has growing in her garden into a bomb ass medicinal tea. I grew up on the stuff and rarely got even a cold," Nate confessed. Karina nodded that she understood as Nate continued.

"She thought it was gas. Everyone did, until the day Auntie Earlene found blood in her stool. Ms. Ruth put her in the car and drove her to the hospital on the spot."

"Ms. Ruth?" Karina queried.

"She's an old friend of Auntie's." Nate took another sip and replayed the early AM wake-up call in her head. "Auntie rarely calls, so when she did this morning, I knew something was up," Nate confessed.

"That's right, the old school letter writer. Adorable," Karina smiled.

"I spoke to my father too," Nate said, pausing for a beat as she recollected the call. "Emails and the occasional awkward phone call are one thing, but now that Auntie is sick, daddy's talking about how he and my mother can't wait to see me."

"After fourteen years, they're finally ready to accept their gay kid? Oh please!" Karina shouted
as the remnants of cocaine rushed down the back of her neck. "You're gonna need back up. Just say the word, and I'm there."

"I appreciate that," Nate grinned. Sure Karina was flying high, but Nate remained grateful that she always seemed to have her back. Despite her many flaws, this was the reason Nate had remained so loyal to their friendship. Warts and all, the two had been thick as thieves since high school. Little did she know, Nate would soon learn an ugly truth about her bestie—one that she would never be able to overlook.

Chapter 4

Apple Jacks

Tru Lee was a butterfly, a true chameleon and that night at the upscale seaside inn, her clients had requested that the dominatrix for hire transform into the classic schoolgirl. The curvaceous half black, half Korean woman dressed in clunky glasses, a short plaid skirt, stilettos and white button-down tied just below her full breasts, Tru was happy to oblige their fantasy. Having just concluded a heated S & M session complete with spankings, sensual massage, and lap dances, the strong-willed twenty-five-year-old was running late and needed to wrap things up.

Followed closely behind by a middle-aged white woman, Tru slipped into a black pea-coat and swung open the double doors leading to the penthouse suite. Tru smirked as the woman with the plump face and pear-like physique tried unsuccessfully to conceal a set of indisputably erect nipples that had moments prior been gripped by the ferocity of metal clamps.

"Incredible," Tru whispered in the woman's ear while giving her round rear a good squeeze.

"So next week, then, Mistress?" The woman, her face flushed and skin red hot, enveloped Tru in a long hug, allowing her hands to roam up and under the short Catholic school skirt.

"Maybe," Tru pulled away. Keep 'em guessing—whether it was personal or professional, this was her mantra and at the present moment, it was paying off big time.

"Maybe?" The woman mimicked Tru, then slid a manila envelope full of cash into her oversized purse, all while pulling her in close for a kiss. Tru was fast. With a nod of the head, she let the woman down with both style and ease as she had a strict no kissing policy.

"A lot going on next week, but I'll email you," Tru said.

"We look forward to it, Mistress!" The woman's lover exclaimed as smoke from a menthol cigarette poured from her mouth. She was around Tru's age, lying in bed and playing with a red ball gag that had minutes ago adorned her wide mouth.

Tru swept the bangs of her short, red bob out of her eyes and winked at the woman's lover. The bulk of Tru's clients were alpha males during the day, but once they left the boardroom, the beards came all the way off. And Tru never judged. How could she? Her subs were relatively easy to handle, plus their checks always cleared. But as a lesbian, Tru got a kick out of being contracted by females, especially hot chocolate femmes like the one lying in bed before her. While Tru was a consummate professional, she was unapologetic about the fact that her line of work came with some incredible perks.

"Take care. Both of you." Tru kissed the older woman on the cheek, then slunk toward the end of the corridor. She was met by a man dressed in a black, three-piece suit and eerie, half-face, skeleton style motorcycle helmet.

"Going down?" He asked, extending his arm and escorting Tru into the elevator. Moments later, Tru was throwing a duffle bag into the trunk of her 1995 cherry red BMW 325i and making a left out of the parking lot as her bodyguard steered his motorcycle in the opposite direction. A legit professional, Tru had mastered the art of the hotel quick change. In under seven minutes flat, she'd managed to swap out wigs and transform her sultry self into a casual cutie. As the cool ocean breeze whisked through the convertible and Tru's now eggplant colored pixie, the custom-built stereo pumped out the most recent episode of Nate's podcast—The Naked Truth with Natty One:

"All night people have been hitting me up with confessions," her Jamaican accent noticeably thicker, Nate's voice poured from the speakers. "Feels good, doesn't it? Go on, let that cat out the bag. Cheating on your girl? Living on the DL? Stole a pound of crab legs?" Nate laughed. "Hit me up and let me know."

Tru laughed along with Nate's podcast then took a long swig from her bedazzled flask. Moments later, the podcast switched to the show's musical segment, an eclectic blend of EDM and island rhythms. Then she glanced down at her dashboard. It was closing in on One AM, and she had promised Nate that she'd meet her at the club by midnight.

"Damn," Tru cursed and used a Kleenex to wipe away the blood-red lipstick frantically. She then texted Nate a single letter at each red light: "L-O-V-E-R."

Keep 'em guessing, Tru shrugged as the line between her professional mantra and personal life continued to blur.

#

Several miles away, Karina, forever the wildest of the crew danced for her life at the infamous West Hollywood club. Across the dance floor, a group of women eyeballed her seductively. "Karina, you need to stop!" Their butch and bubbly friend, Royce, laughed nervously, as Karina delighted in the attention.

"I'm thirsty," Karina smirked.

"Clearly," Royce joked. "So after what, a year of dating, we finally get to meet this mystery
chick?"

"We've met," Karina said, sucking her teeth. "Tru ain't all that. Besides, I wouldn't exactly call bumping uglies under the cloak of darkness, dating."

"You have no chill," Nate huffed.

"Well, it isn't," Karina replied.

"For the millionth time Kar, just because Nate has a girl, doesn't mean she loves us any less," Royce spoke to Karina the way a mother explains to her toddler that she's about to be a big sister. "Tru is not Nate's girlfriend," Karina countered, completely missing the point. Next she directed her attention back at the group of admirers. Using one finger, she beckoned them over. One brave soul, statuesque and dressed in a snapback and designer glasses, actually took the bait. Nate made a spin move so that she could get a better view as the lone lesbian in clunky frames drew near.

"Incoming," Nate giggled, satisfied to at least temporarily be off Karina's radar.

"Three, two, one," with the tall woman rapidly approaching, Karina counted down, then spun around to greet the stranger. "Hey," Karina spoke first. She figured it was the least she could do since the young lady had walked the length of the club to get a closer look.

"You wearing those shorts, ma," the stranger in glasses said, smiling at Karina.

"Thanks, ma!" Karina cooed as she stepped in closer to greet the woman. Taking this as their cue, Nate and Royce worked their way through the dance floor, leaving Karina to chat it up with the woman. Although Karina swore she was straight, male or female, she was here for every ounce of adoration.

It was near closing time at the landmark West Hollywood hot spot. In fact, you could practically smell the mix of desperation and bad decisions in the dense, club air. However, Nate and her crew had it all mapped out. The Club. Get in and get out before those dreadful house lights were brought up and that cutie you had been dancing with all night, the one you swore was a dime piece turned suddenly into a dud.

Once she and Royce reached the bar, Nate checked her phone and immediately assumed the goofiest grin imaginable. "I know that face," Royce laughed as Nate's fingers danced across her smartphone. "Yours Truly, right?"

Nate showed off the text that simply read, "L-O-V-E-R."

"No judgment, but I can't believe you've spent the last year getting done by a dominatrix. Who does that?" Royce asked playfully, socking Nate in the arm.

"So I'm emotionally unavailable and tend to date the like," Nate laughed. "But the more I think about it," she beamed, "the more I know Tru and I would make a dope couple."

"You're gonna make your booty call your boo," Royce teased, then directed her attention toward the bar. "Two shots of Patron and a Heineken." She nodded at the bartender and leaned back, resting her elbows on the bar to further enjoy the view as Nate returned the text message:

"Better had brought me a gift lol. That's the ONLY reason to be late! Matter fact, I just left." Moments later, a tap on the shoulder made it abundantly clear that the jig was up. Nate turned around to see Tru, dressed in a pair of pale purple skinny jeans and a belly-baring crop top. She was casually fine and Nate was thoroughly impressed. "So what'd you bring me?" Nate tossed back her shot of Patron, beaming as she greeted Tru.

"Some sugar," Tru replied, her once ruby red lips, now lubed solely by gloss.

"Word? Well, let me have it!" Nate shut her eyes and puckered up, only to be socked in the stomach with a box of Raisinets. "Real funny," Nate chuckled, pulling Tru in for a tight hug. "Oh, you got that."

"No, you got that," Tru whispered seductively, gripping Nate's ample bottom with a smirk. "I'm saying, Natty, you gotta fatty." Tru's attempt at an island accent was dreadful, but her words had been just enough to stir up the butterflies in Nate's stomach. The two women remained lost in each other's eyes and embraced until Nate noticed Royce gawking, her eyebrows raised unapologetically in their direction.

"This is Royce," Nate said, playing it cool as Royce sipped the cold brew.

"Of course." Tru extended her hand. "I'm Tru."

"And I'm a hugger." Royce rejected Tru's handshake, electing instead for an affectionate bear hug. Tru stiffened at the invasion of personal space. "Yours Truly in the flesh—it's nice to finally meet you."

"It's been hectic. I work a lot," Tru said, pulling away from the unexpected embrace.

"I've heard," Royce laughed knowingly, then redirected her gaze toward Karina. "Bumping and grinding for Grey Goose. Help her, Lord," Royce said, grimacing as Karina downed shots and danced on a mosaic tabletop. "I'm going in," she sighed, then made her way to the opposite end of the club.

"Have fun with that," Tru joked. Utterly uninterested in playing captain save-a-hoe, she grabbed Nate's arm and ventured onto the crowded dance floor, where the two women grooved along to a reimagined seventies soul classic.

"It's about that time, princess!" Royce tried not to make a scene as she screamed over the music and extended her hand toward Karina. Without so much as a "thanks for the drinks," Karina leaped from the mosaic tabletop, all smiles.

Meanwhile, Nate kissed Tru lustfully on the dance floor. "Someone's excited," Tru said, pulling away confused, as Nate—in a year of casual dating, had never been the type to display PDA. Emboldened by happy hour with Karina, followed by multiple cocktails at the club, Nate found it hard to focus. In fact, since learning of Auntie Earlene's life-threatening diagnosis early that morning, thoughts of a return trip home had left her ravaged by anxiety. Thankfully, the sight of Tru paired with an abundance of well-aged Tequila, were temporary, albeit welcomed distractions.

"Didn't think you'd show," Nate slurred and again dove tongue first into Tru's mouth. Pawing at Tru like an enamored newlywed, Nate remained oblivious to onlookers. Embarrassed, Tru pulled away again, but this time she maintained her distance.

"What's wrong? My breath stink?" Her almond-shaped eyes now nearly shut, Nate laughed and swayed from side to side.

"Let me grab you a bottled water," Tru softened.

Across the club, things with Karina and Royce were on the verge of becoming downright dangerous. "I got this!" The tomboy, who Karina had sidelined, hopped down from the tabletop and into Royce's face.

"It's all good. She's my sister," Royce said laughing, and dangling an empty beer bottle lowly by her side as a couple of party people snickered at the thought of the bump and grinding, interracial duo being related.

Convinced that she was being played, the lanky tomboy in the fitted snapback pushed Royce hard in the chest. Caught off guard, the typically peaceful woman's knee jerk reaction was not to turn the other cheek, but in fact, an eye for an eye. With no hesitation, Royce shoved the tomboy back and shattered her empty beer bottle on a nearby table, all in one fluid motion. "Back! Up!" Royce exclaimed, pointing the fractured glass in the direction of the tomboy and her squad.

The crowd quickly growing around them gained the attention of Nate and Tru. Immediately, the women sprinted in the direction of the chaos. Fortunately, by the time Nate and Tru waded through the mess, someone had already broken up what had the potential to become a brawl.

"Let's go!" Karina screamed, grabbed Royce by her hand and led her out of the club. As the crowd slipped quickly back into party mode, Nate and Tru hung back for a beat to assure that the lesbian terror squad didn't try a sneak attack. Her adrenaline pumping, Nate was lost in the moment and had almost forgotten that Tru was by her side.

"Your girl really knows how to ruin a good time," Tru said, tossing aubergine bangs out of her eyes, as Nate snapped out of her adrenaline-fueled haze.

Moments later, Karina decompressed with a hand-rolled clove at a park behind the club while Royce, visibly shaken, prayed aloud to be exonerated, "I completely blacked out. Lord, forgive me."

"You should've cut her!" Karina chuckled. Mercy was not her strong suit.

"That's not even funny!" Nate screeched.

"Keep running all that game and somebody will get hurt," Tru piped in as Nate braced for the exchange. Ever since Nate divulged the details of their steamy, first-time encounter, Karina had made it clear that she did not like Tru. Their late-night hookup had occurred just days after Nate shot down Karina's hot tub advances and had been a real blow to Karina's ego.

Karina was good and plastered, but even when sober the girl had absolutely no filter. Her friends could sense it. She was about to blow. "Nate, check your girl with her cheap wig-wearing ass!" Her statement punctuated by the roar of nearby thunder, Karina took a long drag from her clove and then exhaled in Tru's direction.

"All that's not even necessary," Nate said, rolling her eyes in Karina's direction.

"Damn Kar, chill," Royce replied, raising a disapproving eyebrow.

"What? She don't know me," Karina responded roughly. She had this funny habit of getting all Crenshaw and Pico, even though she was reared in the country clubs of Brentwood. Her friends couldn't help but laugh.

"Easy, killer," Tru smirked, unbothered by Karina's crudeness or the rain clouds in the night sky.

"We're out." Nate hugged her crew and then she and Tru made their departure.

"Good luck on that meeting with Simon tomorrow, love," Karina couldn't resist reminding Nate about the potentially game-changing encounter she'd orchestrated.

"Sleep it off, beautiful!" Nate yelled and waved goodbye without looking back.

"She so wants you," Tru spoke lowly while leaning into Nate as they strolled down the boutique-lined boulevard. "You sure y'all never dated?"

"Hell no!" Nate didn't want to lie but felt as though the omission was necessary. In their fourteen-year friendship, Nate and Karina had shared one drunken kiss in a Jacuzzi. And because they'd agreed never to mention it, Nate felt it was only right she keep her word. "I'd be surprised if she even remembers you were here tonight," Nate said shaking her head somberly. "She's been partying a lot lately.

"You mean more than you?" Tru asked, eyeing Nate. While the near brawl was sobering, Nate,

the light-weight, remained blatantly buzzed.

"Seriously, something's up with her," Nate protested.

"Nothing, a stint at rehab, won't cure," Tru shrugged. "Probably needs a hug and a good shrink wouldn't hurt," Tru smirked, unaware of how true her statement was.

"And what do you need?" Before Tru could answer Nate's question, the skies opened up and began to douse the city of angels in a wicked downpour. Nate grabbed her hand and they quickly ducked under a nearby awning for shelter.

"I'll get the car," Tru said, motioning for her keys.

"No." Nate grabbed Tru's arm. "It'll pass. Let's give it a minute."

"Okay," Tru said, closing her eyes and melting into Nate's chest. "You smell good."

"Don't change the subject," Nate replied with a grin. Lately, Nate talked more and more about becoming an official couple, which was clearly where this line of questioning was heading. "Seriously, what do you need for us to make this work?" Nate queried, her almond-shaped eyes now little more than two narrow slits.

"I think I'm gonna need you to sober up," Tru responded with a playful eye roll. A full four inches taller, Tru looked up to Nate, who, to her surprise, was coming in top speed and tongue first. Even though public displays of affection were entirely out of character for them, the chemistry between the two women was undisputable. Tru allowed herself to go with it and for a beat, they faded entirely into the moment. Oblivious of spectators in honking cars, Tru and Nate kissed feverishly, fondling each other with vigor, as rain poured down from above.

Nate was insatiable. She nibbled at Tru's neck, then spun her around with ease, pressing Tru's chest firmly against the brick, storefront wall.

"It's like that?" Tru smiled, looked over her shoulder and submitted to another wet kiss. Nate was in heaven. Tru tasted like the milk left over after a heaping bowl of Apple Jacks on a Saturday morning and her backside was just as sweet. Standing behind her, Nate pulled Tru in even closer. Nate then allowed her fingers to float from Tru's hips as her hands slipped up and under Tru's shirt, clutching a perky set of C-cups. The cool, damp air on Tru's warm skin was enough to smack her quickly back to reality.

"I have something for you," Tru moaned lowly and spun around so that she and Nate were face to face. The two then took off running hand-in-hand into the rain.

Chapter 5

White Girl Wasted

Outside, a torrential storm rained down hard and boomed with thunder. And although the inside of Karina's industrial home was dry, the vibe was just as bleak. She'd drawn the shades in the tenth-floor loft apartment, making the swanky 2,000 square foot space dank and cold. And lining the concrete floors were the remnants of tonight's look. A pair of solid gold, sequence booty shorts, black lace undies and a single high-heeled shoe led to the downstairs bathroom doorframe. While in the air, her disappointed Armenian mother's distinct inflection rang like cowbells through Karina's speakerphone.

"I'm beginning to see a pattern, Karina. You can't just miss work once a week," Karina's mother reprimanded her via voicemail as Karina clumsily searched the fully stocked medicine cabinet. Advil, Adderall, Tylenol, Zanax, the party girl was locked and still pretty loaded. "Did you think the studio wouldn't call when you missed today's viewing? My clueless child," she groaned. "You begged us to do business with the studios—cried to your father to be lead on this contract. If you won't do the work, your brother is more than willing to take the Herbst account off your hands."

Karina groaned and contemplated who was more annoying, the mother who loved to point out her shortcomings or Tru who had been a pain in her ass ever since she'd come into Nate's life. With a sigh, Karina reached for the extra strength Excedrin, popped the top and shook several into her open mouth, as her mother continued to ride her.

"Yes patrast yem ognel dzez?" Loosely translated, Karina's mother was willing to help her, but wondered when Karina would be willing to help herself." As the voicemail concluded, Karina pressed delete on the message left earlier that day. Like most moms, Karina's had mastered the art of the guilt trip and slipping into Armenian was her signature chokehold.

Karina slammed the cabinet door shut, causing glass to splinter and rain down into the bathroom sink. Unphased by the "sleep it off, beautiful" post it clinging faintly to the top left corner of the mangled mirror, Karina reached for the biggest shard and deliberately sliced a thin layer into her forearm. The fresh wound lay right beside a scar of identical proportion and had punctured the skin just enough to draw blood. Suddenly soothed, Karina took a good look at herself in the cracked glass. Hair matted, makeup smeared and rocking an apropos "White Girl Wasted" tank, Karina Zakaryan was a bonafide hot mess.

"Sleep it off, beautiful," she scoffed after reading the light-hearted, yet inspirational post-it aloud.

Nate had left it there the night she denied Karina's drunken Jacuzzi advances. A disheveled heap and unable to sleep, Karina ripped the post it down and stumbled past the massive soaking tub. She'd converted it into a makeshift bed by fitting it with a blanket and pillows. Karina figured if she had to yack, sleeping as close as possible to the toilet was a safe bet. Next, she stepped over the remnants of discarded fast food leading to the living room, its only source of light—two eerie Jack-O-Lanterns resting on the marble mantel.

Karina, flopped onto the leather sectional and leaned toward the mirrored coffee table. Then she inhaled two fat lines and threw her head back onto the couch as the cocaine went to work. Karina focused on the ceiling fan above her. Its slow, melodic drone was so mesmerizing that she shut her eyes and began to drift. Entranced by their dull hum, the blades of the fan fused impeccably with the melodic beats that Karina recalled Nate laying down just last month at Herbst Studios:

Karina remembered Nate seated behind the audio console, pressing buttons. "I started with this," Nate said, hammering out a spastic melody. She then reached over to the mixer and added a beat, which only seemed to complicate things, but by massaging the tempo, the sound gradually morphed into an edgy aria.

"O.k." Karina began to nod her head to the beat, unaware that Tru was its inspiration.

"Then I went here," Nate replied, adding another layer, this time an EDM and piano mashup.

"Nice! Karina squealed. "You're all boom by day—beats by night." She said, gesturing to Nate's boom microphone nestled in the corner.

"Speaking of beating it up at night," Nate laughed. She had melded two completely different flows into one cohesive vibe in a matter of minutes. "I'm falling, Kar," Nate gushed, biting at her bottom lip seductively.

"I just hope you're able to get up because I'm not convinced," Karina spoke candidly about Nate's relationship with Tru.

"You will be," Nate countered.

"You should go for that intern. You said she's been throwing it at you," Karina pushed knowing full well that hooking up with coworkers had never been Nate's style.

"I'm telling you, Tru could be wifey," Nate said, pausing her handiwork to let a timeless un-manipulated rock steady track play. "Now, this I haven't placed yet, but I know it'll work."

Karina took Nate's cue and shifted the conversation from Tru back to the music. "To think, you've wasted all that time and talent on reality shows." The combination of Karina's backhanded compliment and a producer entering the audio suite without knocking brought the session to a roaring halt.

"Big up! Big up!" The producer entered the cramped audio bay like a tourist, tipsy on Bourbon Street. "Dope beats, Nate," he admitted, "but that sounds nothing like the mixes for Replace My Face." This particular producer got on Nate's last nerve as he insisted on slipping into Ebonics whenever he spoke to her. "Where my mixes at?" He queried.

Nate refused to reciprocate his foolishness. Instead, she pressed stop on the rock steady track and kept her tone professional. "Hey Bruce, I posted them to the server an hour ago. Guess you missed my email."

"If I don't respond to your emails, shoot a brotha a text," he commanded. "It's that simple."

"I'm just saying the mixes are posted every morning at the same time," Nate said, standing her ground.

"So angry," replied Bruce, softening as he looked over at Karina. "Who's she?"

"This is my friend, Karina," Nate replied as she began to talk up her best friend. "She's with Zakaryan Realtors. I know we're looking for some new places to shoot and thought Karina could help. We discussed this last week. You told me to bring her by for coffee." Nate laughed, making herself appear less combative as she walked the fine line of handling both the producer's ego and tenure with care. "You accepted the calendar invite," she tried to jog his memory.

"An email reminder would've been nice," he responded while walking over to greet Karina.

"You just said to text," Nate responded matter-of-factly.

"So sassy," the producer laughed. "How do you deal with this one?"

"I'm always telling her that—you know how it is with some people," Karina replied with evidently no qualms about throwing Nate under the bus.

"Pleasure to meet you, Karina."

"The pleasure's all mine," she smiled.

"Bruce," the smitten producer declared, beaming in Karina's face. "I've already had my coffee, but I'd love to look at some of the properties. Come back tomorrow if you can swing it. I'll connect you and my location team."

"Fantastic! Thank you, Bruce," Karina said, shaking the producer's hand. Unbeknownst to Nate, Karina's plan to infiltrate Herbst Studios was in full swing. Her next order of business would be taking down Simon.

"Perfect! Nate, do me a favor. Text me Karina's contact info and make sure she has the show synopsis," the producer concluded."

"That went great!" Karina howled as soon as the lanky producer was on the other side of the door.

"Some people?" Nate cringed, recalling the loaded phrase.

"You know how it is with these dorky producers, just stroking his ego," Karina maintained.

"You sold the man his house. Just pitch Simon directly," Nate pressed. "Why are you going through Bruce?"

"I don't want to put Simon on the spot," Karina lied effortlessly. "Besides, he's trying to do the job that his dead daddy took decades to master. I'm sure locations is not a priority." Karina approached Nate from behind and began to massage her best friend's neck and shoulders. "I need this. You don't understand what I'm going through," she paused for a beat before continuing. "My parents are constantly on my case, especially my mother—if she doesn't get off my brother's cock, I'm gonna report the both of them to CPS," Karina chuckled.

Nate spun around in her chair to face Karina, unamused. "Do you realize it took me several rounds of interviews in a span of three months to sit in this chair?" Nate quizzed. "You waltz in and get a meeting the very next day."

"When you got it, you got it," Karina said, primping in front of the narrow edit suite mirror.

"Forget it," Nate said, throwing her hands up in defeat.

"I'm joking." Karina spun Nate's chair back around to face her. "You got mad skills! Honestly, that pencil dick producer doesn't deserve you."

"I'll text him your info and I'll email you the show synopsis," Nate said.

"Thank you, thank you, thank you." Karina said, covering Nate's face in kisses. "Once my parents see how much money we can make with these production contracts they'll finally give me a little respect."

"The synopsis, Karina. Read it."

# #

That night Karina did everything but read the show synopsis. She treated herself to a manicure, pedicure and facial. She even binged-watched her favorite show. And while her outward appearance was put together, Karina arrived at Nate's edit bay the next day, completely flustered.

"Dude, your meeting is on the eighth floor in like ten minutes. What are you doing here?" Nate asked while uploading show mixes to the company server. She was just about to text the producer that they were posted for his approval.

"I need your help," Karina said, shutting the door behind her. "I was totally gonna read the synopsis, but I fell asleep. I have hundreds of properties that I can show, but no idea where to start!"

"So now I'm supposed to do your homework?" Nate pressed send on the text message.

"Exactly!" Karina exclaimed with zero shame.

"Last week I pitched the idea of shooting in a Venice Beach bungalow, but pencil dick shot me down. Bruce and the location team said they want really modern, like Bel Air chic," Nate groaned and rolled her eyes at the notion. "Personally, I think it should be less chic and more street. You know folks love flavor."

"That's no help if they hated it. Give me something I can use," Karina insisted.

"Guess you should've read the synopsis," Nate shrugged.

"Too soon." Karina paced the room for a beat, then looked up at the clock and sprinted out the door. "I'll wing it." An hour later, the producer, location director, and Karina entered Nate's audio bay
unannounced and laughing hysterically.

"Right in the middle of something here, guys. Deadline," Nate told them.

Karina slipped behind Nate and removed her headphones. "Sorry, I know you're crashing, but I just wanted to tell you the team loved my idea!"

"Brilliant," the location director chimed in. "Really edgy. I can't wait to check out the Venice Beach properties in person." Typically, a ball of anxiety, Nate hadn't seen the location director this light-hearted in weeks.

"Venice?" Nate probed.

"Very funny. Acting like I didn't run this idea by you," Karina said, standing in front of Nate, commanding the spotlight. "An idea she hated by the way." She knew that Nate wouldn't say anything that would risk her coming off as the angry black woman, so Karina ran with the pitch completely worry-free. "Folks love flavor and Venice Beach is full of it. I'm telling you, the fact that your Bel Air property dropped out will be a blessing in disguise."

"I'll run it by the E.P., but this could be good," said the producer to the location director, folding his arms.

"When I read the synopsis, it just jumped out at me. Less chic. More street," Karina smiled proudly.

"I love it," the location director nodded his head in agreement. "The location becomes a character."

"Fantastic, you guys go scout and please don't forget to send me pics," the location director ordered.

"On it," the producer agreed.

Although it had been a month since Karina secured the Herbst Studio contract, as she sat in her apartment recollecting—all of her senses activated at once. The location director's arrogant tone echoed in her eardrums like the thunder outside her lavish downtown loft. While the funk of Bruce's cheap cologne incited nausea. But it was the series of snapshots stitched together featuring Nate, trying to keep it together that truly put things into perspective. And as Karina watched herself claim credit for Nate's idea, it wasn't the taste of privilege that unsettled her, so—it was the fact that she wasn't strong enough to rebuke it.

Chapter 6

Queen of Kink

After passing out during the rainy car ride, Nate collapsed onto her bed and was soon fast asleep. "No ma'am," Tru said, slamming a glass of water onto the dresser, her skinny jeans now replaced with a pair of peek-a-boo boy shorts.

"I'm up." Her eyes still closed, Nate sat up, tipped the box of Raisinets into her mouth and savored the chocolate treat bestowed upon her earlier that evening. Tru walked toward the bed, eyeing Nate as if she were her last meal on death row. She first hovered and then lowered to straddle position, forcing Nate onto her back. Immediately Nate's hands slid under Tru's eighties style crop top and helped herself to two heaping handfuls.

"Now you're up," Tru giggled. She then forced Nate's hands over her head and slowly licked her way up Nate's neck. Nate's denim jeans colliding with the smooth fabric of Tru's boy shorts produced an undeniable heat. Their bodies moved in unison and as Tru worked her tongue from Nate's neck to her lips, the lovers began to kiss. Tru was ravenous, sucking first the fleshy bottom lip and then engulfing Nate completely. Nate moaned, giving Tru the official green light, and with that, it was all systems go. Tru quickly unbuttoned Nate's shirt, pulling her up and out of her sports bra with ease.

"Yes!" Nate bit down hard and then parted her plump lips.

"Tell me you want it," Tru whispered into Nate's ear before sliding down to meet each breast with a lingering lap. Next, she unzipped Nate's jeans and yanked them just below her toned posterior. The sweet, damp, scent of Nate's excitement tickled her nostrils and signaled what was yet to come. "Tell me you want it," Tru repeated herself. She got a real rise out of watching Nate beg for it.

"I want it," Nate sighed.

"You can do better than that, lover." Tru yanked the fitted jeans off of Nate and plunged face first in the direction of her bikini briefs. Nate bucked her hips as Tru began to rub and nibble Nate through her dampening undies.

"Fucking tease," Nate whined, as Tru bit down hard on her thigh, delivering just enough pressure to let Nate know who was in charge. "Ow!" Directing her pelvis upward, Nate sucked in air through gritted teeth.

"You like it," Tru laughed, pulled Nate's briefs to the side and began to explore. "Beautiful." She licked her lips while fingering the sticky stream of wetness she'd discovered between Nate's thighs. "Tell me." Tru looked up at Nate who could barely catch her breath.

"I want it," Nate panted. Done teasing, Tru pulled Nate's briefs completely off and reached for the box of chocolate-covered raisins. Tru then smiled at Nate as a thin layer of milk chocolate began to envelop her tongue.

"Lover," Nate purred as her knees buckled. The cadence of her heartbeat and the ceiling fan above culminated beautifully into one sultry R&B hook and as Nate's legs collapsed to the sides and drifted further apart, Tru's eager tongue began to do laps; using the candy to first circle and then tickle Nate's blossoming vulva.

Her thighs slick and head spinning, Nate gushed, teetering optimistically close to orgasm. "Damn," Nate let out a gravelly moan, spreading her muscular quads as Tru plunged a set of slippery digits along with her stiffening tongue in and out of Nate's honey pot. Her vocabulary reduced to little more than guttural expletives, Nate locked her fingers around the back of Tru's head and proceeded to bring herself to climax.

"I've been thinking about that all day long," Tru quipped, placing a soft kiss on Nate's lips and then collapsing beside her.

Parched yet satiated, Nate downed the glass of water in one sudden gulp. "Take your shirt off," Nate commanded as she rolled on to Tru.

"So you boss lady now?" The twenty-five-year-old top cocked her head to the side curious at Nate's sudden desire to reverse roles.

"Do it," Nate smirked as Tru pulled the half-shirt over her head, exposing a rack so perky it could only be attributed to God's grace. Next, Nate removed Tru's sopping wet boy shorts and took a moment to admire her frame. Tru was thick and her breasts were all-natural. She had butterscotch-colored skin and rocked the tiger-like stretch marks on her rump like a badge of honor.

Untouched by a scalpel, Tru was a natural goddess and Nate gave thanks for the glory that presented itself in every curve.

Although the two women had been hooking up for a year, much of Tru's backstory remained a mystery. Nate knew that the interracial cutie lived with her Korean grandmother and had never met her black father. Other than that, Tru remained guarded. She'd never even been to Tru's home, far less seen her without a wig. The one thing Tru had been an open book about since they'd met last year was her career. In fact, Nate couldn't get her to stop talking about it.

Tru was a self-proclaimed sexpert and proud of it. In a day, she could give an erotic couple's massage for breakfast, use her riding crop to tan the hides of a room full of executives for lunch and finally round out the evening as eye candy, escorting a high-powered executive to a high-brow event. However, being a latex rocking, whip-wielding dominatrix was her bread and butter. When it came to fetishes, she'd seen and participated in many of them. As a rule, she never allowed anyone to penetrate or kiss her, although, for the right price, Tru had no qualms strapping up to peg submissive men.

"You ready to answer my question?" Nate queried.

"We back on that?" Tru's tone was telling. They'd had this conversation before. "I can't commit right now. It wouldn't be fair to either of us," Tru spoke softly, careful to be easy with Nate's ego. "Besides, we both knew what this was. Don't be greedy, lover," Tru moaned while taking a playful swat at Nate's rear.

"You're right. We're good," Nate planted sensual kisses on Tru's neck, as her breasts melded with Tru's. "But we could be great," Nate took a nibble out of Tru's ear. "Think, Barack and Michelle. Celie and Shug," she cooed.

"You're ridiculous," Tru burst out laughing. "But keep begging—it's hot!" Tru used her leg to pull Nate down on top of her. Next, she spread her legs so that Nate fit like a puzzle piece, perfectly between her thighs. As their pussies locked lips, Nate grabbed two fistfuls of Tru's fleshy cheeks and began to bear down hard.

Tru was close. She bucked her hips harder, as the cream filled center swelling between them sloshed to life. "Yes!" Tru wailed. The chorus of delight had started in her nether regions and worked its way up her belly and chest to eventually pierce the thick coitus filled air of Nate's Echo Park Lake apartment. Tru's left leg, now on Nate's shoulder, provided the perfect amount of leverage. She was completely open and had blossomed like a flower ready to be plucked. Their salty bodies, covered in sweat, became irrigation to their souls as Nate passionately plowed her way to a full-on frenzy.

"I literally see stars," Tru laughed, grabbing a nearby water bottle from the nightstand.

"You are irrefutably the star of this show." Nate rolled off of Tru and allowed the ceiling fan to blow cool air across their clammy skin. Never one for cuddling or sleeping over, Tru chugged the bottled water, hopped up and threw her legs over the edge of the bed.

"Sure you can't stay?" Nate asked, placing soft kisses on Tru's back. "It's pouring outside."

"If I stay, you'll never get any rest," Tru's smile was enchanting. "You've got to be sharp for that meeting with Simon."

"Hold up a sec," Nate pressed, pulling Tru in closer so that they were both lying on their backs. She began to speak without taking her eyes off of the ceiling fan. "I need to apologize," Nate paused for a beat, somewhat embarrassed. "I was twisted earlier."

"Messy is more like it," Tru laughed.

"I got some horrible news from back home," Nate said, turning to face Tru. "Trying to drink it all away, I guess," Nate said, noticeably unnerved. "My Auntie Earlene's sick—pancreatic cancer."

"No," Tru replied softly, taking Nate's hand in hers.

"I'm flying back on Thursday. It'll be like a really dysfunctional family reunion," Nate laughed, nervously.

"How bad?" Tru explored Nate's face, which looked as though she had already slipped back to a really dark place. "How bad?" Tru repeated the question. Outside of knowing that Nate was very close to Auntie Earlene and that despite their strained relationship, Nate's parents continued to supplement her income, Nate hadn't spoken much about her life on the island.

"Imagine a bunch of Jamaicans sitting in the hot sun eating really bad potato salad and under-seasoned chicken," Nate joked.

"That sounds horrendous and also highly unlikely as I know your people know their way around a kitchen," Tru laughed, giving Nate a playful nudge.

"Come home with me," Nate gulped uneasily, her slapdash statement more declaration than a request.

"What?" Tru sat up again. Nate followed suit. "Come on, it's Jamaica," you could feel the vulnerability in Nate's voice. After fourteen years away, her return home would be monumental. Tru was the only person that Nate imagined along for the ride.

"Okay," Nate conceded. "My homophobic mother will make it super awkward, while my father evades, but it's still paradise," she smirked.

"I can't," Tru spoke resolutely.

"Why not?"

"A trip to Jamaica—to meet the family!" Tru exclaimed and connected a playful jab with Nate's well-built bicep. "You're getting soft," she teased.

"It could be fun," Nate shrugged. She then stood up, embarrassed and pulled on a pair of boxer briefs and a tank top.

Tru put on her panties, bra and jeans, but searched the room for the top that she'd lost somewhere between foreplay and her epic orgasm. "We got a good thing going here," Tru professed. "Why ruin it with double dates and family reunions?" She located her shirt entangled in the sex-soaked sheets, but when she caught Nate's reflection in the mirror, Tru softened and crossed the room to join her. "I'm sorry about your aunt, but trust me, we aren't ready for a romantic trip to the Caribbean."

"It's been a year," Nate said, studying Tru's eyes and taking her hand in hers. "You keep me tucked away like I embarrass you."

"Let's not do this," Tru dropped Nate's hand and turned her back on her as she pulled her shirt over her head. The few short years she had spent working in the sex industry had perverted her already struggling intimacy issues. She'd built up a wall to make ends meet, and until Tru turned the page on being a dominatrix, she wouldn't be ready to start a new chapter with anyone. Nate knew this! Why she felt the need to ruin a great evening with talk of family reunions and beach vacations was beyond Tru.

"If this isn't working for you anymore, just say the word," Tru talked tough, but in reality, she wanted to see how far Nate would push it.

"The only thing that's not working for me is your job," Nate laughed as Tru's phone buzzed, signaling a text message. "You've been retiring since we met."

"I have to run," Tru said, reacting to the text message and leaving Nate where she stood.

"You always do," Nate replied, then opened her bedroom door as if granting Tru permission to leave. She was right. Dating a dominatrix hadn't been easy. Late hours. Kooky clients. Dirty money. It was a means to an end and none of this was news to Nate.

"Don't be like that," Tru said, grabbing her purse before meeting Nate at the doorway. "You know the plan. Let's revisit this conversation in…"

"Six to eight months," it was easy for Nate to interrupt, as this had been Tru's go-to line since day one.

The self-proclaimed sexual muse had spent the last few years helping established couples rekindle dying flames and others safely explore their most taboo turn-ons. Tru was the Queen of Kink and with an exclusive list of clientele throughout Ventura, Los Angeles and Orange counties, she'd stacked a grip of money.

"A year in and I still can't compete with your tricks. You never open up. Hell, I don't even know where you live," Nate complained.

"First of all, not everyone comes with a trust fund, so please do us both a favor and stop being a spoiled brat," Tru said as she pushed past Nate and grabbed her car keys from the hallway table. With early retirement on the horizon, she refused to be shamed by Nate or anyone else.

Iced, Nate reacted, "Just forget I mentioned the trip. Sketel, go get your money." This was their first time arguing about anything more serious than what to order for take-out. Tru didn't speak patois, but she knew enough to understand a sketel was nothing nice, and with that, their rendezvous was officially over. Tru blew past Nate, slamming the door without uttering a single word on her way out.

"Damn it!" Nate grabbed the preloaded bong from her cupboard and inhaled the earthy OG Kush.

Chapter 7

Trois

Still pissed at how their romantic rendezvous had blown up in her face, Tru sat nursing a drink at Trois—the same bar she'd met Nate in last year. Tru let out an audible sigh as she bounced, yet another call from Nate, before shoving the phone into her purse. Since their argument, she'd sent Nate to voicemail a dozen times and for now, she was fine letting her sweat it out.

Although Tru and Nate had been hooking up since the first night they'd met, the last couple of months had thrown Tru way off course. Between tonight's argument and the immense PDA, something was definitely awry. Recently, the women had all but abandoned their unspoken rules of casual dating and were now at an absolute standstill.

Sleeping over, however, was one tenet Tru had managed not to break. Tru was convinced that it would give Nate the wrong idea and was wary of establishing false expectations about their relationship. Still, every now and then, Nate would fall asleep in Tru's arms. Although she'd never admit it, these were the quiet moments Tru most savored. Glancing down at Nate, cradled gently in a sex-induced coma, Tru couldn't believe that she'd found someone so special. Someone capable of dating without looking down on her career and understanding that for Tru, being a dominatrix was merely the temporary means to an end.

As Tru sat, sipping Whiskey on the rocks, she recalled the first time she had laid eyes on Nate at the obscure dive bar. Technically she wasn't spying, but Tru was ear hustling like a pro and had quickly surmised that Nate and the woman sitting beside her were on a first date—and their conversation was just getting good:

"I'm not saying I'll never get married, just that it'll be a long, long time from now," Nate declared.

"Aww, someone's been hurt," the woman sounded condescending, but she was sexy and serving up a serious if your girl only knew vibe.

"For now, I have to keep it casual. Between my podcast, making music and my day job," Nate sighed, "I barely have time for friends."

"You sound like my boyfriend," the woman smirked.

"Boyfriend?" Nate repeated as Tru, and the bartender had a good laugh at her expense.

"I'm in an open relationship," the woman admitted. "But, you knew that."

"No, I didn't," Nate replied, then took another sip of her cocktail.

"It's clear as day on my profile," the woman's laugh was like a hyena. Nate felt like an idiot and was convinced everyone in the bar knew it.

"I need to run to the bathroom. I'll tell you all about Quincy in a sec. You'll love him," the woman said, leaning in and planting a full kiss on Nate's lips. She then used a cocktail napkin to wipe away the dark lipstick she'd smudged across Nate's mouth.

A few seconds later, Tru watched a medium built, bearded man walk off in the same direction as the women's restroom. Quincy, she presumed. If Nate couldn't see it, Tru sure as hell could. Nate was being played. Tru could tell that the woman's tight little frame and tomboy swag had caused Nate to forgive any gaffes, so she collected her thoughts and slid over to the seat directly beside Nate.

"Listen, friend," Tru cleared her throat and began to deliver what she considered to be a public service announcement.

"What's good?" Still craning her neck toward the restroom, Nate had yet to lock eyes with Tru.

"She's bad. I'll give you that," Tru conceded. "But come on! Have you not seen her eyeballing that dude?"

Nate turned away from the bathroom, finally connecting with Tru. "Hold up! You're stalking us?!" Nate raised her voice and Tru lowered hers, trying to get a handle on the conversation.

"I couldn't help but overhear," Tru said, staring into Nate's eyes. They were the shape of two crescent moons and as deep as the San Andreas Fault. Noticing that everyone within earshot was looking in her direction, Tru decided to drop it. "You're probably right," Tru laughed. "Let me stop blocking." Tru shrugged and turned back toward her unattended drink.

"Not so fast, nosy." Nate placed her hand on Tru's shoulder, stopping the eavesdropping stranger in her tracks. "I'm listening," Nate admitted.

Tru glanced back in the direction of the restrooms. While several people had entered, none had returned. Next, Tru motioned for Nate to follow her. Nate sipped the last of her cocktail curiously, got up and then walked behind Tru, no questions asked. Once on the other side of the bathroom door, it became apparent that it wasn't a bathroom at all. With its red vinyl walls and come hither mood lighting, what was moments ago a dingy dive was now bringing sexy back in a major way. Tru gave a knowing nod to the strapping bouncer, who was also her personal bodyguard. Dressed in his signature black suit and spooky half-face, skeleton style motorcycle helmet, his presence spoke volumes without him uttering a single word.

"Mistress." A petite woman in a body-hugging bustier ran her hands through Tru's multicolored pixie cut. When she and Nate pushed past, Tru cut her eyes at the woman for touching her without being invited to do so, then made a mental note of the lashes the woman had coming her way. Nate grew enthralled by the scantily clad patrons and the row of narrow, telephone booth like stalls situated before them as they moved deeper into the hidden backroom. One at a time, Tru slid the barnyard style doors open only to be met with giggling from booed up couples that welcomed her interruption with an invitation. The hum of heedless merriment and heavy breathing put a pep in Nate's step and together she and Tru followed the familiar hyena-like laughter to the last stall.

"Are you serious?" Nate swung the door open to reveal her date doing bumps of cocaine off of a key as her bearded lover squatted below, her hairless mound melting into his mouth.

"Told ya," Tru shrugged.

"It's cool, he's my boyfriend," Nate's date laughed, slurring her speech. "Say hi, Quincy." Nate stormed out of the surreptitious backroom, threw a few twenties at the bartender and exited stage left.

"Your nine o'clock just pulled up out back." The bartender covered the mouthpiece of a landline phone and handed Tru her oversized purse.

"Push him to one," Tru said, fishing for the keys to her convertible.

"Will do," the bartender agreed.

Tru quickly tailed Nate outside. "You okay—need a ride or something?"

"I just stepped out of the matrix. I need more than a ride." Nate was visibly shaken. "That freaky little…"

"Let's get a drink," Tru offered.

"I'm fine," Nate pouted, embarrassed yet, quietly turned on by the sex dungeon scene she'd inadvertently stumbled upon.

"That you are." For the first time standing face-to-face, Tru seized the opportunity to take Nate entirely in. She was taller than Tru with cinnamon-kissed skin that meshed perfectly with her funky blond dreads.

"I got catfished!" Nate said, firing up the dating app.

"I'm pretty sure you didn't," Tru replied, watching Nate curiously. "This is not a reality show," Tru laughed as Nate read the woman's profile. Sure enough, in the about section of her profile, it did, in fact, say that she had a boyfriend.

"But come on, no one reads profiles. You skim them. Everyone knows that," Nate conceded, slipping the phone into her pocket. Tru laughed. Nate was a trip, and up until that point Tru had never met anyone who could pull off those drop-crotch harem pants, but somehow Nate had managed to do so.

"By the way, how did you know?" Nate asked. "About the girl, the club, everything?"

"I just..." Tru tried hard not to stare at the beautiful pair of sculpted biceps that fit snuggly under Nate's short sleeve denim shirt and quickly devised a half-truth she hoped would suffice.

"I'm just hella observant." If by observant Tru meant nervous, more sincere words had never been spoken. "I'm Tru Lee." By that point her painted on acid wash jeans had become little more than a denim towel for drying damp palms.

"As in yours truly?" Nate quizzed.

"Perhaps, one day," Tru laughed. "And you are?"

"Nate," she said, taking Tru's hand in hers.

"You like Whiskey, Nate?" Tru probed.

# #

Traffic was absent for a Friday night, which made zigzagging through Laurel Canyon a delightful blur of semi-awkward conversation accompanied by ice gold and green traffic lights. In Nate's angular prescription frames, the Santa Monica Mountains and canyon homes on stilts projected back, but hindsight was an entirely different view.

"First of all, the name of the bar is Trois! You should have known it was for swingers," Tru gibed.

Having spent the last couple of hours boozing on the hood of her 1995 cherry red four-door, she and Nate were good and buzzed.

"So what you're saying is you're a regular, is that right, Mistress?" Nate giggled, unaware of how accurate her statement was. Then she took a long swig of honey-flavored Whiskey from Tru's blinged-out flask.

"How about I save that story for our second date?" Tru asked.

"Is that what this is?" Nate passed the flask back to Tru and then looked toward the skyline, admiring the faint city lights as they sparkled like distant flames.

"Too early to tell," Tru responded matter-of-factly. Well past three in the morning, Tru was due back at the bar hours ago, but as she glanced over at Nate perched as regal as an onyx hood ornament atop her classic convertible, the decision to bail on her client was made for her." You should chill with all that catalog dating," Tru laughed, took a swig and permitted the bourbon to linger in her mouth before swallowing. "Too many crazies," she warned, then ran her fingers across the flask's Korean engraved characters and silently repeated the mantra in her head: "Keep em' guessing."

"I'm just trying to get my beak wet," Nate giggled. "Guess I'm a little rusty." Nate hadn't been in a relationship since the older, married woman she was seeing several months before her impromptu run-in with Tru dumped her. Bottom line, Nate had mommy issues and hadn't been in any healthy adult relationships, largely because she was admittedly emotionally unavailable. All things considered, casually dating a dominatrix was right up her alley. "How about you?" Nate turned to face Tru. "Date a lot?"

Tru bit down hard on her bottom lip, allowing the wetness that had developed in the palm of her hands to work its way down to her voracious hot spot. The typically self-assured young woman let the butterflies doing the Tootsie Roll in her stomach dull to a quiver before making a move. "No, but there's just something about you that makes me want to yank your hair and call you nasty names," Tru laughed.

"I dare you." Nate leaned in close and connected with Tru's pouty, full lips. After close to three hours of chatting that felt more like foreplay Tru's kiss had the veracity of an industrial strength vacuum.

"Slut bucket," Tru laughed, grabbed a fistful of Nate's locks and gave them a good yank. Tru then strategically placed warm kisses on to Nate's neck and lobes until she was positioned directly on top of Nate. The hood of her vintage ride belched underneath the two women as Tru unbuttoned Nate's shirt and exposed a set of perky B-cups, nestled securely into Nate's sports bra.

"If we get caught up here." Nate eyed the deserted scenic overlook and silently contemplated which was more tantalizing—the twinkling city lights or the possibility of being found out.

"Not another word," Tru commanded by placing her pointer finger on Nate's lips. She then freed Nate's breasts and thumbed her stiffening nipples as they proudly saluted the night sky. Next, Tru inhaled the swollen gourds into her mouth. Nate groaned her approval and slowly let her legs drift apart, while Tru quietly thanked the good Lord above for trendy, loose-fitting pants. Tru eagerly worked her way from Nate's breasts to claim another passionate kiss before slipping her fingers into Nate's boy shorts.

"Yes." Nate spread her legs even further apart as Tru's fingers melted into her like whipped butter on hot grits.

Chapter 8

Round Two

Although it had been two weeks since their initial meeting and impromptu romp, Tru and Nate hadn't spoken since. Too consumed with high-profile clients to give their rendezvous much thought, Tru assumed their hookup was nothing more than a fluke she needed to forget. And so as she suppressed steamy images of the one-night stand, Tru quickly began to focus on the matter at hand. Sporting a black couture evening gown, burnt orange stilettos and matching clutch, she slipped out of the passenger seat and shut the car door behind her.

"Just think about the bag. Three hours, 2K," Tru's masked bodyguard reminded her of the fee she would receive for a job well done.

"If I weren't thinking about the bag, would I jump into this room full of sharks?" Tru countered. She felt unsettled and had relied on liquor as of late to help her through gigs. Did BDSM have an expiration date? After three years in the business, Tru was starting to think so. She wanted out but hadn't yet raised enough capital to quit. Tru's bodyguard slowly turned his head to face hers. Although he was Tru's designated driver, he still rocked his signature motorcycle helmet, making him look more like Skeletor than security.

"Early retirement is just around the corner. Stay the course, boss," he said pointing to his tablet with GPS sensors capable of tracking Tru's every move. "I'll be watching."

"Oh please, you'll be on Grindr as soon as I leave," she said, leaning into the window.

"Seriously. Text, if anything," her bodyguard replied, rolling the tinted window up as Tru slipped through the four-star hotel's service entrance unnoticed. True to form, whenever she was on the clock, Tru made a habit of noting all exits, especially stairwells and outlets located toward the rear of establishments. Once in the lobby, she peered out of the enormous picture window and noticed her date, a Herbst Studios Executive Producer, making his way out of a limousine and up the venue's grand staircase. Approximately three decades her senior, the distinguished silver-haired man cut quickly through the crowd when he noticed Tru. Then, he leaned in for a kiss.

"Uh, uh, uh," she hugged the man close and whispered in his ear, electing to rebuff the well-known executive without embarrassing him.

"Mistress," he purred softly and let his hand drop from the small of Tru's back to her fleshy posterior.

"I'm going to have to punish you tonight, aren't I?" Tru turned her palm skyward, revealing a dime-sized button attached to a thin slave bracelet ring.

"Please do," he begged, then clenched his ass cheeks in delight as Tru balled her hand into a fist, triggering an eruption of pulsating heat through the butt plug stashed in the older man's derrière.

"Now let's go raise some funds," Tru grinned, then escorted the executive through the lobby and into the ballroom where they were met by two hundred plus people, all gathered for Herbst Studio's annual auction. With Tru on his arm, the executive was all smiles and gaining tons of attention. A big-time mover and shaker, the television veteran, commanded the room. Immediately, Tru noticed not only the number of people tripping over themselves to shake his hand but the number of people clamoring to meet her.

"This is Kenya," the television executive used Tru's alias and showed her off much as you would a shiny new Ferrari.

"So exotic," one man chimed in.

"Beautiful," another agreed. He then spun Tru around, making sure to get a good look at how impeccably the couture gown clung to her backside.

"Punish me," a third man whispered, dolling out two kisses, each landing too close to Tru's mouth.

"I'm gonna run to the ladies' room," Tru said, ignoring the men's cheap come-ons and focusing solely on her date. "Reign these boneheads in before I do," Tru whispered in his ear. The smile on his face made it clear that after a lifetime of shot-calling, he was happy to relinquish control. Tru continued, only now, she spoke slowly and deliberately loud enough for his cronies to hear. "The best is yet to come," she cooed, then headed toward the restroom. Well aware of the attention her mere presence ordained, Tru put an extra sway in her sashay as she headed toward the ladies' room. When she glanced back, even though she was terrible at reading lips, it was obvious that the executive had talked her up and she had a pretty good idea what the men were saying.

"Got your hands full with that one," the first man laughed boorishly and pat the executive on his back.

"What is she? Oriental? Black?" The second man quizzed, genuinely puzzled.

"Better question, how much is she?" The third and most garish of the group joked.

"If you have to ask, you can't afford it," the television executive retorted without taking his eyes off Tru, which wasn't hard as diversity was visibly missing from the room. As Tru pushed further into the venue, it didn't take long before she was enveloped by the growing sea of sameness. However, what the room lacked in color, it made up for in cold hard cash.

Suddenly the thrill of big money and potential clients eager to part with it was replaced by nausea. Tru couldn't be sure if it was the rank old man's aftershave that seemed to be wafting through the vents or the Whiskey she'd downed on an empty stomach, but as she squeezed closer toward the front of the ballroom, Tru's anxiety ratcheted up a notch. While the Whiskey and aftershave were contributing factors, if Tru was honest with herself, tonight's trepidation had everything to do with a distinct desire to quit her day job. By her calculations, if Tru stuck to the plan, in less than a year, she'd have enough money to launch her start-up and care for her grandmother.

Tru slipped into the private bathroom just long enough to dampen a paper towel and apply it to her neck. After sipping from the faucet and giving herself a mental pep talk, she ventured back into the main hall, where an art auction featuring segregation era movie memorabilia was in full swing. There were props and signed posters of provocative characters like Little Black Sambo, Charlie Chan and Mammy on display. Tru pressed on sickened, yet unsurprised.

"Pardon me," Tru excused herself, then bumped into someone with a bidding paddle, followed by another and another. The auction, complete with a fast-talking, gavel-wielding auctioneer, was officially on its way. Across the room, Tru noticed her date, his chest all puffed out from the accolades he'd garnered, for merely having her brown body on his arm. Suddenly, Tru felt like it was her on the auction block, not the high-priced, Tinsel Town memorabilia. It was eerie and as if she were looking through a fisheye lens. Tru spun around quickly, this time bumping into several women with paddles, before ducking outside for air.

The serenity of the infinity pool and cool, calm air helped settle Tru's stomach and nerves but when she saw Nate, standing with a friend just steps away, she froze. Although they'd exchanged contact information, the two women hadn't as much as texted since their steamy hook up just two weeks prior. The way she saw it, Tru had two choices, either confront a potentially awkward situation head on or slip off unnoticed. Never one to leave money on the table, a total of $1,600 once her bodyguard got his cut, Tru cocked her shoulders back and strutted gracefully toward Nate.

"Hey, it's been a minute," Tru said, smiling awkwardly in Nate's face.

"Tru!" Nate wrapped her arms around her in a hug so warm Tru could've chilled comfortably in that position all night. "It must be fate," Nate surmised.

"A friend of mine invited me out," Tru said, stretching the truth. "He works for Herbst."

"So do I!" Nate exclaimed.

"Cool," Tru lied. This was the antithesis of cool. The night they hooked up, Tru purposely avoided discussing what each of them did for a living. She wanted to keep it casual, and now there she was dressed in a freaking ball gown. "You look great!" Nate's pants matched Tru's burnt orange clutch and shoes damn near perfectly. Plus, the pocket square added just the right amount of pop to Nate's fitted charcoal gray blazer. Scrumptious.

"You look…" Nate paused, searching for the right words. "Well, like a Blasian Tinkerbelle. And your hair. I love it."

"Thanks. It changes a lot," Tru remained gracious.

"I'm Karina," she said, clearing her throat.

"I'm Tru." She extended her hand, but Karina instead slid her arm through Nate's, as if marking her territory.

"I have a cold so," Karina replied matter-of-factly. Sure it was a California cold, but a cold nonetheless.

"No problem," Tru conceded. "You two are a gorgeous couple." She knew good and well that the women weren't a couple, but it was apparent Karina was territorial, so she figured she'd throw a bitch a bone.

"Oh, no. Karina's my homegirl," Nate corrected. "She works for Herbst too. At least she'd like to."

"I'm in real estate and the studio is a potential client," Karina replied. "If only Nate would get me a meeting."

"First, you'll need to convince your folks to want to do business with the studios," Nate said, reminding Karina.

"They're very traditional, but they'll see the light," Karina said as she sized the newcomer up. While it was true that her family's real estate company was well known, they hadn't yet crossed over to television production. That was Karina's pet project and convincing her parents had proven to be quite the challenge.

"Let's hope they come around soon," Tru said with a smile.

"Thanks and nice shoes by the way," Karina continued. "You know I just donated an identical pair. You haven't been to the Good Will on Venice in the last couple of weeks, have you?"

"Karina, chill," Nate said, elbowing her friend lightly in the ribs.

"I'm kidding," Karina slurred, still high off of high-priced blow and top-shelf Vodka. "I'm sure she can take a joke."

"Funny," Tru smirked. She was used to women being threatened by her, but Karina had reacted in record time.

"I'm gonna get back inside, but we should hang soon," Tru said, smiling at Nate. She then leaned in, gave her a light peck on the lips, and began to walk off.

Nate hadn't been laid in months and had been giddy as hell to tell Karina about her initial run-in with Tru just a couple weeks back. Karina, on the other hand, wasn't nearly as amped. She would never admit it, but because she had flirted with and been shot down by Nate just days prior to Nate meeting Tru, the rejection stung like a swarm of Africanized honey bees. While Karina wasn't gay and didn't consider herself to be bisexual, she was undoubtedly possessive and suffering from a severely bruised ego.

"It's you," Karina said, grabbing Tru by the arm.

"What the hell!" Tru exclaimed. Not appreciating the invasion of her personal space she jerked her arm away hurriedly and walked away from the developing scene. Karina followed, defiantly.

"Leave her alone, Kar!" Nate demanded.

"I'm not sure what that putrid hair color is tonight, but it was Mountain Dew green when we met.

"Either way, I still recognize her, Nate," Karina continued to spill the beans. "You hosted a swinger's party a couple of years back in the valley."

"You are legit faded," Nate laughed, trying to diffuse the escalating situation. "Let's get you some water."

"I'm not," Karina said, shirking away from Nate's grip. "This is the sex club chick you were telling me about, isn't it?" Karina cringed, "She's like a dominatrix or something! You better get tested ASAP."

How embarrassing. Tru couldn't place Karina's face, but she wanted to smack the hell out of it, and if her business didn't rely so heavily on class and anonymity, she would've. For Tru, the party was officially over, so instead of smacking Karina into next week, she texted her bodyguard and hightailed it toward the exit.

"Hold up," Karina demanded, again grabbing for Tru's arm. This time, she lost her balance and fell directly into the deep end of the infinity swimming pool. "That hood rat assaulted me," Karina screeched from the pool as Nate extended her arm and pulled her soggy friend in. "I'm pressing charges!"

"Karina, you fell in. No one touched you," Nate reminded her as a crowd of spectators slowly began to develop around the pool's perimeter.

"Kenya, is everything ok?" The television executive asked Tru.

"Kenya? I thought her name was Tru," Karina laughed. "You have no idea who you let hit!"

"I'm fine, just a misunderstanding," Tru whispered, mortified.

"She's a hood rat whore!" Karina exclaimed.

"I want you thugs out of here now!" The executive exclaimed as he approached Nate and Karina, trailed closely by two security officers.

"That chick in the swap shop wig pushed me," Karina complained through labored speech. "I could've drowned! Arrest her!" Karina turned on the crocodile tears just as Tru clenched her fist, initiating the executive's butt plug. Gasping in both delight and embarrassment, he caused a scene, which acted as the perfect diversion for Tru. She effortlessly slipped through the crowd, tossed her wig and hopped into the awaiting car. Next, she began to fire off a series of text messages, including one to her executive client apologizing for her early departure.

A couple of hours later, Tru found herself dressed down and walking along Santa Monica Boulevard with Nate. She had texted Nate, stating that she wanted to clear things up. To her surprise, Nate agreed to meet.

"Purple. I like it," Nate said, admiring yet another one of Tru's pixie cut hairdos.

"It's lilac, thanks."

"Guess you won't be needing this," Nate laughed nervously and then handed Tru a plastic bag containing her wig from earlier that night.

"How Princess Charming of you," Tru replied, shoving the wig into her oversized purse.

"You know you really don't owe me anything. I barely know you, but honestly, each time after we hang—and I know it's only been twice, but I lay down the most amazing beats," Nate sighed, referencing her music production. Then Nate took a swig from Tru's flask as they continued strolling down the Boulevard. "Maybe you're my muse."

"I didn't know you were a musician."

"I didn't know you were a dominatrix," Nate countered, passing the flask back and finally addressing the elephant in the room.

"First of all, I don't have sex with clients." Tru saw the expression on Nate's face begin to ease and then decided to tell the complete truth. After all, she had nothing to lose. "That is, I don't have sex with female clients," she paused, half expecting Nate to run for the hills; alas, Nate didn't budge. "Truthfully, if it's a submissive man and the price is right, I will strap up and do what I have to do," Tru swallowed hard then continued. "It's a one-way street and I'm always the driver—understand?"

"Not really, but I'm listening," Nate couldn't think of anything else to say. She'd never met anyone who worked in the sex industry, and although she knew it was crazy, Nate was oddly turned on by Tru's candor.

"I'm a dominatrix, yes, but I take pride in being a sexpert. I coach couples through intimacy issues and host parties—a lot of them at that club we met at and some at private homes, as your friend mentioned."

"And Kenya's your alias," Nate nodded, trying to understand.

"One of many," Tru admitted before taking a long sip of Whiskey and passing the flask back to Nate.

"Along with Mistress, right?" Nate queried. "No judgments, but wow," she laughed. "You're really letting that freak flag fly."

"People have so many opinions. I usually only discuss business with my bodyguard." Although Tru was divulging the details of her profession, nothing seemed to get a rise out of Nate. It was refreshing.

"Your life. Live it as you please," Nate advised.

"I'm not sure why I'm telling you all this," Tru laughed bashfully, then paused for a beat to collect her thoughts. The last thing she wanted was Nate's pity. "And to be clear, it's not that I'm ashamed of how I get down, it's just that…"

"I get it," Nate interrupted. "People are judgmental assholes. We've got opinions about everything.

Even about people we've just met," she laughed softly. "It's evident from this conversation, you understand, our opinions are not your problem."

"Now that was good," Tru clapped slowly, humorously. "Let me find out you're a musical therapist." Tru joked while running her hand down Nate's muscular arm.

"No, darling, but I sure could use one," Nate laughed.

"Sounds juicy," Tru smiled, taking Nate's hand. "I'll let you save that story for another time, but for now, this is what I wanted to show you."

"First screen, then get in between." Nate read the text painted alongside the STD screening van aloud. "You're serious?"

"As a drag queen in Jimmy Choos," Tru laughed. "Before the other night, it had been close to one year since I'd been intimate with a woman," Tru lowered her voice, almost embarrassed by the confession. "Let's just say I'm ready to make up for lost time." Tru opened the door to the van and gestured for Nate to go first. "After you."

"To second dates," Nate said, raising the flask.

"Let's just call it round two," Tru countered.

Chapter 9

Pum Pum Rock

Barely fourteen years old, Nate made her way through the moist grove, pushing past vines and shrubs as she had done so many times before. Nate had been traveling with her father, Minister Barrington Higgins, for as long as she could remember and absolutely loved it. At first glance, the old St Ann's aluminum plant and abandoned railroad tracks represented a depressed, West Indian economy, but Nate could see beyond the spoiled exterior to its center; condensed milk sweet and Blue Mountain strong. But more than anything, Nate loved that when her father traveled to Kingston, if school was not in session, she and her best friend Jocelyn were along for the ride.

As Jamaica's Minister of Youth and Culture, Barrington traveled to the capital quarterly. In fact, it was his idea to bring the girls along to participate in what he believed were educational field trips. Nate remembered how her father always encouraged her to "look beyond textbooks" and to "learn from real life."

Barrington wanted Nate and Jocelyn not merely to listen in but to participate, as he believed hearing from teenagers when deciding on their best interests was best practice. As Jamaica's Minister of Youth and Culture, Barrington was responsible for uplifting Jamaica's young people. Through aligning himself with community organizations such as churches, private and government-run entities he had spent the last several years working to reform the government's approach to youth empowerment. His goal was to make sure that Jamaica's youth had access to fun events like camps and concerts, as well as programs that promoted professional and life skills. And while Nate and her best friend Jocelyn loved getting out of Montego Bay, sitting in on meetings led by Barrington bored them to tears. However, Barrington remained persistent, often waking them with a sharp elbow or quick pluck to the forearm to stop them from dozing off during summits. Although, it wasn't until a game of tag had gone terribly wrong, landing a lawmaker smack dab on her stately rump that Minister Higgins finally agreed to give up on the whole field trip notion.

"Why you looking so shook, Natty? We good," Jocelyn asserted self-assuredly.

"Good? You know my father's gonna kill me," Nate sighed. "Then he'll tell my mum, and she'll pay off some duppy to resurrect me just so she can do the same 'ting!"

"So dramatic." Unbothered, Jocelyn was clearly the more brazen of the two. "You ran right into councilwoman, had her granny panties exposed for everyone to see," she chuckled. "Big football star like you should be lighter on your feet."

I'm not saying it wasn't funny," Nate laughed.

"Then we good," Jocelyn interrupted. "Enjoy the moment."

"I guess." Nate took several steps forward and moved gingerly through the shaded brush, each inch bringing her closer to the edge of Bog Walk's steep mountain terrain. Unlike the upper-class Montego Bay community in which she resided, the Middlesex County parish offered the sense of community and adventure that Nate craved.

Fast on her heels, Jocelyn followed Nate deeper into the lush island bush. Within minutes Nate began to relax as the full force of the sun's UV rays caressed her chestnut colored shoulders. This was her happy place. Nate craned her neck heavenward, shut her eyes tight and inhaled the sweet yet barely detectable scent of jasmine.

"This never gets old," Nate exhaled calmly. She then opened her eyes, lowered her neck and fully absorbed the view.

Before the two teens and just across the Rio Cobre River, sat the 8th Wonder of the World, Jamaica's Pum Pum Rock. A real sight to be seen, the mammoth rock could not be more appropriately named. With its thick, crescent-shaped innards, positioned squarely between two bulging rock like lips, trips to Pum Pum Rock had always left Nate feeling happy yet somewhat hurt. The irony was agony. Sort of like eating a really spicy meal. It can burn like a mother, but the flavors are so on point, no one cares that you'll need several glasses of water to get through it.

"Hungry?" Jocelyn smiled as she pulled a mango from her backpack. Mangos were Nate's absolute favorite. Jocelyn had witnessed her eat as many as six in a sitting. Instead of waiting for a response, Nate's fruit wielding bestie quickly began to peel the mango. First, she used her fingernails to pierce the fruit's tough skin and tender interior. Then she let her teeth go to work. Nate watched as her ravenous friend peeled back the fleshy fruit's remaining layers with ease until the glistening tropical delight was left completely exposed. "Well." Proud of her conquest, she offered it to Nate.

"I'm straight," Nate replied, her stomach grumbling in clear contradiction.

"Sure you are," Jocelyn smirked and with an unabashed primitive flow, bit down hard until the stone fruit's natural juices began to grace her lips and chin. Embarrassed, Nate turned her gaze back to Pum Pum Rock and tried to ignore Jocelyn as she devoured the fruit. Barely fourteen and thoroughly confused, Nate stared at the effeminate rock formation and the lush thicket surrounding it as her belly began to bob and weave. Nate took a moment to calm her nerves, swallowed the water that had started to develop in her mouth and again turned to face her friend.

"You need a napkin," Nate feigned repulsion as she eyed Jocelyn—her face, fingers and forearms now wet with the mango's pulpy sweetness.

"I'm straight," Jocelyn countered, slurping what was left of the bowed seed with satisfaction.

# #

Several hours later Nate sat at the top of Auntie Earlene's staircase, spying as the one woman who always had her back sparred with Nate's father.

"They running up and down the state building like chickens with their heads cut clear off!" The Minister tried hard to whisper, but Nate heard every word. "What the people 'dem gonna say when Jamaica's Minister of Youth and Culture's own daughter don't know how to act? Bad enough she's a tomboy," he complained.

"Natty is more than a tomboy and you know it," Auntie Earlene insisted.

Visibly unsettled, Nate caught a glance of herself in a nearby mirror. Basketball shorts, white tank top, scraped knees. A natural athlete, Nate was the poster child for sporty, and although her mother was notorious for harassing Nate about her affinity for activewear until now, Nate's father had never called her out.

"You must teach her to practice restraint," Auntie Earlene warned.

"Said the woman whose never raised a child. Matter of fact, when's the last time you had a man around here? It's been what, seven years since Roosevelt passed," Barrington paused for a beat out of respect for the dead. "People are talking."

"Let them!" Auntie Earlene sucked her teeth with the pizzazz of a truly pissed off island woman. Effortlessly using it to punctuate her thoughts while tearing into her baby brother. "Not like I'm the only one around here with a secret," she scoffed. "Only difference is, should yours ever see the light of day it's lights out for you, brethren." She sniffed, the lingering bouquet of marijuana, light, but still apparent on Barrington's clothing.

"Your voice," Barrington lowered his tone and motioned hush to his big sister, but she refused to be muted. Instead, she kicked it up a notch and Nate took the opportunity to creep closer to the action.

"I was talking about your marriage," Auntie Earlene laughed. "Not ganja, little brother."

"Our marriage. Our business," Barrington clapped back.

"It's a business alright," Earlene mumbled as Barrington rose to answer the doorbell, which had momentarily put their familial beef on pause. On the opposite end stood Ms. Ruth, dressed in overalls and a floppy sun hat with a smile that was just as wide.

"Evening, Minister," Ms. Ruth extended her hand toward Barrington, but he bypassed the gesture completely. In fact, if she hadn't wedged her foot in the screen door, it would've shut right in her face.

"The sun's barely set and you've got all types traipsing right through the front door." Barrington seethed, reclaiming his seat at the table.

"You in there, Earlene?" The soft-spoken woman asked, refusing to budge.

"Be right out," Auntie Earlene yelled from the kitchen. In a matter of seconds, her tone had gone from sugar cane sweet to strangely scientific. "You know, Ms. Ruth was just telling me that she read about what she called cross-cultural evidence for the genetics of homosexuality."

"Genetics?" Nate's father leaned in, visibly unnerved.

"Farmers, right? So analytical," Auntie Earlene continued as she used a knife from the butcher block to cut off several small slices of guava tart. "They say it happens to one out of every four family members, but I believe that's an underestimate." Next, she placed the dessert, along with two glasses of sorrel, onto a tray and walked toward the front door.

For the next few hours, Auntie Earlene and Ms. Ruth chatted on the wrap around porch over freshly brewed sorrel and homemade tart. Nate remembered passing out on the couch pondering the genetics of homosexuality—was it really hereditary like Auntie Earlene said? In the wee hours of the morning, she awoke to the roaring of an engine purring to life. The groggy teen wiped the sleep from her eyes and peered out of the living room window just as the sun crept in to signal the beginning of a brand new day. By then, Aunt Earlene was wearing Ms. Ruth's floppy hat and Nate couldn't be sure, but it looked like she was also kissing Ms. Ruth right on her mouth.

Chapter 10

Simple Simon

Karina sat in the massive claw foot soaking tub nursing a nose bleed, as she recalled her mother's instructions: "Pinch here, lean your head forward and suck on these." As a middle school-aged child, Karina often got nose bleeds due to Southern California's rampant dry heat, but nowadays, her bloody noses had less to do with the weather and more to do with her drug of choice and the many toxins used to cut it.

Karina placed several ice cubes from a previously crushed cocktail into her mouth, pinched her nose and leaned forward. The splatters of blood that had moments ago gushed like a spigot onto the sheets and blanket that she'd outfitted the tub with reminded Karina of the early morning news that had broken just last week and would forever change her life:

"Mayrik, I'll be there as soon as I can," Karina spoke into her cellphone, using the Armenian word for mother. Half of Karina's head was pinned up and neatly curled, while the rest lay limp in anticipation of the high heat curling iron.

"Enough excuses, Karina! Your brother has been in the office for thirty minutes already!" Her mom's disgust rocketed through the cell phone.

"Mayrik, it takes time to pull all this together." Karina used a hand towel to apply pressure to the self-inflicted box cutter wound on her forearm. However, the cut was deep, and her blood soaked quickly through.

"If you're not here in thirty minutes, don't bother," Karina's mother concluded their conversation in a huff. Her wound still weeping, Karina tossed the towel into a nearby sink and began to wrap the abrasion in gauze until the image of Simon and Chad Herbst on her television accompanied by a monumental headline commanded her attention:

"Simon and Chad Herbst named new heads of Herbst Studio." Karina unmuted the television and read the caption aloud as an impassioned news anchor began to relay the breaking news. After months of public pushback from board members and despite their lack of television experience, Chad and Simon Herbst would officially be filling their father's shoes. This position had been vacant ever since their father, Paul Herbst, had lost his life in a tragic head-on collision.

Karina listened to the newscast while she hurriedly wrapped the blood stained gauze in an ace bandage before grabbing a blazer and hopping into her luxury SUV. "Call Nate." She used a voice command to get Nate on to the phone, then began to finger-comb her curls until they blended seamlessly into her straight hair.

"What up, Kar?" Nate answered from the audio bay at work.

"I heard the plantation's got a couple of new overseers," Karina joked.

"They finally announced it, but it makes no difference to me," Nate replied candidly. "They've been here since their father's accident this summer. Aside from that initial town hall meeting, they mostly stay in their ivory tower."

"Let the grunts sweat it out in the field," Karina said with a laugh, then laid in on her horn as she swerved to get around a listless driver. The amount of attitude she threw the slowpoke would have been impressive had his gaze not remained fixed on the road ahead. "Good ol boys club," she continued while white-knuckling the steering wheel and accelerating. "We either play the game or get run over."

"While I appreciate that you recognize the bias of this situation, let's be clear. Nepotism is how you got your job," Nate reminded Karina.

"It's not my fault I'm an exotic beauty born on the right side of the tracks," Karina responded smugly, then gunned it just as the light turned red and a pedestrian in the crosswalk flipped her off. "I am a Muslim woman— nowadays, that's almost as bad as being black. No offense." Karina's ability to make any conversation revolve around her was uncanny. "I completely get all the isms. Nepotism, racism, sexism. I feel your pain, sis."

"Do you?" Nate asked, sighing into the phone.

"Of course I do," replied Karina. "You're underutilized, underpaid and underappreciated." She looked at the clock on the dashboard and then made a quick turn into one of Los Angeles' most popular trails. Next, Karina slowed the SUV down to a crawl, and as she came dangerously close to a runner in a hooded sweatsuit, the most unsettling smile developed across her face.

"You produce amazing tracks. They deserve to be heard. As a matter of fact, I spoke to Simon about you," Karina lied. She hadn't spoken to Simon in months, but that was all about to change.

"You did?" The surprise in Nate's voice was apparent.

"I'll fill you in later. Just know that he's dying to meet you." She hung up, and as the hooded man turned to face Karina, she sped up, causing him to leap from the SUV's path. Once the dust settled, and the man was able to compose himself, Karina hopped out of the vehicle, its engine still running.

"What the hell?" Simon gasped, trying to stand. But Karina used her high heel to push the bewildered man back to the ground.

"I've texted. I've called. You can't just ignore me, Simon."

"Did you follow me here?"

"Simple Simon. I sold you the house you live in. Did you think it would be that hard to track you down?" Karina had spent the last couple of weeks trailing Simon and she'd learned that every other morning he jogged Runyon Canyon at precisely this time. It had been several months since Simon assaulted Karina and memories of the attack left her hell-bent on revenge:

"Just let me in," Karina recalled how as she reached the front door, Simon whispered lowly in her ear while nuzzling his stiff shaft against her pencil skirt.

"No!" Karina remembered smacking Simon in the face and how lashing out had only encouraged him. In fact, she could still feel the sting of his open backhand hitting her hard in the face moments before forcing himself upon her.

Karina was incensed and willing to take Simon down by any means necessary, even if that meant sacrificing Nate in the process. And now that he and his brother had officially been named heads of Herbst Studios, the timing was perfect—Simon had everything to loose. Plus, it didn't hurt that Nate had helped Karina secure some contract work with the studio. Thanks to her unknowing bestie, Karina's plan was in full swing and she intended to work it from the inside out. Blood trickling down his forehead, Simon stood up pissed. He grabbed Karina by her injured forearm, but the throbbing pain of his stronghold only acted as fuel to the vengeful woman.

"You're completely unhinged!" He declared, no idea how true that statement was.

"I can scream bloody murder, or you can get in the car," Karina said, looking down at Simon's grasp, then at the crowd of joggers slowly starting to gather. "I'll wait." Noticing the developing throng of onlookers, Simon let Karina's arm go and followed her to the SUV. "Here's what's gonna happen," Karina said, shutting the door behind her. "My friend Nate Higgins has spent the last two years as an audio engineer at Herbst Studios. She's going to call your assistant to arrange a meeting and you're gonna take the meeting. As a matter of fact, you're going to be ecstatic about the meeting. Listen to her podcast. Shower her with compliments." Karina lit up a clove and blew smoke in Simon's direction before continuing. "Now, Nate would be happy just having her tracks included in the studio's stock music library, which is a great place to start, but you and I, see, we're used to getting what we want and what Nate really wants is a record deal."

"A contract!" Simon scoffed, noticing for the first time blood on his hands along with the blood that had seeped through Karina's blazer. She folded her arms, attempting to conceal the reinjured wound.

"I want you to introduce Nate to your connects at Masquerade Records. If not, I'll release the tape," Karina threatened. "Everyone will know that Hollywood's newest television exec is also a rapist." Sure Simon had assaulted her the day of the house viewing, but there wasn't video to prove it, was there? Simon searched Karina's stone-cold poker face. She had to be bluffing.

"Even if a tape does exist, you can't release a thing. You signed an NDA," Simon countered, standing his ground. "You were paid to keep quiet."

"Maybe it'll get leaked. These things happen," Karina said with a shrug.

"You're insane," Simon groaned.

"And you've got a lot to lose." Karina blew another plume of smoke into Simon's face. "You really should be thanking me. Nate's a little shy at first, but the girl is gorgeous. I'm sure she'll be very appreciative of your help."

"How appreciative?" For the first time in their conversation, Simon made direct eye contact with Karina. It was at that point that Karina knew she had him.

Part Two

If Yuh Sleep Wid Dawg

Chapter 11

An Old Broom

Nate clicked the purchase button and then shut down her laptop. In two days, she would return to a home she hadn't been to in fourteen years. Nate wasn't just unprepared. The upcoming reunion left her overwhelmed. Her stomach in knots, Nate began shuffling scrambled egg whites around the damask kitchen plate. Fighting with Tru and worrying about Auntie Earlene had taken a toll. Nate poked at her breakfast a few more times before pushing the plate aside.

Mentally exhausted, Nate exhaled, and as she did, she was transported back to another stress-filled moment in time. She could laugh at it now, but that night as Nate and Jocelyn sat across from each other, while Auntie Earlene manned the head of the table, nothing was funny:

"You know y'all, wrong," Auntie Earlene reprimanded a fourteen-year-old Nate.

"It was an accident, Auntie," Nate moaned apologetically, shifting the position of the untouched food around on her plate.

"Hush, child," Auntie Earlene shut Nate down just as fast as she had opened her mouth. "I heard you mash into the Minister of Health—had her bloomers showing for all the world to see."

"If anything mash up, it's the floor her big behind fell on," Jocelyn joked, but Auntie Earlene didn't even crack a smile. Sure she was a rebel, but talking slick to Earlene was too much, even for Jocelyn. Jocelyn was trying to divert attention from Nate, and although Auntie Earlene found the gesture endearing, Jocelyn needed to be checked.

"Show some respect!" Auntie Earlene exclaimed, grabbing the young girl's face and angling it toward her. "The woman old enough to be your granny."

"Please, Auntie—she's joking," Nate cried out and instinctively grabbed Jocelyn's hand as Auntie Earlene released the girl from her clutches and began to dish out a serious warning.

"You think I'm blind?" Auntie Earlene paused, all but daring the girls to respond. "I see you. Both of you." Auntie Earlene's gaze drifted back and forth between the two friends. She sipped ginger tea and took a moment to settle herself. "A new broom sweeps clean, but an old broom knows every corner." She swallowed another mouthful of the spiced brew as a look of knowing concern gradually began to define her face. "It's not safe, Natty. This country has laws, and if those laws are broken, you pay—sometimes with your life." Auntie Earlene continued as the girls slowly let their clasped hands drift apart. "You understand?"

Nate opened her mouth to respond just as her father's Mercedes advanced up the dirt driveway. She watched while he parked in front of Auntie Earlene's farmhouse and pulled the rearview mirror down suspiciously. It was as if he thought someone was following him, but instead of being tailed, the only thing that shone back was his own blood shot eyes. Nate didn't realize it at the time, but her father was in a post-coital fog. He needed to snap out of it. Alas, flashbacks of an abandoned train yard paired with Island Sweet Skunk and an unidentified lover doling out mind-blowing head dominated Barrington's mental banks.

Nate always assumed something was off in her parents' relationship. She'd even heard Auntie Earlene call their marriage a business, but Nate knew better than ever to broach the subject. Unbeknownst to Nate, her parent's union was one of convenience established many moons ago. An open marriage where affairs were tolerated, yet kept under lock and key. The optics boasted a nuclear family poised to climb the political ladder.

After slamming the car door shut, Barrington inched toward the old Spanish style farmhouse. "Dad, I can explain," Nate blurted out as the kitchen door swung open.

Jocelyn stood to her feet, again directing the attention away from Nate. "It was entirely my fault, Minister Higgins. I pulled the fire alarm. I knew better and I'm sorry."

"We're sorry," Nate agreed, standing as Jocelyn eye-balled Auntie Earlene before taking Nate's hand in hers. Aside from Auntie Earlene, Jocelyn was the only person who consistently went to bat for Nate. Even on the brink of an ass whooping, it was a great feeling. For a brief moment, she felt protected and could care less about the lashes headed her way.

"I'm disappointed, Natty. You both know better," Barrington spoke calmly.

"It won't happen again," Nate promised.

"I know it won't," Barrington agreed. "Now, go on, you know what's next."

Once outside, Jocelyn ran full speed through the farm's North East quadrant, which was littered with young coconuts and canary-colored fronds on their last leg. "Stop playing, before these three lashes turn to ten," Nate warned Jocelyn. She then chased the vivacious sprinter past palms diseased by lethal yellowing and into Auntie Earlene's sugar cane field.

"Live a little!" Jocelyn exclaimed. "We're already in trouble." Nate's fearless bestie looked over her shoulder, just as both girls allowed their bodies to collapse into a thick patch of grass. On their backs and shrouded entirely by eight-foot-tall sugar cane, the girls attempted to catch their breath through laughter.

"Your dad's a softy, and you know it," Jocelyn concluded. "Plus, unless high grade makes a cologne I'm pretty sure he's feeling good."

"You smelled him, right?" Nate giggled. "Maybe it'll mellow him out."

"Girls, let's go!" Barrington's voice bounced off of the sugar-filled stalks.

"Guess not," Nate sighed and began to get up, but her defiant friend rolled on top of her, pinning Nate to the ground.

"Listen Natty, I just gonna say it." Jocelyn took a deep breath and then blurted out a declaration as assuredly as you would your own shoe size. "I think you like me. Matter fact, I know you do."

"What?" Nate attempted to stall but could barely string together a few syllables. "How?" Nate shied away, nervously. She had barely come to terms with her sexuality, and now her gutsy friend was trying to get her to confess her deepest desires aloud. No way. No how. She was cute and all, especially when she undid her topknot and allowed her long, naturally thick hair to fall past her shoulders and grace Nate's face.

"Stop playing," Nate evaded, but Jocelyn was persistent and unmistakably loved to live on the edge. These were undoubtedly Jocelyn's most endearing traits.

"Just tell me I'm wrong, if it's so," Jocelyn stood her ground.

"The switch, now, Natty!" Barrington's voice cut across the field for a second time.

"If anyone finds out, dad will be fired and mom will have to find another sucker to control," Nate sighed. "What's the point?"

"The point is we shouldn't have to hide in a field, Natty! We run 'tings, 'tings no run we." Jocelyn sat up confidently, but Nate remained flat on her back.

"We—like you and me?"

"So you have thought about us," Jocelyn beamed. "I like you, Natty. I want you to be mine." Although younger than Nate by a year, she was obviously the senior. All but daring Nate to make a move, Jocelyn stared down at her life-long friend. "You the one for me, Natty," she declared, "matter fact, from now on, I gon' call you Natty One." Nate and Jocelyn laughed.

"You always talk about guys, so I thought…" Entranced, Nate sat up so that they were face to face, yet still shielded by the tall, sweet shafts. The lines of their friendship forever blurred, Nate pulled her bestie in close, as the two inexperienced teens shared their first kiss.

"How'd you know?" Nate broke away from the embrace long enough to ask Jocelyn a question.

"You never talk about guys, plus you're the best footballer in St. James," Jocelyn laughed after giving Nate's question all of one second to digest. "I've had a crush on you forever," she continued, giving Nate a good squeeze.

Although she was hiding in a sugar cane field, this was the most transparent Nate had ever been. It felt great—until reality set in.

"You heard what Auntie said," Nate lamented. "Jamaica has laws—people are being killed."

"I gonna ask you one more time, Natty One," the self-assured teen whispered into Nate's ear, "be mine." She then gave Nate another soft kiss on the lips.

"I'm pretty sure that wasn't a question," Nate smiled, their lips still locked. "You sound like a caveman," Nate laughed, briefly losing herself in her best friend's coffee-colored eyes. "You would make a cute, Fred Flintstone though."

"So we gonna Yabba Dabba do this or what?" Jocelyn smirked.

Chapter 12

Daddy Issues

Tru strolled into the Beverly Hills bank, rocking a pale green pixie cut and a pair of painted-on acid wash jeans. The headstrong cutie approached the counter like she owned the place. Her eclectic, frame-hugging blazer was cropped just enough to fall gracefully above her derrière with couture ease. All eyes on her, Tru was calculated and had years ago learned how to work a room.

"Deposit, please," Tru said, sliding a piece of paper under the thick plastic divider. The teller made no eye contact. Instead, she sighed and slowly began rolling on a pair of plastic gloves. "Hello," Tru's tone grew louder as she knocked on the bulletproof window.

"Hey," the teller responded dryly. She then read the deposit slip and shook her head in disgust.

"Whatever," Tru retorted. She recognized the teller, and the woman always seemed to have an attitude. From her purse, Tru pulled out several envelopes full of cash divided into various denominations.

"There must be five hundred singles here," the teller sucked her teeth like Tru was forcing her to do long division without a calculator. She then used the money counter to tabulate $2,500 in cash. "What did you say you did for a living?" The teller quizzed, finally making eye contact, not with Tru, but with her plunging neckline.

"I didn't." Unmoved, Tru opened her blazer even wider and positioned her hands on her hips.

"Problem?" Tru fished a lollipop from the plastic Jack-o'-lantern on the teller's sill, unwrapped it and began to suck.

"Daddy issues, clearly. My guess is yours wasn't around much," the teller teased.

"You hateful old..." Tru scanned the lobby as if she was being punk'd, but with no camera crew in sight, it was safe to assume that this was no practical joke. Tru wasn't getting punk'd, she was being disrespected.

"I've made your deposit," the teller hissed, "now please move along." Next, she shoved a deposit receipt under the chunky plastic partition. At that moment, Tru realized she had two choices. Take the paper and the teller's funky attitude, or unleash the stereotype she was begging Tru to assume.

"Over here, sir," the teller ushered the next customer over, removing her gloves in the process.

"Oh, so his money ain't dirty?" Tru quizzed. Y'all see this?" She gave the customers a percipient once over, as they all suddenly had very important matters to handle on their phones. It was cool though. Tru was used to going it alone. She held out a single finger causing the customer to pause mid-stride. "Hold up. I'm not done with Cruella."

"One minute, sir," the teller sighed. "Your type always causes a scene—well, what else do you want?" She asked Tru.

"Loretta, what's going on?" The bank manager approached from behind the teller as all eyes were fixed on the dramatic scene unfolding.

"Your girl was just about to tell me how my type of people always cause scenes," Tru said, filling in the branch manager. "Now, what type is that exactly, Loretta?"

"She made her deposit but refused to leave," the teller's voice quivered. "She'd rather harass me—she's completely out of control."

"No, you're out of control!" Tru exclaimed. Every time I come in here, she has an attitude. Now, she fighting back tears. Girl, bye!" Tru took a beat to surmise the situation. With a long line of curious customers, the teller had started to sweat. Tru decided now was the perfect time to up the ante. "Matter fact, why don't you just close the account," Tru concluded.

"Now, that's the last thing we want you to do," the manager interjected. "Excuse me, Loretta." The teller gave the manager some space and he went to work, playing the computer's keyboard like a vintage Casio. When he discovered the nearly half-million-dollar account balance, he swallowed hard and glared through the teller. "Loretta, take five." The teller rolled her eyes at Tru, then made her way to the employee break room.

"Yeah, Loretta, step," Tru agreed and waved goodbye to the embarrassed woman.

"I see you've been a valued customer of ours for several years now, Ms. Lee. I'm truly sorry for the misunderstanding. We'd hate to lose your business," the branch manager advised.

"I'm sure," Tru said, crossing her arms against her chest.

"I'd like to offer you this $100 Visa gift card and please accept my apology for any misunderstanding," he continued. "I do hope you'll still to bank with us."

"If that teller even looks at me wrong…" Tru's cell phone interrupted her mid-sentence. "Hey, I'm twenty minutes out." As she spoke into the cellphone, Tru's voice went from Friday night fury to easy like Sunday Morning. "I'll call you from the road." She ended the call and returned her attention to the banker. "If she comes at me sideways one more time, I promise I'll walk." Tru grabbed the gift card and exited the bank.

#

A half-hour later, Tru was touring a commercial property with Karina in the middle of downtown L.A. Despite their confrontation outside of the club last night, Nate was right—Karina could barely remember any of it. Instead, she'd attributed anything unbecoming to being intoxicated and they left it at that. Karina knew every property available in the county, and even though Tru didn't trust her, she welcomed her expertise.

"We're in the heart of the financial district, plenty of boutiques, fine dining, and high-end clientele!" Karina gushed. She was in full-on agent mode. "This place won't last long," she warned.

Tru fingered the fixtures, silently envisioning the venue tastefully refurbished. Upstairs the VIP area would overlook a crowded dance floor and on stage, a live soul band—maybe even The Roots! Tru dreamed big, always had. Every night would have a theme—Thirsty Thursdays would feature nothing but fine wine and the realest poets. Get Fresh Fridays would allow resident deejays to spin only the best old school beats. Peep shows would cater to voyeurs, and champagne rooms would provide a place for those who simply had to touch. Soul Saturdays would spotlight live music from underground artists. And to cap off the weekend, Sunday Funday, boasting rooftop views, live gospel brunch, lunch and dinner.

"Nice place," Tru said as she followed Karina up a long, spiraling staircase to a loft that overlooked the expansive lower level. "But for now, let's keep this between us."

"No worries. I love surprises," Karina feigned excitement, and Tru was perceptive enough to realize it. Trusting Karina was a long shot, but Tru was strategic. Even if Karina told Nate that they were meeting, at least Nate would know that she was serious about quitting her job and starting a business that didn't leave her feeling vacant.

"Finally ready to hang up them whips and chains," Karina laughed aloud. "So long dry humps! Beat it, hand jobs!" It never failed. Karina was always gunning for Tru. But because Karina was merely a means to an end, Tru mostly just laughed off or straight up ignored her off-putting jokes.

Karina spoke while checking herself out on her camera phone, "Seriously, the place is perfect. Plus, it's in foreclosure, so it won't last long." Karina tucked her phone back into her clutch, just as Tru's began to ring.

"I'll call her back," Tru said, scrolling through the list of unreturned calls and texts from Nate. Her mind was made up. Her feelings had been hurt, and because of that, her gal pal would have to put in some work.

"Nate?" Karina quizzed.

"We got into it last night. I'm just not ready to talk." Tru let her fingers run across the embossed paneled wallpaper as she reminded herself of the mantra her grandmother had drilled into her all those years ago—keep 'em guessing.

"She's my girl and all, but a little needy, don't you think? Selfish actually," Karina said, smack-talking Nate.

"She wants me to go to Jamaica and meet her family. It's a sweet offer, but Halloween is my biggest gig of the year—she knows this."

"That's a whole lot of singles." Classic Karina, right on cue. She shimmied and popped her round rump up and down to a rhythm only she could hear. While the financial ramifications of leaving town were a factor, so was the nature of Tru and Nate's relationship. Things had gotten complicated quickly. And although Tru was enjoying the ride, she insisted they keep things casual. At least for the next few months.

Tru ignored Karina's passive-aggression and instead took note as she continued to trash talk Nate. "She expects you to leave all that money on the table for a trip to the beach?" Karina quizzed. "I mean, it's been what, a year, and y'all aren't even official. Get your paper, girl!" Exclaimed Karina.

"I've got to get home," Tru replied. "Still not the right fit. I'm thinking more vintage," she continued, abruptly making her way back down the staircase. "But we're getting close." Tru could handle Karina's bitchy nature, but after watching how she so effortlessly threw Nate under the bus it was officially time to lock a new realtor.

"We've seen ten places in the last two weeks," Karina reminded Tru.

"No worries, Kar. There's a sweet commission in your future." Tru looked up at Karina one last time before exiting the 2-million-dollar property.

"No problem, princess." Karina's smile faded as soon as the door shut behind Tru. "Follow her," Tru barked the command into her cell phone, then lit up a hand-rolled clove.

Chapter 13

Make Some Noise

Production had arranged an upscale cooking class for round two of Brown Bag Cutie. The chic kitchen boasted marble countertops, a high-end backsplash, and stainless steel appliances. Laid out on the island were all the ingredients necessary for a delicious date night. With candlelight and flowing libations, the backdrop was ideal for a romantic cooking class. The theme was Autumn in Paris, and the menu was sumptuous: spicy steamed mussels with fennel and tomatoes, steak with braised onions, and roasted rosemary potatoes.

"Sorry I'm late. Car trouble," Nate's audio intern Abby, affectionately known as Junior Mint, said sliding into confessional a full two hours late. She was the director's niece and came from a place of privilege, but Nate had never really seen her use it. She was genuinely more awkward than entitled.

"Your podcast last week. Amazing," Abby whispered. "I loved how you..." Nate shushed the intern and continued to monitor audio levels, as Dater #1 adorned in a bejeweled brown bag spoke to the camera.

"I'm a total boss and I'm gonna do what I got to do to smoke the competition. I'm going to hurt people's feelings. I'm going to laugh when they cry. And I'm gonna love every minute of it," Dater #1 affirmed.

Nate could barely keep a straight face. The assertive dater was a straight-up shark, and she had no qualms about it. Typically, on these dates, producers plied contestants with enough alcohol to sponsor an NCAA Division 1 tailgate, but with Dater #1, that wasn't necessary. A trial attorney by day and maneater by night, Dater #1 didn't need liquid courage because she'd arrived to the venue already on ten.

"I deserve to win," Dater #1 continued as she moved from the confessional to the kitchen. "I'm smart, I'm sexy, and if you pick me, you won't have to beat your meat," Dater #1 joked, then proceeded to tenderize the hell out of the boneless rib eye.

"You're really pounding that thing," said The Picker nodding his head approvingly as Dater #2 interjected.

"Would you believe this is the first meal I learned to cook?" Dater #2 said, sorting through the mussels. She was the only contestant not wearing a mask. "We need to make sure that the shells are closed tight and that the beards have been removed. Right, chef?" Dater #2 said, holding up the perfect specimen as an example.

"Oui, oui. She is correct," their instructor nodded in agreement.

"So you cook?" The Picker asked, sounding thrilled.

"I studied at the Cordon Bleu," Dater #2 responded, discernibly proud but not at all arrogant.

"Oh, she's the help. I get it now," Dater #3 said, trying to rattle Dater #2. "Sexy southerner, tomboy scruff and the help," she concluded, pointing out each contestant starting with herself.

"I try to avoid labels," The Picker piped up, halting the potential girl fight in its tracks. "But I do love Paris," he continued, "I have family in Bordeaux."

"Then, I'm sure you've been to VinExpo?" Dater #2 quizzed.

"Oui, Oui, mademoiselle. J'aime ça!" Exclaimed The Picker.

"English please," Dater #1 sighed, "America first."

"He was just saying how he loved the wine festival," Dater #2 blushed.

"You know what they say about all that wine, cheese and bread. A minute on the lips," Dater #1 playfully poked Dater #2 in her midsection, causing her face to flush in discomfort. Then, Dater #1 smirked and ran her hand across The Picker's well-defined chest. Nate watched Dater #3 all but evaporate.

"Not that you have to worry about love handles," Dater #1 flattered The Picker.

"I feel so bad for the pudgy little thing," Dater #3 spoke directly to the camera in the confessional as Nate adjusted the Southerner's audio levels.

"And the other one, well she's just trying too hard," Dater #3 continued. "Did you see what she did to that steak? Just so mannish," she joked. Dater #3 was sporting a Lucha Libre mask so you could not see the look on her face, but you could most certainly hear the dejection in her voice. "She's probably intimidated. I mean, I'm barely trying, and the guy can't keep his hands off me," Dater #3 said with a shrug.

Southern charm or not, it was evident to Nate that while Dater #3 had no shame in her vain, she had made a valid point. When the mussels were served, The Picker grew hypnotized by her technique of slurping the gooey innards of spicy mussels into her mouth. "There's just no way to eat these and make it look pretty," said Dater #3, throwing her scraps into a pile of discarded shells.

"If only you could see what I see," The Picker replied, then took a long swig of Merlot, as Dater #3 sucked the garlic and herb steeped mussel from its shiny black exterior. Nate was captivated by her confidence. Mask or not, she knew she was pretty, and the way she licked her fingers indiscriminately meant she didn't have to be extra dainty to prove it.

"You make that mask look sexy," The Picker complimented Dater #3.

"Oh hush," Dater #3 replied coyly.

"She looks more like a blow-up doll if you ask me," Dater #1 interrupted but was unsuccessful in getting a rise out of Dater #3.

"Aren't you the sweetest," Dater #3 said, completely ignoring Dater #1's insult. She was was so seductive, Nate found it hard to concentrate. Nate angled the boom mic in Dater #3's direction. Her lips were moving, so she had to be talking, but Nate didn't hear any of it. The more Dater #3 consumed, the more Nate fantasized about being intertwined with Tru in last night's stellar lovemaking session. Nate remembered how Tru used her leg to pull her in close and when their bodies finally touched, it was like two stars colliding.

"Nate, you good?" The intern asked, interrupting Nate's erotic daydream. Then, Nate noticed Dater #2 waiting beside the confessional. Immediately she lowered her boom mic and walked past a couple of camera operators chatting up Dater #3.

"It's simple—you're either going home with beauty or taking home the beast." Dater #3 laughed, gesturing at Dater #1, who was laying it on deep as she flirted with The Picker.

"You do kind of look like a blow-up doll," the cameraman joked with Dater #3. "You know I was watching this video." His crudeness caused Nate's skin to crawl. Daytime fantasies were one thing, she could keep it in her pants and nobody had to know, but coming on to contestants was just plain gross.

Nate lingered for a beat and noticed that no matter how creepy the comment, Dater #3 loved the attention. Nate looked over at The Picker and could tell that although he was humoring Dater #1, he couldn't keep his eyes off of Dater #3. Nate couldn't make heads or tails of the cat and mouse game the contestants were playing, far less the song and dance she and Tru had authored. Tru hadn't responded to any of Nate's calls or texts and it was starting to tick her off. Her look of disgust caught the attention of the boorish camera operator.

"So when are you gonna take off your mask, Nate?" The camera operator probed.

"I'm not wearing one," Nate answered, confused and in no mood for foolishness.

"Sure you are. Try smiling more," the camera operator teased. Nate ignored the unsolicited advice and made her way past her colleagues toward the confessional so that she could supervise the intern as she monitored Dater #2's audio levels.

"It's like just when I think we're finding common ground, one of those two shoves her boobs in his face or talks about how good they are at beating meat," Dater #2 joked.

Dater #2 laughed and for the first time, Nate took a good look at her. She felt like a jerk for not noticing sooner, mostly because the others were just so outgoing and well, scantily clad, but when Nate stopped to pay attention, she discovered that Dater #2 gave off a serious girl-next-door vibe. Dater #2 was pretty with wavy brown hair and sparkling green eyes, plus the fact that she could cook meant that she was a catch.

"Now look who's showing off!" Dater #3 exclaimed as Dater #2 impressed the room with her technique of artfully applying Chantilly Whipped Cream to the bittersweet chocolate soufflé.

"Looks almost too good to eat," The Picker agreed, admiring Dater #2's handiwork.

"Said no one ever," Dater #2 replied, then squirted a smidge of the sweet confection onto the tip of her finger. Next, she licked it off and went in for a kiss.

"Delicious," The Picker laughed, licking his lips and locking eyes with Dater #2. She had come from behind and scored the first kiss of the three-round date. It was a ballsy move that no one saw coming.

"I'm torn," The Picker sat in the confessional and spoke to the camera. "The girls are great, but honestly, Betty Crocker has got to go. She's cool and all, but the other two will be way more fun in the Jacuzzi! Au Revoir."

In her head, Nate had hurled expletives like hand grenades at The Picker, but in reality, she was merely monitoring his audio tracks. She listened as The Picker dismissed Dater #2 to her face, just as callously as he had done in the confessional and observed the audio levels ebb and crest as Dater #2 bravely held back tears of humiliation. Nate hadn't cried when Tru left the night before, but she had come damn close. Nate knew the deal. She and Tru had agreed on casually hooking up, but lately, it felt like more. When she invited Tru back to Jamaica, Nate had hoped Tru would at least consider the offer. No such luck. Watching Dater #2 walk the hall of shame made her wish she had held her cards just a hair closer to her chest last night, but that ship had sailed and appeared to be sinking fast. With a slate of unanswered phone calls and text messages mounting, the ball was absolutely in Tru's court.

"And cut. Nice job, everyone," the director said, removing his headphones. "Talent take five. Party bus to round three leaves in ten."

"I can't believe he cut Betty Crocker," Abby said, leaning in close, her breasts hanging detectably close to Nate's back."

"I know right, she was cool," Nate replied. She then stood up and eyed Abby. Since day one of her internship, it had been obvious that she liked Nate, but it was just a schoolgirl crush. Or so she thought. The typically bashful intern had lately given off a come-and-get it vibe, and as bruised as her ego was at the moment, Nate was considering the invitation.

"I'm thinking about upgrading my workstation. You're using the Motif XF, right?" asked the intern, shoving her phone into her back pocket and exhaling self-assuredly."

"Yeah, I love it," Nate responded.

"I'm on the XF8. It's a sweet set up, but I'd love to check yours out. There's a sale this week, so maybe after we wrap, if you aren't busy, I can come through," she said, tossing her long black hair over her shoulder. Nate stared at the intern like a jigsaw puzzle.

"You're probably exhausted, have a date or something," Abby recanted, suddenly drowning in a wave of insecurity.

"So, what—you ready to make some noise, Junior Mint?" Nate asked with a smirk.

Chapter 14

Holly Berry

Tru slid the key card into the door's magnetic slot. Once the sensor turned green, she exhaled, put on a sexy smile and entered the suite. On the other side of the door, an anxious couple in their late thirties sat waiting. The shirtless man stood and greeted Tru by her alias.

"Kenya, you're even more beautiful in person." He turned back and flashed a smile at his wife.

"Come on over, baby," he encouraged.

"I swear I'm never late," Tru continued, entering the suite. "Wardrobe malfunction."

"We were this close to leaving," The man's wife responded, gesturing with her fingers.

"She's kidding," the man interjected. "So glad you made it." Next, he popped a bottle of champagne and offered a glass to each of the women. Their names were Noel and Holly, and they were new clients. After three years in the game, couples had become Tru's sweet spot.

"Thanks for having me," Tru responded, then slipped out of her dark trench coat to reveal a black leather corset and matching panties. "Noel and Holly, aye. All we're missing is the mistletoe," she laughed. "Not that we'll need it."

"I'm pretty sure all we need is right in this room," Noel agreed and was as giddy as a virgin on prom night.

Holly, on the other hand, would take some work. Tru was a great judge of character and usually able to size a person up with in the first few minutes of a meeting. What she knew for sure was that Holly was reluctant. Tru had been emailing with Holly for the past couple of weeks, but this was the first time they'd met face to face. In the emails, she'd described her husband Noel as a sexy computer nerd, whom she loved dearly. Holly wanted to do something special for his birthday and had gotten her contact information from a friend of a friend.

"Sit," said Noel, crossing the penthouse suite and relaxing into an oversized leather chair as the ladies cozied up on a plush love seat overlooking the crystal blue Pacific Ocean. "You two look like a big ol' bowl of cookies and cream," Noel laughed, smiling at the women. "And I've got your spoon right here," Noel continued, his entire being throbbing in anticipation.

"You're cute. And your wife—Holly, you're gorgeous." Tru brushed blond bangs out of Holly's bright blue eyes. Her nerves more than apparent, Tru knew how she'd have to play her. Like many of her clients, Holly didn't really want to be there. This was Noel's wet dream, not hers.

On the one hand, Tru pitied Holly for compromising herself to please some man, even if he was her husband. But then Tru dug deeper. Here this woman was, about to go all-in, all to please someone she loved. Now, Tru by no means considered herself to be a romantic person, but she'd seen clients make this gesture in the past, and had to admit, the sentiment got to her every time. Tru wondered could she ever love anyone enough to put their needs in front of her own.

"Don't you like the champagne?" Tru probed, gesturing at the still full flute.

"It's ok," Holly responded.

Tru walked behind the couch and began working Holly's shoulders. "Well, how about this?" Tru queried. "Is this ok too?" She made her way down to Holly's breasts and began to tweak her nipples. Alas, Holly started to loosen.

"It's great," Holly moaned, "but it's Noel's birthday, not mine."

"Happy wife, happy life," Tru countered.

"I'll drink to that," Noel agreed, as the fragrant libation slid down his throat with ease.

"Smart and sexy," Tru said, directing her adoration at Noel. The couple laughed at her compliment as Holly indulged in several lengthy swigs of champagne. Tru had officially broken the ice. Continuing the sensual massage, she straddled Holly, her breasts positioned squarely in the doe-eyed woman's face.

Noel refilled Holly's champagne flute as Tru whispered in her ear. "Guess you were right about the mistletoe," Noel joked, nodding at Tru.

"Someone's a happy camper," Tru spoke softly. The inference was that she was talking about the overly giddy birthday boy, but the truth of the matter was this: Tru knew women, and she could feel Holly's heat rising.

"Get him to come over here. Touch him like I'm touching you," Tru whispered in Holly's ear. "I wanna show you something." Tru stood up, remembering a time when she felt more fulfilled. A time when her role in the sexual commerce game was more about flaunting her sexual freedom and making a butt load of cash in the process and less about being bought, sold, and traded like a commodity on the New York Stock Exchange.

"Noel, honey, come sit," Holly demanded.

"Ok, but where's she going?" Noel quizzed.

"I'll be right back," Tru excused herself, then grabbed her oversized travel bag and headed toward the restroom.

The twenty-five-year-old was smart but had relied heavily on her looks throughout high school. Students and even teachers would let her cheat on exams. Tru would write answers on the bottoms of her shoes, brim of her hat—you name it. To her, cheating was an art form, and by senior year of high school, she had pretty much perfected it. Even cheating on lovers gave Tru a rush. She was a scam artist, and by graduating with a 3.3 average, Tru had beaten the system. She had modeled off and on in high school and throughout the years that followed, but her heart wasn't into it. She gave community college a shot, but with no desire to finish, the born hustler gravitated toward the fast life. She made a killing from credit card scams but watching a best friend get locked up made letting that go easy. Then she dipped her toe into the model pool again, only this time she followed the money—escorting VIPS to fabulous events and hosting over the top mansion parties. She even learned the arts of exotic dance and sensual massage, but being a dominatrix, afforded a chance to cash in like never before.

Tru took another sip from her flask, which brought her back to the mission at hand. She then began to listen as the couple spoke in what they considered hushed tones.

"Oh my God, babe, this is hot!" Noel bellowed, showering Holly with sweet kisses. "Thank you!"

"Happy birthday, love," Holly grinned.

"I am so ready for the both of you," Noel whispered seductively.

"You can stop right there," Holly's tone sharpened. "I told you, she doesn't do that, and neither do we."

"But it's my birthday," Noel whined while gently nibbling his wife's neck. "She's a whore. Just offer her more money."

What a dick. On the other side of the bathroom door, Tru rolled her eyes at Noel's comment and took a long sip from her jewel-encrusted flask, running her fingers over the emblazoned mantra, Keep 'Em Guessing. Tru ingested several more mouthfuls of the brown liquor as she mentally prepared to rejoin the couple.

The typically self-confident dominatrix was just a bit off her game. She had been ever since she'd discovered that her bag had been rifled through. Furthermore, the lingerie that she selected for her midday tryst had been stolen from her car's trunk, somewhere between the property viewing with Karina and the home Tru shared with her grandmother. Getting to the bottom of that would have to wait. For now, Tru needed to stay in the moment. She took a deep breath, then ran her fingers through her jet-black pixie, smoothing hairs into place. Next, she made her way to the center of the posh, overly priced room. In her hands, she carried two cupcakes, birthday candles aglow.

"I would tell you to make a wish, but I'm pretty sure it's already come true," Tru said, smacking Noel hard on the face. He loved it. She then pursed her lips and exhaled the redolence of Irish Whiskey onto the flames.

Despite her hardened, in control demeanor, Tru had started to hate her job, but the money, power and flexibility kept the private dancer in the game. Plus, she'd promised herself that once she'd managed to stack a half a million dollars, she'd retire. After a few years of incredibly hard work, coupled with a few wise investments, her career goal was well within reach.

"On your back, birthday boy," Tru commanded. Noel maneuvered with the agility of an alley cat, quickly positioning himself on the floor at Tru's command. Then, she placed a blindfold around his eyes. "Perfect," she cooed. Never once taking her gaze off Holly, Tru let the birthday candle wax drip onto Noel's chest. Immediately Holly stooped to her knees and began to blow and cool the slick waxy trail that had started to form along hubby's tingling torso.

"So, who's hungry?" asked Tru, smashing the frosted strawberry cupcake onto Noel's mouth. Next, she knelt over him and using her fingers, began to massage the frosting onto his bated lips.

"I'm starving!" Noel cried out, licking the strawberry goodness from his lips.

"Feed him," Tru instructed. The horny housewife approached and hovered above her blinded mate before slowly lowering herself onto his sugar-coated mouth. Noel's tongue, firm and probing, gradually plunged in and out of

Holly's tightening pleasure pit. Thrusting her hips, Holly kept her eyes trained on Tru as she melted like cheddar on hot buttered sourdough. Pleased, Tru circled the couple.

Such a dirty girl!" Tru exclaimed. Then she grabbed a fist full of Holly's blunt bob and yanked her head back so that their faces were mere inches apart.

"Now, tell hubby how you feel." Holly groaned her approval, but for Tru, that would never do. She yanked Holly's hair even harder, this time causing the previously reluctant lover to spring a leak. "Tell him!" Tru commanded.

Holly bucked her hips even more, riding the birthday boy's face like Annie Oakley at one of Buffalo Bill's infamous Wild West Shows.

"It feels like a short, fat Christmas cock," Holly laughed, clearly thrilled by her own rawness. "Don't stop!" She screamed.

"Well alright, Holly Berry! Now I'm turned on," Tru joked. She then removed Noel's blindfold, tossed her panties at the couple and sat on the edge of the California king. She was far enough that they couldn't touch her, but close enough for them to witness her whip out the dong shaped vibrator and moisten it in her mouth. Next, Tru spread her legs and guided the toy slowly in and out. There was a time when the natural born exhibitionist got off on getting couples off. However, as of late, those moments were few and far between. Falling for Nate had complicated Tru's hustle. And good as it felt, Tru just needed a little more time before she could go all in.

Chapter 15

Dark Liquor & Dope

"Nate," the assistant called out for a second time. "They're ready for you," he continued, using a remote control to slide the one-way glass office door open.

"Thanks," Nate replied. She then hopped up and popped the collar to her black and gold soccer jacket. Once inside the opulent office, Nate shook hands with the two brothers. After several months of being interim studio heads, Simon and Chad had just last week been named official heads of Herbst Studios. Simon and Chad could open doors for Nate. That was undeniable. Whether they would, remained, to be seen. More than anything, Nate wanted to create hot dance tracks and to score television and film projects. And with that, Nate set her sights on Simon. The fact that he'd left his position as Director of A&R at Masquerade Records—the label that repped Nate's favorite EDM musicians made him an invaluable resource. Although confident in her talent, Nate realized it took a lot more than ability to make it in the music industry. Career success depended on who you knew, and by her estimates, being besties with Karina had gotten her in the door. Now, all Nate had to do was shoot her shot. She handed Simon a flash drive containing her demo, then sat behind Chad's desk as Simon went on about what he believed to be America's first socially conscious reality show.

"We don't want people to be judged based on their skin color or any other identifiers," Simon continued. "We brown bag players on Brown Bag Cutie in hopes of them getting to know each other beyond the exterior and we want the same for our staff. Our team should represent a rainbow coalition of demographics, interests and ideas."

Hold up. Was dude actually talking inclusivity? Nate sat up straight in her chair, excited at the thought of someone who regularly dined on privilege pie volunteering to share a slice. As a black, lesbian immigrant, she epitomized multiplicity.

"I can't tell you how grateful I am to work for a company that embodies so much of what I stand for," she smiled, continuing. "Since you two took over for your father, I read all the new hire emails," Nate told the brothers. "This place has a whole new energy. It's dynamic."

"Right," Chad said, peering over his computer. He then looked at Nate who was clearly more excited about collaborating than he was. The fact that Nate could see the social media platform reflecting in Chad's clunky frames only confirmed her suspicions. Nate was striking out fast and needed to quickly grab their attention.

"This is about music, and music is universal," Nate said, redirecting the conversation to her pitch as she pounded out a beat onto the desk. "It's powerful and knows no color lines. Just like my beats, you'll notice my style is a mash-up of genres," she spoke proudly.

Chad took all of a nanosecond to digest Nate's point of view before delivering his microwave safe yet progressively ignorant speech. "The Herbst Brothers are post-racial, or is that transracial?" He laughed. "I honestly can't keep up, but bottom line, we want to start social conversations with all of our projects.

"And that starts with Brown Bag, nah mean?" Simon smirked, tickled as the sound of his voice overly-emphasized the colloquialism. "We're tired of letting old, white men like our pops run things." He sniffed.

"Rest in power," Simon spoke without looking up from his phone as Chad crossed the room and pointed out framed, weathered faces of the deceased white men who had established and subsequently been tasked with running Herbst Studios.

"I respect what you're saying about embracing diversity. As a matter of fact, let me play my track for you," she said, pressing play on her phone. "You'll hear influences from the Caribbean to Copenhagen.

"Please don't," Chad sighed.

"What Chad means is, we've heard it," Simon continued as Nate stopped the track. "And it's really good."

"We want to shake it up. Cater a little more to our diverse demo, which is why this is our new theme song." Chad hit play on the stereo, triggering an avalanche of bassy, hip-hop percussion.

"Yeah, boy!" The music visibly moved Simon. Exasperated, Nate tried hard to contain an eye roll as an ill-timed rapper with a counterfeit Caribbean accent began to flow: It's the dating show with the brown bag, yo, and if you don't know, you better act like you know.

"That's my boy, Sal Katz. We go back like Bar Mitzvahs," Chad joked and bopped his head to the beat. The rap was awful, but even more than that, what bugged Nate most was the fact that Chad and Simon were so used to shooting people down that they never even bothered to change up their diversity spiel. They'd literally sat across from a black woman, told her they wanted to ramp up diversity, then promptly given yet another mediocre white male a shot at success.

"Sal Katz?" Nate asked, quietly fuming.

"Heard of him?" Chad quizzed.

"Never," Nate replied as she came to terms with the fact that her track had been shot down without Simon or Chad even mentioning it by name.

"He's mad underground. They'll never see him coming," Simon squealed.

"The Herbst Brothers are embracing diversity in a major way," Chad continued. "It's our legacy." He then let his fingers tap dance across the keyboard before shutting his laptop. "Now you tell me, what's more diverse than a Hasidic rapper? It's brilliant!"

"That's right, baby. We started from the bottom now we here!" Simon exclaimed. "I have a dream and in that dream, we're marching in red bottoms straight to the top!" Chad gripped the desk like a pulpit. For Nate, his interpretation of Martin Luther King, Jr. was not only asinine it was offensive as hell.

"What up?" Sal Katz, the doo rag wearing, pants sagging, Kosher rapper swung the door wide open. "Kevin told me you had someone in here, but we boys, so whatever," he continued. Next, Sal slapped hands with Simon and Chad, as the overruled assistant watched from his desk. "My bad, shorty," he said, sizing Nate up. "My music video auditions are next week. You a little early, but you definitely got the part," he beamed, showing off his diamond-encrusted grill.

"Easy, Sal. Nate was just leaving," Chad interrupted. He then took a seat at the edge of his desk, which Nate took as her clue. Although red hot, Nate stood up and tried to play it cool.

"Thank you both for your time," she said, shaking hands with Simon and Chad before turning to exit.

"Don't forget this," Simon replied, tossing Nate the flash drive containing her discarded pitch.

"If you're free tomorrow night, I'd love to continue this conversation." Chad rolled his eyes as his younger brother softened his demeanor and feigned charm.

"Your track doesn't work for Brown Bag Cutie, but there'll be other opportunities," Simon said as he crossed the room until he was standing eye to eye with Nate. And there it was—a glimmer of hope.

"Really?" Nate queried. "Thank you!" She tried not to stare at the glaring ring around the coke nose that had only become apparent when Simon breached her personal space.

"Perfect," Simon smiled. "Kevin will email you the details," he said, resting his hand atop her shoulder.

"Thanks again," Nate beamed.

"Later, love," The rapper smiled for a final time, showing off his multi-colored grill.

"Later," Nate nodded and was quickly on the other side of the door.

Kevin used the remote control to slide the glass door shut before speaking to Nate. "So, how did your pitch go?" The assistant inquired.

"They shot my track down, never even listened to it," Nate grinned.

"Glad to see you're taking it so well," the assistant said, eyeing Nate. Although she'd been shot down, Nate was smiling as though her entire Christmas wish list had just been fulfilled.

"My track wasn't the right fit, who even knows if they listened to it, but Simon did ask me for a second meeting."

"That's what's up!" The assistant exclaimed, high-fiving Nate.

"We're linking tomorrow night. He said you'd email me the details," Nate beamed.

"Tomorrow night?" The assistant asked as he checked Simon's calendar.

"Yup. My girl Karina hooked it up. She works locations for a couple of shows."

"So, she'll be there too?" Kevin probed.

"Just me and Simon," Nate replied, as the clatter of celebratory high-fives and the apparent new show open for Brown Bag Cutie blared from Chad's office.

"It's so bad," Nate rolled her eyes as the self-proclaimed rapper and Simon began to call each other the N-Word in admiration. "They always talk like that?" Nate asked the assistant.

"You know how it is. I'm just happy to be in the building," Kevin answered plainly.

"I get that, but I'll be even happier to have a seat at the table," Nate countered.

"Listen, Chad does a good job at keeping Simon at bay. Since he won't be there tomorrow, you'll have to keep him focused," the assistant assumed a serious tone as he doled out advice. "Do that, and you should be fine."

"Should be fine?" Nate said, questioning Kevin's unsolicited advice.

"Three Cuba Libres," Chad's request for cocktails rang through the intercom, causing the assistant to leap into action. "Slight chance of flurries," he laughed.

"I gotta get back to work," Kevin said, grabbing a tray. He then placed iced cubes into three short glasses and poured the top-shelf liquor atop the frozen cubes.

"Dude," Nate pressed as the assistant breezed past her.

"You're a big girl. Just be careful." He used the remote to open the door and then slid into the office with the celebratory cocktails, a bag of imported cocaine and a bowl of local limes. How the hell was she supposed to be careful at a business meeting? Nate wanted to probe Kevin further, and she would've had he not been busy serving up dark liquor and dope.

Chapter 16

Easter Monday

Nate threw her keys onto the kitchen counter, poured fresh water into the kettle and then turned on the stove. After changing into a pair of sports shorts, she kicked her soccer ball down the hallway and into a makeshift goal. Next, she put on her headphones and let the needle drop on the vintage record player. Then, she used her finger to outline the scalded skin left behind on her thighs as the Heptones classic blend of ska and rock steady rhythms carried Nate back home.

Nate remembered when she was fourteen years old and living with her parents in Montego Bay. It was Easter, and Nate should have been helping her family prepare for their annual holiday feast. Instead, she let the Heptones serenade her and Jocelyn as they seized a private moment. The pair had been inseparable since their kiss in the sugar cane field and, unbeknownst to them, were very close to having their secret exposed.

"What's taking so long?!" Nate's mother, Cassia, quickly climbed the stairs and swung the bedroom door open, just in time to catch a flustered Nate tucking her shirt into a pair of creased khakis.

"Mom, please knock!"

"I oughta knock you!" Cassia said as she turned Jocelyn's stereo off. "You supposed to be helping with Easter dinner. Wah gwaan?" She asked, examining the girls.

"We were just on our way up the road," a flustered Nate spoke through labored breath.

"Let's go!" She managed to eke out before gliding past her mother and down the staircase.

"I can eat," Jocelyn said, grinning at an indignant Cassia, just as Nate began to blow the horn of the older model Mercedes.

"You coming?" Nate's voice vibrated through the tiny island home.

"We coming, Natalia!" Cassia yelled from the small screened-in window. She then walked over to the bed and fingered the ruffled sheets. "I would've thought you pick up a 'ting or two about cleaning from your mother," Cassia commented to Jocelyn. She then shook her head in disgust and slipped past the teen, leaving her stunned by the blatant jab. Embarrassed, Jocelyn snapped wrinkles from the tropically themed bedspread.

#

Later that afternoon, Jocelyn and Nate gently straightened the linen tablecloth and helped dress the ten-person table. "Your Uncle George and his wife, gonna sit over here, next to your parents," Alvita, Jocelyn's mother and subsequent maid of the Higgins household, continued. "But your Auntie Earlene," Alvita smiled through muffled laughter, "she gonna sit way down here." Alvita prepared a place at the far end of the table. "It's Easter Monday, and we don't need no noise between her and your mother."

"Agreed," Nate nodded.

"Now, Alvita, that's enough," Cassia said, entering the dining room. "Today, you're our guest." She smiled and took Alvita's hand in hers.

"I don't mind at all, Ma'am," Alvita replied. She kept her eyeballs glued to the matriarch as Cassia took the stack of plates from her hand and passed them to Jocelyn.

"I insist," Cassia said with a smile as Jocelyn stood motionless.

"Well, go on now, girl, take them," the housekeeper demanded of her daughter.

"Yes, Mommy," Jocelyn took the plates. She watched as Cassia escorted her mother out onto the patio, where the two women soaked up sweeping panoramic views and fell deep into conversation.

"She's telling her, I know it!" Nate grew anxious while the women peered at the girls from the terrace.

"Good," Jocelyn said, sucking her teeth. "I tired of this." The sound of an empty glass slipping from Jocelyn's hand and shattering against hardwood rang through the house. Cassia was right. For someone whose mother was a domestic, the teen really should've had a better command of kitchenware. Nate knelt to clean up the mess, simultaneously pricking her finger on the fragmented glass. At the first sight of blood trickling down Nate's arm, Jocelyn leaped to action—first applying pressure and then wrapping Nate's finger with a linen napkin.

"You okay, Natty?" An apron-clad, Barrington emerged from the kitchen with Auntie Earlene by his side.

"I've got it," Alvita said as she began to sweep shards of glass into a dustpan.

"Here, let Daddy see," Barrington consoled Nate.

"I'm fine," Nate downplayed the injury as Jocelyn continued to apply pressure.

"It's just a scratch," Jocelyn agreed as she continued to comfort her best friend. Tending lovingly to Nate's wound was bad, but when Jocelyn removed the linen napkin and kissed Nate's finger, Cassia's eyes glazed over. Nate recognized that look. Cassia was livid.

"If you have the sense God gave a donkey, you'll stop straight away," Cassia's tone was soft yet authoritative.

"Ma'am?" The teen stood to her feet as she let go of Nate's injured hand.

"I see how you tend to my daughter," Cassia said, snapping her neck in Nate's direction. "It hasn't gone unnoticed."

"We just...." Petrified, Jocelyn froze.

"Now listen, we'll eat and later the three of us can discuss this as a family," Barrington told everyone. The consummate statesman played it cool, but he was mortified at the thought of their family secret coming to light.

"I won't have them ruin Easter Monday. This foolishness ends today," Cassia remained resolute as she latched on to Nate and pulled the two friends apart.

"No!" Nate shook away from her mother's grasp.

"You must be mad!" Cassia declared, taken aback by Nate's insolence. "First you pull the fire alarm at Daddy's job, now you're doing God knows what with this," Cassia frowned.

"Jocelyn. Her name's Jocelyn," Nate said, fighting back tears.

"Cease and settle, Cassia. She's a child," Auntie Earlene interjected.

"Oh please, Earlene, she's the help," Cassia replied, disgusted.

"We're not doing this anymore." Nate took hold of Jocelyn's hand. In fourteen years of life, she had never stood up to her mother, and now there she was, being totally honest with her parents and, more importantly, herself. Nate then blew past her parents and up the staircase, causing Cassia to become so enraged that Barrington had to restrain her.

"Jocelyn, stop this foolishness," Alvita commanded.

"Damn it, Barry, let me go! I just gonna talk to her." Cassia spoke emphatically, as Alvita and Auntie Earlene ran after the girls.

"Cassia, you must cool it," Barrington instructed.

"I just want to talk to her," Cassia promised, and as Barrington loosened his grip, she took the stairs two at a time, following droplets of blood straight to Nate's room. Barrington trailed close behind.

"You're confused, Jocelyn. Stop this at once," the domestic pleaded with her daughter as Nate tossed clothing into a duffle bag.

"I'm not confused, Mommy," Jocelyn maintained. "Natty is the one thing I'm certain about," she grinned nervously at Nate.

"If you willing to gamble with your life, so be it," Auntie Earlene sucked her teeth with natural island pizazz. "Obviously, you a woman now, so you gonna do whatever the hell you want, despite how Auntie warn you."

"I meant no disrespect, Auntie," Nate winced.

"Alvita, please take your daughter and be on your way," Auntie Earlene spoke firmly to Jocelyn's mother, as Cassia stormed into Nate's bedroom, followed closely by Barrington.

"Of course you knew about this," Cassia said, invading Auntie Earlene's personal space. "This defect comes from your side of the family," she smirked.

"If you don't take three steps back," Auntie Earlene held her ground as Barrington wedged himself between the two ladies.

"Stay away from Natalia. You're a terrible influence," Cassia snapped. Clasping Jocelyn's hands in hers, Alvita began to recite a prayer for repentance. "If we confess our sins, he is faithful and just and will forgive us our sins," Alvita continued to recite the prayer as Jocelyn sobbed quietly, waiting for Nate to give her a signal.

Had Nate been a teenaged boy, getting his first taste of heteronormative love, instead of prayers for forgiveness, Nate would've simply gotten gibed for the schoolyard crush. But in Jamaica, puppy love was tricky. Barrington was a high ranking public official of a politically conservative country. Rumors he could handle, but confirmation of Nate's blossoming homosexuality would level his career.

"Cassia, we suspected Natty might be—experimenting," Barrington searched his daughter's face. "But, baby girl, you should know better than to flaunt it."

"No, Barry! I don't accept this mess, and neither should you." Cassia said, shaking loose of his grip. Jocelyn eyed Nate as Cassia calmly approached. If they were going to run, they'd have to do it now.

"Clearly, you've made some bad choices, Natalia," Cassia softened, "we can get through this."
But Nate didn't want to get through anything, so with that, she took off running, Jocelyn in tow.

"Natalia!" Cassia screamed after Nate, but Auntie Earlene blocked her from chasing the teens.

"Why don't you just stone Natty to death as those barbarians did them boys in Kingston." Although Auntie Earlene had warned the two girls, she had always been the first person to leap to Nate's defense. "Maybe hire a battery to grine upon she," Earlene thrust her hips suggestively. "Show her what she'll be giving up."

"If it will knock some sense into her, then so be it!" Cassia pushed past Auntie Earlene like a Category 5 hurricane, dividing her family as Moses did the Red Sea. Within seconds, Cassia stood face to face with Nate, duffle bag in one hand and Jocelyn in the other.

"Lord Jesus, I ask that you show these young souls the light," Alvita said, dropping to her knees in prayer.

"You choose to disrespect your father and me in our own home?" Cassia questioned Nate. "Have you even stopped to think how hard life will be?"

"I'm not trying to make things hard for anyone, mommy—but this is my life." Their grips melded together as the young lovers clutched sweaty palms, hand in hand. "Our life," Nate corrected herself.

"Lord, deliver them from their evil ways so that they live naturally, as you intended." Immersed in invocation, Alvita rocked back and forth with the same soothing ease as the waves breaking on the shores below. A look of calculated contemplation gradually consumed Nate's face as Alvita continued to implore the Lord above, "Father God, I pray you to resurrect them in your image so that these two sinners may be reborn."

"Mom, please!" Jocelyn was beginning to crack. "I love her."

"I swear, child," Cassia warned, "if you leave..." She positioned her hands on her shapely hips.

"Then I never come back!" Nate wailed.

"Enough," Barrington interjected. "You understand our daughter is in love, right? Or don't you remember what that's like?"

Although Barrington and Cassia's marriage had morphed into one of convenience, it hadn't always been. Their attraction was instant and while they hailed from opposing ends of the socio-economic spectrum, they were motivated by many of the same things. As similar as the young couple was, early in their marriage, they realized that for many reasons, a traditional relationship would never work. Instead of dissolving it, they reveled in the perks associated with their public personas and had agreed that as long as their transgressions stayed out of the public eye, they would see other people. However, as much as the couple tried to hide it, people were starting to talk.

Cassia snapped. "She lucky I don't send her to one of them camps."

"I gay, okay." Nate's confession gave herself pause as she had never uttered that phrase aloud. The only thing more audible than Nate's admittance was the sound of Cassia's bare hand landing squarely against her sun-kissed cheek. The open-hand was enough to blind Nate with fear. She stood temporarily dazed as her mother released an arsenal of four-letter words that stung much more than the physical assault. Auntie Earlene acted as a human barrier between the two, while Barrington desperately tried to calm Cassia and Alvita clung to her daughter. In shock, Nate remained oblivious. All around her, chaos erupted, but to her, the room was quiet, and intercut with memories from her past.

Age four: Cassia forces Nate to wear a dress. Age six: Cassia stumbles across Nate making her two baby dolls kiss. Age eight: Cassia catches Nate playing doctor with a neighborhood girl and doles out the whooping of a lifetime.

"You're an embarrassment!" The force of Cassia shoving her into a wall brought Nate back to the moment at hand.

"I said that's enough!" Barrington lost it, pulling Cassia with such vigor that she fell hard on the floor, allowing Nate and Jocelyn to flee. Barrington's howls rang through the two-story home as the front door slammed shut behind the two girls. He'd been married to Cassia for nearly two decades and she'd spent that time molding him into the political powerhouse that he'd grown to become. Together they'd amassed clout, capital and most of all, influence. Once Nate was born, Cassia poured into her, but Nate was stubborn even as a baby. Easter was just another example of Nate's willfulness and Cassia attributed that to her side of the family. She was tough on Nate, but perhaps Cassia would have been more willing to bend if she realized this would be Nate's last Easter on the island.

The sound of Nate's teakettle screaming in concert with the clamoring of her intercom doorbell snatched her from the memory of that Easter back to the present day. Nate had nodded off while listening to old records, but memories of some of her last days in Montego Bay left her in desperate need of a distraction. Nate used her shorts as a towel for her clammy hands, turned the teakettle off and answered the intercom.

"Who's there?" she asked.

Chapter 17

Consider it Charity

"Trick or Treat!" Karina kissed Nate on the cheek as she glided into her apartment, carrying a garment bag and tightly rolled clove cigarette.

"Hey, Kar," said Nate as she shut the door. "You're a little early for Halloween."

"Before you say anything, I know how you feel about uninvited guests, but I was in the neighborhood," Karina said, dropping the garment bag onto the couch as she turned to face Nate.

"You could've called," Nate agreed.

"My phone died. "Plus, I think your doorman's sick. He ran by me, clutching his stomach, so I just let myself up," Karina shrugged. The only reason he'd come down with a bug was because Karina had spiked his iced coffee with ex-lax.

"I should go down there. Make sure he's okay," Nate replied, none the wiser.

"Don't," Karina said, redirecting the conversation. "This is not a drill," she laughed. "The Alexander is high end, and I'm so serious about this. You cannot show up to meet Simon in—what are those— soccer shorts?" She inhaled hard on the hand-rolled clove and exhaled thick white smoke over her shoulder.

"First of all, the meeting is tomorrow night and second, you know better than that," Nate told Karina, handing her an ashtray.

"They smell a lot better than that Nag Champa crap," Karina laughed, "but hey, to each is own." She then took another long puff, extinguished the clove and placed it back into its box. "Valentino." Karina unzipped the bag and pulled out option number one. "Flared wool skirt and stretch herringbone bodice. Cute, comfy, sexy."

"I'm supposed to wear that?" Nate asked, flopping onto the sofa in stitches. "This is gonna be good. What else you got?"

"I've gained a couple of pounds," Karina stated the obvious. In the last several months, she had put on weight, but Nate had no clue that the extra pounds were due to the emotional eating Karina had used to comfort herself since Simon's assault. "It's been a minute since I've worn any of this, but I've got a plan to get back down to my fighting weight," she said, passing the dress to Nate. "So you, my friend, can consider this a loan."

"Too short," Nate countered, running her fingers across the decade old scars on her thighs. "I hate my legs. Next!" She exclaimed, suppressing memories of the fiery car wreck that had claimed her unborn brother's life and disfigured her in the process.

"Gucci." Karina pulled out a casual jersey style dress. "Soft cotton blend, money green, signature webbed striping down each sleeve and even a hoodie, cause, well you're—you." Karina laughed.

"Now that, I may be able to rock with," Nate nodded her head, fingering the soft fabric.

"Picture this with a knee-high black boot. You'd crush it!" Karina exclaimed.

"I'm good," Nate said, shooing the dress away as Karina revealed the third and final selection.

"Carolina Herrera," Karina beamed.

"Kar," Nate responded with an eye roll as the flowy, feminine dress was not at all her style.

"Before you say anything, I know you may think the floral pattern is a bit much, but with a black leather jacket and some riding boots," Karina continued to pitch as Nate doubled over in laughter. This was the final inning, and Karina was striking out fast. "Fit and flare silhouette, knee-length hem, conservative neckline."

"I needed that laugh, Kar. Thank you," Nate grinned. She then grabbed Karina's hand and pulled her down onto the couch beside her.

"Well, if you won't wear my oldies, but goodies—at least do something with that mop," Karina laughed as she reached for Nate's bleach-blond dreads.

"One more time and that's your ass," Nate said, swiftly swatting Karina's hand away.

"I'm just saying girl, them edges could use some TLC," Karina laughed, resting her head onto Nate's shoulder.

"In that case, let me borrow a bundle or two," Nate said, gesturing to Karina's hair extensions. "Lord knows you've got hair to spare."

"Touché, bitch," Karina snickered.

"Now you and I both know I'm not wearing any of this stuff, so what are you really doing here?" Nate inquired.

"Consider it charity—it's the holidays, isn't it?" Karina said with a smirk.

"It's Halloween," Nate replied decisively.

"So you too good for my hand me downs?" Karina asked.

"Basically," Nate said with a shrug.

"Whatever, slim, you can't fit the stuff anyway." Karina playfully nudged Nate. "Real women have curves," she replied with a seductive shimmy.

"You right about that," Nate said eyeing Karina. It was a shame—despite the confident glow Karina tried to portray, Nate knew better.

"So, what else is up?" Karina inquired. "You got your ticket back home?"

"Sure did," Nate sighed. "Thursday night red-eye."

"Halloween, how creepy." Karina cackled as she leaned into Nate's shoulder.

"Seeing as though I'll be resurrecting the ghosts of my twisted past—it seems appropriate," Nate grimaced.

"I told you I'd go with," sighed Karina, grabbing Nate's hand. "Seriously, I could move some things around." Nate imagined Karina tossing her brunette tresses around as if she was starring in a shampoo commercial on the white sand beaches of Montego Bay. Then she imagined Karina saying something inappropriate to the wrong person. Nate shuddered at the thought.

"Maybe next time," Nate let go of Karina's hand when she noticed that her blouse had slipped up her forearm to reveal a nasty cut. "What happened here?" Nate asked and tried to get a closer look, but Karina flinched away.

"An accident," Karina lied. "You know I'm clumsy."

"O.k." Nate paused for a beat. She knew Karina well enough to know that she wasn't being sincere. "I still can't believe I was dumb enough to invite Tru to Jamaica," Nate changed the subject, electing not to push.

"What did she say?" Karina asked, pretending this information was new to her. When in reality, Tru had given Karina the scoop at the property viewing that very morning. Nate had no idea that she was helping Tru find the perfect property for the lounge she'd always dreamed of opening.

"As usual, work comes first," Nate moaned. "I should've kept it casual. I just figured we were on a path to something more."

"Honestly, Nate," Karina sighed. "Why do you insist on dating the unattainable? This is just like the married woman before Tru."

"We're working through some things," Nate evaded, unwilling to admit that Karina had a point. "She'll come around."

"You hope," Karina smirked, gently running her fingers through Nate's dreads. "Is she working today?"

"No idea. Tru hasn't answered my calls or texts since last night," Nate sounded angry.

"You've been iced."

"She's pissed. I called her a sketel," Nate said, throwing her head back onto the couch. "A what?" Karina asked.

"A slut," Nate translated.

"Well, isn't she?" Karina quipped.

"Not funny," Nate moaned. "I was mad, still am actually."

"You should be," Karina had a natural ability to stir the pot. "She's ignoring you like some little girl."

"Right!" Nate agreed.

"I say cut her loose—then get yourself checked out," Karina spoke plainly. She thoroughly enjoyed fanning the flames of contention. "I'm telling you, she's either fucking or suck..."

"Kar, chill! Tru is not about that life," Nate cut Karina off. Although she wasn't entirely sure where they stood, Nate still had Tru's back. So, she lied. Sure, Tru periodically strapped up to please her wealthy boy toys, but Karina didn't need to know that.

"You know I'm right," Karina retorted. She could tell that Nate's mind was racing with images of Tru and how she really earned her money. The two sat in silence for a moment until Karina felt that Nate had stewed long enough. "Well, as they say, the best way to get over somebody is to get under somebody. Any prospects?" Karina tried to lighten the mood.

"Definitely not," Nate replied.

"I may hook up with a friend tonight," Karina declared.

"Which one now?" Nate smirked.

"It's nothing serious," Karina cooed.

"Is it ever?" Nate quizzed, sarcastically.

Karina stood up and walked over to the huge sliding glass door, which overlooked Echo Park Lake and led to Nate's patio. "Not everyone needs a partner to define them." Although the words had come from Karina's mouth, she couldn't be sure if she believed it herself. Karina had a habit of hooking up, but unlike Nate and Tru, her casual encounters had a typical life span of a week or so at most.

"I met this fine, coffee-colored specimen a couple of weeks back," Karina explained. "I had on this banging black dress. Long slit. Plunging neckline," she laughed.

"Leading with your boobs per normal," Nate grinned, knowing her friend all too well.

"He was my Uber driver," revealed Karina.

"Kar, no!" Nate spazzed.

"I was wasted and needed a ride," Karina divulged.

"Apparently," Nate laughed. "And Tru's the whore?"

"May I finish?" Karina inquired.

"Don't stop now," Nate sighed.

"I had him pull over at one of those cheap motels," Karina began to paint the picture.

"If your goal is to be the subject of the next Lifetime thriller, you are well on your way," Nate said, shaking her head.

"I'm an excellent judge of character. He was sane and very sexy," Karina bit her lip, summoning the steamy encounter to her frontal lobe. "It's all pretty fuzzy."

"That's because he drugged you!" Nate concluded.

"We did do some blow, but it was mine," Karina smirked. "I'm telling you, Nate, he went down on me like I was his last supper and when we kissed," Karina sighed, "he devoured me like the sweetest Baklava." Nate sat on the edge of the couch, enthralled. Karina loved teasing her.

Karina recounted the hot and honeyed kisses shared between her and the mystery man; "You love tasting yourself, don't you?"

"He asked you that?" Aroused, Nate unwittingly pressed her thighs together.

"Yup," Karina said, nodding her head emphatically. "And when he finally put it in, good Lord, let's just say this twinkling skyline you have here has nothing on the number of stars I saw that night."

"Sounds hot, but it's not safe, Kar," Nate decided.

"We used a condom," Karina whined.

"You know what I mean," Nate pushed.

"You telling me you never get curious about what it would be like to have a little sausage in your life."

"You've officially outstayed your welcome," Nate was only half-joking.

"I'm serious. Do something new. There must be someone. A neighbor, coworker, anybody to help you get over ol' girl?"

"Who said I was ready to get over Tru?" Nate asked.

"I did," Karina teased. "Hello! Haven't you been listening?"

"Actually, that intern was completely throwing it at me today."

"Not Junior Mint?" Karina laughed. "Alice, right?"

"Abby," Nate corrected. "I knew she had a crush or whatever," Nate confessed, "but she's been coming on hella strong for the past few weeks. Now she wants to come by and check out the home studio," Nate laughed.

"Do it!" Karina encouraged.

"I shot her down. Told her I would bring my keyboard to work," Nate smiled. "She's cute, but I can't."

"So you're just gonna punk out," Karina teased, standing before Nate could respond. "I'm gonna use your bathroom." She headed toward the back of Nate's apartment but continued their conversation.

"What does she look like?"

"She's bad. German, I think," Nate smiled as she conjured up an image of her young colleague.

"Barely twenty-two, short blond hair, baby blue eyes with an ass like a black girl." Nate giggled.

"Jackpot!" Karina squealed as she re-emerged from the restroom. "Just the distraction you need."

"I don't need a distraction," Nate refuted.

"You do," Karina insisted. "I'm heading out, but call me tomorrow after your meeting with Simon. "When you pull yourself together, you're gorgeous. Remember that," Karina said, effortlessly delivering the backhanded compliment. "You deserve everything coming to you."

"Thanks," Nate eyed her friend curiously. "But, honestly, my looks should have nothing to do with Simon helping me get established in the music industry."

"Oh, honey, you're cute. Looks have everything to do with—well—everything," Karina shrugged matter-of-factly. "And leave Tru alone. She's toxic." Karina kissed Nate on the cheek and zipped out the door just as fast as she had entered the apartment. Moments later, Nate cracked open a coldie, but just as the frosty pale ale hit her lips, she noticed that Karina had forgotten her garment bag. Nate laughed at the thought of herself in the femme attire, slipped into her flops and sprinted for the door, garment bag in hand. When she opened the door, her heart skipped a beat because standing on the other side was the last person she expected to see.

"What are you doing here?"

Chapter 18

Gold Star

"Junior Mint?" Nate smiled curiously then popped her head outside of the door frame. With Karina nowhere in sight, Nate resolved that returning the designer clothing could wait.

"Have I mentioned how adorable I think your nickname for me is?" Abby, the intern, blushed. She then placed a bag of delectable smelling food onto the granite kitchen countertop.

"I didn't give you that nickname. Lanie from wardrobe did—we all just went with it," Nate laughed as she shut the door behind Abby. Well, that and you've got a sweet little frame, Nate thought silently, electing to keep that part of the Junior Mint moniker a mystery. "What are you doing here?" She asked, hanging Karina's garment bag on a nearby hook. "Better yet, how'd you get past the doorman?" Nate stared at the intern more confused at the situation than pissed at the blatant disregard for her privacy.

"What doorman?" The intern asked, pulling Mediterranean food out of a plastic bag.

"Forget it," Nate said, recalling that Karina mentioned that her doorman had run past her nauseous and clutching his stomach. "My address—how did you get it?"

"I might've bribed the Production Assistant," Abby smiled devilishly. "But, look—I come bearing gifts. Hope you're okay with Mediterranean." The overzealous intern opened the bag and pulled out roasted pepper hummus, a Caprese salad and a grilled white fish.

"Is that from Orzo's?" Nate's mouth watered as she inhaled the familiar scents of her favorite local Greek joint.

"It is," Abby declared. "See! A few minutes ago, you were about to kick your doorman's butt for letting me up."

"And I still might," Nate retorted, eyeing the woman skeptically. "I thought you said he wasn't
there.

"He wasn't," Abby stuck to her story. "I think you're talented and I wanted to see your studio," she said, peering at Nate with ocean blue eyes.

"So, you came over for a jam session?" Nate quizzed.

"If that's what you want to call it," Abby laughed. The younger woman placed her hand, tenderly on Nate's shoulder. Just as she had been earlier in the day, the typically demure colleague was way more confident than she had been in previous months. Rocking a flannel button-down, tattered denim shorts and Uggs her valley girl flow was effortless.

"Does your boyfriend know you're here?" Nate probed. "How about your parents?"

"Oh, so now you got jokes?" The intern laughed. "What about your boyfriend?" Abby countered.

"I've never even kissed a dude," Nate affirmed, proudly as she had long since kicked the hinges off the closet door.

"A gold star," Abby smirked. "How cute," she continued, inching closer to Nate.

"I'm serious, Abby," Nate feigned contempt. "You shouldn't be here."

"No rule says coworkers can't kick it," Abby stood her ground.

Nate conceded as the blend of Mediterranean spices coupled with the realization that she would soon be seeing a lot less of the intern began to calm her. After noting how Abby had ramped up her flirting in recent weeks and then showed up uninvited on her doorstep, Nate had a pretty good idea of what the young woman's end game was. What the hell, Nate shrugged. She then pulled two place settings from the oak cabinet and with that, decided to roll the dice. The women spent the next hour eating, laughing and debating career paths.

"I'm just saying, I've heard your podcast, downloaded your mixes—you're too good for what they have you doing at the studio."

"So, I should quit my day job, blow off the meeting with Simon and work my podcast full time?" Nate eyed her colleague curiously.

"I'm not saying all that," Abby backtracked, "but this is Los Angeles, the place where dreams…"

"Come to die," Nate interrupted and watched as Abby laughed out loud. It's just too bad Nate was only partially joking. "I'm out here on a wing and a prayer," she sighed.

"And talent, don't forget talent," the intern said, sipping Chardonnay from a stemless glass.

"I appreciate that, but you and I both know that if it takes more than talent to get signed," Nate scoffed. "Three-quarters of the battle is about getting in good with the gatekeepers."

"I think Simon's creepy but hey, do what you got to do to get where you need to be, right?" Abby proclaimed, popping an olive into her mouth.

"Crude, yes," Nate agreed, "but creepy?" The surprise houseguest took a long beat, clearly deliberating on how much she wanted to divulge.

"Let me preface this by saying my roommate is a self-proclaimed attention whore."

"Okay," Nate laughed nervously as Abby began to tell her story.

"Simon and Sasha exchanged numbers at last year's holiday party." Visibly, swept away in memories of a night brimming in hijinks and Hennessy, the intern flashed a full set of pearly whites. "Everyone was loaded—except for Simon," she cringed. "He was surprisingly sober. Calculated, even," Abby continued and as she burrowed deeper into that recollection, her tone grew hushed.

"Simon? Sober?" Nate grew skeptical, recalling how just that afternoon, Simon had stood in her face rocking ring-around-the-coke-nose.

"Yup," Abby nodded affirmatively. "He went out with Sasha a few nights later." She shook her head, perplexed by her own account. "Sasha came home crying her eyes out. Stayed in bed for a week."

"What happened?" Nate leaned in suddenly concerned with her safety as she was scheduled to meet with Simon the following evening.

"Still don't know," Abby shrugged.

Nate began to wring her hands as her overactive mind conjured up at least a half dozen scenarios about Simon and the intern's so-called attention-craving roommate. The problem was without any concrete proof; all Nate could do was speculate. Nate eyed Abby suspiciously. Had puppy love brought her to Nate's doorstep or was there more to it?

"Well?" Abby asked, repeating herself.

"Well, what?" Nate was so focused on trying to pin down Abby's motives that she had completely tuned her out.

"You said three-quarters of success in the music industry boils down to gatekeepers," Abby continued, "so what's the last quarter?"

"Autotune," Nate laughed. After sharing a couple more laughs and opening a fresh bottle of Chardonnay, Abby trailed Nate toward her home studio. "This little thing is a beast," said Nate. "I take it everywhere." She sat behind the workstation and began to press buttons as she talked about the unit's features. "It can handle two stereo audio channels and has an audio input on the keyboard that can be routed through effects." Nate was in her zone. She loved to geek out on tech.

"Okay, nerd, slide over," Abby joked, "let me see what she can do." She let the wine moisten her vocal cords and then began to manipulate the keys on the professional workstation. Nate watched as the woman who had professed to be a novice started to stroke the keyboard with the definitiveness of a seasoned artist. Her fingers long and bowed skipped effortlessly across the instrument as she began with an homage to the incomparable Stevie Wonder: For so long, for this night I've prayed.

Nate sat back as the woman she never saw coming continued to tinker. Abby turned knobs and fiddled with the audio levels adding drum beats and guitar riffs until the classic "Ribbon in the Sky" was remixed beyond recognition.

"So you just wanted to come over here and show off?" Nate laughed, impressed. Her transitions were rushed and her pitch was a hair off, but what the junior mint lacked in vocals she made up for in keyboard abilities.

"A compliment from Natty One. Thanks, I'll take it!" Abby blushed. "Got me over here fangirling," the intern squealed. "I'm stoked for this week's show—you have to do something creepy for Halloween!"

Suddenly everything clicked. Abby was a groupie. Nate had to admit, the boost to her ego paired with the buzz from white wine was right on time. She turned the record player on and carefully counted the grooves of the vinyl until the needle was positioned directly over one of her favorite rock steady tracks. The sublime vocal stylings went to work like a snake charmer, causing Abby to stand and sway on cue: We're having a party tonight. Where everything will be all right. We've got to live some life before we're old.

Nate took the carefree lyrics as a direct order, gripping the junior mint's hips lustfully from behind. Together the two women rode the rhythm like a wave crashing ashore to first mount and finally melt into the sand. For the next couple of songs, they allowed their bodies to bend and stretch until Nate's hands drifted gradually up and under her dance partner's perfectly tattered jean shorts, landing squarely on her plump rump.

Abby spun around with desire in her eyes and pushed Nate backward onto the worn futon. As the fangirl slowly lowered to straddle position, Nate paced herself. This moment was too right to rush. While Nate sipped white wine, her now welcomed houseguest unbuttoned her shirt revealing perky pink nipples nestled strategically into the sexiest lace bra.

"By the way, you're not the only gold star in the room," Abby revealed.

"Word?" Nate eyed Abby, as she steadily began to work her tits with one hand and clench her ample bottom with the other.

"True story," Abby laughed, unclasping her bra. Like a lamb to the slaughterhouse, Nate devoured the tantalizing gourds without so much as a second thought. Flipping the purported newbie onto her back, Nate unbuttoned her denim shorts and yanked them down all in one coarse motion.

"Du machst mich so geil!" Abby cried out.

"What was that?" Nate asked between mouthfuls of the tender breast meat.

The now welcomed houseguest giggled through bated breath, "I said you turn me on." The fangirl was literally begging to be plowed in German! Nate's head was swimming.

"You sure?" Nate asked, hovering as the intern let one leg dangle from the futon. Abby remained quiet. Content to let her actions do the talking, she licked two of Nate's fingers, then slid her panties to the side. Nate took the bait, then proceeded to beat the kitty up like a prize-fighter with seven figures on the line, as Abby bore down hard in delight.

"I'm-so-close!" Abby stuttered in staccato as a wave of pleasure overcame her. Still breathless, Abby sat up starry-eyed. "So much for my gold star," she joked. Then, she removed Nate's shirt and shorts, leaving Nate in a sports bra and bikini briefs that exposed her badly scarred thighs.

"War wounds," Nate was self-conscious about the disfigurement she'd obtained in the car accident all those years ago, but Abby remained gentle. She traversed the entirety of Nate's muscular quads, starting first with her fingers and then with the tiniest of kisses.

"I'm so glad you and your girl split." She said, tasting herself on Nate's cream laced digits.

"My what?" Nate recoiled.

"Tru." Abby continued to envelop Nate's body, but by all accounts, the party was officially over.

"I never mentioned a girlfriend," Nate declared, hopping up. "You should go!"

"You're kidding," Abby rolled her eyes in disbelief.

"Not even a little bit," Nate huffed. Next, she marched to the front door without looking back as the junior mint gathered her belongings and slipped quietly into the restroom to change. Moments later, she disappeared through Nate's front door just as quickly as she'd appeared. This was not how Nate had planned on spending her Tuesday night. Sexually frustrated, Nate fired off a series of four-letter words as she sulked toward the bathroom.

Chapter 19

The Roof is on Fire

A hidden camera aimed at an unknown woman's red-polished toenails slowly tilted up, working its way past her feet and beyond her shins. Her legs ajar and stance wide, the camera was capturing her in the most intimate of acts. Gripping the showerhead with the intensity of a batter with bases loaded, the unseen camera operator zoomed in as the woman deliberately bucked her hips in concert with the pulsating water feature.

Next, the invisible technician switched to a profile angle, capturing the woman mid- thrust. She gradually picked up the pace and raised her leg as the muscles in her apple bottom flexed with each erotic thrust. Back on the initial shot, the woman's hands fumbled with the multi-function nozzle until the pressure began to rain down with a torrential force. The camera again tilted up, past her belly, its gaze settling on a set of Hershey kiss shaped tits.

On the camera's final incline, the operator slid past the woman's collarbone to a full set of lips, parted in ostensible ecstasy. Upon zooming out, the quite capable lens expanded, rendering the woman's identity a mystery no more. Nate's privacy had been invaded! Standing there in the buff, exposed for Lord knows who to see, she let the showerhead slip from her grip. Her mission accomplished, Nate sighed as the camera cut to another profile shot. The voyeur's final frame, Nate, slumped over and fatigued, her body supported by the brawn of the bathroom's Artea tiled wall. Across town, the anonymous ogler used an app, editing the video down to the build-up right before Nate's climax and the few seconds following it. Next, the redux video, along with the cryptic seasonal message: "trick or treat?" was texted to an unidentified recipient.

#

"She kicked me out," Abby, the intern, sat texting in her car outside of Nate's apartment.

"What happened?" The mysterious person on the other line replied, only there was no name, simply a seven-digit number, preceded by an L.A. area code.

"We were really connecting," Abby continued to text.

"What happened?" The person on the receiving end repeated.

"Favorite meal, pum pum shorts, white wine," Abby averted.

"If I have to ask one more time," the mystery person's tone intensified.

"I mentioned Tru, and she lost it," Abby confessed.

"Idiot," the unidentified texter snapped.

"It slipped," the jilted junior mint responded repentantly. Then, she waited as text bubbles appeared, alerting her that the person on the other end was responding and then—nothing. Radio silence. "Lavash!" Abby typed furiously. The faceless texter remained still as the exasperated intern sighed, garnering a final glimpse of Nate's silhouette move past a window toward the far end of her apartment.

"I did everything you said," Abby winced.

"Not everything," Lavash, the now identified texter, concluded, "wait for my call."

#

Across town, Karina sat on the ledge of her twelve-story apartment rooftop, lingering dangerously close to the edge. Gathered high above in the night sky, a cluster of constellations sparkled and seemed to congregate, not merely for Karina's viewing pleasures but also to help her connect the dots. Threatening Simon had worked and he and Nate were all set to meet tomorrow night. She engaged the blade of her box cutter and began to draw an imaginary line from Jupiter to a nearby star cluster.

Nate would likely not wear the clothes that Karina had left behind, but either way, she imagined that Simon would get handsy with an unwilling Nate. The calculating stargazer had all but sworn to Simon that Nate would be receptive.

Wielding the box cutter like a maestro in an orchestra pit, Karina smirked proudly, drawing a long, deliberate line south to the next brightest constellation. She couldn't be sure if Nate would be able to escape Simon unharmed, but she assumed Nate would never let an assault slide. Doing so would put too many people at risk, and Nate didn't have the stomach for that type of guilt.

The box cutter slid southwest through the cosmos as Karina drew one final line, landing on the waning crescent moon. Her plot was rock solid. Once Nate reported Simon, his star would promptly fade as his entire world crumbled around him. The media frenzy would rain down like a meteor shower and Karina would be able to reclaim a small piece of her dignity. She recalled the day that she took his fully erect member into her mouth. Simon hadn't forced Karina to do it, but he insisted oral sex was the only way he'd purchase the multimillion-dollar home from her. What a sleaze.

Karina sat up, pleased with herself and convinced that taking Simon down provided a public service. The predator had to be exposed—moreover, Karina demanded vengeance. She wiped tears from her eyes as the glow from a nearby trash can fire began to illuminate her face. Next, she used the box cutter to slice open a cigar, showering its rank contents over the apartment ledge and onto the unsuspecting people a dozen stories below. Then she began to shake a combination of finely ground cloves and liquor laced tobacco into the empty wrapper as she employed her smartphone.

"Call mom." The smartphone repeated the command and after several rings a somnolent Mrs. Zakaryan's voice crept through the receiver.

"It's after midnight, Karina," Mrs. Zakaryan groaned. "Don't tell me you're already calling out of work?"

"I just called to talk," Karina said as she started the tight hand roll. "I'm not feeling great." Karina wanted to collapse into her mother's arms. To tell her that she'd been violated by Simon five months ago and hadn't been the same since, but her relationship with her parents was strained. This wouldn't be easy.

"If that girl misses work one more time!" Her irritated father bellowed in the background.

"I'll be at work! Tell hayrik to calm down," Karina sighed, using the Armenian word for father. The glow on Karina's face intensified as the conversation became more heated.

"It's too late for this nonsense! Hang up the phone, sirakan," yelled Karina's father, using the Armenian pet name for sweetheart.

"We'll talk tomorrow, Karina," Mrs. Zakaryan, sighed, hanging up the phone.

"Didn't you hear me, Mayrik? I said I don't feel well," Karina swallowed hard, "he hurt me," she confessed, then awaited a response. "Hello!" No answer. Her parents had disregarded her literal call for help.

Livid, Karina used the box cutter to slice two deep gashes into her forearm. "AHH!" She yelped gutturally. Next, Karina lit up the hand-rolled clove and exhaled flavorful smoke toward the celestial plan that she'd plotted. Knowing Simon's time at the top was limited began to soothe her, along with the adrenaline rush she got from the cold blade of steel tearing into her supple, warm flesh.

Karina took another puff, allowing the smooth, flavorsome haze to encompass her lungs. Then she scrolled through her list of contacts until she reached the person she'd labeled, Uber. Next, Karina began to text, leaving traces of spilled blood on her smartphone. "You up?" The mysterious light continued to roar in Karina's direction. Her eyes began to twinkle as thought bubbles popped onto the cell phone screen, indicating a reply, and then the Uber driver stopped mid-text. Karina was fuming. She hopped up onto the ledge and began to pace, exhaling thick plumes of smoke along the way, until a security guard leaped from the shadows startling Karina in the process.

"Ms. Zakaryan, you can't be up there." Startled, Karina tripped over her own two feet, but the security guard reacted quickly enough to pull her in. However, in reeling Karina in, the night watchman also hauled in a handful of blood.

"Are you ok?" The guard's glance oscillated between his blood-stained palms and Karina's tear-stained face.

"I'm good. Just an accident." She used her hand to cover the wound and then pushed past the man. In her rush to disappear into the shadows, Karina dashed past the small blaze that roared in the trash can.

"Ms. Zakaryan," the night watchman's final call for Karina unreturned, he used his metal baton to fish out the source of the fire. To his surprise, a badly burned and barely recognizable piece of lingerie clung to his nightstick. And just like that, the mystery of Tru's missing negligee was solved. Stolen from her trunk earlier in the day, the nightie was now being used as kindling for Karina's forbidden rooftop bonfire.

Chapter 20

Jamaican Jedi

Nate smiled wide in her sleep as childhood memories moved beyond her impromptu coming out and slipped toward the romantic beach rendezvous that awaited her post bedlam. Easter Monday. 2007. Having barely escaped Cassia's wrath, fourteen-year-old Nate and Jocelyn, her childhood crush, took delight in a bonfire. After they fled Nate's parent's house, the teens hitchhiked to the solitude of Montego Bay's Sunset Beach. Although Nate had packed enough clothes to last a week, she was hardly gone twenty-four hours. In that short amount of time, Nate and Jocelyn discovered a closeness with each other that they would never again duplicate. And as the teens bid farewell to their virginity, the lines of their friendship were forever blurred. That was the first time Nate had experienced an orgasm with anyone other than herself! It was hot and sticky like a guava tart. And as she lay there, sand against her back, Jocelyn literally wrapped around her fingers, Nate—was—free.

A roaring beach bonfire, dozens of twinkling stars overhead—in twenty-eight years of life that Easter Monday was unquestionably Nate's best night of sleep. The evening had started terribly but concluded coconut rum sweet. Nate hated to see it end. In her dreams, Nate remembered it like yesterday. The warmth of the morning sun rising from the Caribbean Sea. The crick in her neck from sleeping on the sand all night, and the sweet sound of Jocelyn whispering in her ear.

"Rise and shine, Natty," Jocelyn snuggled up to Nate as the beach slowly came to life.

"No, you can't make me," Nate laughed. "I ran away." Her eyes were still closed and focused very much on the mosaic of mental pics she'd stitched together from last night's seaside encounter.

"Ran away?" Jocelyn laughed. "We're ten miles from home and have no money." She rolled on top of Nate. "Time to face the music, Natty One."

"Five more minutes," Nate pleaded, but Jocelyn was relentless.

"Wake up! Wake up! Wake up!" Jocelyn laughed and attacked Nate with tickles.

# #

Back in her Echo Lake apartment, Nate leaped up from her bed and was snatched back to the present moment. Stirred awake by her childhood memory, Nate quickly began to pound digits into her phone.

"Good Morning, my love." Despite it being a quarter to six local time, Auntie Earlene sounded surprisingly alert.

"Sorry to call so early. I just wanted to let you know that I got my tickets. I reach first thing Friday morning," Nate advised.

"That's all well and good, but go on and tell Auntie what vex you, because me hear it all in your voice." The woman knew Nate better than anyone else. Nate exhaled gratitude and began to recount the tale of Abby, the uninvited guest.

"My Lord," Auntie Earlene laughed. "The child showed up at your door in pum pum shorts, carrying your favorite meal." Auntie Earlene's labored laugh quickly turned into a raspy cough.

"It's not funny, Auntie. 'Dis woman could be crazy!" Nate's accent suddenly grew thick and tropically delicious, a direct correlation to speaking with Auntie Earlene.

"If yuh sleep wid dawg, yuh ketch im flea," Auntie Earlene warned.

"Yes, Auntie." Nate had heard her Auntie Earlene use that exact expression hundreds of times before.

"Remember Natty, any dutti waata kool hat iron." Loosely translated—even dirty water will cool a hot iron, this common Jamaican phrase was a metaphor for relationships, in that not everyone who says they're your friend really is.

"I never called her a friend, Auntie."

"Once you understand that," Auntie Earlene's voice had grown noticeably weary.

"Yes, Auntie."

"Rest now, my love," Auntie Earlene paused. "You're safe. You're breathing. You got this," she said reciting the mantra that she had instilled in Nate all those years ago.

Exhausted, Auntie Earlene disconnected the call, as Nate grew mesmerized by Karina's monogrammed garment bag hanging beside the front door. Her mind cloudy and gripped by the words of wisdom imparted by the Jamaican Jedi, Nate's head began to spin. Any dutti waata kool hat iron. Then despite her better judgment, Nate grabbed her car keys and was quickly on the other side of the door.

Part Three

Stranger Danger

Chapter 21

No Strings

Nate awoke startled by tapping on her window and reached immediately into her driver's side door pocket for the pink knuckled stun gun that she kept there. It was early, barely Six AM in West Hollywood, and the streets had slowly begun to purr. Thick morning fog hovered high above the city as the Laundromat shopkeeper cupped his hands against either side of his face and peered into her hybrid vehicle.

"You can't park here," yelled the shopkeeper as he used his worn broom to tap on Nate's driver side window. Realizing that she was not being carjacked, Nate loosened her grip on the stun gun and let it slip back into the car's side pocket. Not long before the shopkeeper woke her up, Nate had fallen asleep in her car while waiting for Tru to emerge from Club Trois. Unsure if Tru was even in the club, Nate had decided to park across the street and wait. However, she drifted off to sleep before being awoken by the Laundromat shopkeeper. After a year of hooking up, Nate didn't even know where Tru lived, and now here she was practically stalking the woman outside of the covert swinger's club.

"Du machst mich so geil!" Nate remembered how earlier in the evening Abby had pleaded to be plowed in German. Although leery at first, Nate eventually warmed to the idea and happily bedded the infatuated intern. Hours later, she reeled with regret and sat casing Tru's place of employment from a distance. Nate felt desperate. She hated it.

"If you're not gone in five minutes, I'll call the cops," the shopkeeper yelled again as he used his worn broom to tap on the driver side window. Exasperated, Nate wiped the sleep from her eyes and rolled down the window.

"I'm going," Nate grumbled as the man lowered his broom and walked back toward the fluff and fold Laundromat in a huff. Once the shopkeeper moved, Nate noticed that the bouncer outside of Trois was the same one that stopped her from entering the establishment last night. Arms folded across his barrel chest, the brute shook his head and smirked, just as he had done when Nate had tried to enter the venue late last night.

In sports shorts, flip-flops and a hoodie, Nate approached the crowd of club-goers—most donned in latex and leather. Shoulders back and with pride in her stride, Nate cut the line in front of Trois but was promptly shot down by the bouncer. After noticing several club goers point their smartphones in her direction, Nate backed away. Unwilling to go viral for acting a fool, she decided to return to her car and wait for Tru to emerge from the club.

"I'm just thankful we're on the same page," Tru said a couple of months after they had first started hooking up. Nate remembered how at peace Tru looked when she uttered those words.

"No strings," Tru declared.

"No drama," Nate said, finishing Tru's thought, which had been easy to do at the time. However, that was months ago. Since then, things had spiraled. Nate remembered a time early on in their courtship. She and Tru sat perched at an overlook above the San Fernando Valley just as the sun began to rise.

"I'm just getting out of this situation," Tru admitted and then she rolled onto her back, allowing gravity to take hold of her natural, bare breasts.

"Sugar mama?" Nate asked as she studied every inch of Tru the way a new lover gazes when emphatically smitten.

"She was a distraction," Tru sighed, recalling her dream to become a fixture in Los Angeles' nightlife scene. "I need to get back on track, start this next chapter."

"The club," Nate responded, well aware of the multiple times Tru had been turned down for bank loans.

"Lounge," Tru corrected. "Once the small business loan finally comes through, it's on," she continued. The freckles on her face seemed to sparkle as Tru divulged a dismal moment from her not-so-distant past. "She was cute. Iranian with dark skin and powder-white hair."

Nate remembered that while she was content with their casual encounters, she was in no mood to hear about Tru's ex-girlfriend. However, convinced that

Tru needed to get something off her chest, Nate tempered her ego and allowed Tru to continue. "We dated for a couple of months, if you can even call it that," Tru's tone grew soft. "She introduced me to some really big spenders and never asked for a cut. Didn't need to. She was loaded." Nate sat up, engrossed as Tru painted a gruesome picture.

"It was all good until she tried convincing me to trick," Tru spoke truthfully. "She constantly brought it up. She hit me once, but was so apologetic." Tru's eyes began to water as she fiddled nervously with the pink knuckle stun gun that she had gifted Nate earlier that evening.

"So, you stayed?" Nate quizzed, trying hard not to sound judgmental. She was surprised at how heavy the subject matter was as their conversations typically ran pretty light.

"I had to," Tru said, wiping a tear from her cheek. "She was deep in the life."

"Drugs?" Nate asked. She stared down at Tru, much more accustomed to her aloof persona than the softer side that their early morning encounter had stirred.

"Sex trafficking—I was this close to getting caught up," Tru said, swallowing hard. "Imagine pocketing a thousand a night for hosting and beating the hell out of really burly men, who aside from a few S&M terms spoke only in Arabic."

"Scary," Nate shivered.

"It was, but I needed the cash. Still, do," Tru whispered, recalling how the pursuit of bankrolling her own private lounge had nearly cost her life. "It didn't take long before things went left."

"How so?" Nate asked.

"Someone was accused of cheating during a high stakes card game that I was hosting. The next thing I know—pop, pop, pop." Tru paused for a beat as she remembered with crystal clarity the distinct thrum of bullets piercing flesh. "After that, I cut all ties with my ex and her shady business partners."

Nate's memory of the encounter at the overlook faded when she heard the sound of laughter at the entrance of Trois. She looked out of her driver side window and saw the bouncer slap hands with a man decked out in a dark suit and skull helmet. Unbeknownst to Nate, that man was Tru's bodyguard. Seconds later, Tru strolled from the club, followed closely by a woman, dressed in all black and sporting an Anderson Cooper crew cut.

Nate slunk down in her seat, then looked back toward the fluff and fold as the shopkeeper tapped his watch. Nate knew that if called, it would take the cops at least five minutes to arrive and with that, Nate decided to risk it. She spent the next few minutes in the car watching as Tru lingered and chatted outside of the club. And then, things got really interesting. The boyish woman with white hair approached Tru who stood inches from the brick wall checking messages on her phone. Nate immediately hit the button on her cell phone assigned to Tru and grew pissed when she watched Tru bounce the call and stuff the phone into her purse. The woman lit a cigarette and leaned in even closer, causing Tru to inch back against the wall. Nate felt her skin growing red hot as the two women got cozy. Oh, hell, no! This couldn't be the abusive, sex trafficking ex—could it?

The mystery woman exhaled cigarette smoke into the early morning air as Tru smiled and ran her fingers through the silver fox's cropped mane. Tru had always used sex to control situations. This moment was no different. Nate watched angrily as the woman submitted to Tru's tender touch. Slowly, fear began to consume Nate. Did Tru have any real feelings for her or was Nate simply just another sucker Tru was manipulating?

Next, the older woman leaned in close, and from that distance, Nate had no way of hearing what she whispered into Tru's ear, but it was enough to garner a long hug. Frantic, Nate channeled all of her will power. She did not want to approach the women like a forlorn lunatic, but watching them together had Nate fuming. Nate took a deep breath and began to recite her calming mantra, "I'm safe, I'm breathing, I got this." The calming breaths and positive self-talk were working. This had to be part of Tru's act. Tru was without a doubt in character and with a client.

Moreover, the white-haired woman was surely not her ex. It couldn't be. Nate tried hard to convince herself. But in reality, the woman didn't just look like Tru's ex—she was her ex. Nate, however, had yet to connect the dots. Then, it happened. Still holding the cigarette in one hand, the woman with the cropped haircut let her left hand brace the wall. Then she pressed her body against Tru's and went in for the kiss. Nate had seen enough. She touched the ignition button and peeled out of the parking space just as a black and white police squad car pulled onto the scene.

Chapter 22

She-Man

After watching Nate and Jocelyn wander off hand in hand that Easter Monday, Cassia had given Alvita—their maid and Jocelyn's mother, a small severance and promptly dismissed her. Their family forever fractured, Cassia remained intent on separating Nate from Jocelyn, her most immediate temptation. Following their all-nighter on the beach, Nate returned home early the next morning, expecting the worse. Instead of being berated by her mother, she received the complete opposite. Silence. It was deafening. For two full days afterward, Cassia simply refused to talk. Moreover, with Barrington out of town on an amorous tryst, disguised as official government business, the house had roared to a hush. Aside from Cassia's silent treatment, it was business as usual—school assignments, band practice and football. April in Montego Bay was ideal for tourists and locals alike. With temperatures averaging a pleasant eighty-one degrees, outdoor activities were plentiful, especially football.

Fourteen-year-old Nate leaped into the air and let the football spring from her head toward her long-legged teammate. Then she took off running down the field, her eyes fixed firmly on the goal ahead as two boys in hot pursuit attempted to keep up. She smiled, picked up the pace, and then made a quick left turn, cutting clear through a strategic line of defense—and then it happened. Nate's teammate broke away from the pack and kicked the ball over the heads of several players. Nate again vaulted into the air, but this time she received the pass by stopping the high-flying ball with her chest. Then she let it slide down her athletic frame before maneuvering the ball between both knees. Next, she barreled down the field. From the sidelines, Jocelyn made an

L on each hand using her pointer finger and thumb. Her fingers forming a frame, Jocelyn followed Nate's every move as she glided across the field. The crowd of neighborhood spectators erupted as she kicked the soccer ball past her competitors and into the goal.

"Game!" Nate shouted. She raised her arms into the air having just scored the winning goal, while a handful of male teammates rushed over to congratulate her in the spontaneous street scrimmage. After a few laughs at their competition's expense, Nate slapped hands with her team and jogged over to the sidelines to speak with Jocelyn.

"Natty, you bad," Jocelyn gushed, handing Nate a bottle of water. "You should be playing for that prep school of yours."

"They weak as hell," Nate shrieked, knowing all too well that the reason she wasn't on her school's soccer team was because Cassia believed the sport was too mannish.

"Precisely," Jocelyn joked. They could use some girl power!"

"You sure she's a girl?" Asked a lanky sore loser with auburn dreads.

"She can't be," the shorter player piped up. "Look at that face," he said, laughing.

"Maybe we should check," joked the lanky dude with dreads. Next, he stiffened his middle and pointer fingers in the direction of Nate's nether regions, but she swiftly pushed his hand away.

"Don't," Nate snarled! Her eyes bounced from one bully to the next. For as long as she could remember, the Campbell brothers loved teasing her.

"They just mad, Natty," Jocelyn interjected. "Little boys with fragile egos." Jocelyn positioned herself between the guys and Nate.

"Poor little rich girl," The light haired bully said rolling his eyes at Nate. "Forget her," he said looking Nate up and down as if she were standing between him and an after-school snack. The trash talker then shifted his attention to Jocelyn. "So, when going out?" He sized the teen beauty up.

"Let me help you out here, bro," the shorter boy butt in. "Girl, you so sweet me wanna add you to porridge." He said, circling Jocelyn.

"I would climb a Macca tree naked for you", the taller brother chimed in.

"Nobody wants to see that," Jocelyn gibed. She crossed her arms and gave the boy a good once over, garnering a big laugh from bystanders.

"This is stupid," sighed Nate. "Let's just go." She grabbed Jocelyn's hand and pulled her away from the growing cluster of spectators.

"Keep hanging with that 'ting, people gonna start to think you funny too, Jocelyn," the taller boy cautioned.

"The only 'ting funny is your face," the insult slipped from Nate's mouth faster than even she could process it. The boy's ego momentarily checked by Nate's retort and the roar of spontaneous laughter gave the girls just enough time to slip away from the scene.

"Watch out for that she-man!" The shorter brother urged Jocelyn, who intuitively let her hand fall from Nate's. It had only been a few days since they'd hooked up on the beach and the two were still very much on the down low. It was one thing to come out to their parents, but the neighborhood kids inherently came with a different set of challenges.

"The Campbells are idiots," Jocelyn broke her silence after the two friends had walked for a few minutes in complete stillness. "Forget them," she sighed.

"I hate this place," said Nate kicking an empty can down the road and into a rubbish-filled ditch with the same artful precision that she'd mastered the football. "Once college starts, I'm getting as far away from here as possible."

"Careful what you wish for, Natty."

"What's that supposed to mean?"

"Come on, Natty. We know how this ends. You'll end up at some far away university, a place I can't even afford to dream of," Jocelyn laughed. "You'll never look back and can't nobody blame you." She stared beyond the busy Montego Bay intersection as if prophesying. "I gonna miss you."

"You sound like we don't have another three years of high school," Nate said, laughing, unaware of how much truth lay nestled in Jocelyn's prediction. "Plus, you don't need money. You'll earn a bunch of scholarships." Nate smiled, although she could tell Jocelyn wasn't buying it.

"Don't need money?" Jocelyn asked, sucking her teeth. "Okay," she laughed and changed the subject. "I need to pay down the layaway on my birthday dress. Come with me."

"I better get home. My mom is still ignoring me," Nate sighed.

"That's perfect," Jocelyn concluded. "You rather her fuss at you?"

"I'm not trying to give her a reason. Besides, your birthday isn't for another two months," Nate teased.

"You remembered," Jocelyn cooed. "What I suppose to wear, pum pum shorts?"

"It's not a horrible idea," Nate smiled, and Jocelyn lit up like Blue Mountain Pine on Christmas.

"Fine," Jocelyn sulked. "I'll catch you later." She turned to exit, but upon second thought, decided against it, as Jocelyn had one final morsel to drop. "The other night on the beach was…"

"Yeah, I know," Nate interrupted, sure to maintain her distance. While homophobic bullies had already spread rumors about her, they couldn't prove anything, and for now, Nate was intent on keeping it that way.

"I would've frozen time if I could," Jocelyn smiled. After making sure that they weren't being watched, she gave Nate a peck on the cheek. Then made her way deeper into town. As PG as it was, the kiss had come from left field and had given Nate a sudden case of butterflies.

"Cool," Nate said, placing her hand on her cheek as she watched Jocelyn melt completely into the horizon. Once out of sight, Nate fished an iPod from her backpack, slipped on a pair of headphones and headed home.

As Nate marched away from the hustle and bustle of town, the reggae in her ears was a glaring contradiction to the road ahead. Covered in red dust, it ran alongside what had years ago been acres of lush forest. The past several decades, steeped in bauxite production and corporate gluttony had done significant damage, but for as long as she'd been walking these roads, Nate hadn't seen the parish any other way.

Oblivious to the fact that she was being followed, Nate took in the landscape while using an imaginary drum set to play a rhythm only she could hear. Next, she cut across the railroad tracks whose line was erected solely to shuttle bauxite for aluminum manufacturing to a nearby port. Then Nate made her way under the overpass, just as the faintest sound disrupted her island rhythm soundtrack. Was someone calling her name? She removed her headphones and looked over her shoulder just in time to see the two young tormenters from earlier running straight for her—the Campbells. Paralyzed with fear, Nate dropped her iPod and ran, but it was too late.

"She-man! Waa gwaan?" The shorter bully teased Nate and then moved in until her back was against the overpass.

"Dude, chill," Nate commanded. "I know you not still mad about the game." She rolled her eyes and deepened her voice.

"You know she's not that gross. Gimme a paper bag. I'll bust that 'ting open," he continued, laughing in Nate's face.

"What is this batty boy crap?" Now wearing Nate's headphones, the taller brother with dreads screamed as vintage Heptones blared into his eardrums.

"Shut up," the shorter bully said, pushing his brother in the chest. "Someone will hear you." He motioned for the taller boy to remove Nate's headphones and that's when Nate took off running. Her sprint, however, was short-lived, as the ruffians were able to quickly tackle Nate into a patch of red mud. As the two brothers stood over Nate, she scanned the environment for a way out.

"Don't worry, she-man. We're here to help," the taller bully asserted, sweeping dreads from his face.

"I'm not playing with y'all!" Nate screamed. Having landed on something hard, Nate used her elbows to prop herself up and relieve pressure from her aching back.

"Ain't nobody playing," the shorter brother asserted. He then approached as Nate planned her getaway. She knew she could outrun them, but first, Nate had to get to her feet.

Chapter 23

You've Arrived

Inches from clipping Simon's receptionist, Nate laid in hard on her brakes outside of Herbst Studios. Since she'd heard about Auntie Earlene's cancer diagnosis, Nate had been haunted by both good and bad memories of home. As she shook off the memory of her childhood tormenters, Simon's receptionist Kevin scurried to pick up a file folder containing the scattered legal documents that he'd dropped in a panic. Nate immediately threw the car into park and hopped out to help.

"I'm sorry, Kev," Nate apologized while kneeling to assist with the mess. "My head was somewhere else."

"Are you kidding me right now," the assistant sighed, exasperated. Then he wiped dirt from the paperwork as Nate took the opportunity to browse some of the verbiage: Unauthorized Disclosure of Information, Injunction, Indemnity. There was also a name that seemed to leap from the page, Sasha Harper. Nate couldn't place it, but the name rang a bell and would prove to stick with her.

"My bad. I can't be late for this meeting with Simon," Nate said, standing with the assistant as he used the trunk of her car to neatly shuffle papers.

"The meeting isn't for another three hours," he exhaled, likely calmed by the fact that the legal documents hadn't suffered any permanent damage. "Chill."

Chill? This was no time to chill! If anything, Nate needed to get fired up. Tonight's meeting with Simon was her chance to impress him to such an extent that he'd be dying to connect her with the executives at Masquerade Records.

If Nate wanted to be signed, she'd need to convince Simon that she was the next big thing. She had to focus. Between dealing with Tru's distance, Auntie Earlene's cancer diagnosis and pitching her music, Nate's mind was a million places. While Simon had already said that the theme song she composed for Brown Bag Cutie wasn't the right fit, that didn't negate the fact that the Herbst family remained connected throughout Hollywood. A green light from Simon was a guaranteed kick start to Nate's career as a composer and music producer—all she had to do was get him to believe in her sound.

"One more," Nate said, handing the assistant a final legal document.

"Thanks," he said, sliding the paper into the pile and placing them into the accordion-style, filing folder. "By the way, I checked out your podcast. Simon had me pull it in preparation for tonight's meeting."

"That's what's up!" Nate squealed. The thought of Simon listening to the Natty One Show—her podcast, featuring original music, plus a talk segment, where Nate encouraged listeners to walk in their truths got Nate fired up.

"So the music, that's all you?"

"Who else would it be," Nate responded smugly. The thought of Simon preparing for their meet and greet had gone directly to her head.

"Cool," Kevin said, carefully tucking the file folder under his arm. "I've got to get this to Van Nuys." The assistant sighed, clearly turned off at the thought of being anywhere near the 405 Freeway during rush hour. "But I have some ideas. We should talk." He turned to exit.

"About?" Nate grew curious.

"I'm producing a short film, and your fusion of EDM and reggae speaks to me." Suddenly filled with inspiration, his smile lit up the dim parking lot. "You ever think about scoring," asked the starry-eyed assistant.

"Doesn't everyone?" Nate responded matter-of-factly. Of course, she'd thought about it. Scoring film and television had been a lifelong dream. Hell, she'd prayed for it, but there was just one caveat—Nate wanted to work on big-budget projects, and although she was too civil to say it aloud, the thought of collaborating on an indie short seemed somehow beneath her. Nate didn't realize how wrong she was.

"We should link up," Kevin said, handing Nate his business card.

"I'm pretty busy. But yeah, I guess," Nate said, shoving the card into her back pocket without so much as a second look." Try as she did to be polite, Nate's response came off as phony.

"Okay." Kevin's smile faded as Nate's lackluster reply sucked the enthusiasm right from him. "Peace," he said flatly.

"Later." Nate nodded her farewells and then hopped back into her car to head home and freshen up.

The truth of the matter was that Nate had told herself that she was too good for independent film. And in doing so, had greatly undervalued the benefits of connecting with artists like Kevin. Nate preferred to partner with Hollywood saviors, like Simon, as opposed to delving into the trenches with guerilla filmmakers. Let the assistant have all the Image Awards he could stomach for the urban award circuit would sadly never satiate Nate. Her sights were set echelons higher—on a golden boy named Oscar and the city of angel's musical matriarch—Grammy.

##

After stopping at her place to shower and change, Nate made her way to a swanky Beverly Hill's hotel. Having tossed her keys to the valet, Nate walked toward the entrance and couldn't help but feel as though all eyes were on her. From the valet who made no qualms about checking her out as she strode into the hotel, to the doorman who escorted her in as though she were a B-List celebrity to the multiple bellhops who stumbled over themselves to assist her.

"Oh my God, you look just like me," Karina squealed. She had peaked up from her cocktail at the precise moment that Nate entered the chic hotel lounge and spoke loud enough for anyone within a twenty-mile radius to hear her. "When you snag that first Grammy, you're taking me as your date! You owe me!" Karina engulfed Nate into her arms, making it evident by her tone and slurred speech that she was in good spirits. Nate felt dwarfed and suffocated by Karina's drunken embrace.

"Sure thing, Kar," Nate told her friend.

"My mini-me," Karina gushed. Although Nate was rocking Karina's money green Gucci, jersey-style dress, she'd funked it up by adding a cropped leather jacket and vintage riding boots. "Two more Cabernets," Karina demanded, snapping her fingers.

"I should stay clear-headed." Nate frowned as the bartender placed the bold red wine in front of the women.

"Drink," Karina said, raising her glass and daring Nate to defy her. "Just a little something to take the edge off."

"I'll start with water," Nate responded.

"Suit yourself." Karina shrugged and then sipped the savory Sauvignon.

"Don't you think it's a little weird, meeting at a hotel," Nate asked, remembering Abby's story of how her roommate came home in tears after a date with Simon. She wanted to share this story with Karina and to tell her all about her uninvited houseguest, but Nate knew better. Gossip this juicy would only be a distraction.

Nate's knees knocked with nervous energy as she ogled the fashionable lounge patrons. Karina smiled, placing her hand on Nate's leg. "Look around," Karina grinned. "You've arrived." They took a moment to survey the scene— a dimly lit, modern chophouse with people in designer clothing downing overpriced tapas and expensive wine. "Welcome to Beverly Hills."

"I'm just saying a conference room would suffice," Nate cleared her throat, attempting to get the bartender's attention. Then she thought back to Abby's story. Could Abby be trusted? She was, after all, the same person who'd shown up to her apartment unannounced. She also knew about Tru, despite Nate never mentioning her. Although anxiety was mounting, in Nate's mind, the reward was greater than the risk.

"Could you be any greener," Karina joked? "Listen, love. This is how it's done." Karina took another sip and then began to walk Nate through what to expect at her meeting with Simon. "You'll have drinks, probably poolside or at one of the private cabanas—and let him do the talking. Rich guys love the sound of their voice," advised Karina.

"I already told you, I want to stay sharp tonight," Nate interrupted.

"That's not an option," Karina warned. "The last thing you want to do is offend the guy by ordering water or some nonsense like that."

"Whatever. I'll tell him I'm on antibiotics," Nate countered.

"You'll do as instructed!" Karina's head jerked in the direction of Nate, who at this point couldn't tell if she was joking or if the egregious stank eye was somehow premonitory.

"If you could take it down like ten notches!" Nate said, growing more irritated by the second.

"Why is it so hard to get this guy's attention? Bartender!" Too busy chatting up a pair of twenty-somethings, the barkeep nodded and held up his index finger.

"I'm just saying. It's not like you're meeting Simon at the Motel Six," Karina sneered.

"So, it's not just a room with two queen beds and one red light bulb," Nate smirked.

"I'm an idiot. Of course, you've never been inside a presidential suite." Karina shook her head, knowingly. "Just think of it as a really nice apartment."

Nate's sarcasm had been lost on Karina. Instead of going for her friend's jugular, Nate took her frustration with Karina out on the staff. "Bartender!" Nate blurted out at the top of her lungs. He again smiled and held up his index finger.

"Hello!" Karina screamed. She then repeatedly clanged a steak knife against her glass, spurring the bartender to action. "Water, now, sparkling," Karina commanded, prompting the bartender to race over with a bottle and pour two glasses for the ladies.

"Apologies for the wait," The bartender sounded distressed and gave Karina his complete attention, even though it was Nate's request that he'd ignored.

"Whatever, man," Nate said, glancing down at her watch. "He should be here in fifteen minutes."

"Men like that are never late. So, I'm gonna go," Karina said, dismissing the bartender like a peasant with one wave of her commanding hand.

"You aren't staying to say hello," Nate quizzed?

"Trust me. You got this", Karina said, smiling. "Meet us at the club afterward. I want to know everything."

"That's because you're nosy," Nate joked.

"Either way, tonight is all about you," Karina beamed. She then lifted the mouth-blown glass toward Nate, who was again haunted by Auntie Earlene's words: "Any dutti waata kool hat iron." While Auntie Earlene's opinions hadn't always been welcome, they were typically warranted. Tonight's telekinetic counsel was no different. Nate took a closer look at the sparkling water. And when she did, it wasn't the faint particles of God knows what floating about that caused her to shudder—but Karina's eerie, waterlogged profile.

Chapter 24

Me Too

Karina was right. Upon arrival, Simon suggested he and Nate start their meeting in the privacy of one of the high-end hotel's cabanas. Cylindrical in nature, the private cabana was wrapped in a luxurious, 360-degree aquarium.

"You must have thought Chad and I were real jerks, giving you the whole diversity spiel and then hiring a white rapper," Simon laughed, referencing how just yesterday Nate had unsuccessfully pitched her music as the theme song for their new reality dating show, Brown Bag Cutie.

"I actually thought…"

Simon cut her off, and Nate listened as the young executive filled the high-end hut with half-baked ideas on race relations.

"Chad and I thought how forward-thinking it would be to feature a Hasidic Jew on the BBC track."

Simon used a steak knife to segment the bloody top sirloin, as Nate's anxiety ticked up a notch. "It's like everyone expects a black rapper, and then boom, we hit 'em with Sal! It's the ultimate form of appreciation," Simon boasted.

"You mean appropriation," Nate mumbled. She understood that black culture sold products and that despite how Simon tried to spin it, contracting Sal was in no way a homage to the culture. Either way, Nate was on a mission, and ensuring Simon remained racially sensitive was not part of her plan. Tonight, Nate was out for self.

"So what part of the Caribbean is he from," Nate pivoted.

"Caribbean?" Simon spoke, visibly tickled as he washed the protein down with a top-shelf, citrus-flavored vodka.

"The accent, where's he from?" Nate queried.

"Sal? Oh, God, no. He's an old family friend from Brentwood," Simon admitted. "The Caribbean thing is a shtick."

"The business of show," Nate responded, nonchalantly.

"Precisely. Chad and I were hooking a brother up. You know how it is," Simon's blatant attempt at infusing an urban edge into his voice was irritating, but it gave Nate an idea. Beat the condescending rich boy at his own game.

"Well, if you're really in the mood to hook someone up, hook a sister up!" Nate laughed, steering the conversation back toward her. "Not to be cocky, but my sound's just different."

"We're all a little cocky. Embrace it," Simon instructed as he fanned his legs in and out beneath the table.

"I will," Nate agreed. She then pulled a cellphone from her messenger bag and hit play on one of her original beats. The perfectly imperfect marriage of electronic dance music and lover's rock poured from her speakers. Nate watched Simon groove along to the instrumental track for a bit before asking his opinion.

"Banging, right?" Nate figured infusing a bit of slang into her question would make her seem relaxed. "Oh, come on! You're an A and R guy," she laughed. "Don't you want to discover the next big thing?" Nate asked, pointing to herself.

"It's a hot track, but a hot track isn't enough," Simon sipped. "Every day this town cares less about talent and more about relationships," Simon replied while topping off his glass with premium Vodka. "Like it or not, we all have to scratch a couple of backs." He concluded by offering Nate a drink, of which she politely shot down.

"I'm all for paying my dues," Nate continued to pitch. "I've got some tracks that would be perfect for the studio's music library—I just want to be heard."

Simon doesn't answer. He instead skips ahead to the next track, an infectious, head-bopping fusion of EDM and lover's rock. And as Simon swayed in his seat, Nate let her eyes drift beyond him and into the tropical fish-filled tank. Despite the manmade enclave, the fish swam opposite the current as if in their native, salt-water environments. The scene was in fact so instinctive that Nate watched wide-eyed as a nerf shark ascended from the cloak of coral reef and tore into a spotted white fish.

"So you're from Jamaica, right? I hear the influence in your sound," Simon continued, as his reflection on the tank melded with the trail of carnage behind him.

129

"I am," Nate declared, "Montego Bay."

"Perfect. If you won't drink with me, you'll at least have a smoke," Simon said, referencing the fact that throughout dinner, despite his insistence, Nate hadn't consumed any alcohol. "You smoke, right?" Simon laughed. "Of course you do—it's your national pastime," he joked. Nate swallowed her words. Had she been sitting across the table from anyone else, she would've told them where they could go with that national pastime mess, but this was Simon, and as far as she was concerned, he was her golden ticket.

"I have some in the room," Simon continued. "Let's roll."

"The conversation was just getting good," Nate said, skipping ahead to another up-tempo dance track on her phone. "I'm fine down here," Nate spoke directly.

"That's just it," Simon laughed. "You've got your feet planted firmly on the ground, but I'm trying to take you sky high," he smirked. "Isn't that what this meeting is about—taking your music career to the next level?"

"No doubt!" She agreed. "I know you've got friends in high places," she laughed awkwardly.

"And, I couldn't be more ready. I'm taking direction, leads, referrals," she grinned, "once the road leads to a record deal, I'm good."

"So let's talk creative," Simon continued, leaning in. "Your podcast is good, but it can be fire, nah'mean?" There it was again—Simon's bastardized attempt at Ebonics. Nate cringed as he stood and yanked the bottle of premium Vodka from the bucket of ice. "Come up, we'll have a smoke, listen to your music and I'll tell you what I have in mind," Simon insisted.

Nate lobbed her napkin onto the table, while Simon pulled back the cabana curtain. Because their conversation had been entirely professional, Nate decided to continue the meeting upstairs. "Have room service send up dessert," Simon said, nodding at the waiter stationed outside of the intimate dining outlet.

"Yes, Mr. Herbst." The waiter held the curtain open even wider as Nate and Simon emerged. Simon proceeded to take the long way to his room, purposely parading Nate past bellhops, the concierge and wait staff. It was as if Simon wanted each of them to see him with Nate, his presumed date for the evening. Within minutes Simon was shutting the door behind him as he and Nate advanced into the plush presidential suite.

"This place is amazing," Nate said as she sat her messenger bag down. She then walked over to the picture window, which overlooked an expansive infinity pool and several gleeful guests, who from, twenty stories up, echoed spastic goldfish.

Simon used his laptop, wirelessly routed to a set of HD monitors, to pull up clips from Nate's podcast. "Your beats are banging," Simon conceded. "I'll give you that." He pressed play on Nate's
latest episode and then began to pour bottled water into a bright red bong.

"Thanks." Nate flashed a smile as Simon observed Nate slip out of her leather jacket, then bounce to a beat of her own making. "Music's always been my passion."

"I see that," Simon said, as he watched Nate groove. Nate again turned to look out the window as Simon's gaze narrowed in on Nate's tight waist and ample backside. "It's hypnotizing."

"You think?" Asked Nate.

Simon nodded affirmatively as he packed the bong with Humboldt County's finest—a hybrid blend of Sativa and Indica cannabis. "The problem is the main focus of your podcast is music, and it shouldn't be—not yet anyway," Simon weighed in. Next, he grabbed a lighter from the side table, lit up the herb and took a nice, long pull. "The show needs to be more…" Simon started to cough, and Nate watched almost amused as the big shot had a coughing fit.

"You good?" Nate handed Simon a bottle of water from the marble countertop. Simon laughed and took another hit. "Gotta cough to get off," he replied, exhaling skunk into the air. "As I was saying, you need to infuse more you into the show. It should be twenty percent music, eighty percent Natty One," he advised, referencing Nate's on-air persona.

"I much rather the music speak for me," Nate retorted. "The talk segment is just something I do as a gag."

"Cute." Simon took a sip of water before continuing. "I'm gonna keep it real. You have what, fifty, sixty subscribers?" He questioned, well aware of the answer.

"Something like that," Nate responded, ashamed by the fact that in two years of podcasting, she'd gained an audience of only a few dozen people.

"That's nothing," Simon said, laying out the cold hard facts of industry life." Before we can present your demo to Masquerade or any other label, you have to have a following. And how you get that is through more of this." He passed the bong to Nate and pressed play on a talk segment from her podcast: "Not only am I dating two sisters, but I gotta man," the caller said, laughing. "Damn, it feels good to see people up on it! You feel me, Natty One," the caller quizzed Nate.

"Okay. Brownie points for the Biz Markie reference," Nate said jokingly, taken aback by the classic rap lyric. "But it sounds like you're doing way too much." Nate's accent, distinctively heightened by the fullness of her podcast persona ripped through Simon's sound system. "The Natty One Show is, of course, a walk in your truth zone. So no judgments, but you better be playing it safe. If not, trust, your ass will be burned. Fire hot!" Nate warned. "Next caller!"

"Two chicks and a dick!" Simon pressed pause. "I love that! Shorty was getting it in," he said, laughing! "But you dropped the ball, Nate. You missed an opportunity to exploit some real dyke drama," Simon lectured.

Dyke drama? Nate's skin crawled. In her opinion, this term was the equivalent to using the n-word. Phrases like this were okay to say if you were a member of the subjugated group, but if you weren't—fall back. Especially when in mixed company! Nate used her thumb to gently press the weed back into the ceramic bowl. Then, she lit up and inhaled the high-grade hemp. "You're saying I should be on that Jerry Springer tip?" Nate queried. Rather than tell Simon where to go she decided to smoke his weed and hear him out.

"Ding-ding-ding! That's what people want to hear! That's how you get your subscribers up, and that's when we introduce you to the labels," he concluded. Nate took another hit, thankful that no matter how crass his delivery, Simon had at least given her career some consideration." And by the way, you need video," Simon said, nodding in full agreement with himself. He then placed the bottle of water onto a nearby table and approached Nate. "People want to see you, and I can't blame them." Simon put his hand on Nate's shoulder, causing her to turn around and stumble back a bit." I've given this some thought, and what you're missing is that good cop—dirty cop element," he said, glancing at the clock mounted on the wall—it was minutes to nine. Then Simon grinned and opened a drawer containing a plate with several lines of cocaine on it. "Your online persona is totally butch, but tonight, baby, you've thrown me for a loop. I knew you were cute, but damn, who knew you had all that body?" He inhaled two lines of the nose candy. "I mean, at first I thought maybe pair you up with another chick. Someone feminine so that you too could play off of each other, but seeing you in that dress tonight," Simon said, rubbing his chin happily. "Maybe we see what your chemistry is like with a man. That could be hot." Simon leaned in and groped Nate's breasts as the bong slipped from her grip and shattered against the tiled floor.

"Definitely not what I had in mind," Nate's voice was stern as she pushed past Simon and made her way toward the door. Had Simon not have used a remote control to lock the door, Nate would've been home free. Nate was stuck and knew the last thing she could afford to do was panic. She turned back around to face him and plotted a way to reach her messenger bag.

"So maybe we got off on the wrong foot," Simon said, softening his tone. He then hopped back on the computer, minimized the podcast and opened a folder with a single file in it. "How about a movie?" He double-clicked the file and pressed play, causing Nate's naked image to splash across all three high definition monitors. Although her face was not in the frame, watching herself star in last night's self-pleasuring session caused a wave of nausea to saturate what had become a hostage situation. "You've been to my house?" Nate asked, fighting off the mounting queasiness as she silently ran through her mantra: I'm safe, I'm breathing, I got this.

"You know Ferraris are my favorite import, but you are a close second," Simon groaned and adjusted his manhood as Nate's eyes stayed glued to the screens. She watched in utter shock as her hips rocked in unison with the all-purpose showerhead.

"So, you like to watch," Nate's captor laughed as the clock struck nine. "Me too." He positioned himself in an armchair and as the door to what Nate had assumed was a closet swung open, a camera-wielding man dressed in all black and a single-horned headdress hopped out.

"What kind of sick shi…" The sound of Nate's voice dulled in comparison to the beat of her racing heart.

"Simon says, consider this your audition!" He commanded.

Chapter 25

Pour Me Another

Simon pulled a wireless headset from the plush wing chair's side pocket and tossed them at Nate. "Simon says," the predator insisted. He then spread his legs and leaned back into the comfort of the high back chair as the headphones landed at Nate's feet. Noticing that the masked camera operator was positioned in front of the palatial suite's only exit, Nate bent down and picked up the headphones in silence—she needed to buy time.

"Put them on," Simon said, motioning for Nate to approach as the cameraman moved from the door to capture a closer angle. His mask was creepy. Single-horned and West African inspired, that left the bottom half of his face exposed.

"Listen, Simon. I'm the last person to judge your…" Nate struggled to find the right words.

"Kink?" Simon interjected.

"I was gonna say fucked up fantasy," Nate replied with a nervous chuckle, trying to squelch her anxiety as she scanned the room for her messenger bag.

"Funny," Simon adjusted in his seat as his tone grew more deliberate. "Put—them—on." Nate's gaze floated past Simon to the concealed cameraman, as he used the manual zoom lens to focus in on Nate's frantic expression. Then she recalled everyone who had seen them make their way up to his suite—the waiter, the elevator man, even room service. Simon had purposely paraded her past hotel staff, who if questioned, would no doubt say that Nate had consented to whatever was about to go down. Slowly, Nate placed the headphones over her head and let them rest on her shoulders as Simon leered at her. "That a girl," he grinned.

Simon then poured two shots as the cameraman gave Nate a slight shove closer toward the predator. She now knew for certain that the only way Simon would champion her career would be if she first scratched his itch. Noticing her messenger bag beside the bottle of liquor, Nate thought fast.

"So about Masquerade Records—favor, for a favor?" Nate's terse statement spoke volumes and Simon was well versed.

"Does it work any other way?" Simon asked with a shrug. Next, he downed the high-end spirit as Nate inched closer and placed the shot glass to her mouth. While the warm liquor slid gradually down Nate's throat, her heart raced loud enough for her to wonder if Simon and the masked assailant could hear it.

"I'm safe. I'm breathing. I got this," Nate ran silently through her mantra as she covered her ears with the headphones, sank to her knees, and was immediately transported back to the abandoned Montego Bay train tracks and the first time she'd ever faced assault. Propped up on her elbows, fourteen-year-old Nate let her knees drift apart as the shorter assailant beamed, his pants already unzipped. Just as he motioned to mount her, Nate took the red-tinged, aluminum-rich rock that she'd landed on and let it connect hard with the back of his head. Next, she pushed the bloody boy away and took off running. Then, Nate's mind returned back to Simon's presidential suite. Nate was ready to fight again.

"Pour me another," Nate said, plotting and slowly taking command of the room.

"Yes, ma'am," Simon agreed eagerly. He then unbuckled his belt as his head eased into the wing back chair.

"Man, I hate you," the cameraman said with a chuckle. Having covered Nate's profile shot, the crass videographer circled enviously behind Simon to capture an over the shoulder angle as Nate put the shot glass to her lips.

"You got next," his smile wide and eyes already shut, Simon retorted with anticipation. The cameraman laughed out loud, and Nate watched as the light from the television monitors seemed to ricochet off his diamond-encrusted grill.

"You're that cornball rapper!" Nate gasped. They'd only met that one time, yesterday in Simon's office, but even through his terrifying mask, Nate recognized that cheesy rainbow grill. "Sal Katz!" Nate shrieked as the rapper's name suddenly came to her.

"What the fuck, Sy?" Completely taken aback, the cameraman's voice cracked as his smile faded. Shook, he let the DLSR camera dangle by his waist side as Simon eyed Nate curiously. The path to the door now clear, Nate seized the opportunity, quite literally refusing to go down without a fight. She reached across Simon's lap, then placed the empty shot glass on the table, grabbed her messenger bag and jumped to her feet.

"Hold up!" Simon yelled and yanked Nate by her wrist, but her plan was already in play. She spat unconsumed liquor into his eyes, briefly blinding him. Next, she pulled the stun gun from her messenger bag and used it to light up the rapidly approaching, masked man, causing him to drop the camera and fall directly to his knees.

"Nate, wait," Simon cried out, rubbing his still stinging eyes and standing to approach her.

"You're disgusting!" Nate asserted defiantly. Invigorated by the shift in the room's power dynamic, she snatched a handful of Simon's junk and let the stun gun go to work. As the men lay doubled over and reeling in pain, Nate grabbed Simon's laptop and raced for the exit.

# #

Less than twenty minutes later, Nate hopped from her illegally parked car and cut through gobs of costumed club-goers searching for Karina. She had a million questions and was sure that Karina had an answer for each of them.

"Mini-me," Karina sounded happy as hell to see Nate. Adorned in a pair of flashing red devil horns, Karina raised her glass in Nate's direction. "I told you. Doesn't she look adorable in my hand me downs?" Karina queried their mutual friend, Royce.

"Why, Karina?" Nate asked, smacking the drink from Karina's hand. "Are you that jealous or is it genuine hate?"

"What the hell are you talking about?" Karina asked, appearing more pissed at the wasted alcohol than anything else. She stood to her feet.

"He tried to rape me!" Nate screamed over the blaring club music. "They both did!"

"Oh, my God!" Dressed in medical scrubs and a stethoscope, their costumed friend gasped and took Nate by the hand. "Who?"

"Simon and that cornball rapper," Nate explained, still gripped by fear.

"You're joking," Karina scoffed, feigning shock.

"Do I look like I'm joking?" Nate got in Karina's face. "He had footage of me in my apartment," Nate said, swallowing hard. "Naked."

"We have to report this," Royce declared. As she attempted to pull Nate toward the exit, Nate shook free, growing more consumed in adrenaline and rage the more she looked at Karina.

"She's right. If anything happened, we need to tell the cops," Karina agreed. Her plan to destroy Simon was in full effect. She was elated but knew better than to show it.

"If?" Nate eyed Karina curiously. "What, you think I'm lying?" Nate asked, fuming. "I know you had something to do with this."

"That's not what she meant," their friend Royce said, rubbing Nate on the back. "Karina, tell her you had nothing to do with this."

"I had nothing to do with this," Karina lied. "Powerful guys like this prey on women all the time. You can't be his only victim."

"I just don't know how he got footage of me," Nate said, refusing to cry.

"You have all types of weird artists in and out of your place all the time," Karina made-up a lie with the effortless flow of a freestyle emcee. "It's not that hard for one of them to plant a camera." Karina continued her hypothesis as if nothing could be more obvious. "I'm sure you let them use your bathroom, whereas I would send their asses down to the lobby," Karina smirked. "I've warned you about being too nice."

"I never said the footage was from my bathroom," Nate spoke lowly, epitomizing the calm before a torrential downpour. "You did this." Karina looked at her friends as her silence said more than denying it ever could.

Chapter 26

Persistence of Memory

"Fuck it. I knew about the video," Karina continued, suddenly liberated by the truth. "Simon's a predator and you were the perfect bait." Karina swallowed hard. The look of utter disgust staring back at Karina assured her that neither Nate nor their friend, Royce was remotely prepared to handle the truth—so she switched gears, opting for a softer approach.

"But I have no idea how he got the video," Karina lied, as the devil horns she rocked for a costume blinked rapidly. For her, deceit was relative and the truth was merely a state of mind she'd over the years learned to bend, shift and shape at will. "Do you really think I could do that to you? Karina paused for dramatic effect and then continued to question Nate. "After all these years?" As her tone grew shallow, Karina tapped into a skill she'd mastered by the tender age of four—the crocodile tear.

Nate quietly studied Karina. First, she imagined clocking her—and then— she recalled their years of friendship and how like Dali's "Persistence of Memory" their bond seemed to be melting into a pile of mismanaged time.

"What would make you think this is ok?" Nate quizzed.

"He hurt me," her first time admitting it aloud, Karina surprised herself with the confession. "Help me take him down, Nate," Karina pleaded.

"Hurt you, how?" Asked Royce, hanging curiously to Karina's every word.

"I sold Simon his house, but for him, it couldn't just be about business. He made it sexual," Karina said, recalling the day of the house viewing. "If I wanted to seal the deal, I had to suck him off—simple as that—and you know what?" Karina laughed maniacally." My father got most of the commission, so it wasn't even worth it."

"Sounds like your typical Saturday night to me," Nate sucked her teeth. She was pissed and taking the high road was not an option.

"Whatever, goodie two shoes!" Karina exclaimed. Then she wiped tears from her eyes as she tussled with the fact that the best day of her career had also been the worst day of her life. "I agreed to blow him, but the asshole took what he wanted."

"Being slutty is not the same thing as being kidnapped!" Nate spat venom and as her temper flared, so too did her frequently stifled Caribbean accent. "I was scared to death tonight, Karina. You did this," Nate winced, shaking with rage.

"No, Simon did this!" Karina grew incensed by flashbacks of the time Simon assaulted her. She stared through Nate recalling how small she felt on her knees as Simon towered over her with a fistful of what had once been a flawless up-do in his grasp. " He raped me. He deserves to rot," Karina proclaimed as she remembered how Simon delighted in gagging her with his cock." Don't be so selfish, Nate. You and I can't be his only victims!"

"You hooked Simon and me up after he assaulted you and I'm selfish?" Nate yelled, pushing Karina in her chest and causing her to stumble backward. "I could've been raped!" Nate's voice crept up to a level that was not only loud enough to command Karina's attention but to garner that of a couple of nearby bouncers as well.

"But you weren't, so let's stop fighting about who did what and nail this clown," said Karina, grabbing Nate's hand like she gave a damn. To Nate, the paradox could not have been more off-putting.

"You think this is a joke," Nate said, ripping her hand from Karina's.

If only it were that simple. *One blow job for one fat ass commission check*. Those were Simon's exact words. Karina presumed the proposal was a business deal, of which she accepted the terms. She'd made her choice and had been tormented by it ever since. Traumatized and humiliated, her body must've gone into instant recovery mode because try as she might, much of what she remembered about that day was foggy. Could she really classify this as assault? Or was this, as Nate suggested, more of Karina's typical slutty behavior.

"Well—say something!" Nate raised her voice, redirecting Karina's focus.

"Damn it. I want revenge!" Karina snapped. "And so should you."

"You're twisted!" Livid, Nate screamed at Karina as an unrelenting sense of betrayal burrowed deep into her soul. She then leaped into Karina's face and gave her just enough reach to pull Nate in for a tight bear hug—her full-figured frame all but swallowing Nate whole. Karina spoke lowly into Nate's ear, "And you're broke and black." Karina was at least half right. Sure, Nate was black but broke? Not by a long shot. After more than a decade of friendship, Karina had asked little about Nate's background, and Nate, so distressed by her upbringing, remained wary of discussing her politically entrenched, monthly stipend wielding family.

"If we don't go to the police station, right now I promise—things will get really bad, really quick," Karina said, swallowing hard. Nate scanned her face, waiting for the punch line, but one never came. Instead, Karina continued to lean in close, speaking low enough for only Nate to hear. So much for Karina's softer approach. Instead, she leaned in closer, speaking low enough for only Nate to hear. "Security's right behind you." Karina held onto Nate even tighter as Nate tried to wiggle her way out of the one-way hug. "I'll release the whole damn video. Try me," Karina said, smirking. "Your abysmal career will be as good as dead—just like your rasclat Auntie."

"Fuck you!" Nate yelled as she broke free of Karina's grip and tackled the backstabber to the ground.

"Y'all need to chill!" Their friend Royce screamed as she attempted to pull Nate off of Karina

"Lock that hood bitch up!" Karina screamed at the top of her lungs as clubgoers aimed their smartphones in the direction of the ruckus.

"Why are you manhandling me?" Nate pleaded as the dark-haired bouncer ground his knee into her back and pressed her face onto the sticky club floor. "She started it!"

"Well, I'm finishing it!" The bouncer screamed while snatching Nate up by her dreads and onto her feet like a weed from its roots. "Out! Now!" He said, pointing toward the exit as the bouncer with salt and pepper hair helped Karina to her feet.

"Both of you can go to hell! You've always been jealous!" Karina screamed and tossed the devil horns from her head at Nate as she exited the venue, followed closely by Royce.

"Let's get you on your feet," the older bouncer said, attempting to help Karina up.

"Hands off!" Karina screamed, flailing her arms and shaking free from the bouncer. She then made her way through the crowd of costumed partiers and exited toward the club's rear, using her cocaine laced bullet every step of the way. Karina swore she knew Nate better than Nate knew herself. There was no doubt in her mind that Nate would turn Simon in. That was a given.

Once outside of the club, Karina marched through the parking lot, hopped into her car and shot off a simple, two-word text to an unnamed person in her cell phone: "game time." In the time it took Karina to light up a hand-rolled clove and initiate the sunroof, the texter on the other end responded—using only the red-faced, horned ogre emoji. Next, Karina rifled through her glove box, tossing its contents, including a box cutter onto the floor mat until her trembling fingers eventually pulled out a CD case. She was frantic. The amount of shame that rocking a jailhouse jumper would bring to Karina's family had the backstabber on the verge of breaking down.

"Call Simon!" Karina barked the command into her Bluetooth and as the phone began to ring, she emptied cocaine onto the case and pulled out a metal straw from her business card holder. Then the call was declined. Karina growled like a mad dog and again commanded the Bluetooth into action. "Call Simon!" She said, inhaling two fat lines as the call was sent to voicemail several more times. "Damn it!" Karina cursed the situation as the streetlight reflecting off the box cutter caught her attention. She reached for the tool and as she gripped the cold steel in her warm hand, Karina exhaled deliberately and again engaged the smartphone. "Call Simon." Noticeably soothed, Karina waited until finally, there was an answer.

"We have nothing to say to each other," Simon groaned as his voice reverberated through Karina's luxury ride.

"That's where you're wrong," Karina objected. She then flicked the button of the box cutter so that it's razor-sharp blade projected into the dense night air.

Chapter 27

Halmoni

It was Tru's first night off in weeks, but instead of relaxing, she used the downtime as most entrepreneurs do—planning her next big move. Tru was determined to open up her lounge and beyond ready to turn the page on her dominatrix duties. Having scouted a dozen locations with Karina, she clicked through pictures on her laptop of The Carlyle—a dilapidated old hotel that she'd stumbled across a few months back on her own.

During the 1960s, music legends like Lena Horne, Ray Charles, and even Celia Cruz had graced The Carlyle's stage. Several decades later, the hub was reduced to little more than a shell of its former self. Just thinking about the amount of work needed to revive the timeworn venue gave Tru heart palpitations. On the other hand, because the neighborhood that housed the historic hotel was undergoing significant gentrification, The Carlyle could be an excellent investment.

Tru had driven past the hotel at least a dozen times in the year or so that it had been on the market, but it wasn't until one early morning after hosting an older couple's sexcapade that something propelled her to hop the fence and give the place a good once over. Tru used the trackpad to maneuver past picture after picture of six stories that overlooked an old swimming pool and a mangled cluster of overgrown landscaping. The ballroom was also a disaster with its musty, abandoned furniture and graffiti-covered walls, but it hadn't always looked like that. Tru visualized the Queen of Salsa backed by the infamous Tito Puente Orchestra belting out the classic Guantanamera to a full house. It was magical. The place had charm, history and quite possibly a future.

"That one's a real fixer-upper," Tru's grandmother whispered into her ear as Tru navigated across the still images. "Keep the faith sonnyeo," she continued, using the Korean term for granddaughter, "that small business loan is right around the corner—I dreamt about it."

"Thanks, Halmoni," Tru replied, using the Korean word for grandmother, "but I don't really feel like talking," Tru whined and pushed the prescription glasses back up the bridge of her nose. Makeup free, wig-free and sans contact lenses, the natural beauty exuded authenticity yet extreme vulnerability.

"Oh, please," Tru's grandmother retorted. "You pay rent, but my name's on the deed."

"Yes, Halmoni," Tru conceded as she rejected yet another call from Nate.

"Five missed calls?" Tru's grandmother pried. Nate was relentless. Since their fight, she'd reached out via voicemail and email. But the texts were genuinely unnerving: "Marley, Garvey, Montego Bay. My treat." Tru dealt with the pressure the best way she knew how—avoidance.

"I'll call her later. Keep 'em guessing, right," Tru smirked, quoting the phrase that her grandmother had drilled into her head from a young age.

"If you're going to quote me, please get it right," the sassy matriarch stipulated as she placed a pile of mail onto Tru's desk. "Nate's your friend, right? The one you won't let me meet?"

"It's not that I won't let you meet her, Halmoni. It's just that we haven't had the chance," Tru said, minimizing the photo application on her laptop. Afterward, she cracked open a beer and turned to face her grandmother.

"Mantra is not meant for friends. Mantra is meant for suitors," the bubbly senior responded. She then picked up one of Tru's brightly colored wigs and began combing it as Tru raised the frosty bottle to her mouth and took a swig of the local IPA. "Unless," Tru's grandmother paused deliberately before continuing, "Nate's more than a friend."

Tru's grandmother tried on the neon wig, while Tru, so embarrassed by the inference, nearly choked on the microbrew. "We're just friends." Tru lied, not because she suspected her grandmother was homophobic, but because admitting the truth to her grandmother meant admitting the truth to herself.

"Smart, private, can't hold your liquor," the older woman teased. "Just like your mother," she laughed. "My Yooni was so secretive that I didn't even know you existed until she was seven months pregnant."

"Yes, I know Halmoni," Tru continued. "I'm sure she beat herself up for getting pregnant during what should've been a carefree, one-night stand."

"On the contrary." Tru's grandmother took off the wig and walked over to Tru so that they were both staring into the mirror positioned behind Tru's desk. "Yooni loved you from day one, but because she thought me and granddad would not accept our beautiful, brown grandbaby, you gestated in secrecy." Tru's grandmother dipped her fingers in a coconut-oil based moisturizer and began to run each finger down the parts of Tru's cornrows. "I couldn't admit it then, but she was right. Yooni was unwed and pregnant by a..."

"Black sailor," Tru interjected. Although she'd never met her father, Tru had heard the story multiple times and was easily able to finish her grandmother's sentence.

"Exactly," Tru's grandmother sighed. You could hear the guilt in her voice. She then dipped her fingers in the moisturizer again, taking the time to phrase her words carefully. "We were ignorant. Too concerned about what other people thought. But that all changed with hal-abeoji."

In all the times her grandmother had told the story, her grandfather was never a principal player.

"Grandpa?" Tru inquired, suddenly astute.

The matron nodded affirmatively. "Three hours after you were born, Yooni passed, and I lost my mind." She laughed, recalling the memories as if yesterday. "I jumped right into funeral plans while grandpa stayed with you at the hospital day and night. It was love at first sight."

"I can't believe grandpa slept somewhere other than his bed."

"It's called sacrifice. And like grandpa, when your mom found out the cancer was back, she refused chemo because even though it might've saved her life, it wasn't good for her baby girl. That's how much she loved you," Tru's grandmother professed.

"I'll never forgive myself," Tru said fighting back tears.

"Oh, Truly, this story isn't meant to make you feel guilty. It's a cautionary tale," the matriarch continued. "My Yooni was supposed to be a great architect. The first in the family." A sense of pride consumed the older woman as she spoke about what could have been. "She wanted to get married, have a family, travel the world. Instead, she spent the last year of her life fighting cancer." The matriarch paused, taking a moment to mourn her deceased child.

"I can't imagine." Tru wiped away tears as an alert on her laptop beeped—Hallows Eve Fetish Fest. She scrambled to hide the reminder, but her grandmother never missed a beat. She knew full well that Tru did a lot more than model, but the older woman didn't see the point in bringing up something Tru was clearly hell-bent on keeping hush-hush. She did, however, find no qualms in hinting.

"You are a strong woman like Yooni, but careful not to be so strong you don't let anyone in." Tru's grandmother ran her finger down the last part in Tru's head and then screwed the top back onto the moisturizer.

"I understand, Halmoni." Tru wiped tears from her eyes as she began to sort through the pile of mail.

"Do you?" The grandmother continued as Tru nodded affirmatively. "She would have been fifty this Friday."

"What's this?" Tru held up a 6x9 manila envelope addressed to her from her dearly departed mother.

"You know in this family. Birthdays are more about giving than receiving," Tru's grandmother reminded her.

"Tradition."

"Very good, Truly. And in keeping with that tradition, a gift from Yooni to you." She wiped tears of awe and joy from Tru's eyes. "One of her last wishes was that I mail this the week of her 50th birthday."

"You're serious?" Tru asked, examining the handwriting. She then ran her hand carefully across the envelope as if it were brail.

"I'll leave you with it," Tru's grandmother smiled.

"Should I wait until Friday to open it?" Tru's voice was suddenly full of unease, but her grandmother gave her a calming kiss on the top of her head and then let the door close behind her.

Tru placed the envelope down beside her computer, took another swig of the now room temperature beer and then she looked down at her phone. Five missed calls and one voicemail, all from tonight and all from Nate. Consumed by thoughts of the mother she never knew, Tru sat there for a moment, her gaze shifting from the envelope to the cell phone and back. Finally, she pressed play on the voicemail from Nate.

"I know we aren't exactly speaking, but if you were ever my friend, please call me." Tru listened closely as Nate continued, her pace rushed and tone frantic. "I was attacked. Karina set me up," Nate spoke through sobs. "I'll be at the field. I need you."

Tru rewound the message several times. "I was attacked. Karina set me up." Tru reacted without thinking, first grabbing her wig and keys and then heading for her car. So much for her night off.

Chapter 28

EGO

Tru entered the car wash code and then pulled into the drive through as an older model sedan exited. Once positioned in front of the sensor, the light turned red and Tru threw the car in park as high-powered hoses began to fire water from every angle. Tru wanted to run to Nate—to comfort her, but a combination of pride and fear rendered the dominatrix oddly inflexible. So, she stalled, electing to hit the car wash before meeting Nate at the soccer field.

And so as the blue rags spun in circles and slapped soap against Tru's cherry red ride, she too yearned to come clean. She had never said it aloud, but Tru was slowly beginning to realize that she'd outgrown their casual friendship. She wanted more. However, at this stage in the game, the chronic business planner wasn't ready to broach the girlfriend topic with Nate. Not until she crossed a few things off her list. Namely, her job. Tru simply could not manage her clients and a serious relationship, but she was working on that.

The next cycle initiated and the hoses began to rinse away soap suds. Tru remembered how her abusive ex-girlfriend had suddenly shown up at Trois nightclub late last night, begging for forgiveness. Despite how volatile their short-lived relationship had been, something told Tru to hear the woman with the Anderson Cooper crew cut out. Because her ex-girlfriend understood that time was money, she booked the remainder of Tru's shift so that they could talk.

Tru listened as her ex-lover explained that she had been sober for only a few months and had spent much of that period apologizing to people she'd hurt. Tru was the last person on her list. She had come to the club last night, not to indulge in kinky fantasies, but to beg for forgiveness. By the end of their conversation, Tru couldn't be more thankful. Tru had consistently been denied small business loans and the woman knew that. And so in addition to atoning for her shortcomings, she showed up to the club to connect Tru with her personal banker—one word from her and Tru's small business loan was a go.

"She's expecting your call," Tru's ex said, handing her the banker's business card. "It's all legit."

Tru was ecstatic. She'd dreamt of opening a lounge her entire life and now her aspirations were well within reach. Tru had even settled on a name for the venue—EGO—Eternally Grateful Optimist. She couldn't wait to tell Nate. However, first, she needed to find out what happened to her. Then she'd, of course, have to kick Karina's ass or better yet, hire some round-the-way girls to do it for her.

Feeling increasingly protective, Tru looked up to see what cycle the wash was on and was startled by someone standing at the exit dressed in black nylon pants and an eerie unicorn mask. The person had a small frame and she wore a creepy shirt with a jack-o'-lantern design. Tru sized the mysterious female up and told herself that, if the woman did anything crazy, she would accelerate. Tru then gripped the steering wheel as the assailant brandished a machete from behind her back and slowly approached Tru's vehicle.

"Oh, hell no," Tru said. She then punched the gas but grew shocked when it would not move. So consumed in grandeur dreams of entrepreneurship and being in a loving relationship with Nate, Tru hadn't noticed the veiled prankster place a cinder block in front of her tires. Without warning, the masked assailant hit the system's power down button and then accelerated, landing on the hood of Tru's car. In full-on survival mode, Tru instinctively threw the hybrid in reverse but quickly discovered that the rear tires had been barricaded by cinder blocks as well.

"Shit." Tru braced herself and prepared to fight, as the disguised goon used the butt of the machete to bang on Tru's windshield. Realizing that the machete could at any moment slice through the Beemer's soft top, Tru began to blow the car's horn in a desperate attempt to gain the attention of anyone within earshot.

"Gotcha!" The horned trickster said, bursting out in laughter. She then rolled quickly off the hood, dropping her cutlass in the process. Next, she re-engaged the rinse cycle and fled through the rear of the carwash. Once Tru zeroed in on a shopkeeper approaching from the front, she hopped from the car and tossed the cinder blocks that were obstructing her front tires aside.

"You okay in here?" The shopkeeper quizzed as he disengaged the wash, which had left Tru soaked in a matter of seconds.

"Halloween prankster," Tru said, catching her breath. She then examined the discarded knife and immediately realized that it was fake.

"She left this behind," Tru said as she tossed the dime store prop toward the shopkeeper. Just a few blocks away, a dressed down and sweaty Nate played soccer alone, kicking a ball into a net. Nate remembered the look on Simon's face as he lay there cowering in pain after she zapped him with the stun gun. Then, Nate thought of Karina and how she'd repeatedly betrayed her.

Would Tru ever show up? Did Karina deserve to go down? The woman was mad but as crazy as Karina sounded, she was also Nate's first American friend. Despite their eye-opening altercation, Nate felt an underlying loyalty to Karina. As for Simon, although he'd kidnapped her, everyone had seen Nate go willingly up to his room. Why would the police take her word over Simon's?

"I got your message," Tru's voice was soft and as she knelt down, Nate sat immediately up, surprised by Tru's presence.

"You're here," Nate said, collapsing into the shelter of Tru's chest. "I'm sorry." Nate laughed nervously and wiped tears from her eyes. "You're soaked."

"Just tell me, what happened. Are you ok"? Tru asked. "Who attacked you?" She checked Nate for injuries. There were no bruises and aside from Nate's emotional state, no visible proof that anything had gone awry.

"Simon did it! Him and that rasta-imposter. They had this camera, and the suite had a remote control door," Delirious, Nate took a moment to compose herself and then laid out everything that happened that night. How Simon and his henchman had kidnapped her and how she was able to escape thanks to the stun gun that Tru had gifted her. Nate told Tru all about the masturbation video and how Karina admitted to setting the whole thing up.

"Say the word, and I'll put out a call," Tru said, scrolling through the contacts in her cell phone. "I know people that can make a person disappear," she said, snapping her finger. "Simon Herbst and Karina Zakaryn. Whereabouts unknown. I'm just saying."

"You're sweet," Nate laughed, letting her guard down as she nuzzled into Tru's shoulder. "But you're no killer—unless you count lady killer," she joked. The mood needed some lightening. The reunited gal pals laughed, and for a moment, grew lost in the stillness of the night sky.

"Seriously, I don't care how long you've been friends or what reason she gave you for putting you in the lion's den," Tru said, helping Nate to her feet. "The bitch has a screw loose. We're reporting both of them."

"You know how this goes," Nate interrupted. "I can't just go up there and say billionaire boys club kidnapped me. Not to Rampart P.D.," she scoffed. "With these dreads and highly melaninated skin, I need tangible proof." Nate was interrupted by a ping from Tru's cell phone. "Go ahead. I know you need to answer that," she instructed.

"Off the clock tonight. I meant to leave it in the car," Tru said, glancing at the phone before shoving it back into her purse.

"The laptop," Nate responded numbly. Simon's laptop was in her car. She had almost forgotten that she'd stolen it from his suite. Suddenly Nate grew curious about what else lived on that laptop.

Chapter 29

Simon Says

"That video was for your eyes only, Simon! An appetizer," Karina said, screaming into the phone as she headed north on the Los Angeles Freeway. "Nate was the main course! And why you thought it was a good idea to involve your idiot friend is beyond me."

"Nothing about this is hard to understand, you pudgy little…" Audibly unnerved, Simon took a moment to composes himself. Five months had passed since he assaulted Karina at the house viewing, but because Simon had ultimately purchased the home, in his opinion, they were even. In addition to the commission from the sale, Karina had signed an NDA stating that she'd never mention their sexual encounter. She'd all but disappeared from his life until recently.

"I should've known you were bat shit crazy when you rolled up on me at the park last week," he laughed. "I humored you, and dear Lord, I can't tell you how much I regret that, but I'm done. I want nothing to do with you or that bitch with the stun gun," he sighed.

"Stun gun?" That was news to Karina.

"She lit me up!" Simon groaned.

"You let that happen?" Karina asked, laughing, "You are dumb!"

"And your head game's weak," Simon spouted off.

"You're deranged," Karina scoffed while careening in and out of the expansive freeway lanes. "I know Nate and I can't be the only ones you violated. Don't make me start digging," Karina threatened.

"Let's cut to the chase here, honey. Your services are no longer needed at Herbst."

"You have no legal grounds to terminate my contract. None that you can prove anyway." Karina paused. "My father's lawyers will..."

"It's done," Simon interjected. "You can expect a parting gift from LAPD tomorrow morning," he scoffed. "Simon says, consider yourself restrained." He hung up the phone.

"No!" Karina slammed her fist hard against the driver side window, catapulting herself back to the day of the Hollywood Hills house viewing. She remembered how infinitesimal she felt, her knees raw and blouse covered in Simon's spunk.

"You're a mess," Karina recalled the playfulness in Simon's voice as he tossed her a kitchen towel.

"So, we've got a deal?" Karina quizzed.

"I'm a man of my word, but we're not done—not yet anyway," Simon said loosening his tie and stepping toward Karina.

"Simon, no!" She mustered up the most authoritative voice possible. "If I'm not back at the office soon, my mother will send a search party," Karina said in her last-ditch effort to evade further sexual advances, but even the fear that someone could at any moment knock on the mega mansion's front doors did not stir Simon.

"You can't just leave," Simon whined. He then pushed Karina hard against the kitchen wall. Karina tensed to her core, remembering and reliving the moment. His breath. His energy. His scent. Overcome unexpectedly by nausea, Karina exited on to Riverside Drive and white-knuckled the steering wheel. She sniffed and swore she could smell Simon's rank aftershave. Panicked by his reflection in her rearview, she turned to examine her backseat only to discover—nothing.

"I'm bugging," she said to herself. Then she continued a quarter mile up the road to Egret Park as the mental tug of war continued in her head. Karina remembered Simon's words as clear as day: "Relax." Those were Simon's words, but up until this very moment, she hadn't been able to remember what happened next. "No!" Karina said, but Simon stifled her voice with his body.

"Oh, come on," he sighed into Karina's ear. "Simon says, play nice."

"Simon says." That was it. Karina repeated the phrase aloud, then drove as far as she could into the park. The fact that he had uttered those same words during the assault and had also ended their phone conversation with the phrase had proven one thing: the predator had a pattern.

Karina got out of her car and meandered the bicycle path for a beat on foot. Once the L.A. River was in her sights, she climbed down the concrete embankment and tossed the burner phone into the raging water with a grunt. Twenty minutes later, she used several crisp bills to bribe Nate's stand in doorman. She assumed that the regular guy had called in sick since she'd gifted him a laxative laced iced coffee just last night. After taking the elevator to Nate's floor, she slipped on a pair of disposable gloves and used a credit card to break in. Once on the other side of the darkened apartment, Karina promptly thanked God for YouTube—there wasn't much that couldn't be learned on the free site. Next, she slipped quietly into the bathroom and snatched up the two hidden HD cameras that she had planted. Karina slithered through the unlit apartment with the stealth of an alley cat, reached for the doorknob and was almost home free until...

"Hey," Karina said, bumping into Nate's neighbor upon exiting the apartment. "Anthony, right?"

"Ant," the long and lean man replied, looking over Karina's head into the quiet apartment.

"Whatever." Karina slammed the door behind her and then continued, "Nate's not here."

"I was just returning these," he responded, holding up a set of borrowed records. However, Karina could care less. She pushed past him and fled down the stairs, taking two steps at a time. Moments later, the elevator at the end of the hall dinged and opened as Nate and Tru rushed out.

"Nate!" Yelled, Ant.

"Can't talk," Nate said, hurrying toward her apartment.

"Your records," he said, holding up the vintage vinyl with a smile.

"Keep them," Tru answered for Nate as she took Nate's hand in hers and rushed toward the residence.

"Cool," Ant said, reaching for his doorknob, and then, he remembered. "Hey, you just missed Karina." This tidbit was enough to stop Nate and Tru in their tracks.

Chapter 30

Sasha Harper

"This is exactly why we should've gone straight to the cops," Tru groaned. In search of a hidden camera, she used a stepladder to access the top of the bathroom vanity. "We're wasting time and getting our fingerprints on everything," she said, hopping down from the ladder.

"She didn't leave any prints," Nate replied fingering the doorframe for hidden objects. "Remember, Ant said Karina had on disposable gloves."

"Then we're tampering with evidence," Tru responded calmly." We've torn this bathroom apart. Let's get to the police station." Tru hit the light switch and ventured into the hallway. "She must've taken the camera with her."

"Or maybe she moved it to another room," Nate said, swinging the studio door open as if she expected Karina to be waiting there. "She's probably watching us now," growing more enraged by the second, her typically subdued accent bubbled like lava to the surface. "Bumbaclott!" Nate craned her neck and flipped Karina the bird, just in case she was still spying.

"I doubt that," Tru said as she turned on a nearby lamp and began to thumb through Nate's records. "She's smart and trying to cover her tracks," Tru grimaced. "So is Simon for that matter."

"I can't believe that bastard broke into my car," Nate whined. She then collapsed onto the futon. Its windows bashed in and back seat littered with glass, Nate recalled how she and Tru had found her car vandalized outside of the soccer field.

"It's not here!" Nate searched for the laptop. After escaping Simon's suite, she had hidden the laptop under a crate of records, and now it was nowhere to be found.

"He must've had the tracker on," Tru said, slamming the trunk shut. Now, about an hour after realizing that the stolen laptop had been reclaimed, Tru took a seat beside Nate on the futon and spoke with a sense of urgency, "I'm telling you, the sooner we report everything, the better."

"The fact that you think these cops give a damn about my black life is mind-boggling," Nate sighed.

"I know you not about to let these privileged assholes walk," Tru reasoned.

"I just need proof," Nate sat up suddenly empowered.

"Maybe Simon's assistant has something to say. You said he was acting weird, almost warning you."

"And bite the hand that feeds him? Not likely." Nate stared off into the distance. "Unless." She doubted Simon's staffer would squeal, but Tru had sparked something. Nate hopped to her feet and began to pound the keys of her laptop with the ferocity of a court reporter.

"What are you looking for?" Tru asked.

"Kevin—Simon's assistant, dropped a bunch of legal papers earlier today. One of them said, in-demnity," Nate struggled to pronounce the word.

"Indemnity," Tru repeated effortlessly.

"Yes! Indemnity." Nate continued to type.

"It's basically compensation for damages," Tru rattled off the definition as Nate googled it and was left staggered by the depths of her legal prowess. "What?" Tru shrugged. "A lot of my clients are attorneys."

"Another one of the papers had a woman's name on it," Nate said, navigating to Facebook. She then began to type a series of names in hopes that something might look familiar. "Sarah, Sandy, Sophia—Sasha. I think that's it."

"How about the last name?" Tru pushed.

"Something with an H—Hancock, Harrison, Hanson—damn! I'm drawing a blank," Nate groaned.

"Well, at least we know Simon is paying Sasha off. Keep trying. Something will click," Tru encouraged.

"Harvey, Henderson, Hill." Nat grew frustrated and began to waffle. She looked at the digital wall clock. In twenty-four hours, Nate would board a flight back home. She'd nurse her sick Auntie Earlene and deal with the skeletons she left behind. Nate didn't have the bandwidth to handle any more drama, and with that, she exhaled and quietly shut her laptop.

"I'm good," she concluded.

"You're not," Tru said, opening the laptop. "You escaped, but what about the girls that didn't?"

"Now you sound like Karina," Nate sighed. "Whose side are you on?"

"You aren't seriously asking me that," Tru said, refusing to dignify Nate's question with a response.

"I'm saying, Karina was practically begging me to go to the cops. I guess I feel bad for her if it's true that Simon assaulted her," Nate got up from the computer and spoke while peering out the window onto the quiet streets below. "But why does this fall in my lap?" Nate asked turning to face Tru again. "If something happened to her, she should've reported it right there and then."

"A lot of people don't," Tru reminded Nate of a fact, they both knew all too well.

"Shame, guilt, embarrassment, fear of retaliation," Nate sounded off as she backed away from the window.

"Or worse, fear no one will believe them," Tru added to the growing list of reasons many victims exercise their right to remain silent. "I by no means agree with Karina's methods, but she was right. You're the perfect bait," Tru professed, as she pulled Nate's chair out for her. "She knew you wouldn't let Simon slide. It's not in your character."

Nate humbly accepted the seat and conceded with a smirk, "Where would I be without my moral compass?" She then continued to type. "Holmes, Holt, Hardy." This went on for a good while longer before Nate typed in the six letters that would prove to drastically change the trajectory of her night— Harper.

"Sasha Harper?" Tru leaned over Nate's shoulder, peering at the screen.

"I think so," Nate said, nodding her head.

"Great, there are only twenty-eight people with that name, so start narrowing it down. How many live in Los Angeles? Any mutual friends?"

"A lot of these accounts are private, but I'll check." Nate began sorting through the multitude of social media profiles as Tru laid on her back, tossing a soccer ball up into the air.

Nate used the mirror positioned above her computer to glance at Tru. "Thanks again for coming," Nate smirked and continued studying the random profiles, unsure of what exactly she was looking for.

"You said you needed a friend," Tru responded as she continued to toss the ball up and down casually.

"I guess that's all we'll ever be," sighed Nate.

"Ouch!" Tru winced.

The pink elephant in the room had now taken center stage and would prove impossible to reign in. Nate went with it. "I get it. We said no strings and now I'm the one changing course, but it's been a year," Nate groaned and spun around in her chair to face Tru.

"Let's focus on one thing at a time," Tru said as she cleared her throat and skirted the issue with the grace of a newborn giraffe. "Like the man that attacked you and the bestie who set you up," she redirected. "How many Sarah Harper's live in L.A.?"

"Fourteen," Nate responded rapidly. Even though the tone was casual, she was by no means done with her inquisition. "I'm just saying—I needed you tonight and I love you for showing up." For the first time, Nate had confessed her love for Tru and the declaration caught them both off guard. "Have you thought any more about Jamaica?"

Tru began to sweat. "You know Halloween is my biggest check of the year. I'm booked throughout the weekend," Tru reminded Nate.

"No pressure," Nate lied.

"I just need a little more time before I'm ready to take a romantic trip, meet the family and all that."

Tru could feel her heart racing as she spoke. "I'm this close to..."

"Early retirement. I know," Nate finished Tru's statement. "You've been retiring for as long as we've known each other."

"Yes, but you have no idea how close I am—how close we are," you could hear the excitement in Tru's voice. "It needs a lot of work, but I think I found the perfect property. I even settled on a name," Tru laughed, proud of the perseverance and tactical planning that had gotten her so close to actualizing her dream. "And I won't believe it until the ink dries, but a friend of mine said she'd hook me up with her banker. I'm finally gonna get approved for that loan."

Nate believed that by "friend", Tru meant an ex-girlfriend, and for good reason. Just that morning, she'd seen the two women cozying up outside of the club where Tru worked. But for fear of looking like a stalker, Nate elected to keep that to herself. Was Tru playing her, or was the thought of making their relationship official just as thrilling for Tru as it was for Nate?

"I'm happy for you," Nate sulked as she tried to read Tru's face.

"It sure doesn't feel that way," Tru replied, acknowledging Nate's long face. "Did you not just hear what I said? I found a place for the lounge and my friend hooked me up with her loan officer."

"My sick Auntie put a lot of things into perspective. I just don't want to waste time. Mine or yours."

Nate had no idea where she was going with the conversation. It was as if her body had been snatched and she was a passenger, merely along for the ride as some alien who knew not how to bite her tongue artfully steered the most direct conversation of Nate's life. "It's ok to say you don't want what I do."

"I'm just asking you to be patient," Tru replied.

"And I'm just asking you to be honest," Nate paused just long enough to let her insecurities get the best of her. "So, who's your friend?"

"What are you insinuating?" Tru queried, growing more irked by the second.

The reality was, there was nothing that Tru could tell Nate that would appease her. Nate knew that she had a plan and was committed to ending one thing before starting the next. Being more strategic than spontaneous, Tru was following a judiciously designed blueprint—retire from the dominatrix business, find a venue, open the lounge, then commit. Nate was asking that she skip steps and as tough as Tru was, she simply wasn't brave enough to take uncalculated risks. To make matters worse, Nate was insinuating that Tru had a side chick. She had some nerve! Tru opened her mouth to speak just as a knock at the door interrupted her. She took the opportunity and bolted for the door as Nate yelled from the studio, "Just leave it. It's probably, Ant."

Too late—Tru swung the door open and was greeted by someone she recognized instantly as the machete-wielding prankster from the carwash. The trickster was dressed in the same Jack-O-Lantern mid-drift along with black, Nylon disco pants and had ditched the mask and machete for a bottle of Pinot and a bag of what smelled like Nate's favorite takeout. "You!" Tru snarled as her face flushed with both fear and venom.

Part Four

Truth Be Told

Chapter 31

Lavash

Nate buckled her seat belt, checked the rearview mirrors and then pulled away from the tranquil, tree-lined street into the chaos inherent in her morning commute. After a quick left, Nate inched into the long line of cars on Riverside Drive and, too, began to head north. As her compact hybrid withstood the ebb and stagnant flow of rush hour traffic, Nate recalled last night. So eager to escape an uncomfortable conversation about the future of their relationship, Tru had made a mad dash to the front door. Nate assumed it was her neighbor Ant knocking, but once she heard the sound of a woman screaming, she knew it was anyone but. Frantic, Nate called out to Tru and rushed toward the front of the apartment. Once at the doorframe, Nate stepped over a bag of abandoned take-out food along with a bottle of premium Vodka. Nate remembered how she slowly stuck her head out of the apartment, looking first left and finally right, afraid at what she might encounter. There at the end of the hallway, Tru stood confronting a hysterical Abby.

Nate remembered how she'd called out, too scared to approach for fear of what Tru and the barely legal intern she'd bedded just forty-eight hours ago could be discussing. She recalled how Tru had remained in the young woman's face, all but daring her to lash out. Once neighbors began to pop their heads out of their doors, Nate had no choice but to react. She sprinted toward the commotion and wedged herself between the two women. Nate assumed the argument was about her hooking up with Abby, but she would soon learn that this beef had nothing to do with casual sex. After noticing several of her neighbors, cell phones in hand, and no doubt ready to report the disturbance,

Nate insisted they return to her apartment. Once back at Nate's residence, Tru immediately locked the door and propped herself against it as if she were a human barricade.

"Talk," Tru demanded Abby spill every bit of the twisted backstory that had brought them all to that moment.

Abby looked at both women, then smiled nervously before speaking. "The machete thing was a joke," she affirmed. "Lavash put me up to it."

"Lavash?" Tru repeated the name aloud.

"It's an Armenian flatbread," Nate said, recalling how the traditional unleavened bread accompanied damn near every meal she'd eaten as a teen at Karina's.

"Karina," Tru mumbled, allowing her body to slip down the heavy door and melt into the Autumn themed floor mat. "She claims they've never met."

"We haven't," Abby interjected, biting her bottom lip nervously. "We've only communicated through text, DMs and a couple of phone calls."

"Do you always get this cozy with randoms online?" Nate asked.

"I haven't met half of my online friends in real life," Abby's admittance was indeed a sign of the times. "Besides, Lavash isn't random," Abby continued her confession. "She said you'd been friends since high school, that you love Halloween and that each year you one-up each other. So I helped her with a couple of harmless pranks." The intern came clean about everything. "The carwash gag was a prank and so was stealing lingerie from your trunk."

"That was you?" Tru yelled as the pieces of the puzzle came together before her eyes.

"It was a joke," Abby shrugged before directing her attention at Nate. "She knew everything about you."

"Including my favorite place to eat," Nate sighed, eyeing the bag of untouched Mediterranean food on the floor.

"This is all a misunderstanding—I'm here to cheer you up. Lavash told me the meeting with Simon didn't go well tonight."

"Didn't go well?" Tru repeated, rolling her eyes.

"That's putting it mildly," Nate agreed.

"I told you Simon creeped me out," Abby took a deep breath and studied the room before continuing. "Bottom line, Lavash said that you liked me, so I shot my shot." Abby paused for a moment, hopeful. "Lavash was just trying to help."

"How romantic," Tru laughed. She then cracked the seal to the Vodka that Abby had brought over and took a swig.

160

"You haven't told her?" The intern's question caused Nate to break a sweat. At that moment, Nate realized—her night could not get any worse.

"She's amazing, but you already know that," Abby conceded with a smile, her starry-eyed vision obscured purely by puppy love. I thought we were heading in the right direction, after, well—our milestone," Abby smiled awkwardly as Tru read between the lines.

"Milestone?" Tru asked, trying to mask her jealousy. "Oh, so you two been kicking it," Tru scoffed. And you got the nerve to ask me about my friends?"

"We just," Nate stammered, as she strung together a succession of monosyllabic pronouns and verbs. "It was one time."

"It was Tuesday and it was everything," the intern smirked cautiously. "Listen, ladies. I'm not trying to get in the middle of whatever this is," she continued as Nate and Tru tried desperately not to look at each other. "It's all here. Every message," she said, pulling up first a text message stream that went back a good thirty days, followed by a direct message conversation that was just as old. The correspondences had started at the same time that Karina began working with the studio. Abby handed Nate the phone, then walked across the room, allowing her to examine the messages while Tru remained seated on the floor.

"This isn't Karina's number but everything she said is here."

"Fan-fucking-tastic," Tru said, sounding more enthusiastic about her second swig of Vodka than she was about the intern's multiple revelations.

As Nate pulled up to Herbst Studios that Thursday morning, she remembered how depleted Tru looked sipping Vodka straight from the bottle and how guilty she felt for being the source of her anguish. Then she exhaled hard and tried to push all that down. Nate hadn't slept a wink or gone to the cops. She did, however, plan out exactly what she would say when she saw Simon. Before reporting him to the authorities, Nate wanted to put Simon on blast in a public place in hopes of emboldening any other casualties—only, she hadn't anticipated what would come next. Nate punched in her security code several times, but the studio gates would not open. Next, she beeped her horn, until finally, a security guard carrying a box hopped from his guard shack and approached her vehicle.

"Hey, buddy," Nate said nodding at the guard. "My code's not working. Can you buzz me in?"

"Actually, I can't," the guard placed the box atop Nate's roof before continuing. "You aren't allowed on the premises."

"What?"

"I'm gonna need your badge, too," he continued.

"I'm fired?" Nate quizzed.

"Looks that way," the guard said, grabbing the box of Nate's belongings. "Pop the trunk." Nate did as instructed, first unlocking the trunk and then removing the lanyard containing her badge without a word. "I'm sorry," he said, looking back at the line of cars that had started to develop behind her. "You should go." He took the badge from her hand, prompting her to wince at the irony of uttering those exact words to Abby late last night.

Nate had suggested Abby leave, having concluded that the text and direct messages were all the proof she needed to confirm that Karina had devised a shady plan to not only destroy Simon but to get between her and Tru.

"I'll go," Abby sulked, "but what's Harper have to do with this?" The intern asked curiously as she glanced at Nate's computer screen and observed the list of Sasha Harper profiles.

"You know her?" Tru asked, finally moved to her feet.

"I know her," Abby replied assuredly, positioning the mouse over the familiar face. "She's my roommate. The one I was telling you about."

Chapter 32

Correction

Despite being an iconic Los Angeles landmark, the Hollywood Bowl was owned and operated by the Department of Parks and Recreation, which meant concert or not, the park was public. So after leaving the studio unemployed, embarrassed, and personal effects in tow, Nate headed in the direction of the Hollywood Bowl. The century-old, open-air amphitheater would allow Nate to sit with her thoughts and make a few calls.

"This is Nate—again," she said, clearing her throat. "I get it. You don't know me." Nate switched the cell phone from her left to right ear as she moved further into the famed venue on foot. "I know Simon Herbst attacked you. I can't get into it on the phone, but call me. Please." Nate paused for a beat before ending yet another unreturned voicemail to Sasha Harper. "I have a plan," Nate stretched the truth. There was no plan in place. Her goal was to humiliate Simon—that much was certain. The how, remained to be seen.

Nate stood at the base of the majestic 18,000-person venue and craned her neck skyward. Aside from a few landscapers milling about in the distance, she was completely alone. Taking comfort in the isolation, Nate began to climb, and with each stride—her next steps became even more apparent. Although she'd told Tru that she would not let Simon get away with what he'd done to her, the truth of the matter was, she had let predators go unchecked before.

Nate continued her ascent up the stairs, and as the orchestra pit became but a blip in her rearview, the knots in her stomach grew more and more taut. Nate followed the steep incline up—past rows D, E and F. She remembered smacking the childhood bully in the head with a jagged red rock and sprinting home, never once looking back. Too pissed to talk and too scared to cry, Nate never mentioned the incident to anyone other than Auntie Earlene. Nate scaled The Bowl, and although the early morning fog was still thick, the sun had started to break through. Even as the salty sweat from her brow began to intermingle with the tears she'd been too angry to shed all those years ago, Nate remained unrelenting in her hike.

Nate passed rows J, K and L recalling not only the assault that happened when she was a mere fourteen-years-old but the conversation between her mother and Auntie Earlene that followed. When she entered the home and didn't talk to either of the women, that was enough to set Cassia off.

"Come in my house without speaking again," Cassia mumbled under her breath as she poured herself an Appleton Rum straight up. "The girl is rude."

"Natty!" Auntie Earlene walked to the foot of the staircase and called out to her niece. Nate didn't answer. Instead, she let the sound of piano chords and heavy EDM synthesizers bouncing against her bedroom walls speak for her. "That's not like, Natty," Auntie Earlene grimaced, taking a seat at the far end of the ten-person table. "Want me to talk to her?"

"What vex Natty is no secret to me," Cassia said, sucking her teeth.

"Well, tell me then. What vex Natty so?" Auntie Earlene probed. Cassia picked up the bottle of rum again, admiring it as if she had never before laid eyes on the local libation. She took her time, first retrieving cubes from the ice bucket and finally dropping them one-at-a-time into her glass. "Cassia, please." Auntie Earlene couldn't be sure why Cassia was stalling as the women were barely on speaking terms. Auntie Earlene had only stopped by the house to pick up a few items for Barrington, as he and Cassia hadn't spoken since the fireworks on Easter Monday. As a matter of fact, shortly after Jocelyn and Nate ran away, Barrington left too. The only difference was the girls returned the next morning and Barrington was on day three of his hiatus from the Higgins home.

"Those two talentless brothers that Natty plays soccer with. I forget their names," she said, taking a minute to sip and savor the spiced rum. "The younger one is tall and goofy with dreads, while the other pickaninny is too short to take a shit by himself."

"The Campbells," Auntie Earlene nodded knowingly, her voice now raised in deliberate competition with Nate's stereo. "Winston and Jeffrey. Their grandmother and me go to the same church."

"Winston and Jeffrey Campbell," Cassia agreed. She then dove into the candy jar taking her time to free dark chocolate from its brash, albeit essential wrapper. "Their mother called, said Natty smacked the little one with a rock."

"No," Auntie Earlene gasped as she watched her sister-in-law suck rum raisin flavored candy from her slender fingers.

"Yes. Gave the boy a concussion," Cassia continued, doling out a recap of the story as if the incident hadn't happened to Nate but to a character on a novella she barely watched. "The Campbell's, of course, have no insurance, so came calling with their hand out."

"Natty wouldn't just haul off and smack the boy, unless he had it coming." Auntie Earlene replied, her voice still in blatant opposition to the frenzied EDM coming from Nate's room.

"I was trying to correct a situation," Cassia said, fidgeting with the recently upgraded diamond that resided on her ring finger.

"You didn't?" Auntie Earlene asked, almost afraid of the answer. This was the side of Jamaica that tourists didn't get to see—where homosexuality is not only a crime but deemed a mental deformity, curable by corrective rape. After taking a slight pause, Cassia nodded her head affirmatively, causing Auntie Earlene to explode and toss Cassia's still full glass of the national liquor against the hardwood floor.

"Don't be so dramatic," Cassia scoffed.

"Damn it, Cassia!" Auntie Earlene began to pace the room. "If I weren't saved, I would beat your rasclat ass right now!"

"Oh, please, Earlene. Trust, you don't want to ramp with me," Cassia countered. "This is about legacy, so I suggest you fall back. Nate is our daughter, not yours."

"You hired someone to violate her! My God Cassia, the girl is fourteen." Nate remembered how Cassia took a momentary pause when she saw Nate's reflection peering back at her from a mirror across the room. Instead of changing her tune, the sight of her daughter only caused the matriarch's commitment to intensify.

"Had she stayed, she might've liked it," Cassia said sucking her teeth and staring directly at Nate in defiance.

"I swear before God, if they hurt Natty, I will come for you," Auntie Earlene spoke, still unaware of Nate's presence as Cassia locked eyes with Nate, damn near daring her to speak. Nate froze, refusing to humor even a blink. "They will have to put me under the jail! You over stand?"

"Instead of threatening me, you should talk to Barrington," Cassia countered. "Maybe if he spent more time home Natty wouldn't seek attention from trash. "She's fallen for the help, for God's sake."

"Natty is a good girl and Jocelyn is her best friend," Auntie Earlene said as she got into Cassia's face. "How dare you do this?" She eyed Cassia with legit concern. "She's your child, Cassia."

"Exactly. My. Child," Cassia stressed. "For the hundredth time, you are not Natalia's mother!" Cassia had always felt jealous of the relationship between Earlene and Nate. "Everything I do is out of love for Natalia."

"If that was true, you would guide her. Encourage Natty to tone it down, to be more discrete," Earlene countered.

"A makeover," Cassia mocked. "Why didn't I think of that?"

"You're joking, but I can't imagine sacrificing my own daughter just to save face," Auntie Earlene sighed.

And then the memory of her mother and Auntie Earlene faded into the background as Nate again found herself racing through the Hollywood Bowl in the early morning. She reached row M and just as she had done so many times in the past, stopped to take in The Bowl's best vantage point of the emblematic Hollywood sign. As an ill-adjusted teen, Nate had always imagined herself free of her antiquated hometown, but never in a million years did she believe her dreams of escaping to Los Angeles would manifest. And yet as she gazed out on to that iconic sign and the domed concert stage nestled snuggly beneath it, Nate took a breath. This was where she was meant to be.

As she stood there, reeling from the nightmare of her youth and gazing upon The Hollywood Bowl's expansive forest green backdrop, Nate refused to be broken. Tonight, she would board that plane to Montego Bay and face her past head-on. Nate took a moment to collect herself in the nosebleeds as her childhood memories continued bubbling to the surface. She remembered it all. The sound of Cassia shattering the bottle of Appleton against the wall in a huff. The echo of Auntie Earlene's feet clamoring against hard wood while she scrambled up the stairs to console Nate. Nate even remembered hearing the bathroom door slam shut followed by Cassia's whimpers. Albeit it muffled, Cassia was undoubtedly crying. She really did want to accept Nate. She just didn't know how to. Cassia had been born and bred in a country that criminalized homosexuality and celebrated homophobic song lyrics. Like it or not, homophobia was a well-ingrained part of the culture.

After nearly two hundred steps, Nate had made it to the iconic venue's peak, and it was at that moment a wave of calmness washed over her. Unlike her fourteen-year-old self, twenty-eight-year-old Nate was a warrior, and with her sights trained firmly on Simon, she knew what she had to do.

Chapter 33

The Missing Link

"You know nothing about me. Stop calling!" Nate sulked as she read Sasha Harper's text message while stopped at one of Hollywood's busiest intersections. Although it was not the reply she wanted, Abby's roommate, Sasha, had at least gotten back to her. The legal papers addressed to her from Simon made it apparent that the young woman was being paid off for something that Simon wanted to keep quiet.

As a group of teens dressed in Halloween costumes raced through the crosswalk, Nate re-read the text message, "You know nothing about me." Technically while Nate didn't know everything, she did know a lot. Sasha Harper had come home devastated after a date with Simon. Shortly afterward, she traded in her bus pass for a brand new BMW, and then there were, of course, the court documents addressed to her. Thanks to Abby, Nate had found one more person to corroborate Simon's predatorial nature. Sasha Harper was the missing link. Now, if only Nate could get her to talk.

"I just need a few minutes…" Nate began to reply to the text but was interrupted by a row of cars beeping behind her. "Please call me," Nate finished the text, pressed send and was promptly hit with a response: "Leave Me Alone!" The combination of certain defeat and blaring car horns acted as triggers, carrying Nate back to her youth and the confines of her bedroom.

After confiding in Auntie Earlene about the attempted assault, Nate had made her swear not to press the issue. Since the attackers were unsuccessful and Nate had managed to escape, Nate convinced herself that it wasn't that big of a deal. Like many survivors, Nate wanted to move on. She and Auntie Earlene knew how things would play out because they'd seen it happen in the past. If she reported the attack, authorities would likely say it was Nate's fault, call her a sinner and tell her to repent. Auntie Earlene refused to let Nate go through that. So, the secret stayed in the family, and Nate's healing mantra was born: I'm safe. I'm breathing. I got this.

Afterward, Auntie Earlene left home with a suitcase full of Barrington's belongings, and Nate eventually drifted to sleep until Cassia's car horn jolted her awake. Stirred to her feet, Nate peered out the second-story window just in time to see Cassia shoo a groundskeeper away. Next, she signaled for Nate to come outside.

"I need you to help me carry a few items inside," Cassia said, grabbing her designer purse and shutting the car door behind.

"Okay," Nate replied. She then jogged down the porch steps, looked into the trunk and pulled out a top of the line keyboard workstation wrapped in gold, black and green ribbons. "This is mine?"

"You happy now?" Cassia replied.

"Very!" Nate exclaimed, resting the keyboard momentarily against the car to hug her mother.

"It was the most expensive one they had at the store," Cassia's hug was awkward and clumsy, so much so that the way she engulfed Nate was more akin to how a politician greets a constituent.

It was at that instant that Nate realized her happiness could be bought and consequently sold. Nate had convinced herself that she hated her mother and had spent the afternoon in silent protest. However, once Cassia presented the keyboard, the picket signs became little more than firewood and Nate became an official scab.

"Thank you!" Nate continued, accepting the peace offering while doing her best to mask an air of quiet self-loathing and tapered excitement. With Barrington oscillating between crashing at his sister's house to his private tryst, disguised as official government business, the tension in the Herbst home had been as thick as the fat meat on a pork rib.

"You can't live like this—not in Jamaica," Cassia concluded.

"I know," Nate sulked. She'd always had crushes on girls, and no matter how hard Nate tried to suppress it, it simply was what it was.

"Mommy just wants to see you thrive," Cassia said, lifting Nate's head so that their eyes met. "That means no more Jocelyn."

"But we're best friends," Nate whined.

"It's over," Cassia insisted. "You must correct yourself."

"I've tried, mommy," Nate sulked.

"So have I," Cassia countered.

Cassia truly believed that by enlisting Nate's attackers, she was doing right by her daughter. She'd seen gay people on the island lose everything from their livelihoods to their lives. Aside from ruining Barrington's political ambitions, homosexuality was not the life she'd envisioned for Nate, so Cassia paid the Campbell brothers to cure her. From Cassia's perspective, it needed to be done, and because of that fact alone, she would never apologize. With her olive branch accepted and order restored, Cassia had regained the upper hand.

Nearly fifteen years had come and gone since Nate had been manipulated by Cassia and bribed with the high-end keyboard. As Nate sat in her home studio, she laughed out loud, recalling that first song that she'd composed on the keyboard workstation. It was untitled, but after spending a full five hours locked up in her room, Nate had disassembled several EDM hits and reggae classics only to repackage them together into one hot mess of a track. Nate could not help but smile as she remembered her mother's candid reaction.

"What you think you can just mash up a bunch of songs and call it music?" Cassia asked, laughing, never one to pull punches. "It's rubbish."

"I'm experimenting," Nate replied. Years later she chuckled, finally admitting to herself that the track was indeed awful.

"Listen, Natalia, wasting time is a commodity Jamaicans can't afford, so I gonna be straight up with you." Depleted, Natty watched Cassia pour piping hot tea into a ceramic mug as she continued. "Music, piano, in particular, will look great on your university applications, but it isn't a career—not for you."

"You're joking, right?" Nate began to list some of her hometown idols. "The Heptones, Grace Jones, Bob Marley," Nate shrugged. "Any Marley actually."

"You know what those artists have in common that you don't?" Cassia queried.

"Tell me."

"Originality," Cassia concluded. She then placed two sugar cubes into the steaming cup of ginger tea before continuing. "All you've done is copy and paste a bunch of songs together," she laughed while stirring in the lumps of sweetener. You don't even have lyrics."

"Not all songs have lyrics, mommy."

"The good ones do. Now I know me never raised a quitter, so I want you to go back up and massage whatever that was you played me. Write some lyrics and let me hear it again," Cassia instructed. She was hard on Nate, but only because she genuinely wished the best for her.

"I want daddy to hear it first," Nate whined.

"Do it look like daddy here?"

"He promised he'd be home tonight," Nate complained.

"Promises make the sweetest lies, don't they?" Cassia asked, fiddling with her wedding band. "I'm gonna tell you like this, if you want people to listen to your music, the least you could do is have something to say." Back in her Echo Lake apartment, Nate sat up in her chair, recognizing instantly that she did have something to share and tonight's Halloween podcast was the perfect platform to do just that.

Chapter 34

Hallows Eve

Nate screwed the pocket-sized video camera into the mini tripod and positioned it directly beside her keyboard workstation. While she hadn't taken Simon's advice about enlisting a partner to co-host, in hindsight, she agreed that Simon was on to something when he encouraged her to film her podcast. His advice ricocheted like a game of pinball in her head—"People want to see you," and as fate would have it, not only did Nate want to be heard, but tonight, she also wanted to be seen.

Nate used a tiny remote control to press record on the HD camera, which immediately caused her face to appear on the monitor mounted in front of her. Next, she slipped on her wireless headphones and began a countdown: "3, 2, 1. Check, check." Satisfied with the clarity and synch of video and audio, Nate used the small remote control to zoom to a close shot of her face, followed by a medium shot and finally a wide shot.

After noticing that the soccer ball Tru had left behind was in the frame, Nate walked over to the sighed and rolled the ball out of the camera's sightline. Next, she tidied up a bit, first fluffing pillows and then tossing the empty camera box out of her shot. Often forced and typically fabricated, this was the exact reason why Nate preferred working behind the scenes. She hated the picture-perfect pomp and circumstance that accompanied video production.

After freshening up and packing a week's worth of clothes, Nate changed into a vintage tank top and a pair of black skinnies. Next, she draped her fanny pack to the handle of her suitcase and wheeled the luggage to the front door. With the clock ticking, Nate took one final look at her cell phone. The last text was from Sasha Harper. It had been sent earlier in the morning and its meaning couldn't be clearer: "Leave Me Alone." Nate responded with a link to her podcast along with a simple phrase borrowed from a timeless yet poignant piece of literature: "Lend me your ear."

Next, Nate lit an incense stick, dimmed the lights and collapsed onto the floor. She then leaned back against the futon cushions and shut her eyes. She had about five minutes before the show's start and thought about calling, Tru, but after how things ended last night, that wasn't an option. Having acquired Sasha's phone number from Abby, Tru and Nate advised her to leave the apartment. Mortified, Abby left without looking back, and Tru promptly shut the door behind her, unaware that she too would be dismissed.

"I got it from here," Nate's tone was direct.

"So, you don't want me to go with you to the police station?" Tru asked, confused.

"I'll go alone," Nate said, slowly slipping into self-sabotage mode.

"But I'm here," Tru replied, taking Nate's hand in hers. Nate hadn't just stalked Tru; she'd practically begged her to come back. And when Tru did, Nate found a way to derail the reunion. She'd hooked up with Abby. Given Tru shit about her timeline. And was currently letting a case of cold feet get the best of her.

"I'll call you," Nate said, forcing a strained smile.

"You asked for my help," Tru sounded genuinely perplexed. "Is this a game to you?"

"I wish it were," Nate's voice cracked. Subconscious or not, Nate was testing Tru's resolve.

"I'll call you," Nate responded knowingly. "Promise."

"If I walk out that door again," Tru's eyes began to water as Nate's hand fell from hers.

Less than twenty-four hours later, Nate was in her home studio, preparing for her podcast while re-living what was perhaps the last conversation she'd ever share with Tru. Too amped up on insecurity, ego had yet again allowed Nate to push Tru away. With sixty seconds on the clock, Nate popped up, stood behind her workstation and fired up the camera. Then she gently placed her headset over her ears and watched as the digital clock on the wall began to count down the seconds until the start of the show: 5, 4, 3, 2, 1.

Nate pressed play on the show's reggae-inspired intro and then leaned into her shoulder as she gradually began to cut and scratch between the intro and Michael Jackson's "Thriller." Bopping her head along to the beat, she

173

seamlessly blended the two instrumental tracks, but once Jackson's chilling iconic single took center stage, she slowly faded the volume down and assumed her place in the spotlight.

"Wah gwaan, everyone? This is Natty One on the ones and twos, and tonight, we are live and in living color!" The Natty One persona fit Nate like a well-worn glove. She was self-assured and expressive as hell. Being on the mic meant that the Caribbean twang she typically stifled was amplified and free to roam.

"Welcome to our first-ever video live stream, bredren! Happy Halloween!" Nate again leaned into her shoulder and spent the next minute intercutting the creepy Jackson track with an EDM cue that was just as eerie. On the laptop beside her, the podcast's social media page was blowing up with comments. Eventually, the EDM track had overridden "Thriller," and Nate once again lowered the volume, settled into her seat and began to speak.

"As always, I appreciate you tuning in, especially on a holiday. You looking good by the way." Nate said while scrolling across the party pics that listeners had begun sharing of themselves in costume. "As you know this is a no judgment zone. Good or bad each week you come on and tell your truth." Nate used the remote control to switch from a wide shot of the studio to a medium shot of herself. "I swear, sometimes I feel like a pastor behind the confessional wall," she said laughing. "You've inspired me to walk in my truth. So tonight for Halloween I've ditched the mask, because" Nate said, leaning into the camera. "It's my turn to confess."

Nate took a deep breath as she watched the headcount of the people listening ramp steadily up—23, 24, 25. "All I've ever wanted to do is make music. My best friend knew this and took advantage of me." Nate recalled how Karina made her feel stupid for even suggesting that it was weird she and Simon were meeting at a hotel. 33, 34, 35—the number of listeners increased as Nate, exposed her truth to everyone within earshot.

"I was almost raped last night. My best friend was behind everything. She set me up with a well-known television executive who has major music industry connects. What she neglected to tell me was that he sexually assaulted her. She knew he was a creep. Hell, she had first-hand experience," Nate tried to squelch nervous laughter. "This isn't even the first time that I've been assaulted," Nate continued. "But this is the first time I've spoken out." Nate cut to the close-up angle of her face and spoke directly to the camera. 98, 99, 100—as Nate's testimony intensified, the number of listeners had ticked steadily up.

"And if this podcast causes you to feel even an ounce of the fear that you put me through, well then that's a start—but I promise, it ain't the end."

Chapter 35

But You're Always Late

"We can't let predators skate, even if they are our friends." Nate's voice cut through Karina's apartment like a serrated knife through whipped butter as Karina continued to gut an heirloom pumpkin.. While she listened to the live stream on her phone, Karina meticulously used an X-Acto knife to follow the outline left behind by the black sharpie on the pumpkin's grainy orange flesh.

"You should be thanking me!" Karina replied to Nate's podcast as she removed the top of the pumpkin and began to pull out its slimy, pulpous insides. "Mention my name just one time, and I'll sue for slander," Karina threatened while flinging pumpkin guts into the stainless steel farmhouse sink.

"In her own twisted way I actually believe she was trying to help," said Nate. With her listeners now well over 1,000, Nate continued from her home studio. "But baby girl, please know that you don't sacrifice a friend to take down a predator."

"Are you kidding me?" Karina jabbed the X-Acto knife into what was quickly becoming the Jack-O-Lantern's mouth. "He deserved to be taken down and if you got scared or heaven forbid had your feelings hurt in the process, that's on you." Karina again reached into the pumpkin and used the knife's blunt end to knock excess pumpkin trimmings into the sink. "I'm the victim here!" She shouted.

Growing increasingly unnerved, Karina moved onto the Jack-O-Lantern's eyes, repeatedly thrusting the knife into the stringy carrot-colored flesh. Next, Karina moved onto the nose. Completely bypassing the sharpie's rendering of two circular nostrils, Karina plunged the knife into the gourd's center and elected for a more asymmetrical cut. As she carved away at the snout, Karina remembered how the snowflake colored cocaine she'd snorted that morning—yen, as her dealer called it—singed the fine hairs of her nasal cavity. To pass the time, she'd done several bumps in the parking lot of her family's real estate business before entering the building. After the scuffle with Nate, she hadn't slept a wink and felt the incessant need to self-medicate.

#

Standing there, elbow-deep in pumpkin waste, Karina recalled how she couldn't just saunter in early or even on time for that matter. After last night, she had to stick with her routine. Her paranoia level already on ten, Karina needed everything to look as normal as possible. So instead of entering the suite at Nine AM, Karina strolled into the office at half-past Nine.

Karina's hands began to tremble as she struggled to complete the final touches of the Jack-O-Lantern's menacing mouth. She would give anything for just one more bump. Alas, Karina was out, so for now, memories of the premium product would have to do. She recalled how the narcotic numbed her throat and how its pristine composition had left her equally aloof.

Upon entering the building, Karina barely greeted her colleagues before shutting the door to her glass fishbowl of an office behind her. She then hopped on to her PC and leaned on work as a distraction. 650 K, Brentwood, one bedroom. 999 K, Westwood, two bedrooms. 1.2 million, Beverly Hills, two bedrooms. Mother-in-law chalet included. Not even a full five minutes into reviewing the latest property listings, the office's receptionist pinged Karina on the company's internal messenger application: "You're needed up front."

Before Karina could respond, she looked up from her computer and locked eyes with two of Los Angeles' finest. As Karina searched her kitchen pantry for tea lights, she remembered the taste of fear in her cottonmouth. With no desire to create suspicion, Karina swallowed the trepidation like a wad of bubble gum and rose immediately to her feet. When she noticed the onslaught of lookie-loos that were suddenly walking back and forth in front of her see-through suite, Karina squelched her instinct to behave indignantly. Instead, Karina nodded in agreement as the Sheriffs doled out the conditions of Simon's restraining order. The officers were in and out rather quickly. However, it wasn't until she walked the officers through the mounting sea of co-workers that the situation got truly awkward.

"Why were those police officers here?" Karina's mother probed as soon as the authorities had exited the building.

"Nothing, Mayrik. Just a couple of speeding tickets," Karina responded to her mother as she observed the officers climb into the black and white squad car.

"Speeding tickets?" Karina's father asked, laughing. "But you're always late." Karina thought about laughing along with her father, but quickly recognized she was too frightened to fake it. Instead, she remained stoic, convinced her laughter might meld into tears. "It's nothing, hayrik," Karina lied to her father.

"It's always something, so tell me, Karina," her father prodded, as an entire office intently watched the scene unfold.

# #

The pumpkin now carved to completion, Karina placed several tea lights into the creepy gourd and lit them. In the background, she could still hear Nate on her show, encouraging others to speak out. "She can't prove anything, and neither can he," Karina said, glancing down at the holiday's mauled mascot. She then grabbed the restraining order and turned off all the apartment lights. "I was careful." Aside from the glimmer emitted from the live stream on Karina's phone and the ominous candlelight, her apartment was in complete darkness. Karina took a deep breath and then stuck the packet of papers into the Jack-O-Lantern allowing the blaze to creep slowly up the official order.

Next, Karina recalled all the ways that she'd covered her tracks. There was the ditched burner phone and hidden cameras, plus she'd never met Abby face to face. And then there was Simon. As far as Karina was concerned, it was his word against hers. Sure, she'd spiked the doorman's ice-coffee with a laxative, allowing her to go up to Nate's apartment unannounced, but no one could prove that. She'd also convinced Abby to bribe the fill-in doorman after her club beef with Nate. But if confronted, would the minimum-wage employee ever admit that he'd accepted money from Abby? Karina didn't think so. Convinced that she was in the clear, Karina grew enamored at the orange and blue flames that were slinking steadily toward her fingertips. Then she remembered her father's voice.

"It's always something, so tell me, Karina," Despite the chill in his voice, Karina had for a split second considered collapsing into her father's chest and sharing with him all of her woes. But she couldn't. As the blaze flickered and glowed, an image of Ant, Nate's neighbor, flashed before her now bulbous eyes. "Shit!" Karina screamed aloud as the fire burned her fingertips, completely engulfing the restraining order. As it turned out, she had not done her due diligence. Karina had nearly forgotten that she'd ran into Nate's nosy neighbor just as she had finished breaking into Nate's apartment. She needed to go back and stop him from talking to Nate if it wasn't already too late.

"Damn it!" Karina sprinted toward the back of the apartment, passing an image of Nate on her phone as the suddenly liberated podcaster began inviting her audience of now more than ten thousand listeners to call in and share their stories.

Chapter 36

Ten Stacks

"It breaks my heart to hear how many of you have been assaulted," Nate spoke lowly, using the video camera's remote control to switch from a medium angle to a wide shot. She then stood to her feet and continued her story.

"The week that I moved to the states from Jamaica, two boys jumped me." Filled with the nerves brought on by recalling this story, Nate began to pace. "I'll never forget how helpless I felt. They were strong, but I was smart and I knew in order to escape, I'd have to outrun them," Nate said, evoking images of herself crisscrossing a soccer field as she unwittingly averted her would-be attackers. "After they tackled me on a deserted backwoods road, they starting laughing, debating who would get to go first. The argument was short-lived as neither one of them had much of an attention span—idiots," Nate spoke through anxiety-ridden laughter.

"The shorter one moved in, while the taller boy watched from the sidelines. "Don't worry, She-Man," he told me, "you gonna thank us," Nate thickened her accent to parrot the island twang of her young, vertically challenged assailant.

"His smile was unnerving. How could such a young man already be full of such venom?" Nate shuttered at the remembrance as her tone grew sharper. "And then it hit me, or rather it hit him," she chuckled. "The boys had tackled me and in the struggle, I'd landed on a jagged piece of bauxite rock. That thing tore my back up." Nate's voice grew raw as she was reminded of the sense of empowerment that overtook her the instant she committed to salvaging her narrative.

"When I tell you I smacked the hell out of that boy with a stone—man, I thought for sure I killed him." Reliving her great escape, Nate paused for a beat in the middle of the studio to collect herself. "I remember crawling up from under him as the look of complete shock consumed his brother's face. Blood was everywhere. He must've thought I killed him too," Nate said, laughing.

"You would've thought I was Usain the way I bolted out of there," Nate said, settling back into her seat behind the workstation as listeners chimed in, at record number on the show's social media page. "After a half hour sprint, I reached the safety of home. I was sweaty, dirty and in complete shock, Nate pressed a button on the remote, framing herself instantly in a medium shot. "Isn't it funny how you can be completely honest with a room—make that, live stream full of strangers, and be scared as hell to share the same sentiments with your so-called loved ones?"

"You gone be cured," Nate again ratcheted up her accent to mimic the shorter boy's declaration. "Those were the last words he said before mounting me. Like he was doing me a solid by violating me on that dirt road," Nate sucked her teeth in disgust. "Later, I found out that someone who should've been taking care of me, someone whose job was to simply love me unconditionally, had paid them to rape me." Although she was fighting back tears, Nate cut to a close up. She was completely vulnerable and refused to hide from the authenticity of this moment. Hell-bent on reclaiming her narrative, Nate needed to be as unfiltered as possible.

"It's called corrective rape and it happens throughout the world. Jamaica is one of the countries where it's most rampant. People actually think that slipping a lesbian a bit of dick will set her straight. Ignorance. It's a hate crime and I hate that my own mother enlisted those young boys into something so evil." Nate paused for a beat letting the fact that she had just outed her mother sink in. "I was barely fourteen-years-old, and I hated myself because I couldn't change myself. Dyke, batty boy, she-man, I've heard it all," Nate shrugged indifferently.

"I never thought I'd tell my story to anyone, let alone the 12,000 people that are listening now." Nate cut to a wide shot and was seen scrolling across the comments left behind by viewers. "The attack has eaten away at me for years and I get it. I understand why people stay quiet, but I can't tell you how good it feels to tell the truth," Nate concluded.

#

Thirty miles away and nestled between the Pacific Ocean and Pacific Coast Highway, Tru sat listening from the driveway of a pristine beachfront mansion. So consumed by Nate's listeners sharing their personal tales of survival, Tru was practically oblivious to the scene developing around her. Partygoers, some costumed, many in the buff, and all in masquerade masks, traipsed in and out of the two-story estate's annual Hallows Eve Fetish Fest.

It was still early at a few minutes to ten, but some guests had already started to get things going. One couple danced and fondled each other alongside the infinity pool. And at the far end of the courtyard, two men sandwiched a woman between them. With only a wall for support, their naked bodies collided like waves against a sea wall.

"People are starting to ask for you," Tru's masked bodyguard said, hopping into the convertible's driver's seat as Tru remained perched on the cherry red hood like a provocative hood ornament. Dressed in a dark royal blue latex catsuit with a plunging neckline, Tru was the definition of dom. The confident cat woman had paired the skintight suit with an iron rod eye mask and cat ears combo.

"You coming?" The bodyguard asked.

"Let them wait," Tru responded. So engrossed in the current caller's story about being assaulted by his Sunday school teacher, Tru hadn't bothered to look over her shoulder to make eye contact with the man whose sole responsibility was to have her back. Both Tru and the guard remained quiet for the next several minutes as callers continued to weigh in. Assaults at the workplace. Attacked during early morning jogs. Date rape. Date drugs. Each story of survival was one that should have never been authored at all.

"You know I'm thinking seriously about sitting this one out," Tru spoke, still staring off into the distance, as unapologetic revelry developed swiftly behind her.

"Now, I know you're bugging." The masked man turned off the live stream, hopped from behind the wheel and met Tru at the car's helm. "I know you're not about to leave ten stacks on the table. Not for a booty call," he said, laughing as though the notion was as far-fetched as unicorns that crap rainbows or pigs that fly.

Her attention finally stirred, Tru stood up and ran her hand across the bright blue pixie cut which for the evening's festivities she'd slicked back with a sleek and shiny finish.

"We wait all year for this check," Tru's bodyguard stated the obvious. "You know I need it."

"And I don't?" Tru moved suddenly from her hair to the holster on her back, pulled out a riding crop and let it slap down hard into her bare hand.

"I'm saying—if you leave, I lose." The bodyguard complained.

"I'm gonna give you a pass because I know you help with your brother's tuition, but if you don't turn my stereo back on," Tru replied sternly, settling back into her role as a glorified hood ornament while the guard did as instructed. Promptly Nate's voice could again be heard coming through the car's sound system—only now Nate was giving out a hotline number for sexual assault survivors.

"Is this a damn PSA?" He joked. "I'm telling you if she would've just slobbed the knob, then the rich boy, whoever he is, would've hooked her career all the way up."

Tru climbed into the passenger seat and cut the bodyguard a lethal look. So immersed in his own bluster, he missed it and the man in the skeleton mask continued to dig his own grave. "Now she's jobless and reduced to crying about it online," he said, lighting up a cigarette and finally noticing Tru's stifled body language.

"My bad," he said, as plumes of gray smoke escaped through gritted teeth. Next, the veiled bodyguard extinguished the Marlboro Red and pushed it back into its carton as a few more people found their way to the pool, and several more stumbled onto the dance floor. The inside of the house had also begun to swell with swingers living out their sexual fantasies. Entirely glass, the open floor plan was a culmination of anonymous, multi-hued breasts and biceps. Tru's bodyguard took it all in, looking back and forth between Tru and the imminent orgy as several luxury two-seaters and SUVs pulled onto the property.

"Three nights, ten stacks," the bodyguard softened his tone as if trying to hypnotize Tru, but the way she leaned into the stereo while cranking the volume up ensured that she was already entranced.

"This is Sasha Harper," the caller cleared her throat, her nerves more prominent than stank on a skunk. "His name is Simon Herbst and he did the same thing to me. The only difference is, I couldn't out run him."

Chapter 37

She Who Can't Hear

Feeling accomplished, Nate tossed her luggage, a single backpack and suitcase into the trunk, slid her fanny pack around her waist and then hopped into the driver's seat. As she made her way south down Glendale Boulevard, reality began to set in. Nate had shared all the details about how she'd been accosted at the hotel, then escaped only to be fired the very next day. Nate hadn't mentioned his name, but Sasha had. In fact, she'd publicly corroborated Simon's predatorial nature. In complete shock that Sasha had even called into the live stream, Nate remembered how her voice quivered as she recalled the assault: "Everyone saw me go up to his room. In fact, I think he purposely took the long way—parading me around the hotel like some trophy. It sounds funny, but I was flattered." Sasha spoke of being wined and dined by Simon, just as Nate had been. "He was hot, older, successful. Every staff member knew his name. I was impressed and he knew it." The recollection of Sasha's voice resounded emphatically—as if she were sitting in the passenger seat alongside Nate.

"I thought we might hook up, but he pushed. He wanted to take it further, and I said no," Sasha spoke through sobs. "One minute, he was giving me a shoulder massage, and the next, he was using his necktie to strangle me. I must've blacked out because when I came to, Simon was inside of me," Sasha paused for a beat as images of her being defiled no doubt inundated her memory banks. "I swear I begged him to stop, but he wouldn't. Simon says you love it," she said, imitating the predator whose family name had allowed him to prey on the weak for far too long.

Haunted by Sasha's admission, Nate pulled up in front of the notorious Rampart Police station and put the car in park. Immediately her stomach began to knot up like an army of clenched fists. The controversial station was anchored in a legacy of scandal that ran so deep, it was no wonder Sasha had declined Nate's offer to join her. Sasha's head was still whirling from recounting the assault to an audience of close to thirteen thousand people— Nate's biggest tune in ever. She was thankful that Nate had pushed her and while filing a police report wouldn't happen that night, they both agreed it had to happen soon. To combat mounting nausea, Nate popped a ginger candy into her mouth and continued to watch the processional of accused criminals.

Back in the late nineties, Rampart's anti-gang unit was mired in corruption. The precinct was all over the news and the source of much theatrical fodder for crimes like falsifying evidence, drug dealing, robbery, perjury and assault. They'd racked up over $100 million in lawsuits, destroying countless lives in the process. Rampart's illicit happenings were the stuff rap songs were written about and movies were made. However, while she knew about these police scandals, aside from the hyped up security guard who had accosted her last night after arguing with Karina, Nate had never experienced an unpleasant run-in with the law.

So why was she tripping? Nate knew how to talk to people. Hell, she was born with a silver spoon in her mouth and, good or bad, unlike the so-called thugs being hauled into the station before her eyes, Nate had never experienced deprivation. Desperation had never driven Nate to commit a crime, and although she knew little about street life, Nate still reeled from its effects. Nightly news, pop culture and world history were saturated with people of color being violently battered by people in power. Whether plantation, street corner, or football field, to Nate, the similarities between overseer, officer and owner were rampant. Nate had been hurt in the past by those who were supposed to protect her and wondered if Rampart P.D. would be any different.

Nate slipped another ginger candy into her mouth, threw her shoulders back and then marched through the front doors. Yet, once inside the station, Nate was underwhelmed. The lobby was quiet and reminiscent of a DMV. Most people sat in hard metal chairs grimacing, while others paced about nervously as an officer behind a glass barricade kept a sharp eye out. Nate strolled up to the bulletproof partition while an officer in street clothes manhandling a teenager blew past her, pushing the handcuffed adolescent through a side door.

"May I help you?" Nate hadn't heard the officer behind the panel speak, but from his tone, she presumed that he was tired of repeating himself. "May I help you?" He asked again, clearing his throat.

"I'm here to report a crime," Nate said, swallowing hard as the officer held up his pointer finger before looking over his shoulder to relay her request to a fresh-faced rookie. Within moments, the rookie was on her side of the glass and chauffeuring Nate through that same side door. The lobby's silence faded and was quickly replaced by chatter from overly-tatted police officers, low-end prostitutes and convicts just shy of their third strike—all the images pop culture had imprinted on her psyche in living color. Even the young boy she'd seen being maltreated just moments ago was present, only now his stiff upper lip had started to quiver as the same plainclothes cop howled obscenities and pointed directly in his face.

"We're in here," the rookie motioned toward a room that felt more like a closet than an office. "Have a seat," the rookie said, pulling out a chair for Nate.

"I have a flight to catch," Nate replied, refusing to sit.

"Okay," the rookie responded, his arms folded suspiciously. "So, you aren't here to report a crime?"

"Everything you need to know is here," Nate spoke while retrieving a thumb drive from her pocket and sliding it across the table.

"That's not how this works," the rookie said with a laugh as he slid the thumb drive back in Nate's direction. "Haven't you ever been in a police station?"

"What would make you think that I have?" Nate queried, returning the officer's loaded question with one of her own.

"Listen, I need a written statement," he said, dismissing her question.

"And I need your help," Nate said, sliding the thumb drive back across the table, before turning to exit.

"Hold on. Please," the rookie appealed to Nate.

"I'll be in touch in a couple of days," she replied.

Nate ignored the young officer's request then moved swiftly through the door and down the hallway as the rookie succumbed instantly to curiosity. He took a seat behind the prehistoric PC and breathed a sigh of relief, thankful it had a USB port. After plugging the flash drive in, he noticed that the miniature storage device contained two folders: Simon Herbst and Karina Zakaryan. To the rookie, Karina was a nobody, but the Herbsts' were legendary. Based solely on familiarity, the inquisitive cop double clicked Simon's folder and pressed play on its contents—an mp3 entitled 1031 podcast.

It took just about thirty minutes for the skies to open up in a fierce downfall and for Nate to reach the extended parking at LAX. Once parked, she pulled on her hoodie and boarded a shuttle to the Montego Bay bound flight's assigned terminal. A weight lifted from her shoulders, Nate felt tremendous about turning Simon over to the police. However, she had disregarded every attempt the authorities had made to reach her. Voicemails, texts, phone calls—all ignored. Nate hadn't even bothered to listen to or read the messages.

She needed a minute to marinate on the past twenty-four hours, not to mention the good, bad and undeniable ugly that awaited her in Montego Bay. Nate looked out the rain stained shuttle window as the cramped bus finessed its way through the snarl of bumper-to-bumper LAX traffic. Nate smirked, contrasting the scene in front of her with what she remembered of Montego Bay. Quiet, lush and far from the concrete jungle, she now called home. And as tail lights refracted through dewy droplets and puddles of water, Nate was brought back to her Auntie Earlene's farmhouse.

#

It was the time of year where the sun lingers forever and tints the sky with awe-inspiring shades of blood orange and magenta. "They don't even love each other," a fourteen-year-old Nate spoke while watering the herbs in Auntie Earlene's garden. "Poppy show." Sitting there in that densely populated bus, Nate couldn't recall what her parents had done to piss her off, but her Auntie's reaction had stuck with her for years.

Like an undocumented foreigner, Auntie Earlene moved with stealth and resilience. First snapping a stalk of aloe between her nimble fingers and then splitting it down the middle with her nail before finally rubbing a heap full of its pungent contents inside of Nate's mouth.

"Auntie!" The hose dropped from Nate's hand as she spat out the jellied goo.

"No, sir." Auntie Earlene scooped another heap into Nate's mouth and all but dared her to spit it out. "She who can't hear must feel," Auntie Earlene turned her back to Nate so that she wouldn't see her laughing at the situation. "And stop wasting my water!" She exclaimed. "Now you can confide in me all you want, but disrespecting your parents is where I draw the line. You hear?"

"Yes, Auntie," her puckered mouth barely able to contain the bitter aloe Nate aimed the hose at the herb garden, allowing the cool water to saturate the plot of land that with its numerous natural remedies was more pharmacy than farm. As Nate made it through airport security, she remembered how Auntie Earlene took pride in the many medical benefits that her crops possessed. Lemongrass, peppermint, ginger, you name it—if the plant had a known healing property, Auntie Earlene was sure to propagate it.

"My brother and his wife may have a peculiar way of showing it, but trust, everything they do is for you—private school, private maid—you'd be hard-pressed to name just one thing you ever wanted but didn't get."

"Yes, Auntie," Nate replied as the succulent's unsavory innards began to take up residency on her tongue.

"It's natural to be vex with your parents now and then, but the key is forgiveness. Remember, not even you, my sweet niece, gets it right 100% of the time." Auntie Earlene pointed in the direction of the row of soursop trees and Nate began to douse the soil and leaves.

"Grudges will eat you up inside, but only if you let them," Auntie Earlene plucked several of the tree's prickly green fruit along with a handful of its leaves and placed them neatly into her basket." She then laughed quietly to herself as Nate grimaced at the tang of raw aloe—a unique punishment that Nate would never forget. "All right, chile, go on and spit."

#

As the lights in the first-class cabin dimmed, Nate threw the hoodie over her head so that it hung lowly over her eyes, while Karina let the hood of her rain jacket fall to her shoulders as she made her way down the long hallway that led to Nate's apartment.

Chapter 38

Breaking and Entering

Dressed in a white hooded cashmere rain jacket, fire engine red lipstick and black thigh high-boots, Karina approached Ant's apartment. Remembering that he had seen her leaving Nate's place last night, he was the final loose end that she needed to tie up. Dead-set on doing whatever it took to make sure Ant stayed quiet, Karina placed her hand into her jacket's deep satin-lined pocket. Then she allowed her thumb to gingerly graze the box cutter's shaft, continuously coaxing its steel blade in and out of hiding. She'd been light-headed on the drive over, but despite mounting wooziness, Karina ran through a few possible scenarios. Because she realized Ant was attracted to her, Karina would start by sweet-talking him. If that didn't work, she'd flash the wad of cash that was nestled snuggly in her other pocket.

"Karina?"

"Anthony," Karina answered as her last loose end stepped from his apartment. She contrived the biggest smile she could muster while unclasping the single button that was responsible for keeping her jacket closed, "Just the man, I wanted to see."

Karina permitted her jacket to fall open, and Ant raised an eyebrow taking it all in, just as two police officers exited the apartment behind him. Rocking a fiery, cherry red strapped cage-inspired lingerie set with plunging neckline and sleek garter belts, Karina had come to seduce.

"It's her," Ant said, more interested in helping Nate, his neighbor, and friend than he was in humoring Karina.

"Ms. Zakaryan, we have a couple of questions for you," the female officer took a step toward Karina, who had already begun to back up. "Please, come with us."

"That's not gonna happen," Karina responded. She then struggled to close her jacket. She fumbled first with its sole button but eventually gave up, permitting the jacket to fall open, leaving her body on full display.

"Ms. Zakaryan, please. It's just a couple of questions," the male officer replied while taking a few steps toward Karina.

"About what?" Karina raised her voice and again stepped away from the officers as her unsteady legs moved like marmalade beneath her.

"Breaking and entering—don't act dumb! You're on tape," incensed, Ant barked at Karina. "You poisoned the damn doorman!" Ant exclaimed, referencing the apartment's incriminating surveillance video. It showed Karina chatting up the doorman as he sipped a laxative-laced iced coffee moments before racing to the restroom.

"Sir, please. Let us do our job," the female officer spoke to Ant but kept her eyes glued to Karina, observing as she slid her hand into the rain jacket's deep, satin-lined pocket.

"Take it up with my lawyer," Karina protested. The officers couldn't be sure if Karina were inebriated or if it was her sense of entitlement that was handicapping her, but Karina's increasingly slurred speech was undoubtedly a red flag.

"Fucking K-Mart cops." Karina turned to exit as the female officer lunged. Without thinking, Karina pulled the blade from her pocket and sliced the top of the female officer's hand, causing her to recoil.

"Drop your weapon!" The male cop exclaimed, grabbing instantly for his Glock twenty-three and pointing it at Karina.

"I'm not going anywhere with you!" Karina wielded the box cutter high over her head, causing the belled sleeves of her rain jacket to slide to her elbow and reveal both fresh and old cuts on her forearms.

"Let us get you some help," the female officer spoke lowly while eyeing the trail of blood that had begun to spill from the self-inflicted wounds on Karina's arms.

"I don't need your help," Karina spoke lowly and used the wall to prop herself up. "Stop harassing me," she pleaded as the female officer used a handkerchief to apply pressure to the cut Karina had inflicted upon her.

"Your weapon, now!" The male officer kept his gun trained on Karina, who had hit an artery and was losing blood fast.

"Horizontal means you'll see another day. Vertical cuts you pass away," Karina smirked as a feeling of tremendous loss consumed her. Then, she used what little strength she had left to point the blade in the cop's direction. Her best friend was gone, a court case was looming, and no matter how well off her family was, Karina was certain that they'd sooner disown her than deal with the repercussions of her actions. On the bright side, if the cops killed her, she'd at least live on in the minds and memories of Los Angeles folklore forever.

"Just do it!" Karina exclaimed, still pointing the now blood-soaked box cutter in the officer's direction.

Chapter 39

Leaving on a Jet Plane

As the 747 glided high above middle America, Nate lay reclined and in the midst of a dream that brought her back to Montego Bay, age fourteen. After sneaking Jocelyn up to her bedroom, the two teens had spent hours talking and making music on Nate's new keyboard workstation. Although Cassia had forbidden Nate from seeing Jocelyn and had even fired her mother, their housekeeper, Nate needed a comfort that only Jocelyn could provide. While the keyboard workstation had temporarily placated her, Nate was ravaged by post-traumatic stress. The assault had happened just that afternoon and more than anything, Nate needed to be held. While Jocelyn could glean that Nate being upset had something to do with Cassia, Nate refused to detail the assault.

"Man, I wish my mom felt guilty more often!" Jocelyn said as she allowed her fingers to dance across the pricy keyboard.

"I just wish my mother felt period," Nate sighed. "She's pretty much a robot."

"So I guess you won't mind if I take this off your hands," Jocelyn said, lifting the keyboard.

"Yea, right," Nate laughed.

"Yea, I thought so," Jocelyn said, sucking her teeth. "You lucky, Natty. Your mother tough as nails, but you have everything you could ever want." While Jocelyn had a point, Nate was in no mood to hear it. She simply wanted to forget about the events of that day and to take comfort in the girl who was not only her best friend but her first love."

"There is one thing I want that my parents can't give me," Nate whispered, then leaned in and kissed Jocelyn.

"Now I know you're mad," Jocelyn said, pulling away and walking over to the window that she'd snuck in through. "All we need is for your mother to open that door."

"It's locked," Nate smiled, rising to her feet. She then walked over and planted another kiss on Jocelyn, only this time she didn't pull away. Jocelyn, instead, leaned in, kissing Nate deeply. The young lovers took delight in exploring each other intimately late into the night. After drifting asleep, the teens awoke in a panic just before daybreak. Jocelyn should have been gone hours ago.

"I'll see you after school," Nate planted one final kiss on Jocelyn's lips and watched as she slipped out of the bedroom window. What Nate didn't realize was that while Cassia was enjoying a spliff in the gazebo, she'd seen the girls kiss good night. There would be no more second chances. Nate needed to pay.

When Nate returned home from school the following afternoon, she headed straight for the soccer net in her backyard. After the attack, she wasn't ready to face the Campbell brothers and planned to avoid local parks for a while. After using the net set up alongside her home to run a few soccer drills, Nate found herself overcome with thirst. Nate tucked the soccer ball under her arm and retreated toward the house to quench that thirst. Exchanging the warmth of the Montego Bay sun for the cool confines of her childhood home Nate entered the foyer, nearly tripping over her keyboard and a suitcase full of her belongings. The designer bags were situated at the bottom of the staircase, and on top of them, a first-class, one-way ticket to Los Angeles. Confused and suddenly nauseous, Nate kicked the soccer ball toward the back of the house and followed the sound of a whistling teapot toward the kitchen.

"What's this?" Nate asked, waving the one-way ticket in her unresponsive mother's face. "Mom, please!"

"You can't stay here." Her face expressionless, Cassia broke her silence. Nate watched as her mother added two cubes of sugar, stirred and then blew steam off of the teacup before sipping.

"You're kicking me out?" Nate slammed the ticket on the table in front of her mother. "This flight is tonight!" Nate exclaimed. Steadfast, it was clear that Cassia's mind had been made up for some time now.

"You'll stay with your Auntie and Uncle in Los Angeles. It was either California or conversion camp." Cassia sat at the table, sipping hot tea and shaking her head in disgust. "I'd say you got off easy," she sighed.

"What about school? My friends?" Nate continued, "I can't just leave!" Frustrated, Nate ran upstairs. Unsure of what exactly she was looking for, she went to her parent's bedroom and discovered that Barrington's closet was completely cleaned out. Next, she tried calling him on his mobile phone, but soon realized that Cassia had disconnected the service. At that point, Nate's anxiety began to rage.

"I'm safe. I'm breathing. I got this!" Nate flew down the stairs, taking them two at a time until she reunited with Cassia in the kitchen. "So what, you fire Ms. Alvita, chase daddy away, and now I next?" Nate asked, her heart racing uncontrollably.

"You best mind yourself!" Cassia freshened her cup of tea with hot water.

"What? Your batty boy daughter embarrass you?"

"I said hush, now!" Frustrated, Cassia slung the tea kettle hard against the wall.

# #

Jarred awake by the sweet dream that had metamorphosed into a bitter nightmare, Nate shot up like a projectile from a smoothbore cannon. Her heart racing and eyes bulging, she could barely catch her breath as the passengers in the VIP cabin began to stir around her.

"We here already?" Asked a man seated beside Nate as he removed his eye mask. For a moment, Nate just stood there, staring straight ahead and rubbing her blistered thighs through the rips in her skinny jeans. "Ma'am, are you ok?" He asked as Nate dealt with both the physical and mental scars left behind from her childhood.

Unable to breathe or talk, Nate unbuckled her seat belt and fumbled through her fanny pack. It was empty! Unbeknownst to Nate, in addition to planting hidden cameras in her bathroom, Karina had stolen her inhaler, leaving the anxiety sufferer's health in the hands of fate. Her heart racing and body overcome with chills, Nate climbed over the businessman seated to her right and began to pace the aisle of the cramped cabin. As her damp hands tingled with numbness and the prick of needles, Nate shook them spastically, garnering the attention of a flight attendant.

"Miss, you need to be seated," the flight attendant commanded, and as the plane shuddered through a spit of turbulence, Nate attempted to ground herself. First by pacing the floor and focusing on the carpet's indigo and ashen patchwork and then by running through her mantra in her head: "I'm safe. I'm breathing. I got this."

"Miss, please take your seat," the attendant again directed Nate to sit, only this time, the panicked traveler looked away from the textured carpet and locked eyes with the flight attendant, who was finally able to discern that something wasn't right. Nate was several shades lighter and drenched in perspiration.

"I can't breathe," Nate somehow managed to eke out the obvious as her chest continued to rise and fall in a disconcerting loop.

Chapter 40

5150'ed

The rookie officer that had taken Nate's flash drive stood with his arms folded outside of Karina's hospital room, accompanied by a veteran officer. The older officer was bald, blunt and proudly scoffed at political correctness. Karina could be seen through the small window. Her make up smeared and hair tussled, she lay shackled to a metal bedpost yet was still somehow able to emit an air of defiance.

"Zakaryan," the older officer thumbed through a file folder.

"Yup, huge in the real estate game," the younger officer replied.

"I thought that last name sounded familiar," the veteran responded with a nod of the head.

"Her dad and brother's faces are plastered at just about every bus stop between Brentwood and Malibu," the rookie reported.

"So poor little rich girl's got a screw loose," the veteran continued with a sigh. "Sure is cute, though."

"Hot and crazy go hand-in-hand," the younger cop agreed.

"Having a mess of bloody, self-inflicted wounds and leaving home in lingerie isn't a crime," the older officer stated the obvious.

"But attacking a cop and breaking and entering is," replied the rookie.

"Precisely," the veteran agreed and rubbed his clean-shaven head while working through the case aloud. "Security camera footage of her entering the apartment coincide with the neighbor's report of running into her leaving Ms. Higgins' unit—plus the fact that she works with the studio and Simon Herbst filed a restraining order against her proves they're connected."

"I just wish Ms. Higgins hadn't bailed on us," the younger officer said while tossing Nate's flash drive into the air.

"Know when she'll be back?" Asked the veteran.

"No idea," the rookie responded with a shrug. "Said she'd reach out in a couple of days."

"At least she left a trail of bread crumbs," the older officer ran his hand through his salt and pepper goatee.

"I want my phone and cloves now!" Karina tugged at the tight metal cuffs and yelled as loud as possible, but no one responded.

She then threw her head back in the chair so that she was staring at the ceiling, which had been painted with fluffy white clouds. Her high-end rain jacket now balled up in a plastic bag of confiscated belongings, Karina couldn't help but squirm in the hospital bed as her skin grew irritated by the polyester infirmary gown. She was an exhausted shell of herself and staring at those puffy snow-white clouds allowed her mind to drift back to the confrontation with the police outside of Nate's apartment. She'd lost a lot of blood and her arms were bandaged from the artery she'd slashed through. While Karina had undoubtedly cheated death, she believed that her demise would have been a much easier out.

She'd fainted shortly after pulling the box cutter on the officers and they'd rushed her immediately to the hospital. After seeing the self-inflicted wounds, both the medical staff and the police agreed that it was best Karina be 5150'ed under California's Lanterman–Petris–Short Act mandating involuntary civil commitment to a mental health institution. This seventy-two-hour involuntary hold would give medical professionals enough time to evaluate Karina's mental state. As Karina continued to stare at the hospital ceiling, her memories drifted between being thrown on a gurney, rushed through the hospital doors and assaulted by Simon. How attempting to take down a predator had landed Karina in handcuffs was beyond her. The hypocrisy was crippling—she was pissed and reacted with a guttural howl.

"You don't have to hang from a tree to be a nut," the veteran said, shaking his head coldly as Karina's scream ripped through the hospital room.

"I guess," the rookie responded as his gaze slipped from the veteran officer and settled on the reluctant patient. "As far as Herbst, I could be down there in thirty minutes."

"Stand down, rook. We'll roll in the morning after Richie Rich has had his latte," the senior officer said while slapping the file folder into the younger officer's chest. "Simon's old man produced every Star Wars. Did you know that? Every last one."

"You've mentioned it," the younger officer replied, rolling his eyes at the blatant fan boy.

"In a galaxy far, far away…" the older officer deepened his voice and assumed the style of a sci-fi narrator.

"Simon is still an asshole," the rookie interrupted.

"Was he an asshole when he donated money to upgrade our squad cars or renovate the break room you spend way too much time in?" The veteran queried.

"I just meant, this isn't the first time he's been accused," the younger officer countered. "Maybe it'll stick this time."

"And maybe it won't," the older officer's tone grew stern.

"But the live stream," the rookie continued. "That woman, called him out by name—Sasha Harper," he said, reading the name from his notepad.

"Live stream, you're joking, right?" The vet replied with irritation, turning his back on Karina so that he could see eye-to-eye with his subordinate. "Guys like Simon don't need to rape women. Now, as I said, we'll stop by in the morning," he continued, completely disregarding the younger officer's point, "not like he's a flight risk."

#

Meanwhile, across town, Tru had thrown a hoodie over her fetish attire and had relocated her car to a spot just down the road from the Halloween party. Parked along the Pacific Coast Highway, she hopped from behind the wheel of her car, picked up the small box that was resting in her passenger seat and sat on the warm hood of her car. After opening the container, she pulled out a chocolate cupcake topped with vanilla frosting and rainbow sprinkles. Next, she dug into the pocket of her hoodie and pulled out a lighter and birthday candle. Then she lit the candle and stuck it into the single-serving dessert.

"Happy Birthday, Eomma," Tru said, smiling to the stars, before blowing out the candles for her deceased mother. She then took a giant bite and placed the sweet treat next to her on the car. After licking her fingers clean of frosting, she dug into her other pocket and fished out the envelope from her mother. "Gifting on your birthday, just like Halmoni." Tru again craned her neck heavenward, before ripping into the envelope. She stuck her fingers into the package quickly but was almost afraid to pull out its contents. After a deep breath, curiosity got the best of her, and in she went to retrieve its contents—an expired passport.

"Okay." Tru handled her mother's expired passport with both confusion and care. First, getting a kick out of the dated photo of a woman who looked just like her, only several shades lighter with bone straight hair. Upon thumbing through the official document, she quickly discovered that it had never been stamped. Tru had, spoken to her grandmother many times in an effort to learn more about Yooni, the mother she never knew. In those conversations she'd learned that as an only child, Yooni loved to travel and looked forward to road trips with her parents. Together they'd driven as far East as New York City and had stopped at countless tourist destinations in between.

Tru imagined that her mother's passion for travel coincided directly with her love of architecture and was ultimately the reason she decided to study the art form. Sadly, outside of domestic trips and images in textbooks, she'd never laid her eyes on the awe-inspiring structures from around the world that moved her to pursue architecture as a career. Tru continued to flip through empty pages of the passport and out fell a handwritten note.

"No way," Tru said aloud as she began unfolding the letter, which read:

"Baby girl, travel is never a matter of money, but of courage, so today, on my birthday, I wish for you the gift of seeing the world. Be fearless, be yourself and above all else, remember time is not on your side."

Tears streaming down her face, Tru again looked toward the starlit sky as a double-decker Airbus floated high above the Pacific Ocean and raced through the pre-dawn sky.

# #

Miles away and thousands of feet in the air, Nate had stopped hyperventilating and was again seated in her chair. After nearly fainting, the flight attendant gave her a paper bag to breathe into, which had helped. However, what really saved the day was the kindness of an older woman with a rich Jamaican accent who reminded her of Auntie Earlene. She'd given Nate her lavender aromatherapy nasal inhaler and encouraged her to relax. Then she talked to her for close to an hour as Nate sat there listening and inhaling. The woman lived in Negril and told Nate all about her well-off son, who insisted on flying her first-class multiple times a year so that she could spend time with her grandbabies. By the end of the conversation, Nate knew the children's names, ages and favorite television shows. The woman's son was a hotshot lawyer, so she'd also given Nate his business card because "you never know when you might need it," the woman said with a smile.

Nate couldn't be sure if it were the woman's soothing familial vibe or the anxiety-reducing inhaler, but the panic attack had subsided and Nate had again drifted off to sleep, only to be awakened by the Captain's omniscient voice: "We'll be touching down in Montego Bay in approximately twenty-five minutes. The local time is half-past six in the morning, and the temperature is a perfect seventy-six degrees."

Nate swallowed hard and shook her head from side to side as the flight attendant offered hot tea and coffee to her, and the man seated beside her. She then glanced outside the window. The sun had scarcely started to make its presence known, but even still, the aerial view was breathtaking: Crystal clear water consisting of several shades of turquoise, white sand beaches, and a lush mountain range. Over a decade had come and gone since she'd last stepped foot on her island home, and now that she was back, her stomach was tumbling more than Simone Biles at the 2016 Summer Olympics. Nate took another long sniff of the lavender inhaler as the Captain continued.

"If you're on vacation, try the rum punch, and if you are returning home, let me be the first to welcome you back."

Part Five

Roots. Rock. Reggae.

Chapter 41

Alvitazen

By the time Nate had snaked her way through customs at the congested Montego Bay Airport, she'd broken a sweat. Fourteen years removed from the tropical heat and humidity, the tiny beads of sweat that had begun to form on her brow were like long lost relatives. Nate peeled off her jacket, draped it over her luggage and scanned a long line of drivers holding signs with various surnames: Winston, Thomas, Chin—but no Higgins.

"Need a ride, princess?" a virile yet slightly weathered cab driver asked as Nate exited the airport.

"No, thank you," Nate replied, gently settling into her native tongue and tone. "I'm good, brethren," she shot down a few more cabbies and surveyed the scene. There was traffic but nowhere near what she'd grown accustomed to in Los Angeles. And as far as the eye could see, billboards lined the sky—advertising everything local—from rum to elections and the endless tourist destinations in between.

The air was dotted with the distinction of livestock. Goat, Nate imagined. Her mouth watered at the thought of Auntie Earlene's signature Sunday meal—curried goat, cabbage, peas and rice. Next, the boldness of Blue Mountain coffee delighted her senses. Alone, the fragrances were unmistakable. Together they epitomized home. Nate checked her watch and then paced the length of the sidewalk. Next, she turned on her phone and was bombarded with text messages from several friends who'd heard about Karina being placed under psych evaluation after her run-in with the police. Details were scant, but after listening to a voicemail from Ant, her neighbor and eyewitness to Karina's assault on the female officer, Nate was able to fill in many of the blanks. Nate was taken aback by how fast things had blown up as she continued to scroll through text messages.

Suddenly, an ice, gold, and green minivan stopped several feet in front of her, and to Nate's shock, out popped Jocelyn—her former best friend and forever first love. Jocelyn ran top speed, leaped into Nate's arms and wrapped her lean legs around her waist. Nate inhaled deeply. Jocelyn smelled good enough to eat, re-heat and turn into a bomb chicken and dumpling soup.

"Natty, it's so good to see you!"

"J?" Nate queried, pulling her head away so that she could get a good look at her old friend.

"Surprise!" Jocelyn exclaimed as she slid down Nate's body but continued the embrace. "Auntie Earlene wanted to surprise you." Since Barrington had told Nate to expect a car service, seeing Jocelyn at the airport was indeed a shock.

"Well, it worked!" Nate beamed as she sized up Jocelyn. In fourteen years, she had fully embraced womanhood. Her hair was still long and thick and the extra inches she'd amassed in height enabled any prior baby fat to settle into all the right places. When Jocelyn tossed Nate's luggage into the van, Nate tried hard not to stare at how nicely her oldest friend's derrière filled out her leggings. Then it happened. Jocelyn caught Nate checking her out, and just like that, Nate felt as nervous as her fourteen-year-old self.

Mortified, Nate shut the door and buckled up as Jocelyn pulled out of the parking lot, heading in the hospital's direction. The parrot bottom was just as chatty as she'd always been. Nate embraced the warmth familiarity.

"Y'all love social media," Jocelyn said as Nate's phone chirped several times. "You a real Yankee now, huh?"

"I was just texting my dad," Nate lied. In actuality, she was sorting through text messages from Rampart police detectives. They were eager to question her about the thumb drive she'd left, which featured last night's live stream and detailed Simon's assaults to both her and Sasha.

"Why? I'm taking you to the hospital now. Relax, enjoy the view," Jocelyn replied with a smile. She was a knockout, but, in the words of Bob Marley, her sexiest curve was always her smile.

"You look good, Natty." Jocelyn patted Nate on the thigh as she headed south on Gloucester Avenue.

"You too, friend," Nate said as her phone slipped temporarily to sleep. "This is like a dream." She averted her gaze from Jocelyn to the scenic resort and tree-lined route. "I'm back."

"Fate has a funny way of placing us precisely where we need to be," replied Jocelyn.

"We owe a debt of gratitude to Auntie Earlene," Nate's sentiments slipped from the passenger side window as salty sea air caressed her brown skin.

"For our reunion and so much more," Jocelyn continued. "I hate that she's sick, but Auntie Earlene's a fighter," Jocelyn said, resting her hand atop Nate's. "I stopped by her room last night."

"How she look?" Nate queried. She then trained her eyes from their intertwined fingers to Jocelyn's face.

"She's lost some weight, but overall, she's in good spirits. Over there cussing nurses and worrying too much about her garden."

"That's Auntie," Nate said with a laugh. "There's some hospital in Miami that specializes in oncology daddy wants to send her to, but you know Auntie don't fly."

"What about the Oncology Centre in Kingston?"

"Have you met my father?" Nate teased.

"Sure have! Your parents are bougie as hell," Jocelyn giggled. "But the Oncology Centre is still a great, local option."

"The test results are due today," Nate continued. "We'll know our next steps soon."

"Either way, keep it positive," Jocelyn replied.

"Good vibes only," Nate agreed as her phone chirped, signaling an incoming call from the police. Nate's phone was full of missed calls, texts, and voicemails from officers that needed her attention. Unfortunately, they would all have to wait. Nate switched the phone to airplane mode and resigned to stay in the moment.

"So what have you been up to? This all you?" Nate asked, motioning to the tricked out tourism van.

"This is the Ice Gold and Green Machine," Jocelyn said, tapping on the dashboard. We have a fleet of five," Jocelyn said proudly.

"We?"

"Yup, I co-own Alvitazen Tours with a friend of mine." Jocelyn paused for a beat before continuing. "She's an army brat. We studied together at ECC."

"Excelsior," Nate said, recalling the community college she hadn't thought about in years.

"Guess you were wrong about me getting a scholarship to some big-time university," Jocelyn smirked as Nate quietly tried not to choke on her silver spoon. "My business partner's family is from the states," Jocelyn continued, "but her parents spent years stationed in Germany."

"Okay, I get it. Alvitazen," Nate said, nodding her head.

"It's German for until we meet again," Jocelyn explained.

"Alvita is also your mom," said Nate, redirecting her gaze from the picturesque Montego Bay Cricket Club as Jocelyn continued along Cottage Road.

"Yes," said Jocelyn, keeping her eyes on the road while tears welled up. "She was."

"I should've been here for her funeral," Nate's voice cracked.

"You're right," Jocelyn used sarcasm in an attempt to lighten the mood. "Relax, it's been years." She continued, massaging Nate's shoulder. "So tense," Jocelyn said, frowning. She then gave Nate another firm squeeze on her neck as she pulled into the regional hospital's parking lot. "Remember, good vibes only."

"I'm safe. I'm breathing. I got this." Nate quietly ran through the calming phrase.

"Auntie's mantra," Jocelyn said, smiling as she threw the van into park. "That's a throwback."

"So are you," Nate laughed, hopping from the van, anxious as hell.

"I'll pick you up from your parent's house," Jocelyn spoke as she pulled Nate's luggage out of the vehicle. "Noon, okay for lunch?"

"Perfect," Nate agreed, and as Jocelyn pulled her in for a warm hug, Nate's arms gently roamed the length of Jocelyn's spine.

"Natty One, back on the island," Jocelyn sighed. She had given Nate that nickname years ago, and Nate had subsequently run with it, embracing the moniker as her online persona.

"I was sure you'd never look back," Jocelyn spoke softly.

"Guess you were wrong," Nate replied, again inhaling Jocelyn's scent, an intoxicating mixture of sandalwood and soft vanilla.

"Too early to tell," Jocelyn laughed as Nate tried unsuccessfully to read between the lines. "By the way," Jocelyn changed the subject. After all these years, she was still able to ease Nate's jitters with a joke. "I haven't spoken to your mom since she fired mine," Jocelyn snickered. "Tell her and your daddy, I said whap'am."

"You're crazy," Nate said with a wave as Jocelyn pulled away from the hospital. She then looked up at the expansive ten-story building and again verbalized her mantra. "I'm safe. I'm breathing. I got this."

Chapter 42

A Rude Awakening

The rookie officer swallowed hard as he took in the enormity of Simon's Hollywood Hills home. The exterior was modern with fantastic up-lighting and a slanted art deco-inspired roof that would give even the world's most capable skateboarder a run for his money. As the young officer surveyed the property, his veteran partner quietly shut the squad car's door behind him and approached the home. It was early in the morning, barely Five AM on the West Coast and the house looked quiet. However, on the inside, an entirely different scenario was unfolding.

"Every news outlet is running this story. Leave now!" A voicemail from Chad, Simon's older brother, scored the scene as the frenzied television executive stuffed articles of clothing and wads of cash into a duffle bag, recalling the few minutes of pleasure that had brought a world of pain to his doorsteps.

He remembered everything just like it was yesterday. Karina was giving him a tour of the home that he would eventually go on to purchase. She was incredibly detailed about all the work that went into the house—Central American Ipe wood flooring, marble countertops and custom copper fixtures throughout. He even remembered Karina pointing out the high-price home's security system.

"Clearly, the place is built for a king, but it's best asset is a state of the art security system, featuring cameras in every room." Simon kicked himself for not caring more about this detail at the time.

"What's so hard to understand about NDA?" Simon asked, punching his fist through the bedroom drywall. He then clicked a link on his phone, and there it was clear as day—Simon was having sex with Karina, and although her face had been digitally obscured, there was no denying the act. High definition security cameras had captured multiple angles of the assault. In her final act of defiance, Karina had programmed the video file to auto-upload to every local news network and police station's social media pages at precisely Four AM. Nate's thumb drive containing her live stream had been a great start, but it was Karina's automatic upload that genuinely propelled the police to act. Originally they'd planned to question Simon at a decent hour, specifically after his morning latte, but Karina's video evidence changed everything.

Simon's mind was racing: "The bitch agreed to a blow job. She knew what was coming next." Could he turn back time, Simon would've taken Karina to the hotel where he'd assaulted Nate, Sasha and countless others, but as it stood, the narrative was out of his control and would be very hard to manipulate.

Frantic, sweating, and moving way too fast, Simon backed into a lamp and shattered it against the imported hardwood. The commotion was enough to wake the two women that had fallen asleep in his plush California King bed.

"Come back to bed, baby," said the doe-eyed brunette.

"It's time to get up!" Simon yelled, without looking at the women as he pulled a black hoodie over his bare chest and slipped into a pair of sweats.

"Not gonna happen," the second woman replied, cuddling up to the brunette with clearly no intentions of rising as Chad's voicemail continued in the background: "I've made arrangements in San Bernardino. You know the spot." Simon deleted the voicemail and text message chain between him and his brother and then proceeded to unleash a verbal assault on the women.

"Both of you! Get the fuck out now!" Simon inhaled several fat lines of cocaine and rubbed the remainder on to his gums as the two naked women hopped out of bed and clumsily began to throw on their clothes.

Outside of the estate, a second squad car drove past the gated entrance and parked directly in front of Simon's sports car. Out hopped two more officers, who immediately made their way to the back of the home—one opting to enter from the east side of the house and the other from the west. The rookie rang the doorbell as his partner, the veteran, backed him up, making sure that his hand was in close proximity to the butt of his GLOCK 22. There was no answer. After waiting a few seconds, the rookie laid in on the doorbell and began to knock aggressively on the French doors.

"Simon Herbst, this is LAPD! Open up!" The rookie peaked into several of the windows, but they were mirrored, so he could only see his reflection along with that of his partner, and then it happened—the door swung open, and out walked the two women.

"Where's Simon? Is he with you?" The rookie inquired forcefully, peering past the women, who were too surprised by the early morning police presence to respond.

"Is he in the house?" The veteran officer exclaimed, his hand still positioned securely on the butt of his GLOCK.

"I don't know where he is!" The brunette responded.

"He told us to leave through the front," the second woman nervously chimed in while the veteran officer moved past the women and stepped carefully into the foyer.

"LAPD!" He screamed, just as the garage door opened, allowing Simon to peel out on his motorcycle.

"Stop! Police!" The rookie exclaimed and then took chase as Simon ducked under the garage door and buzzed toward the end of the driveway. Had the squad cars not impeded his path, Simon might have been able to escape. In his attempt to maneuver around the vehicles, the rookie reacted. First sprinting and then leaping into the air, the officer tackled Simon right off of the vintage Ducati.

"What the hell!" Simon exclaimed just as the other three officers approached, guns blazing. Several minutes later, Simon found himself handcuffed in the back of an LAPD squad car. "You have no right!" Simon was fuming. "I swear if there's so much as a scratch on my bike." Simon doled out empty threats as squad cars exited the gated community, parading him past a long line of paparazzi, eager to shoot the tainted television executive.

Chapter 43

Boy Wonder

The hospital room's primary light source came from a flat-screen mounted high on the drab beige wall. Aside from that were sporadic claps of lightning and the flicker of monitors tasked with overseeing Karina's recovery. Now thoroughly sedated, Karina zoned out while two television reporters gushed over paparazzi video of Simon's arrest.

"Herbst Studios is responsible for some of the greatest moments in television and film point blank, but it was music, not movies, where Simon really shined," the male anchor swooned as Karina's mother stroked her daughter's bandaged forearms.

"Simon Herbst is the boy wonder of a famous family. As Director of A&R he was responsible for grooming some of the biggest artists at Masquerade Records," the male anchor continued as Karina's father erupted.

"What does any of this matter? The man is a rapist! Brrnabarogh!" Karina's father exclaimed while placing his hand atop hers. "You should have come to us sooner, sirelis." He called her sweetheart—sirelis—when he most wanted her to listen. "Even with video, it will be hard to prove."

Karina lay expressionless and handcuffed to the hospital bed as the female anchor spoke, "This isn't the first time allegations have surfaced about Simon Herbst."

"Yes, but that was last year and the claims were later retracted." Karina stared out the rain-stained window as the male anchor offered his rebuttal.

"This is aghb—trash. I'm turning it off." Karina's mother grabbed the remote control, but Karina insisted she let the broadcast play.

"No, don't," Karina pleaded through her drug-induced haze as her handcuffs clanged against the metal bedposts.

"Simon Herbst has a history, that's all I'm saying," the female anchor continued while the blurred video of Karina being assaulted played out.

As the sedatives began to take effect, Karina fought sleep with all her might. She wanted to hear what the news anchors were saying, but her eyelids were growing heavier by the second. Her blinks too much to bear, Karina eventually succumbed to sleep while old memories played out in her mind. As a teen, she was a real handful—constant partier, class cutter and disrespectful as all hell. Like countless of other teens, Karina was looking for attention in all the wrong places. To get noticed, she even sold sizzurp to her affluent classmates and had many of them hooked on the combination of codeine, grape soda and jolly ranchers. The money was nice, but Karina's primary motivator was an increase in popularity. The fact that these weren't friends but merely high schoolers looking to get hooked up, made no difference to the chubby, self-conscious teen. From distributing sizzurp to discovering that cocaine suppresses appetites, Karina became a functioning addict and climbed deep into a rabbit hole that she'd yet to escape. Looking back was hard. Shackled to her hospital bed and deeply sedated, Karina recalled the first time she had been hospitalized. At the age of fifteen, Karina's parents checked her into rehab after OD'ing at a high school party. During that three-week stint, Karina roomed with a young tatted up teen that drastically changed the trajectory of her recovery.

"People try to off themselves all the time around here," Karina's roommate said, scoffing as she hopped from the top bunk bed and took a seat beside her. "There's a chick two doors down that ransacked the pharmacy. Threw herself a pill party. Unfortunately, she had no idea what she was doing—they pumped her stomach, and sadly, she lived."

"For the hundredth time, this was an accident," Karina whispered as she sat up in bed. "I wasn't trying to kill myself."

"Good, because if you were, you suck at it," Karina's bunkmate laughed and then angled her pointer finger into a hook. Next, she cautiously pulled out a razor blade that she'd tucked beside her cheek. "This is how I take the edge off," the teen spoke lowly as she pressed the blade halfway between her elbow and wrists, slicing instantly through her Minnie Mouse tattoo.

"What the fuck?" Karina recoiled as blood began to seep from the bisected Minnie Mouse caricature.

"Try it," her roommate said, offering the bloody blade to Karina.

"Hell no," proclaimed Karina as she sat shaking her head in disbelief.

"The endorphins are sick," her roomie explained, again pressing the blade to her flesh and slowly pulling the razor across her already-scarred skin. "Horizontal means you live to see another day. Vertical cuts you pass away." Karina's roommate smirked at the morbid rhyme as she tilted her head toward the ceiling in delight.

Haunted by visions of herself aged, hardened and behind bars, Karina began to toss and turn in the thin hospital bed. Nate had been the only friend to visit Karina during that first rehab stretch and the two that followed. In fact, when Nate abruptly moved to the states as a teen, she and Karina connected immediately. Nate's thick accent and island culture made her an easy target for bullies and an even easier mark for Karina as authentic friendships had never been her forte. Despite being chain cuffed to a hospital bed for betraying Nate, Karina remained unmoved. Even in her pharmaceutical stupor, Karina couldn't be swayed by the fact that when diagnosed with antisocial personality disorder, Nate was the only person within whom she felt comfortable confiding. Although, for Karina, loyalty had never been a priority. She just wasn't built that way. If Nate couldn't see that in setting her up with Simon, they could take down a predator, Karina was willing to let the friendship dissolve. Her freedom, on the other hand, was the one thing she wasn't ready to let go of.

"Wake up, sirelis," Karina's mother whispered, shaking Karina as she whimpered in her sleep. "You're dreaming."

The truth of the matter was none of this was a dream. Karina's very calculated steps had gotten her to this precise moment in time. She'd lost her best friend and, in the process, had almost lost her life. Karina was in danger of going to jail, but scarier than prison was the thought of her privacy being invaded. She dreaded having her personal demons blasted onto the front pages of American rag mags and celebrity news shows. As Karina's eyes fluttered open, her mother wiped tears from her flushed face.

"It's Mayrik—mommy's here." Karina's mother dabbed at the tears on her daughter's face as Karina got a glimpse of her father talking to their family lawyer in the hallway. He'd gotten her brother off on drunk driving charges in the past and was able to find a loophole when Karina got busted for distributing in a school zone, but would Karina's privilege again be enough to free her of mounting criminal charges?

Chapter 44

Stage IV

Nate stepped out of the elevator on to the tenth floor, shoved the lavender inhaler back into her fanny pack and followed the signs toward room 1032, Aunt Earlene's room. After hanging a right by a set of potted plants, Nate passed the nurses' station and then paused as she reached a set of empty gurneys swathed in stark white sheets. When she made it to the corner, a man in all black that Nate recognized instantly as government security whispered something into his two-way radio. At that point, the reality of seeing her family became all too real.

Nate froze and, for a second, actually considered fleeing. Despite its many perks, her parents' high status in the community had always been somewhat off-putting. After all, one of the reasons why they rejected Nate—their prodigal queer daughter—was because they needed to maintain appearances. She could simply book the next flight out of town, but how would that look? Returning to Los Angeles meant turning on the woman who'd always had her back, and for Nate, this was most certainly not an option. Auntie Earlene was everything to her. So instead of bolting, Nate took a calming breath and pressed on. After passing an expansive floor-to-ceiling wall of glass that overlooked the Caribbean Sea, Nate came to the end of the hallway. Positioned outside of room 1032, an attractive middle-aged man—also wearing an all-black suit and holding a two-way radio—signaled Nate to approach.

"I'm here to see my Auntie Earlene and because the men-in-black are here, I'll assume my dad is too," Nate laughed.

"You look just like your mother," the man said, extending his hand. "Natalia, right?"

"Right."

"They're all inside with the doctor," the man opened the door and stepped aside for Nate to enter. Nate took a deep breath and forced herself across the threshold. Immediately, she was hit with the sweet smell of flowers cut fresh from Auntie Earlene's garden. Throughout the room, tropical arrangements of local blossoms had been strategically placed, enveloping the space in warm shades of crimson and lavender.

"Natty!" Barrington exclaimed as he raced toward Nate and scooped her up into his arms. "To God, be the glory." He looked good—tieless and rocking a dark tailored suit, closely cropped fade and an uncomfortable smile.

Temporarily tearing down the emotional walls between her and Barrington, Nate melted at the sight of her father. "Daddy," she whispered like a lost cub reacquainting with its pride.

"Earlene, you see this? Look how tall she get." Barrington twirled his daughter around. "Gorgeous too," the proud father roared.

"Yea, mon. Little Natty done grown like a weed," Although her noticeably paler skin had lost much of its elasticity, Earlene beamed with joy as Nate approached the hospital bed and laid across her chest. As a child, Auntie Earlene's breasts had been a place of refuge and comfort, but now as Nate draped her body across her Aunt's frail frame, she could tell things were different. Her once full cup size was now downsized. And while Auntie Earlene was not rail thin, she had lost a staggering amount of weight.

"My God, Natty you left a nash little 'ting and came back all woman," Auntie Earlene coughed a small amount of blood into a mauve kerchief as she laughed at her own joke.

"I was never nash, Auntie," Nate laughed to keep from crying.

"Please!" Auntie Earlene sucked her teeth. "This girl was thin as a blade of grass." She smiled at her doctor while adjusting her Kente cloth head wrap.

"You looking good too, Auntie." Nate tried not to be obvious as she assessed Earlene. Despite her illness, her Aunt looked regal in her green, gold, and red East African head wrap, matching blouse and just a pop of pink lipstick. The oxygen cannulas attached to her nose would, however, take some getting used to.

"What Auntie tell you about lying?" She asked while taking a playful swat at Nate's rear.

"I'm Dr. Samuels," the physician took Nate's hand in hers as she stood to greet him.

"Natty."

"The big-time, Hollywood music producer," Dr. Samuels replied as Nate locked eyes with Barrington and wondered which of her parents were responsible for the career embellishment.

"My girl has skills, very talented. Always has been," Auntie Earlene boasted. "Even has her own radio show."

"It's just a podcast, Auntie," Nate grew flushed.

"Have you worked with anyone I might know?" The doctor inquired.

"Probably not," Nate deflected as the doors to the attached exterior patio slid open.

"My long lost pickney in the flesh." Framed beautifully by the French Doors, Cassia had barely aged a day. With long golden locks, the lioness looked more like Nate's older sister than her mother. In her flowing yellow blouse and linen pants, she was regal yet distant. Nate didn't respond and dared not move.

"It's been a long time," Cassia said, stepping further into the room. Nate opened her mouth, but she was speechless. "Come to me, child. Come greet your dear mother."

Auntie Earlene gave Nate a slight pinch, prompting Nate to action. Slowly, she slipped past her father then walked the length of the room to receive her mother. Their hug was oafish, icy and about a dozen years too late.

"Good morning, mommy," Nate whispered into Cassia's ear as she stared through the French Doors in wonderment at the tranquil yet lethal Caribbean Sea, trying her best to channel its strength. "It's good to be home." Nate inhaled the faint scent of marijuana that clung to Cassia.

"My little tomboy," Cassia said while stepping back to get a good look at her daughter. "All these years and still not a stitch of makeup."

"The child just reach. Give it a day or so before you start picking her apart," Auntie Earlene coughed softly then soothed her throat with a sip of the hot bush tea.

"A little lipstick never hurt—even a natural beauty like Natalia," Cassia smiled, lifting Nate's chin so that they were eye to eye.

"Natty's naturally striking and need not concern herself with imposed standards of beauty," Barrington spoke, using a pocket square to dab the developing beads of sweat from his temples—a dead giveaway that this reunion was already a lot to bare.

215

"Let's talk treatment," the doctor interjected as Nate battled her desire to sprint like a gazelle on an open plain. "As you know, Cornwall Regional has a close relationship with Sylvester Comprehensive Cancer Center in Miami. There's a bed ready and waiting for you, Earlene."

"Well, they gonna be waiting a long time because you know I don't fly," Auntie Earlene said, sucking her teeth loudly.

"You're too stubborn for your own good," Barrington complained.

"What if I fly with you, Auntie?" Nate asked.

"Not even if Jesus himself were pilot," Auntie Earlene said with a laugh.

"Couldn't she cruise there?" Cassia blurted out.

"Too long and too risky," the doctor's voice grew more urgent. "This is stage four pancreatic cancer," he paused solemnly. "The imaging results show that it's spread. We have to act aggressively."

"Stage four?" Nate's eyes welled up, but this time she didn't fight it. Instead, she gave in to her natural inclinations and permitted the waterworks to flow.

"Come here, baby." Auntie Earlene placed the medicinal bush tea on the nightstand while a sobbing Nate crawled into bed beside her.

"How long does she have?" Barrington asked with his back to the room as he used the pocket square to wipe away tears.

"Earlene, if you're absolutely sure that you want to decline further treatment, I'd say..."

"You're good, doctor," Earlene interjected, "but only the good Lord can answer that." "Now, to be clear, I have not decided to decline treatment. I simply wish to put it on hold for a spell. I have business to tend to—after that, we'll revisit the Oncology Centre."

"Honestly, sis, Kingston?" Barrington rolled his eyes, exasperated.

"It's a fantastic option and has comforted many Jamaicans," the physician placed his hand on Earlene's shoulder as he looked directly into her eyes, before continuing. "Again, time is of the essence. I'll let you all talk as a family." The doctor shook hands with everyone before exiting the room.

"What business can be more important than your health, Auntie?" Nate asked with a sniffle.

"First off, Natty, you can rest assured that our Lord and Savior is the almighty healer and master architect of all things." Auntie Earlene paused before continuing, "She is clothed in strength and dignity…"

"And she laughs without fear of the future," Nate finished the Old Testament Proverb that Auntie Earlene had drilled into her years ago.

"Very good, Natty," Auntie Earlene continued with a girlish giggle. "Today, we celebrate! Look around! Did you think you were here for a funeral?" She asked with a laugh as Nate again scanned the room.

There were vases upon vases of local lilac, royal red dwarf Poinciana, and adorning Auntie Earlene's bed, an elegant arch made of pale orange bougainvillea.

"I'm getting married!" Auntie Earlene proclaimed.

"Stop playing, Auntie." Nate forced a smile while using the back of her hand to wipe away tears.

"Technically, it's a commitment ceremony," advised Barrington.

"Wait, hold up?" Nate winced as she started to put the pieces together. "Commitment ceremony as in two brides?" Nate laughed.

"Not this again," Cassia moaned.

"Yes, this again!" Auntie Earlene exclaimed. "If you don't like it, please feel free to excuse yourself."

"Barry, you know we can't be here for this," Cassia spoke to her husband. "The rumor mill is already working double time as is." Cassia lowered her tone as she caught a glimpse of Barrington's handler on the other side of the door.

"What's at stake, couldn't be any clearer," Barrington tried to keep his voice down. "I'm the one with everything to lose," he declared.

"Quite honestly, this isn't about either of you," reminded Auntie Earlene. "I don't need anyone's permission to live fully." Auntie Earlene coughed into her handkerchief. Then her gaze drifted toward Nate with a smile. "I do, however, have one wish to ask of you, Ms. Natty."

"Anything, Auntie," Nate spoke through bated breath as her homecoming continued to unravel.

"I don't just want you to be a guest at my wedding," Auntie Earlene continued with a smile. "I want you to be my maid of honor. Will you do that?"

Chapter 45

Homecoming

"I'm happy for you and Ms. Ruth, Auntie. Shocked, but very happy." Nate leaned in and gave Auntie Earlene a loving kiss on her forehead. Watching her beam like a honeymooning twenty-something-year-old, Nate couldn't help but wonder. Had Auntie Earlene always been gay and, if so, had the man she'd buried after twenty plus years of marriage been her beard?

"But where are the other guests, your church sisters and them?" Nate queried.

"Let's just say folks haven't been the most supportive," Auntie Earlene said with a shrug.

"This is crazy," Nate whispered, half expecting Auntie Earlene to confess she'd been joking about the entire thing.

"No, this is complicated, but such is life," Auntie Earlene laughed. "Ruth will be here soon. She's excited to see you."

"We're all excited for you, Earlene, but honestly, the optics will kill us," Cassia said, approaching Earlene's bedside. "I mean no offense, but certainly, you know we can't stay for this." Cassia laughed aloud at the thought.

"I stopped being offended a long time ago," Auntie Earlene replied resolutely.

"Then we're on the same page," Cassia breathed a sigh of relief as she grabbed her designer handbag and motioned toward the door. "Natalia, I'm sure you're hungry. There's a place just down the road. We'll catch up over Ackee and saltfish."

"I'm not hungry," Nate lied.

"Not hungry?" Cassia paused at the door and then turned to face Nate before continuing. "After a seven-hour flight?"

"I'm staying," Nate responded with certainty as she rose from Auntie Earlene's bed.

"Trust, it's best we all leave together, like a family," Cassia declared, approaching Nate, her hand extended.

"We haven't been family in years," Nate blurted out the words faster than she had even thought them up.

"Natty, please," Auntie Earlene implored her niece. "Cease and settle."

"That's fine, Earlene," Cassia said with a sigh, withdrawing her hand. "You're an adult. I won't belabor the point, but as for daddy and me—we can't be seen at a gay wedding, commitment ceremony or any such foolishness."

"I've decided to stay," Barrington approached his wife and responded softly. Nate had rarely seen Barrington stand up to Cassia and wondered if he had done so just a little more often when she was growing up, would life have been different.

"I'm not sure what's more surprising," Nate said as she eyed Barrington. "The fact that you're finally standing up to her or that in fourteen years," Nate continued, redirecting her gaze to Cassia, "you haven't changed a bit."

"Yes, that backbone looks good on you, brethren," Auntie Earlene joked, as Cassia ignored the jibe.

"We've been over this," Cassia replied, shocked at Barrington's sudden change of heart. "It's an election year, Barrington," Cassia's voice quivered. "Think about the repercussions—all these nosy nurses. Something's bound to slip."

"Give them some credit. These are medical professionals," Barrington scoffed, trying his best to downplay Cassia's concerns. "Afterward, we'll go for breakfast in town so that everyone can welcome Natty home." He went on to paint an optimistic picture, "Smart, successful hometown girl, back in Jamrock to help her father's campaign. Constituents will love it."

All eyes on her, Cassia studied the room before placing her purse on a nearby sectional. "Give us a minute," she replied, walking Barrington onto the patio and sliding the door closed behind her before speaking.

"Natalia—on the campaign trail?" Cassia asked, frowning at the thought.

"It could work," Barrington sounded like he was trying to convince himself more than his wife.

"You aren't thinking rationally." Cassia hovered over Barrington like a dark cloud as she continued to speak with her hands, "The child belongs in a closet, not a campaign ad."

"I'm not letting you chase her away again," Barrington replied as he caught a glimpse of Earlene's Bride entering the room. She was dressed neatly in jeans and suspenders over a pressed white button-down, but what really made the outfit pop was her lavender boutonnière. Lignum vitae—the national flower—was pinned to her lapel as both a sign of pride and intrigue. Clutching a worn Bible, the Reverend entered next. She was as cheerful as she was plump, and aside from the rainbow-hued scarf draped over her shoulders, the Reverend was dressed entirely in black. A young nurse was the last to enter the room. Fresh-faced and somewhat intrusive in nature, she wheeled her cart over to Earlene's bed and promptly began checking her blood pressure.

"We done?" Barrington asked.

"I was just about to tell you to kiss me backside," Cassia exaggerated her accent for emphasis.

"Is this really the homecoming you want to give to, Natty?" Barrington sulked as Cassia studied his face. "My God, woman, you have no sense of decorum, tact or timing." Barrington turned to face the sea below while running his hand across the silver waves atop his head.

"And you have no sense, at all," Cassia proclaimed, plucking Barrington in his temple, not once, but twice. "How about I come down to the capital and embarrass you at your job as you did me in our home—in front of the help no less?"

"Do what you gotta do," Barrington called Cassia's bluff. Airing his dirty laundry meant that she too would have to relinquish each perk that came along with being married to Jamaica's Minister of Youth and Culture.

"Come test me," Cassia said with a laugh and island twang that was snatched straight from the ghettos of Spanish Town. "You just had to bring that bastard back to my house," she sighed emphatically.

"How can my son be a bastard?" Barrington spoke softly.

"Damn it, Barrington, there are rules to this!" An open marriage was one thing, but a child in primary school was straight up disrespectful.

"I made a mistake," he responded, grabbing her hands into his while everyone in the hospital room tried to ignore the commotion.

"No, you got sloppy," Cassia pulled her hands from his grip as Barrington watched the nurse peel the blood pressure cuff off of Auntie Earlene and laugh at what was no doubt one of his older sister's crass jokes.

"Please, wait in the car," Barrington spoke softly before closing the door behind him and exiting to greet the women. Cassia watched with aversion as Barrington offered the nurse and Reverend handshakes. He then bestowed upon Earlene's bride a sincere hug to which she replied with a smile that more than personified her willingness to wed.

Like Auntie Earlene, Ms. Ruth was a farmer. The strong silent type, Ms. Ruth had always presented more masculine than most women. In her early sixties, Ms. Ruth was also more soft spoken than her vocal wife-to-be. For years, Auntie Earlene and Ms. Ruth had kept their relationship surreptitious. Denying romantic rumors became a way of life until Earlene's recent cancer diagnosis. At that point, improving Earlene's quality of life became a priority, and that meant kicking the hinges right off the closet door.

Cassia lit up the remainder of a spliff she'd started earlier that morning and watched as the group laughed and absorbed the magic and romance inherent in this moment. Cassia took a few quick puffs to calm her nerves as she watched Ms. Ruth undo Nate's top knot and place a handmade, floral headband onto Nate's crown. The embellishment instantly feminized Nate and gave Cassia a glimpse at what could have been. Next, Cassia turned her attention to the young nurse. She'd been in and out of that room at least three times that morning. Cassia assumed the nurse was a gossip and hated that Barrington was too blind to see it. Cassia took one final drag before flicking the roach over the balcony, donning a bogus grin and making her way into the hospital room.

"Good Morning, Mrs. Higgins," the nurse greeted Cassia, who replied merely with an affected smile.

"Congratulations," Cassia said, glancing in Auntie Earlene and Ms. Ruth's direction.

"Shame you can't stay, Cassia," Ms. Ruth replied while wiping a smudge from her clunky glasses.

"People and their opinions," the Reverend scoffed. "Life's too short."

"It's just a shame I had to become a sick old lady before I understood that," Auntie Earlene laughed.

"If we knew then what we know now," Ms. Ruth sighed, commiserating with Auntie Earlene as the nurse checked her levels.

"You would have done things exactly the same," Cassia chimed in. "Being an adult isn't just about making decisions. It's about living with them," Cassia countered.

"And sometimes there's absolutely no decision to be made," Nate paused before continuing. "Sometimes you have no choice but to play the cards you've been dealt."

"My optimistic baby girl." Cassia looked Nate up and down, her blond dreads now long, flowing and topped off with a crown arranged from the finest blossoms in Earlene's garden. "Punchdrunk off the American dream," Cassia laughed. "What's it feel like to be so free?"

Chapter 46

Here Come the Brides

After receiving the signal in the form of a head nod from the Reverend, Nate pressed play on the small boom box and out came the most enchanting music she'd ever heard. Nate positioned herself alongside Barrington. Ms. Ruth stood beside Auntie Earlene as she lay in her hospital bed and they gazed into each other's adoring eyes. As the couple held hands, the room filled rapidly with melodic chords, captivating guitar riffs and lyrics about love and sacrifice. Once the song finished, the Reverend cleared her throat and began to speak.

"Marriage. Matrimony. Nuptials," she paused a beat and then continued. "In the beginning, it had little to do with wedded bliss and everything to do with money and stability—in fact, in many cases it still does," the Reverend laughed.

Meanwhile, at the hospital entrance, a chauffeur held the door open for Cassia, allowing her to slide into the back seat of the luxury car.

"Because you see when you walk by faith and remain committed to the Lord, you find peace where there is war. Joy, where there is sorrow. Life, where there is death. Good or bad, our circumstances do not define us," preached the Reverend.

"Yes, Lord," Auntie Earlene spoke lowly as she humbly consumed the Reverend's word.

"Second Corinthians, four, verse sixteen," the Reverend thumbed the pages of her worn Bible and then began to read. "Though outwardly we are wasting away, inwardly we are being renewed day-by-day. That is why we never give up," she said, smiling, "for our light and temporary affliction is producing for us an eternal glory that far outweighs our troubles."

"Amen," Ms. Ruth whispered approvingly as the Reverend placed the Bible on the side table.

"Ladies, you've written your vows. Now, who would like to go first?" The Reverend queried.

"What can I say that I haven't already said? What can I give you that you don't already have?" Ms. Ruth inquired as she clutched Earlene's hand firmly. "My heart, soul, mind and body are already yours. They have been for years now, and so today, I promise to continue what we've started."

While Ms. Ruth pledged her undying love to Auntie Earlene, Nate's emotions got the best of her. Her eyes welled up, and as she began to weep silently, all she could think about was her wedding day. Nate imagined herself in a fitted diamond white tuxedo jacket with black lapels and matching trousers. Opposite the tranquil turquoise sea, Nate envisioned Jamaica's Blue Mountains as the backdrop while she awaited her bride at the end of a long aisle covered in tropical petals.

"I'll try my best to make you laugh when all you want to do is cry and to lift you up so that you can fly, Ms. Ruth continued. "I vow to be your best friend and your rock. I promise to live out loud and to love you with all my heart. To be faithful and forthright, forevermore." Barrington swallowed hard and clasped hands with Nate as he watched his big sister look the happiest he'd ever seen her.

"Thank you, Ruth. Beautiful," the Reverend's smile lit up the room. "Earlene, you have the floor." Auntie Earlene sat up as straight as possible, took a deep breath and began to recite her vows as images of Nate's dreamlike nuptials played out in her head. Nate imagined Tru in a vintage laced wedding dress. Her formal wear sexy, short and backless, Tru was a vision of loveliness, even though her face remained obscured by a long, running veil.

"From the moment I first saw you, I knew you were special. It was a Saturday and Linstead Market was packed. A lot of people sold cane, but yours was the sweetest," Auntie Earlene maintained, baring a suggestive smile. "We struck up a conversation and quickly became friends. The fact that I was married at the time meant that we could spend years laughing and learning about each other. When my husband passed, you were the first one there. A true friend, you stood by my side, patiently, lovingly as I mourned". Nate gradually began to recall all the times that Tru had been there for her, including this very week as Auntie Earlene continued.

"You wiped my tears and opened me up to the possibility of real love—romantic love for the first time in my life," Auntie Earlene giggled, remembering the many stolen moments and forbidden encounters she and Ms. Ruth had shared. "Because of you, I want to carry on. You inspire me. Challenge me, make me want to do better. With you by my side, I no longer have to hide. I'm so grateful to God that after all these years, I can finally call you my bride," Auntie Earlene concluded, and by then, there was not a dry eye in the room.

"The rings please," the Reverend said, smiling at Nate, who promptly pulled a small box containing two gold bands from her pocket. "Thank you," the Reverend nodded at Nate as she proceeded to explain the significance of the ceremonial bands. "Circles are infinite, and just as your love, there is no beginning or end." The Reverend passed one of the rings to Ruth and continued. "Please, place this ring on Earlene's finger and repeat after me. With this ring, I bind my life to yours." Ruth echoed the Reverend, and Nate imagined slipping a wedding band onto the well-manicured finger of her own bride one day.

"With this ring, I bind my life to yours."

"Perfect," the Reverend said as she passed Ruth's ring to Earlene. "Please, place this ring on Ruth's finger and repeat after me. With this ring, I bind my life to yours."

Auntie Earlene tenderly placed the band on to Ruth's finger while reciting the symbolic phrase," With this ring, I bind my life to yours."

"You may now salute your bride," the Reverend grinned as Ms. Ruth arched her neck toward the hospital bed to meet with Earlene's lips.

Nate imagined her first kiss as a married woman: slowly pulling the veil back, up and over Tru's face; the lace would float, but instead of Tru's looming lips, Jocelyn stood puckered, primed and ready for a second chance at love.

"Congratulations," Barrington blew a party horn, which shifted Nate's fantasy back to reality.

"Congrats, you two!" Nate threw a handful of Bougainvillea petals at the happy couple as she laughed off thoughts of marrying her first love.

"Thanks," Auntie Earlene replied, leaning in and giving Ms. Ruth a deep kiss. "Catch!" Auntie Earlene threw her bouquet toward Nate. Without giving it a second thought, Nate stuck out her right arm and caught the blossoming arrangement against her chest.

Chapter 47

Rules are Rules

Nate used Auntie Earlene's old Polaroid camera to take several selfies with her. Then she took a few candid shots: Auntie Earlene adjusting Ms. Ruth's boutonnière, Ms. Ruth fine-tuning the knot on Earlene's majestic head wrap and dad tossing bougainvillea petals like confetti at Carnival. As the vintage camera spat out developing frames, Nate placed each one on a side table. After she photographed the Reverend and Barrington, Nate pointed the retro device toward Ms. Ruth and Auntie Earlene as the couple lovingly embraced.

"Get a room," Barrington said, laughing as he witnessed Ms. Ruth and Auntie Earlene's first-ever public kiss. After one final family photo op, Nate slipped a selfie of her and Auntie Earlene into the outside compartment of her suitcase. She then said her goodbyes to Ms. Ruth and the Reverend. After promising to return tomorrow for lunch, Nate scooped Auntie Earlene up into yet another tender hug.

"I'm proud of you, Auntie," Nate whispered into Auntie Earlene's ear.

"You never know how strong you are until being strong is your only choice," Auntie Earlene whispered the celebrated Bob Marley quote into Nate's ear and then she gave her a tender kiss on the cheek.

After one last look back, Nate slid on her backpack and wheeled her luggage into the hallway as Barrington fished an envelope from his pocket and handed it to the Reverend. "Thank you," he said, shaking hands with the devout woman. "We appreciate you standing with Earlene and Ruth today when so many others would not."

"And I appreciate you, Minister Higgins," the Reverend responded while placing the check somewhere between first Corinthians, thirteen, four and Ephesians six. "May God continue to bless you."

"I'll be back with Natty tomorrow for lunch if that's fine with you, sis," Barrington said, offering his ailing sibling a forehead kiss.

Drained from all the excitement, Auntie Earlene smiled her approval, before letting her head and body retreat into the comfort of the mattress and lux goose down pillow. As Barrington walked out of the room, the Reverend grabbed Auntie Earlene's right hand, while Ms. Ruth grabbed her left. As the three women bowed their heads, the Reverend cleared her throat and prepared the room to receive God's grace, "Let us pray."

Still rocking her floral headband, Nate slid into the elevator, followed by Barrington and his handler. Once outside of the hospital, they strode through the parking lot only to be surprised by a reporter from the local newspaper. "Good Morning, Minister Higgins," the wiry reporter said, emerging from behind a minivan into the direct path of Barrington. "Delroy Lloyd with the Jamaica Observer." He walked backward as the group picked up the pace. "Hate to bother you."

"Then don't!" Barrington snapped.

"Alright, Daddy! There goes that backbone again," Nate joked.

"Minister Higgins is having a private moment with his family. A little respect, please," Barrington's handler spoke up.

"Understood. I'll make it quick," the reporter pulled a handheld recorder from his shirt pocket and pressed record. "How do you feel about your older sister marrying a woman?" The journalist smiled as he used air quotes around the word marrying.

"No comment," Barrington's handler put his arms around Nate and Barrington and made a beeline toward the awaiting black car, but the writer remained persistent in his line of questioning.

"Don't Buggery Laws apply to everyone, even if they are related to government officials? And how about The Cabinet, Minister Higgins, is there an official stance?"

"No comment, no comment, no comment," Barrington's handler answered for him, then helped Nate into the front of the car and Barrington into the back.

"Rules are rules, Minister Higgins," the journalist replied while snapping several quick pictures of the fleeing family.

"I warned you," Cassia spoke with exasperation, although it was obvious the woman delighted in being right. "Change of plans. Driver, please carry us home." Cassia raised the tinted window and pulled on a pair of dark designer shades. From the front seat, Nate watched the side mirror as images of Barrington's handler berating the tenacious reporter shone back.

In less than a half an hour after traversing the island's scenic north coast, the driver pulled up to the peripheries of Nate's childhood home and entered the secret code into its keypad. Seconds later, the gate swung open, allowing the driver to maneuver the black car past the guard shack and up the long, curvy driveway. A canopy of bougainvillea bent and stretched eastward, marking the property's entrance. The landscape lush and full of life, a gardener utilized the island's established mango picking technique. Hoist. Twist. Tug. He locked eyes with Nate as the car continued uphill. Angling the long pole over his head, he allowed the tool's teeth to sink into the branches of the tree. With a few yanks of his pole down came a basket of the fleshy sweet fruit.

Cloaked in a delicious daydream, Nate recalled how she'd mastered this skill as a youth and how she'd spent hours perched high above in the security of braided limbs enjoying the tropical succulent. She never gave it a second thought as a child, but looking at it now, the house was more exquisite than Nate remembered. It wasn't until just then that Nate began to absorb its true opulence. Tucked into the mountains of Montego Bay, the sprawling baby blue and white Victorian cottage was magnificent. Once parked, Nate, her parents and the driver each hopped from the car. However, Nate remained cautiously close to the vehicle. After fourteen years away, Nate could hardly fathom that she was home.

"You coming in?" Barrington spoke from the top of a long staircase while holding the door open for Nate.

Chapter 48

The Best of Me

"I'm safe. I'm breathing. I got this." Nate silently ran through her mantra as she ascended the staircase leading to her childhood home. Wracked with nerves, she washed her clammy hands in the powder room. Then she took a couple of relaxing puffs from the lavender inhaler that the woman on the plane had gifted her. And while the herbal remedy helped, Nate wasn't quite ready to see what her parents had done with the house's living quarters. Instead, she ventured into the library to discover that everything had been updated.

A wall-to-wall bookshelf was now the room's main focal point, along with a view of the well-manicured front lawn. Beside the vast picture window sat a desk and mounted above it, a high definition monitor with several small quadrants tasked with keeping careful watch over the property. Wafting from the kitchen, the heavenly aroma of traditional island favorites made itself known: sautéed onions and tomatoes paired with scrambled Ackee and a savory saltfish were on the menu.

Approaching the mantel, Nate let her hand slide against its wood grain while scanning an array of framed degrees and photos. There were pictures of Barrington and Cassia on their wedding day and at various political events, along with several shots of Auntie Earlene and her late husband. Sprinkled throughout these mounted moments in time were images that captured Nate's early childhood. However, once Nate reached her teens, the homages abruptly ended. Standing as a testament to Barrington's legacy was a picture of his father getting sworn in as Jamaica's Minister of Transport over forty years ago. But out of all the photos, the one that stood out most was an image of Cassia.

No more than five years old, she played with friends in the photograph, fully embracing their beloved Spanish Town yet remaining seemingly oblivious to its squalor.

"Breakfast will be out as soon as your father gets off the phone," Cassia said, entering the room with a fresh pot of ginger tea.

"Okay." A sharp contrast to her mother's current state, Nate put the picture of Cassia back in its place on the mantel and watched her mother curiously. As Cassia sweetened the hot tea with condensed milk, Nate searched for signs of that vulnerable street kid in Cassia, but alas, there were none to be found.

"I swear lately he's on the phone more than a teenager," Cassia rolled her eyes as Barrington was heard full-on belly-laughing in the next room. He was on the phone with his son's mother and although Barrington had yet to admit it, the signs were as clear as day. This was no casual fling. Barrington had fallen in love. While she had always suspected her father might have someone on the side, Nate had no idea about her parent's complex open relationship. As Cassia prepared the tea and pretended not to be bothered by Barrington's blatant disrespect, Nate observed her. It was like witnessing a barista during the morning rush—a dash of cinnamon, splash of vanilla, a little milk, and just like that, tea good enough to make you forget all your troubles, at least until you got to the bottom of the cup.

"Here you go," Cassia said, handing Nate a mug. She then took a seat on the couch nearest the picture window, while Nate sat on the edge of the desk, her arms folded. For a moment, the two women sat simply in silence. Like one of those standoffs in an old cowboy movie, the tension was thick and underscored by the sound of a ticking grandfather clock and the faintest roar of the salty Caribbean Sea.

"Well, what is it, child? You just gonna sit there staring or you ready to speak your peace?" Nate unfolded her arms and slowly stood to her feet. She had gone over this moment multiple times in her head.

"I just think," Nate stammered. "I mean, you've always been so…"

"All that fancy education and you can't formulate a complete sentence," Cassia teased.

"You've always been so hard on me and I have no idea why. At this point, I don't care. Just know that no matter how much you hurt me, you never broke me."

"Wasn't nobody trying to break you. If anything, I was trying to build you up. The problem is you're spoiled. You honestly think we're supposed to be friends, braid each other's hair, 'tings like that," Cassia scoffed. "A real mother calls their children out when they do wrong—and does whatever it takes to correct them."

"Including corrective rape," Nate countered, refusing to cry.

"There's a lot that I'm not proud of, but I swear before God, everything I did—everything I do is for the good of this family. Our legacy." Nate listened intently as Cassia's voice cracked with emotion. "Sure, your father came with a pedigree, but the man had no ambition. I carried him to the top. Shaped and molded him, just as I tried to do with you. I put you in ballet. You opt for football. I arrange play dates with little girls. You try to bed them," Cassia laughed. "I made those elitists down at the capital respect me; their wives revere me. But when it came to you, Natalia—you were the one thing I couldn't fix."

"So, you hired the Campbell brothers to do it for you?" Nate approached her mother and stared as if she were capable of gazing at her soul through those deep-set eyes. "How do you sleep at night?"

"Like a baby," Cassia responded rapidly. She then paused for a beat, taking a moment to blow hot steam from her tea. "You see, I know what it's like to go without—I've survived rape, poverty and prejudice. You, my privileged, baby girl, have no idea. And your father knows even less," she said, laughing. "You were both born on pedestals, while I had to claw my way out of the ghetto." Cassia's eyes began to fill with tears so much so that one blink would undoubtedly lead to a full-on display of emotion. She then walked over to the mantel and stopped in front of the picture of her young self in the Spanish Town slums. "With no parents and only a primary school education, Barrington was my way out."

"So this is all a scam," Nate gestured to the opulence of the sitting room and lush compound, visible through the window. "I wonder how the press would feel if they found out your marriage was a business."

"You are your mother's child," Cassia smirked.

"Unfortunately." Nate's tone was calm, but on the inside, she bubbled like lava until she finally exploded in the form of a jab aimed at a framed family photo. "None of its real." She cut herself accidentally. The cut wasn't deep, but it was enough to break the skin and draw blood.

Without hesitation, Cassia grabbed several Kleenex and applied pressure to Nate's surface wound as she spoke. "When your little brother died in my womb, you were all I had left," Cassia continued to apply pressure to Nate's hand. "You are my child and I love you because you're the best of me. I just don't love what you've become."

"But, this is who I've always been," Nate said, shirking her hand away from Cassia. "And you know it."

"You made a choice, and now, my dear, you must live with it," Cassia resolved.

"The only choice I've made is to live authentically," Nate responded while again taking a seat on the edge of the desk. "I won't apologize for loving women." She caught a glimpse of Barrington on the monitors, only now he'd moved his conversation from the house to the front porch.

"And I won't apologize for keeping you at bay all these years. Your father's work has impacted the lives of thousands of Jamaican youth. We've had tremendous success. None of this would've been possible if there were signs of rampant faggotry in the Higgins household." Cassia took another sip of the hot tea before continuing. "One day I pray you'll learn real love isn't that mushy gushy stuff they show in Hollywood movies. Real love is sacrifice. You could have chosen to forgo women, but you didn't. It seems the sacrifice was too great."

"I'm proud of who I am. I am a black, lesbian immigrant living in colonized America. You have no idea what I've been through," Nate spoke while applying pressure to the cut on her knuckles.

"Oh, I don't?" Cassia took a moment to contemplate whether or not she should continue. "My cousin was murdered for being a batty boy. He was fourteen years old. The same age that you were when we sent you away." Tears began to slip from Cassia's eyes as her voice trembled, giving Nate just the slightest glimpse of Cassia, the helpless street kid from the photos.

"Perhaps I'd be a little more accepting of your lifestyle if I hadn't witnessed my cousin and countless others get beat down for living as you say, authentically." Cassia paused to collect herself and it was at that moment Nate realized she had never seen her mother be anything but stoic.

Despite the years of anger harbored toward Cassia, at that moment, Nate wanted nothing more than to wrap her arms around her mother, but something in Nate wouldn't allow her to do so.

"What happened to your cousin was terrible, but things have changed," Nate sounded cautiously optimistic. That was then, and this is now."

"No, this is Jamaica, that is your father, the Ministry of Youth and Culture and homosexuality is a national offense." As Cassia pointed at Barrington on the monitor, Nate noticed Jocelyn's tourism van pop up in one of the quadrants.

"Oceans, miles and years apart, and yet somehow you still manage to defy me," Cassia jeered.

"You expected me to come all this way and not see Jocelyn?"

"If yuh sleep, wid dawg, yuh katch im flea," Cassia shrugged.

"Good thing I don't mind a little itch," having gotten everything off her chest, Nate smiled at her mother then exited the home, her luggage in tow. On the monitors, Cassia watched as Nate hugged Barrington goodbye and hopped into Jocelyn's van.

Chapter 49

Luminous Lagoon

It was barely noon, and dressed way down in sweats and a hoodie, Tru was almost unrecognizable. In fact, she barely recognized herself and hoped that the gesture she considered romantic wouldn't come off as stalkerlike. Either way, at this stage of the game, it was too late. Tru was more than thirty thousand feet in the air and beyond the point of no return. Plus, the fact that she was unable to reach Nate due to her phone being in airplane mode didn't help matters.

After landing in Montego Bay, Jamaica, Tru headed to the airport bathroom to change. She wiggled into a polka dot romper and slipped on a pair of wedges that showed off a set of shapely legs. And on her head, she wore a crown of long, natural cornrows, replacing her signature, multi-hued pixie cut wigs. Tru's natural new look was stunning. Content with her look, Tru pulled her flask from her purse and examined it. During the flight, she had used an airplane knife to amend the keep 'em guessing inscription to simply read, "keep 'em." She laughed, unscrewed it, and then took a long, deliberate sip of liquid courage. It didn't take long for her to find the town's hospital and to learn Auntie Earlene's room number. Nearly ninety minutes after she landed, Tru knocked on the door to Auntie Earlene's hospital room.

"Come in," Auntie Earlene said, sitting up in her hospital bed.

"Hi. I'm Nate's friend Tru," she entered the room and was immediately greeted by Auntie Earlene and Ms. Ruth cuddling in the tight hospital bed and enjoying the Polaroids snapped earlier.

Meanwhile, across the island, Jocelyn weaved through traffic while Nate sat in the passenger seat, filling her friend in on the specifics of Auntie Earlene's commitment ceremony.

"I can't believe Auntie came out to you before telling me."

"Maybe if you came home a little more often," Jocelyn teased.

"Because clearly my parents and I can't get enough of each other," Nate chuckled as she looked down at her freshly scraped knuckle.

"Oh, so your parents are the only reason you have to visit?" Jocelyn had always been a flirt.

"I wrote you letters for a full year," Nate replied. "You never responded to any of them."

"Cause I was mad!" Jocelyn exclaimed. "You left me here to rot."

"Like I had a choice," Nate grimaced.

"I know that now," Jocelyn said, slapping Nate playfully on her thigh. "My thirteen-year-old self may still be vex, but I forgive you, Natty." She smiled. After driving and reminiscing for a few more miles, Jocelyn and Nate stopped at a roadside eatery.

"Cheers!" Jocelyn smiled as she and Nate clinked ice-cold bottles of the national nectar. "To telling mommy dearest to F-off!" She smiled while Nate downed half the bottle with one swig.

"Cheers," Nate laughed as she raised the bottle of Red Stripe back to her lips and again began to sip. Officially two beers in, she had changed into a look that was much more befitting of her celebratory mood—board shorts, backpack, a tank top and flops.

"Order up," the chef yelled at the roadside stand, scooping their meals into two Styrofoam containers and beckoning Jocelyn over. After paying for their meals and two more beers, the two women walked down a narrow, winding road that dead-ended at a high-end resort.

"This is nice," Nate said, straightening her posture as she watched high-end cars and clientele pull in and out of the valet station. Jocelyn responded with a smile for Nate and a knowing head nod to one of the valets. The two women then used the service entrance to access the property, which meant traversing the bowels of the five-star resort. The hallways were long and snaked like a maze. But Jocelyn seemed to know every turn—even more impressive was that everyone they passed along the way seemed to know her just as well. Jocelyn greeted each bellhop, maid, and frontend employee with warmth and familiarity as the sound of sweet reggae music drew them toward a staircase.

"Why does this feel like a horror movie?" Nate looked over her shoulder at Jocelyn as she slowly climbed the stairs.

"So now you don't trust me?" Jocelyn asked Nate in return. She then gave Nate a slight slap on the ass for motivation. "Mash!" She laughed as Nate slowly pushed the heavy door open to reveal a blinding white light. Soon the two childhood friends were enjoying the comforts of a poolside cabana.

"You have to let me have this one," Jocelyn gawked at the selfie Nate had taken in the floral headpiece.

"It's yours," Nate tore into the jerk chicken while they sat in the midst of a scene that would make even heaven look like the hood. An infinity pool overlooked white sand beaches and a turquoise sea, while a steel pan band provided authentic island rhythms.

"Good looks, good job—you sure you aren't snatched up?" Jocelyn queried.

"Correction, I had an ok job."

"Had?" Jocelyn probed.

"I'll spare you the details," Nate replied as she reached for the vase in front of them and pulled from it a Lignum Vitae. She refused to revisit Simon's assault and her subsequent firing that followed.

"Temporary setback." Jocelyn brushed blond dreads from Nate's face and for a split second, a tidal wave of guilt washed over Nate accompanied by memories of her and Tru during less complicated times. Picking up on the energy shift, Jocelyn backed off.

"I have a friend," Nate revealed, "but she's not my girl. We're taking things slow." She kicked herself for the steady stream of TMI flowing from her mouth. "How about you? Anyone special?" Nate asked, shifting the attention to Jocelyn's love life.

"You know how it is. I work a lot, plus the scene is abysmal," Jocelyn laughed. "A couple of underground clubs here and there, but I'm not a big partier, so it's tough."

"I get that," Nate said as she plucked a single lavender petal from the island's national flower.

"My soul mate's out there somewhere," Jocelyn said with a sigh, and as she threw her head back and began to sway to the music, her long black hair slipped past her shoulders and graced her back. Nate was enthralled and watched slyly as beads of sweat began to roll down Jocelyn's breasts, like a runaway roller coaster.

"Rum punch, compliments of the bartender." The server stuck his head into the cabana, simultaneously breaking Nate's trance.

"Thanks," Jocelyn raised the complimentary pitcher in the direction of the bartender, who waved back.

"Is there anyone here you don't know?" Nate quizzed.

"I'm pretty much the mayor of MoBay," Jocelyn laughed.

The two friends spent the remainder of their time at the resort drinking and bouncing back and forth between their cabana, the sea and the pool. The sexual tension was undeniable, and although they'd both thought about getting physical, neither was willing to make a move. Instead, they laughed and danced along with the band as the day inevitably slipped away. The party vibe was official, and the music spoke to the girls, especially Jocelyn. She couldn't help but wind her waist as she backed her ample bikini-clad bottom into Nate. Together, their bodies fit like lock and key—yet another reason why it was indeed good to be home.

"There's one more place I want to take you before I drop you at your hotel," Jocelyn said while buckling her seat belt.

"Let's roll!" Nate felt like she'd downed at least a gallon of rum punch all on her own.

"Decisive, I like that." Jocelyn lit up a spliff, took a couple of puffs and passed it to Nate. They then drove up the coast, listening to Peter Tosh and chasing the setting sun until shades of orange and tangerine gave way to a mystical magenta sky. Eventually, Nate fell smack dab into the arms of the Sandman and an enchanting dream:

She was underground and navigating an intricate jumble of hallways similar to the one below the resort she and Jocelyn had just left. The ground was covered in lavender Lignum Vitae petals, and from above, it looked a lot like a Keith Haring pop art print. A single flower in hand, Nate followed the bed of perennials as it crisscrossed the mysterious labyrinth, dropping petals and playing the love game along the way.

"She loves me. She loves me not." Nate followed the trail and continued the game until she reached a door. "She loves me," Nate said, dropping the now petal-less stem at her feet as she pushed the door open. Next, she followed the sound of running water and petals through a bedroom and into a bathroom.

"You coming in?" Unsurprised by Nate's visit, Jocelyn spoke calmly from the shower. Nate undressed and entered without saying a word. Face to face with her first real love, even in her dreams, Nate realized instantly that any phrase she tried to formulate would undoubtedly fall flat. At a loss for words,

Nate decided body language was her best bet. Nate leaned in, and when their lips met, to say it was fireworks would be a severe understatement. This kiss was like the Fourth of July meets every war ever. Explosive and erotic, their tongues insatiably explored each other. With fourteen years in the rearview, this was the moment to make up for lost time.

#

Back in the realm of reality, Jocelyn's timing was perfect. She and Nate arrived at Falmouth's luminous lagoon just as the skies succumbed to a torrential downpour.

"We're here," Jocelyn said, rubbing Nate's thigh.

"Must've dozed off," Nate responded with a huge smile as she recalled the erotic dream, which had left her highly aroused. "Wow, I haven't been here since that field trip back in elementary school."

It was like a scene from a sci-fi movie, only this supernatural event was happening in the flesh. The old friends watched in silence as science unfolded before them. It was as though bright blue neon lights were submerged below the lagoon's surface, causing the water to radiate for as far as the eye could see. As the downpour slowly began to subside, the luminous lights too started to dim.

"It's now or never," Jocelyn yelped. She then cranked the stereo, peeled off her sarong, hopped from the vehicle and made a mad dash for the water. When she jumped in, the lagoon lit up like some sort of futuristic baptismal. Nate followed suit, diving headfirst into the sacred space to be reborn.

"They say a dip in this lagoon will add inches to a man and turn a B cup into a C cup," said Jocelyn.

"Well, you must be here all the time because your cup runneth over," Nate laughed.

"You noticed," Jocelyn replied with a smirk.

"I uh," Nate stammered.

"Uh-huh." Jocelyn splashed water at Nate. "I can't believe I spent years pissed at you," she continued. "As a kid, all I knew for certain was that we should be together." Jocelyn swam over to Nate. "I loved you."

"I loved you too," Nate cradled Jocelyn into a tight hug and whispered in her ear.

"Do you ever think about what would've happened if you stayed?" Jocelyn's warm breath tickled Nate's neck as the classic Heptones jam, "Fatty Fatty" crept lowly from the van's stereo.

"More than you know," Nate confessed.

"I look for you in everyone," Jocelyn affirmed, breaking free of the hug. "There's just something about us," she sighed. "I can't let go." And like Coco bread sandwiching a Jamaican patty, Jocelyn laid it on thick. Their connection was paranormal. Being ravished by Jocelyn's luscious lips was like kissing the ghost of Easter Monday's past. And as her hands drifted to Jocelyn's waist, Nate found herself swiftly surrendering to Jocelyn's spell.

Chapter 50

Ain't No Mountain

Although little more than a peck, the intimate act, fourteen years in the making had thrown Nate entirely off course. "I'm sorry," she sighed. "I can't." Nate pulled away from Jocelyn's kiss and swam the short distance to shore. Jocelyn followed suit.

"Did you really just ditch me—again?" Jocelyn tried to make light of an awkward situation. She then wrapped herself in a sarong and peeled off her wet bikini. Embarrassed, Nate looked anywhere but at Jocelyn's body. "Old habits die hard, aye," Jocelyn continued.

"Not funny," Nate pivoted. "It's been a long day. I'm buzzed, exhausted and haven't even checked into my hotel," she laughed half-heartedly, although the sting of rejection was blatant.

"Buckle up," Jocelyn said as she rammed the key into the ignition.

"With my luck, they probably gave my room away," Nate responded while reluctantly switching her phone out of airplane mode. She wasn't ready to confront the unresolved drama left behind in Los Angeles, but reality had already set in. Just as expected, once her phone began to roam, Nate was bombarded with voicemails and text messages from LAPD. Those could wait, but what she wasn't expecting was the slew of messages from Barrington and Tru. Nate began to sweat like the weed man confronting a K9 unit as she ran through the stream of missed messages from Tru alerting her that she had landed in Montego Bay.

"You good?" Jocelyn inquired, noticing Nate's apparent unease.

"Daddy left a bunch of messages," Nate's tone was flustered. "Something's wrong with Auntie." Nate began to search her contacts for Barrington's number just as she received a phone call from him. The news was urgent and easily the worse Nate had ever obtained.

"It happened in her sleep," Barrington explained. "Auntie's gone, Natty." He had been mentally preparing for his sister's death, but the finiteness of her passing was brutal. "Get to the hospital now," he concluded.

From that moment on, everything seemed to play out in warp speed for Nate. Jocelyn made it back to Montego Bay in record time. That was the easy part. But, Nate's call to Tru could not have been more arduous. Jocelyn listened to one side of a conversation between the two lovers as they agreed to meet at the hotel. However, when Nate and Jocelyn rushed into the hospital, Tru was waiting at the main entrance, and just like that, Nate's past and future became one.

"I couldn't let you go through this alone," Tru said as she hugged Nate while eyeballing Jocelyn. Nate hurriedly introduced the two women and then scurried to Auntie Earlene's room. The men in black were there just as they had been earlier that day. However, the hallway leading to Auntie Earlene's room seemed so much longer. When they reached the room, they saw Ms. Ruth sobbing softly into Auntie Earlene's Kente cloth head wrap while Barrington slumped over her body wailing. Jocelyn and Tru hung back as Nate approached her deceased Auntie Earlene, and she too began to cry at the sight of her lifeless body and mostly bald head. Then Nate caught a glimpse of her mother pacing the patio and was motivated by something profound within to join her.

"I've seen you cry more today than in my entire life," Nate said as she slid the patio door closed behind her. "What, are there cameras and reporters out here too?" Nate was a sopping wet ball of emotions, and as callous and out of character as it was, attacking Cassia provided a comforting effect.

"Today's been full of firsts," Cassia hit the spliff, then passed it to Nate. Her parents had for years smoked in secrecy and now Cassia was offering Nate weed.

"Herb?" Nate asked, looking down at the lit spliff in Cassia's outstretched hand.

"Please, child. There's no need to act new," she countered as Nate took the joint and inhaled warily. "Your father and I have been married for thirty years. And I've known Auntie Earlene for just as long. Believe it or not, I always respected her. And if you ever repeat this, I'll deny it to my grave," Cassia said with a laugh. "Truth is, I was always jealous of the relationship you and Auntie shared. I wanted that for us. Still do."

"It's not too late, mommy. I can forgive you—for everything. Daddy too," Nate's declaration surprised Cassia just as much as it astounded Nate. She'd spent years harboring a grudge against her mother, and in an instant, she was ready to absolve Cassia from all misdoings. "I would love to put the past behind us," she continued. "I'm just not sure you're able to."

Nate took one final puff from the joint then passed it to Cassia, who promptly turned her back to Nate. The sea wasn't visible, although the sound alone lingered ominously in the night air. As Cassia contemplated the political ramifications of fully accepting her daughter, Nate watched Ms. Ruth drape the Kente cloth over Auntie Earlene's stiffening body.

"It's not that easy, Natalia," Cassia exhaled.

"Nothing worth having ever is," Nate exited the patio and searched the hallway for a water fountain. Splashing cold water on her face brought her instantly back to Falmouth's luminous lagoon and the magical kiss shared with Jocelyn. Nate remained haunted by Jocelyn's declaration: "I look for you in everyone."

"Nate," Tru said, approaching from behind.

"I'm so sorry," Nate sobbed, collapsing on Tru's shoulder. "I can't believe you showed up after I acted like…"

"A spoiled brat," Tru laughed. "It's all good. You've got a lifetime to make it up to me." Then, Tru smiled at Nate and escorted her to a nearby bench.

"Right now, let's just focus on what's in front of us," Tru said, as Nate rested her head on Tru's shoulder.

"I should've stayed here with her," Nate wept gently.

"You couldn't save her, Nate," Tru sighed. "I'm just glad you were able to see her, and now, thank God, she's at peace."

Tru and Nate spent the next half hour or so cuddled up on the bench, fighting sleep until they drifted off peacefully in each other's embrace.

"Natty," Jocelyn said as she approached the bench, clearing her throat. "They're ready to take her if you want to say one last goodbye."

Nate groggily took to her feet. She'd fallen asleep and in the span of a catnap had almost completely forgotten where she was.

"Thank you," Tru stood, her hand extended. "It's Jackie, right?"

"Jocelyn," she corrected, shaking Tru's hand.

"Jocelyn is my oldest friend in the world and Tru is..." Nate froze. She felt as out of sorts as a prostitute approaching the pulpit.

"I'm her girlfriend," Tru declared.

"Yes, Natty mentioned you. I'm glad you were able to get off of work, was it?" Jocelyn quizzed.

"Luckily, I was able to move some things around." Tru gave Nate a look that she wasn't quite sure how to interpret. Tru was either un-amused that Nate had put her business in the streets or she was simply marking her territory. "Nate's so private. She rarely mentions home—not the good parts at least."

"I'll be the first to admit we've got a lot of small-minded people on the island. Life can be tough here for a lot of us, but still, there's something extraordinary about this place," Jocelyn paused for a beat. "Things in Jamaica may not be great, but from what I've seen, we as real as they come."

"Auntie Earlene was definitely as real as they come. She didn't start that way, but she made sure that's how she went out," Nate declared proudly, as she watched two orderlies enter Auntie Earlene's room to retrieve her body. "No more suffering, Auntie," Nate whispered as Tru took hold of her hand.

"I'm glad you're here," Jocelyn said, swallowing hard as she glared at the newly minted couple and their intertwined fingers. "Natty's my oldest friend, but right now, she needs more than that. As we lay Auntie's soul to rest, Natty, I pray you can lean on your soul mate. That kindred spirit destined, designed and perfectly aligned for you," Jocelyn said, smiling as tears welled up in her eyes. "Clearly that's you," she said, shifting her attention to Tru. "You the one—I mean, why else would you come all this way?"

"You don't need me to tell you how special this one is," Tru said as she sized up Nate and Jocelyn. From the looks on both of their faces, it was apparent that the women had history. Still, Tru had traveled nearly three thousand miles and was unwavering in holding her ground. "Ain't no mountain high enough. Ain't no valley low enough," Tru recited the sixties soul lyrics with an awkward smile, grasping Nate's hand even harder.

"The truth is that everyone's gonna hurt you. You just have to find the one worth suffering for," Jocelyn retorted with a famous quote of her own.

"Brother Bob," Nate replied, verifying the quote's author as a tear slipped down Jocelyn's cheek.

"Good, Natty. Still a yardie at heart." Jocelyn wiped the solitary tear away with a smile. "My deepest condolences," Jocelyn said, pulling Nate in for a hug. "Al vita Zane, Natty One."

So much for second chances. Jocelyn bowed out gracefully and as she made her way to the elevator, Tru and Nate walked the opposite direction hand-in-hand. Nate's mind was flooded like the roads after a catastrophic storm and littered with matters of the heart. Stuck between what could have been and what was very much her reality, Nate cringed and shut her eyes tight. After fourteen years, fate had led her back to her first love. And then there was Tru. She had dropped everything to be with Nate. And had given Nate precisely what she asked for—a commitment. While spending the day with Jocelyn had been magical, moving back to Jamaica and her messy family dynamic would be brutal. Life with Tru just made more sense. Together they'd take on the drama between Simon and Karina that awaited her in Los Angeles. Tru would eventually open her lounge—EGO—Eternally Grateful Optimist, and Nate would, of course, be a resident deejay. Together they'd hob knob with L.A.'s finest and enjoy the meteoric reboot and rise of Nate's career.

As Nate reached the doorway, she looked over her shoulder to see Jocelyn pressing the elevator button—it wasn't until that very moment that she began to wonder. Was Jocelyn the one who got away? In truth, the more that she considered this, the more Nate started to see the similarities between Jocelyn and Tru. Both women were A-type, entrepreneurs who knew exactly what they wanted from life. As Nate put the pieces together, the more it seemed that she too had spent the last half of her life looking for some semblance of Jocelyn in her partners. However, today was Auntie Earlene's day, and for the moment, Nate's love life would have to wait. One loss was hard to bear, but two in the same day would be something Nate could never come back from. Squeezing Tru's hand, Nate yelled out to Jocelyn at the elevator doors.

"Jocelyn, wait!" To Nate's surprise, Jocelyn waited, and as she began to walk toward her and Tru, Nate searched for the right words to say, but there were none. Instead, Nate took both of their hands in hers. Determined to have the two loves of her life by her side, friends at the strangest, most beautiful end, the three women walked into the hospital room to pay their final respects and to face the mysteries of life to come.

# #

In the two months since Auntie Earlene's death, Nate had spoken to her parents a handful of times, which, when you did the math, was a way higher frequency than they were accustomed to. Despite reconnecting, Nate still didn't know that Barrington had made her a big sister or the extents he and Cassia had gone to secure their foothold in Jamaica's Parliament. While their relationship was a work in progress, shrouded in enigmas, Nate and Jocelyn's relationship had completely stalled out. Although they had promised to keep in touch at Auntie Earlene's funeral, it became impossible to do so. Instead, the two old flames had concocted an unspoken pact aimed at keeping temptation at bay.

Then there was Simon. It was a week before Christmas and a roundtable of newscasters practically salivated as they analyzed the news that had broken earlier that week. Simon had been found not guilty of sexual assault charges due to insufficient evidence. While Sasha and Karina had reported their assault to the police, their refusal to testify hadn't helped their case. And on its own, in the eyes of jurors, Nate's testimony was not enough.

"Boy wonder skates again," the female anchored sighed.

"Simon Herbst was judged by a jury of his peers," her male colleague retorted. "Clearly, the evidence wasn't there."

"Evidence?" She queried. "You saw the video and heard the podcast! What more do we need?"

"I'm not saying these women were opportunists, but where's the tangible proof? And since when does a business meeting end in a hotel room?" The male anchored quizzed, "I'm just saying, we have to do better."

Across town Karina sat on the edge of her bed, clutching her trusted box cutter as the telecast played out. While Nate had dropped the charges, they hadn't spoken since their club altercation. Mortified, Karina listened as the anchors continued to spar.

"Celebrity or not, anyone who violates another person deserves jail time," the female anchor

concluded, as Karina let the sharp blade slide in and out of its sheath.

"Couldn't agree with you more, but was it rape or rough sex?" The male anchor probed crudely. "Obviously, in the eyes of the jurors, the Zakaryan video is inconclusive."

Karina exposed the blade and pressed it against her forearm, but she couldn't do it. As she released the box cutter from her grip, a guttural groan bubbled from her stomach and spewed like molten lava as the device fell hard to the floor. Then, Karina collapsed backward onto the plush California king, and as she allowed her gaze to drift to the nightstand, her eyes settled on the fourth pregnancy test she'd taken that morning. The night that she'd been 5150'ed, doctors confirmed Karina's pregnancy. She couldn't wrap her mind around it then, but now there was no denying it. With a baby on the way, Karina had six months to get her shit together.

Meanwhile, Nate listened to the news report through earbuds as she carefully hung the neon club moniker in the middle of a jet black wall.

"All these protesters in front of the man's home and place of business," the male anchored sighed. "This is ridiculous."

"No, this is America—and you need to acknowledge your privilege," the female anchor replied sharply. "I'm just not sure you're brave enough to take off your blinders."

"Hello! Earth to Natty One," Tru plucked the earbuds from Nate's ears. "I said, which color do you like?" Nate turned around to see overalls clad Tru covered in a menagerie of paint splatters. Beaming with optimism, Tru was adorable, and just the light Nate needed to distract her from this gloomy newscast.

"Well?" Tru asked again. Nate looked past her and saw that Tru had painted the wall several shades. Deep red, bright blue, forest green, canary yellow and a royal purple.

"I can't decide," Tru chuckled. "I love them all." Watching Tru laugh like that had a calming effect on Nate, and as she climbed down from the ladder, she decided from that moment on she'd make ever adversity an opportunity for personal growth.

"It's perfect," Nate said as she wrapped her arms around Tru's waist. "As a matter of fact," Nate continued while pulling a remote control from her back pocket. "Check this out." Nate pressed a button, allowing the neon sign to flicker instantly on. Its big, bold cursive letters spelled out E.G.O. And below it, the acronym's translation—Eternally Grateful Optimist."

"I love it," Tru squealed.

"You embody it," Nate whispered lovingly into Tru's ear as she envisioned her future. Despite it all, the best was undoubtedly yet to come.